"So here we are, the pair of us, out here hiding in the dark. Two people who don't wish to marry"—he gave a sly wink—"anyone in *that* ballroom."

Exasperated, she shook her head slightly and grinned at him. "You won't give my secret away, will you, Mr. Woodward?"

"If you promise to call me Alex and I can call you . . . Caroline, was it?"

"Caroline," she repeated.

"Well, *Caroline,* since we know some secrets about each other, we should be on a first-name basis, don't you think?"

"I think, *Alex,* that we have a deal then," she agreed with a teasing smile, looking up at him. He reached for her, gently taking hold of both her small hands. She let out a little gasp of surprise, but she did not pull away.

Tiny tingling sensations began to build inside her as his hands held hers. Oh, she definitely should have left her gloves on! For now she could feel his warm skin and his strong yet soft fingers that held her gently but with a firm pressure. It was difficult to breathe because her heart was beating so rapidly. She had the oddest feeling that something very special was happening. She lifted her gaze to meet his eyes, those dark eyes, and had the sensation that she was suddenly falling off a very, very steep cliff.

His voice was a whisper. "Shall we seal our secrets with a kiss?"

Without a second's hesitation, he pulled her closer lowering his mouth over hers . . .

SECRETS
OF A
DUCHESS

KAITLIN O'RILEY

ZEBRA BOOKS
Kensington Publishing Corp.
www.kensingtonbooks.com

ZEBRA BOOKS are published by

Kensington Publishing Corp.
850 Third Avenue
New York, NY 10022

All Kensington titles, imprints, and distributed lines are available
at special quantity discounts for bulk purchases for sales promo-
tion, premiums, fund-raising, educational, or institutional use.

Special book excerpts or customized printings can also be created to fit specific needs. For details, write or phone the office
of the Kensington Special Sales Manager: Attn. Special Sales
Department. Kensington Publishing Corp., 850 Third Avenue,
New York, NY 10022. Phone: 1-800-221-2647.

Zebra and the Z logo Reg. U.S. Pat. & TM Off.

ISBN-13: 978-0-8217-8092-3
ISBN-10: 0-8217-8092-1

First Printing: February 2007
10 9 8 7 6 5 4 3 2 1

Printed in the United States of America

For my mother, Joan.
I miss you more than you know.

ACKNOWLEDGMENTS

I want to thank my sisters, Jane, Maureen, Janet, and Jennifer.
I couldn't have done this without all of you.
Note to Riley: You are the angel of my life.

CHAPTER 1

London, England
May 1865

Lord and Lady Maxwell's ballroom was decorated with colorful garlands of fresh flowers perfuming the air and countless flickering candles lighting the room. Long oak tables, draped with the finest linen cloths trimmed in Belgian lace, were laden with shining sterling silver platters piled with delicacies and refreshments of all sorts and sparkling Irish crystal champagne flutes arranged artfully along the side, ready for toasting. A myriad of obliging servants were there to accommodate the slightest need of the hundreds of invited guests, the crème de la crème of London society, arriving in their most formal attire. The full orchestra, hidden behind a delicate Chinese screen, played melodiously at the end of the room near the dance floor. The steady buzz of voices in animated conversation was punctuated with bursts of merry laughter echoing through the elegant crowd of young debutantes, hopeful parents, eligible bachelors, social climbers, and society matrons. For the first grand ball of the Season, a general feeling of excitement and expectation was in the air, and everyone was in high spirits.

Olivia Fairchild, the Dowager Countess of Glenwood, had wasted no time in introducing her two granddaughters to the sons and grandsons of her aristocratic friends, and soon both Emma's and Caroline's dance cards were filled.

"Now, girls, try to remember everything your Aunt Jane and I taught you," Olivia intoned in an encouraging whisper.

At her insistence, both granddaughters had been dressed painstakingly for their debut. The preparations had taken nearly all day. As young girls traditionally did at their first ball, Caroline, although considered somewhat old at twenty-two, wore a gown of soft white satin with small, capped sleeves, which accentuated her fair skin and slender figure. Her long, honey-colored hair was pinned up loosely on her head, and tiny white rosebuds were arranged there, forming a delicate crown, while stray tendrils of hair curled softly around her face. The effect was casually elegant, but it had taken what seemed like hours to get it just right. Armlength white gloves and white satin slippers completed the ethereal ensemble.

As Caroline Armstrong twirled the white satin ribbon that held her card, she dreaded the part she knew she had to play when the first gentleman came to claim his dance. In spite of her grandmother's hopeful predictions for her, a brilliant Season with scores of promising gentlemen vying for her hand in marriage was not in Caroline's future. She would make sure of that. She had to.

When Sir Edward Winslow extended his arm to

her, Caroline gave him a half-hearted smile and lowered her eyes demurely as he escorted her to the dance floor. He was a nice-looking young man of average height with a shy grin. Within a matter of minutes, she was thanking heaven for every dance lesson she had endured, because she needed all her resources to follow Sir Edward Winslow's jerky, erratic movements. Too enthusiastic a dancer to simply waltz, Edward marched her awkwardly about the floor, pulling on her arms with a determined look of concentration on his long face. As she struggled to stay in step with his clumsy gait, she wondered if the boy had ever had a dance lesson in his life.

"It is a pleasure dancing with you, Miss Armstrong," he declared while panting with exertion. "You are like dancing with an angel from heaven."

"Thank you." She looked down at her poor, trodupon feet in their brand-new dainty slippers, and she bit her lip. The experience was quite the opposite of heavenly! Yet Lord Winslow seemed very kind, and feeling somewhat sorry for him, she hadn't the heart to put her secret plan into effect and simply let him fall under the impression that she was extremely shy. Not daring to engage him in any conversation, she did not speak again, only nodded her head in answer to his polite questions and marched the remainder of the waltz with him.

Her next partner, however, was fairly begging to be set down a notch or two and appeared to be an apt subject upon which to implement her untested method of deterring suitors. Caroline became much more blatant in her discouragement of him, if only to save herself from ever having to be near the man again. *Oily* was the only word she could think of to describe Lord Arthur Kingston. *Maybe a snake,* she thought, as he eased her to the dance floor. His hard fingers pressed tightly against her arms, and his too-bright smile seemed avaricious. Some women might have found him handsome enough in a slick sort of way, but the pair of thin, wet lips under his fashionable set of whiskers and the calculating gleam in his sharp eyes unnerved her. Not quite sure why she felt so instantly repulsed by him, she reasoned now was as good a time as any to turn him away.

"You, Miss Armstrong," he whispered heatedly in her ear as he squeezed her tighter, "are the prettiest girl here tonight. I thought I knew all the prettiest girls in London. Where have you been hiding all this time?"

And without compunction for this ungentlemanly gentleman, Caroline put her secret plan into effect.

Wishing to escape another unwanted dance partner, Caroline managed to slip away from the ballroom unnoticed. Her aunt and uncle were engaged in conversation with Lady Maxwell; her sister was dancing a reel with a rather short, blond gentleman; and her grandmother was having an animated discussion with Lady Weatherby. She would not be missed for a moment or two. She passed the card room, where the older ladies and gentlemen were playing whist and faro, and ambled aimlessly down a long hallway, taking a moment here and there to admire the formal Maxwell family portraits displayed on the walls. No one paid any attention to her as she ascended a short flight of stairs and stepped through a set of French doors, which opened onto a marble balcony overlooking a well-manicured garden.

A full moon bathed the balcony in a silvery light, and Caroline breathed in the fresh air, which was perfumed with the scent of blooming lilacs. The cool air felt refreshing after the stuffiness of the ballroom. Because she was so warm and still unused to wearing them, she peeled off her long, white gloves and stuffed them into her small reticule, reminding herself to don them again before she returned to her grandmother. Olivia would certainly disapprove of her granddaughter being gloveless.

Relieved to finally be alone, she leaned against a tall marble pillar, which felt deliciously cool against her warm skin, and breathed deeply. It was quiet here; she could barely hear the faint strains of music from the ballroom. Gazing up at the glowing full moon, her thoughts drifted, and a slight sigh escaped her.

The mere fact that she was attending a ball in London at all was still unbelievable. Only months earlier she lived with her father and sister in a little cottage in the country. When her father died last October, he left her and Emma penniless, and Caroline had just accepted a position as a governess with a family in Sussex. Then her grandmother, Olivia Fairchild, the Dowager Countess of Glenwood, arrived, rescuing her and Emma from an uncertain fate and bringing them into a new world. She consequently met a family she had never known. During the past six months, she had grown to love her grandmother, as well as her mother's brother, Uncle Kit, and his wife, Jane, and their young son, Teddy. This new family was a soothing balm to help ease the ache of being left orphaned by the death of both her parents. Now after months of training in etiquette and deportment with her grandmother and Aunt Jane, she was finally making her Season debut in London, as all well-bred young ladies of society did. The ultimate goal, of which, was to find a suitable husband.

She had agonized for weeks over what to do about this situation. Would she be able to deter any suitors without causing her grandmother to become aware of her true intentions? Would her newly devised plan actually work? Could she extricate herself from the possibility of marriage without arousing suspicion of the truth?

The truth that still haunted her night after night. The truth that she could not marry anyone.

"Such a beautiful young lady shouldn't look so sad on such a beautiful night."

Almost jumping out of her skin, Caroline was startled by the sound of a deep male voice. With her hand on her pounding heart, she turned and saw the tall figure of a man leaning against another white marble column in the shadows at the far end of the balcony.

"I apologize for startling you."

After taking a shaky breath, her hand still on her heart, she murmured, "No, I am sorry, sir. I had no idea anyone else was out here. Forgive me if I have intruded." She turned to leave.

"No apologies are necessary. There is no reason for you to go," he said, his voice distinctive in its resonance. "We can both enjoy this incredible full moon."

As he moved forward and the moonlight fell across his face, Caroline saw that she did not recognize the man standing in the shadows. In fact, she was quite certain that she had never met him, because she would have remembered seeing that face.

Oh yes, she definitely would have remembered seeing that man's face before. Her heart skipped a little beat as she stared up at him, startling her more than his voice had just done. He was quite tall and powerfully built. He possessed a muscular body that was evidently used to a great deal of physical activity, and he held himself with an easy confidence. A suit of the finest quality fit his masculine form elegantly, without being fussy. Dark black hair covered his head, and piercing blue eyes peered astutely from his classically chiseled face. He was not sporting a set of whiskers, as was the current fashion for men, but was clean shaven, which set off his features more prominently: an aquiline nose; a strong, angular jawline; and dark, expressive eyebrows framed eyes that projected honesty, intelligence, and humor. He was handsome with a very commanding presence.

The man was perfect looking.

"Why aren't you inside, trying to find a husband like all the other girls?" He stepped toward her, stopping about a foot away, and leaned himself casually against the white marble railing.

She saw him smile and then realized he was teasing her. Oddly unsettled by his physical presence and more than a little irked by his condescending comment, she offered back with slight sarcasm, "Maybe I don't want a husband."

With a smirk on his handsome face, he cast a doubtful look in her direction. He uttered somewhat scornfully, "In all my life I have yet to meet a female that didn't want a husband."

Now Caroline was irritated. He had actually smirked at her! Moreover, he certainly harbored a low opinion of women. "Well, there is always a first time for everything. I am Miss Caroline Armstrong. And I do not want a husband." She curtsied in mock politeness, a contemptuous look on her face, certain that she had broken quite a number of rules of etiquette on the proper introduction to a gentleman. "I am pleased to meet you."

Picking up on her little game, he bowed most elegantly, his eyes flashing at her. "I am Alexander Woodward, and it is, indeed, an honor to meet you, Miss Armstrong." Each word dripped with disdain.

His name sounded vaguely familiar to her, but then she had been introduced to so many people in the past weeks that all the names had blurred. "Congratulations, Mr. Woodward. You have finally met a woman who does not wish to get married." Then she added impetuously, "I do hope you don't faint."

He shook his head lightly and grinned at her with a wry look. "I find it very difficult to imagine that a young lady such as yourself has no interest in getting married."

"Then you obviously have a very poor imagination."

He laughed out loud at that. An appreciative laugh, deep and full of mirth. Then, with an intense stare, he questioned her. "Why are you having a Season then, Miss Armstrong, if not to look for a husband?"

"Because my grandmother expects me to." The truth was out of Caroline's mouth before she could consider what she was saying. It was a relief to finally be honest about how she felt. Even to a complete stranger. And a very handsome stranger at that. "She, along with everyone else in society, seems to think that it is of the utmost importance for me to get married as quickly as possible."

"You don't agree with that sentiment?"

"Not particularly, no."

"What if a suitable young man offers for you? What will you do then?"

"That won't happen because I shall not encourage anyone. I'll be a bluestocking, deadly dull, a boring old spinster." Now she had confessed her plan to him. What *was* she thinking?

"I don't think you could convince anyone that you are a boring old spinster."

"My, but you are full of opinions, Mr. Woodward."

"As are you, Miss Armstrong. But I stand by my opinion that you couldn't convince anyone that you are a boring old spinster. Not with your looks, anyway." His eyes moved over her, and her cheeks warmed under his regard.

"You didn't see me dance with Lord Kingston earlier. I think he found me most disagreeable." She grinned in satisfaction at the memory of the repellant man scurrying away from her after their brief dance. "In fact, I'm positive he did."

"Arthur Kingston?" Alex muttered in disgust, his dark brows creasing into a frown. "I should say you would want to stay away from that lame excuse of a man. Though I cannot imagine he let you go so easily. How did you manage to escape?"

She gave him a superior glance. "Listen." He watched with interest as she screwed up her face in a surprisingly sour expression, affected a high-pitched nasal voice, and said with great condescension, "I couldn't possibly marry anyone who isn't able to quote Plato's *Republic* or Sophocles's *Antigone.*" She topped that off with a sentence in Greek.

"Quite an unattractive little voice you have there," he quipped.

She laughed and resumed speaking in her natural

voice. "That's what I was hoping for. Anytime Lord Kingston asked me a question, I answered him in Greek. I'm not sure if he even understood what I was saying, but he looked utterly horrified. He couldn't leave me fast enough when the music stopped. Coughing in his face probably scared him off as well."

"You coughed in his face?" he asked in astonishment, pushing himself from his casual position at the railing to stare at her.

Caroline nodded with an exhilarated grin. "It would be rather frowned upon by the etiquette books."

"I should say so."

"I thought it quite inspired."

"If anyone deserves that kind of treatment, it's definitely Arthur Kingston. That's the best bit of news I've heard all day. I admire your spirit."

An unexpected thrill coursed through her at his compliment. "Thank you." She went on to explain with an air of satisfaction, "I am sure by now the word is out that I am an original bluestocking and terribly ill-mannered and no one will want me."

"That point is still debatable," he said, eyeing her carefully.

Once again her cheeks grew warm, and she glanced away, suddenly shy. There was a brief moment of silence between them.

"You actually told him that he disgusts you?" Alex asked with quiet deliberation.

"You understand Greek?" The surprise registered on her face. She had not expected this from him.

"Yes, I happen to know some Greek, among other languages. And it is obvious that you are very well educated." Alex paused deliberately and gave her a teasing look. "For a female."

She rose to the bait and frowned at him. "Yes, I am very well educated, as a female *should* be."

"And how did you come upon this vast education, Miss Armstrong?"

"Unlike most people"—she tossed him a disdainful glance—"my father was an enlightened and unprejudiced man who believed in educating women. He taught me everything he knew. History, literature, art, botany, astronomy, and philosophy. As well as Latin, French, Spanish, Italian, and of course Greek." She couldn't resist smiling proudly.

He gazed at her. "Appallingly few women are as well educated as you are, Miss Armstrong. I am very impressed. With you and your father."

Rather taken aback by his reaction, she had the wind taken out of her sails for she had been prepared to spar with him over that point. To her immense surprise, she was again thrilled by his unexpected praise. Most men did not care for intelligent women. That fact was now her secret weapon against unwanted suitors. Arthur Kingston and two other gentlemen practically ran from her when she demonstrated her academic knowledge. It was oddly gratifying to learn that this man, this very handsome man, approved of her unusual education. Caroline murmured a simple, "Thank you."

"Your father sounds like a man I would enjoy meeting."

"Oh." She hesitated. "My father . . . he passed away last fall. And my mother died when I was twelve."

"I'm terribly sorry." His voice was filled with genuine concern, and the teasing look that had been on his face earlier disappeared. For some reason, that touched her. "You have my deepest sympathies, Miss Armstrong. My own father passed away last summer."

She sensed his emotion and looked up into his dark eyes, and her heart thudded in her chest. "I am sorry for your loss as well."

"Thank you."

Tearing her gaze from those dangerous eyes, she clarified, "I live with my grandmother now."

"Ah yes." He nodded his head in acknowledgment. "The grandmother who insists upon you having a Season." His eyebrows arched with interest, and the tender, sad moment between them passed. "Why put yourself through all this nonsense? Why not simply tell your grandmother that you do not wish to marry?"

Caroline shook her head. "You don't know my grandmother. She would never understand the fact that I don't want to marry anyone. She means well, but she doesn't quite approve of my 'vast' education. In her eyes, a young lady's only goal in life is to secure a successful marriage to a suitable man. That is all she can envision for my future."

"I see." Alex folded his arms comfortably across his broad chest and leaned back against the railing in a relaxed pose. "I am very intrigued. Please tell me, Miss Armstrong, what other strategies do you have planned for ridding yourself of unwanted admirers?"

"That's it, I'm afraid. Aside from acting dull and academic, I wanted to wear spectacles and a very unflattering gown this evening, but then my grandmother would have surely seen through my plan." It made no sense, but she could not seem to stop herself from telling him any of this.

"Yes, I can see where that would make her suspicious. Still, I think it would be very difficult for you to conceal your beauty, Miss Armstrong. Even with spectacles." His appreciative gaze caused her skin to tingle.

Caroline gently shook her head and protested, "Besides, I'm too old to interest anyone. I'm twenty-two already!" Why was she confiding in him? How did he make her feel so at ease? Yet it was good to share her feelings openly with someone. She had held the burden of too many secrets for far too long. What did it matter if she told a stranger anyway?

He grinned at her, feigning shock. "As old as twenty-two, are you?"

"Yes . . . I'm almost a spinster for certain. No one could possibly be interested in me."

"I think you would interest many young men in that ballroom, Miss Armstrong."

Although the look he gave her caused her stomach to flutter, Caroline stated emphatically, "Well, Mr. Woodward, I can assure you that I have no interest in marrying anyone in that ballroom."

"Aha!" he declared in triumph, eyeing her keenly, challenging her. "Then it's just this particular ballroom that holds no interest for you."

She scoffed at him, "Don't be ridiculous."

"Now wait a minute, Little Miss I-Don't-Want-a-Husband. I think we have just come to the real reason that you say you don't want to have a Season. It's not that you don't wish to marry. It's that you don't wish to marry anyone *here*." Alex grinned knowingly, like the cat that ate the canary. When she made no response to the contrary, he continued with his theory. "I believe that there is a someone. Someone who is not here, whom you are very interested in marrying. This would also explain your sadness this evening. Am I correct, Miss Armstrong?"

"No, Mr. Woodward, you are not correct. In fact,

far from it." She uttered the words coolly, belying the fact that she was a little unnerved that he had so nearly guessed her secret. He knew way too much about her already, and she couldn't afford to divulge any more information. Instead she turned the tables on him. "Why are you here tonight, Mr. Woodward? Are you looking for a wife?"

"Lord, no!" He looked at her slyly and raised one eyebrow. "Not in that ballroom, anyway. But what makes you think that I'm not married already?" he asked, his eyes lingering on hers.

"You don't act as if you are married."

"And just how does a married man act?"

"I'm not sure exactly"—she regarded him carefully—"but I have the distinct feeling that they don't act the way you do. I have the impression you're hiding."

"Now what would I possibly be hiding from?" he asked with a charming grin, which caused her heart to skip a beat again.

"Most likely you are hiding out here to avoid the husband-hungry ladies and their mothers in the ballroom." Glancing up at those dangerous eyes, she thought he certainly was handsome enough to have all those women falling at his feet.

"You are absolutely right, Miss Armstrong," he conceded easily. "I am only in attendance tonight to fulfill a promise. I'm out here because I am most definitely trying to avoid the ladies in the ballroom." After a moment, he added, "Now we know each other's secrets."

Idly running her fingers along the cool marble railing, she whispered, "It seems we do."

"So here we are, the pair of us, out here hiding in

the dark. Two people who don't wish to marry"—he gave a sly wink—"anyone in *that* ballroom."

Exasperated, she shook her head slightly and grinned at him. "You won't give my secret away will you, Mr. Woodward?"

"If you promise to call me Alex and I can call you . . . Caroline, was it?"

"Caroline," she repeated.

"Well, *Caroline*, since we know some secrets about each other, we should be on a first-name basis, don't you think?"

"I think, *Alex*, that we have a deal then," she agreed with a teasing smile, looking up at him. He reached for her, gently taking hold of both her small hands. She let out a little gasp of surprise, but she did not pull away.

Tiny tingling sensations began to build inside her as his hands held hers. Oh, she definitely should have left her gloves on! For now she could feel his warm skin and his strong yet soft fingers that held her gently but with a firm pressure. It was difficult to breathe because her heart was beating so rapidly. She had the oddest feeling that something very special was happening. She lifted her gaze to meet his eyes, those dark eyes, and had the sensation that she was suddenly falling off a very, very steep cliff.

His voice was a whisper. "Shall we seal our secrets with a kiss?"

CHAPTER 2

Without a second's hesitation, he pulled her closer, lowering his mouth over hers. When his lips touched hers, Caroline felt a shock go through her entire body, as if someone poured liquid fire directly into her veins. His lips were hot, searing. They moved deliberately, purposefully, intently over hers. He tasted faintly of some spice she couldn't name. She was unable to breathe and was overwhelmed by him, yet did not want the feeling to end. There was a tingling and a tightening sensation deep down in her stomach. Her mouth opened of its own volition, and he seductively slipped his tongue inside. She accepted him readily, savoring the taste of him, maneuvering her tongue to meet his. Slick. Warm. Swirling. Amazing. This was no hurried kiss. He was taking his time with her.

His hands, having released hers, slowly, deliberately slid up the length of her bare arms and shoulders, softly caressing her warm skin. Like a whisper, his fingers paused at the back of her neck, stroking, barely touching the sensitive area. She trembled in response to the feel of his hands on her body, her neck, her skin. Then his hands moved leisurely down her spine, pressing her body full against his. Her arms, which had been hanging motionless at her side, suddenly found the will to reach up and encircle him, drawing him nearer to her.

Caroline knew it was highly improper for this man to kiss her. She should not even be out here alone with him at all, let alone confiding her deepest secrets in him, laughing with him, allowing him to hold her hands so intimately. Her grandmother would be scandalized at the very thought of Caroline in the dark with this man. A stranger, no less! With the exception of his name and that he did not want to get married, she knew nothing else about him. She knew only that she responded to this man on some level. That she could trust him somehow. He would keep her secret safe.

The thought that her behavior was scandalous vaguely entered her mind as his kiss deepened in intensity, causing that thought to flutter away much like a feather in a puff of a breeze. She couldn't seem to keep a coherent thought in her head at all. She could do nothing except kiss him back. And feel: his lips, his tongue, his hands, his heat. Alexander. His name tumbled over and over in her mind. Alex, Alex, Alex.

Pressing herself closer against his chest, her hands traveled behind his head, hesitantly touching his thick, dark hair. A slight moan of pleasure escaped his mouth, and he pulled her tighter, causing her to melt completely against him, her breasts crushing against his chest. Temptation and desire coursed through her. She was dizzy with it. Almost drunk with it. His body was strong and hard, yet she was enveloped in the incredible warmth and softness of him. Lost. She was completely and utterly lost in this man's embrace. She didn't care if she was never found.

Abruptly Alex pushed her away from him.

Feeling somewhat dazed, as if she were waking from a dream, she reluctantly opened her eyes to see him staring at her intently. He was breathing as hard as she was, and their eyes locked together. Too stunned by their powerful reaction to each other to speak, they simply gazed into each other's eyes for what seemed like an eternity, trying to catch their breaths and make some sense out of what had just happened. He reached for her hands again and held them tightly in his own.

Smiling faintly at him, Caroline struggled to breathe. She felt hot and shaky, not at all herself. The desire to have him kiss her like that again ran rampant in her veins and left her trembling and without the ability to speak. To say something. Anything. Instead of standing there willing him with her eyes to kiss her again. Gazing up at him, she knew he knew exactly what she wanted from him. She should be embarrassed to the tips of her toes, but for some inexplicable reason she was not embarrassed at all.

They were still staring at each other, not saying a word, when a young man and woman, whispering and giggling together, stumbled out onto the balcony, interrupting their little reverie. Caroline barely noticed them, but Alex quickly dropped her hands.

"Oh, excuse us, Your Grace. We didn't mean to disturb you," the young man apologized nervously, as the red-haired girl he was with stared at them with wide eyes, both of them suddenly subdued.

Alex flashed them a friendly smile. "It's quite all right. We were just going inside. Good evening."

He quickly guided Caroline through the French doors and back into the house. In the candlelit hallway, he placed a gentle kiss upon her forehead. "Please forgive my behavior. I shouldn't have taken such liberties with you," he apologized, but his eyes said he had no regrets.

She merely blinked at him.

"Well, Caroline, it seems our secrets are well sealed and quite safe now."

"I'm not sure the etiquette book would approve of this . . ." she murmured.

He grinned ruefully. "No doubt you are quite right. You had better return to the ballroom. Although I must say that I enjoyed our little . . . conversation . . . immensely."

"Yes . . . thank you very much." *Did I just thank him for kissing me?* Caroline thought she was losing her mind completely. "I'm sure my grandmother must be wondering where I am by now," she managed to whisper, as she quickly turned and made her way on shaky legs down the dimly lit corridor.

Somehow, she found an unoccupied alcove, partitioned with heavy velvet drapes, in which to sit for a moment. Her breathing still had not slowed, and her head was spinning wildly with thoughts and feelings she didn't know she possessed. Feeling strangely giddy and bubbly, she was amazed at her brazen behavior. She had a sinking feeling that had Alex not ended the kiss when he did, she very well might have let him take further liberties with her, because she had certainly been incapable of stopping him at the time. The thought had not even entered her mind to stop him.

Mortified by her feelings, she covered her heated cheeks with her hands. She wanted to scream and giggle and cry all in the same instant. How could she have behaved so disgracefully? What had come over her? She had not wanted his kiss to end. She had wanted it to go on and on, and when it did end, she wanted to cry out with the loss of it. How could she feel this way about a complete stranger when Stephen's kisses had never made her feel this way?

Stephen!

She clutched her stomach and rocked back and forth, now feeling slightly ill. Not once had she thought about Stephen Bennett. Oh, she was shameful. Dreadful. She had no business kissing another man. A man she didn't even know!

Yet that was what was so extraordinary. Alex didn't feel like a stranger.

Caroline couldn't shake the sensation that she knew him. But that couldn't be. She had only just met Mr. Alexander Woodward.

Your Grace.

The young man on the balcony had called Alex "Your Grace." That was the form of address for a duke. And there was only one duke she knew of that would be at the Maxwells' ball tonight.

This could only mean that Alexander Woodward was none other than the Duke of Woodborough.

The well-known, handsome, wealthy, sought-after Duke of Woodborough had just kissed her passionately in the moonlight. She couldn't suppress a bubble of feminine pride from rising up within her, and she giggled. Then she suddenly stopped.

The Duke of Woodborough was practically engaged to Lady Madeline Maxwell. At least that's what everyone was saying.

Then what was he doing, hiding on the balcony at the home of his intended betrothed, saying he didn't want to get married, and kissing Caroline? What was he about with his heated kisses and his wonderful hands on her when he was practically engaged to another? A tiny pang of jealousy pricked her at the thought of him marrying that haughty Madeline Maxwell.

Laughing at herself and the ridiculousness of the situation, she wondered idly whatever happened to the reasonable, sensible Caroline. Quite sure she didn't know, she sighed deeply, knowing she had better hurry back to the ballroom. She quietly returned to her grandmother, seated in a dim corner. The loud music and steady hum of conversation now irritated her already frayed nerves, so it was not difficult for her to feign an illness when Olivia asked where she had been.

"I just went out for some fresh air. I have a crushing headache."

"You do look a little flushed," Olivia noticed with some concern, smoothing her hand across Caroline's forehead. "And you look more like your mother than you will ever know," she said with a bittersweet smile. Then she became stern. "Lord Summerton came to claim his dance with you."

"I'm sorry, Grandmother, but I fear I'm not up to dancing at the moment. I feel ill," she murmured, placing her hand to her temple. Sensing her grandmother's disappointment that she was not making the great impression expected of her, she truly felt ill and was no longer capable of acting her role of the boring old spinster this evening. She had just been kissed by a complete stranger and was stunned by the impact. How could she now dance with awkward boys and pretend to be a bluestocking? Nervously, her eyes scanned the room hoping to catch a glimpse of Alexander Woodward. Yet she feared that she would. For whatever would she say if she did see him?

Then she saw him.

Her heart began to thud in her chest, and her stomach fluttered in a nervous reaction that was new to her. Alexander Woodward was standing across the room, speaking with Lord Maxwell. In the light, she was amazed by just how strikingly handsome he was, even in profile. The sight of him took her breath away. The strong line of his jaw, the aquiline nose, the chiseled features—it was as if he were carved from marble. His black hair gleamed. His eyes flashed. He seemed taller than she remembered, because he practically towered over every man in the room. He had an energy around him that fascinated her. There was a distinctly displeased look on his face at the moment, however. He seemed more than irritated. His sensual mouth was set in a grim line. The unusual thought that she would never want to cause him to look at her that way flickered briefly through her mind. She preferred the way he looked at her after they had kissed. It was an intimate, knowing look. It made her feel special. She couldn't help but wonder what so displeased him now with Lord Maxwell. Surreptitiously she continued to watch him over the brim of her white lace fan.

Alex didn't seem to notice her at first, but then, as if feeling her gaze, he deliberately turned and looked in her direction. He smiled as their eyes met across the room. It was a secretive smile. A suggestive smile. A smile that said nothing at all, yet spoke volumes. It flooded her with a feeling she couldn't describe, but that feeling reached all the way down to her belly, almost taking her breath away. She smiled back, unable to do anything else. Then embarrassed, she quickly averted her eyes and chatted absently with her grandmother. When she dared to look up again, he was nowhere in sight.

CHAPTER 3

"I have absolutely no intention of marrying your daughter. I do not appreciate being placed in this awkward position. You must put a stop to your wife and daughter's gossip and misleading statements about me, or I will. And if I am the one to end it . . . Well, you know what that could do to her reputation. But this must end," insisted Alexander Woodward, the seventh Duke of Woodborough, as he stood in the elegant, if rarely used, library of Lord Albert Maxwell, while hundreds of guests were downstairs dancing in their crowded ballroom. The only reason he was attending this ball tonight was to clear up this situation once and for all.

"Your father and I always thought that you and Madeline would make a fine match, Your Grace. Madeline was the toast of London last Season and held off many offers of marriage with the understanding that she would eventually marry you," Lord Maxwell mumbled, a note of sadness in his tone. He was a very short man with a paunchy middle, typical of his years. He had a round red face, from which bulged pale, watery blue eyes, and his mostly bald head was topped by thin wisps of white hair. His white tie was askew, adding to his usual rumpled appearance, for which his wife, Ellie, was forever berating him.

Alex sighed in weariness. "I understand you were a good friend to my father, and I am sorry that you were given the impression that I was going to marry your daughter. But I made it very clear to my father before he died that I would find a wife of my own choosing. However charming Madeline is, I do not think that we would suit each other. I have known her since she was a child, and I have no interest in her. Since my father died last summer, your wife and daughter have deluded half of London into believing that I am about to offer for her. Even my own friends are beginning to believe it!" Noticing the expression on Lord Maxwell's face, he tried to reiterate it more kindly. "Madeline is a lovely young lady and will make a wonderful wife for some man. I am simply not that man. And not at any time have I ever led her, or you, or my own father to believe otherwise."

The last thing he wanted was a marriage to a spoiled little society chit like Madeline Maxwell. Everyone had heard the stories about her childhood and the excess to which her parents had spoiled her. The Maxwells had given their little girl her own miniature pony and cart at four years old, an extravagant Worth gown from Paris made especially for her at age ten, and a diamond and ruby tiara for her sixteenth birthday. How would one ever satisfy a wife with those expectations?

An uncomfortable silence ensued before the duke added, "If you do not wish to inform Madeline of my true intentions, I will discuss the matter with her personally."

"It is just that she has her heart set on you and I don't know how to break the news to her." Lord Maxwell's small, beefy hand shook as he took a gulp of whiskey. "Or to my wife."

The duke ignored that last statement. "Tonight we can say that Madeline has changed her mind and that she does not wish to marry me."

Lord Maxwell scoffed at the very idea. "Who would believe that?"

The duke knew that Lord Maxwell was correct. At thirty years old he was the most sought-after bachelor in London. The good Lord had graced him with innumerable assets. A keen intelligence, a charming magnetism, and a vast fortune were just a few of the features that made him attractive to the opposite sex. The Duke of Woodborough was an uncommonly handsome man and well aware of it. Yet he did not flaunt or take advantage of its powers. "Well, she could say that she dislikes me. She could say that I am a cad, a rake, a drunkard. I really don't care how she explains it. Blame everything on me and I will not say a word against her."

"Everyone just assumed that you and Madeline would marry, especially since your father passed away. But I suppose I could just let the word out that there will be no marriage." Lord Maxwell conceded sadly, his fat jowls sagging in misery.

The duke said, "Well, it is not as though there has ever been a formal announcement about it."

"And what sort of announcement would that be?" a playful, girlish voice asked.

Lady Madeline Maxwell, a petite vision of femininity in a baby blue silk gown that accentuated the pale blue of her eyes, breezed into the library. She tossed her yellow curls and smiled sweetly at her father, then turned her full attention upon the Duke of Woodborough.

"Uh . . . Madeline . . . darling . . . The duke and I were . . . just . . . discussing . . ." Lord Maxwell stammered weakly.

The duke, looking directly at Lady Madeline, explained without pretense, "The fact that there will be no marriage between us."

The bright smile vanished from Madeline's pretty face. "Whatever do you mean, Your Grace?"

She was confused. This was not going at all how she intended. The duke, after settling matters with her father, was supposed to ask her to stroll in the rose garden and while there become so captivated by her charm and beauty that he would propose marriage. Ask her to be his duchess. The Duchess of Woodborough. That was what was supposed to happen. But now . . .

She did not like the look of his eyes. They were frosty and hard. Ice blue. She was accustomed to gentlemen looking at her with longing and appreciation. Men always did what she wanted them to. They were so easy to manipulate. A flutter of her long eyelashes, one pretty pout, a toss of her curls, and they were hers.

The duke was not behaving correctly. She had been positive that he was in love with her when they spoke last Christmas at the Talbots' Holiday Ball. He had smiled at her and commented that she had grown into a lovely young lady and that she was no longer the little girl he remembered teasing. She mentioned that their fathers hoped that they would marry someday, and he said he was aware of their wishes.

Everyone thought that they should marry. Everyone said she was perfect for him. His own father had wanted him to marry her, knowing full well that she would make a beautiful duchess. Every man wanted her. He would be crazy not to marry her! Yet he did not look like a man about to propose marriage now, standing before the mantel with his handsome features set in a dark scowl. So what had gone wrong?

"I mean, Lady Madeline, that I do not appreciate the gossip about us. However lovely you are, I have never mentioned marriage to you, or anyone else for that matter. You and I have not even seen each other in months. I am sorry to put this so bluntly, but I have no intention of proposing to you," the duke stated, his eyes locked with Madeline's.

An anguished moan escaped from Lord Maxwell. He sank heavily into a rich leather armchair, taking another long gulp of whiskey as he went.

Lady Madeline was stunned. Utterly stunned. No one had ever spoken so rudely to her before. How dare he! Her mind raced feverishly as she struggled to get her thoughts around the meaning of his words.

He did not want her.

He did not want her. *Her.* How could he not want her? Why, she was the one that everyone wanted! Didn't he just say that she was lovely? But wasn't she the loveliest, the most charming, the most fashionable, the most graceful? How could he not want her? There must be some terrible mistake.

"But everyone believes that we will be betrothed, Your Grace." She posed dramatically with her hands to her heart, hoping that he would notice how attractive her bosom was in her low-cut French gown.

Ignoring her affected posturing, he asked

with quiet determination, "Whose fault is that, Lady Madeline?"

"Papa?" Madeline turned to her father for confirmation that this man did not want to marry her. The idea was completely preposterous. The duke could not treat her this way. Surely her father would make him marry her. Her father always got her what she wanted.

Lord Maxwell could not meet his daughter's eyes and sank lower into his chair. "I'm sorry, my dear." He finished off his whiskey and stared at the empty glass.

This is impossible, Madeline thought. Everyone knew that they were getting married. She was going to be the Duchess of Woodborough. Her mother had said so. Her father had said so. Her friends had said so. Yet here was the duke himself saying it was not true.

He was not going to marry her.

What in heaven's name was she going to say to everybody? How could she ever show her face again?

If he didn't love her, her mind reasoned quickly, he must be in love with someone else. But who could it possibly be? There wasn't a girl in the *ton* who even came close to matching her in beauty or style. There had to be somebody though. Nothing else made sense. Madeline would find out who she was eventually. There could be no other logical explanation for him to spurn her. White-hot tears of humiliation stung behind her eyes, but she held them back. She clenched her hands so tightly her fingernails cut into the flesh of her palms. She would not cry.

Her pride and vanity bolstered her now. No one could think that the duke turned her away. No, no, no! *She* had to be the one to turn *him* down! Yes, that was it! Wouldn't that be something? The beautiful Lady Madeline Maxwell refused the Duke of Woodborough's hand in marriage! Why? She simply did not love him! And, oh, but he was devastated, completely crushed by her rejection! The gossips would love that. She would be renowned. Gentlemen would flock to her, wanting to be the one she chose in his place! Yes . . . Yes. This could work.

However, she would have to marry very quickly to give the impression that she was in love with another all this time, that she had just been torn between her parents' wishes and her true love. But who? Who . . . ? John Talbot? He was young and handsome but would only be a baron. Besides, he was too serious. Maybe Oliver Parkridge? He was rich, young, somewhat handsome, and would at least become an earl when his father died. She could win him over in no time since he was in love with her already.

Yes, Oliver Parkridge would have to do.

She promptly composed herself and faced the duke. "Well then." She smiled brightly, while smoothing the silk ruffles of her blue gown.

From the depths of his chair, Lord Maxwell offered in a thin voice, "We can say you refused his hand, my dear."

Madeline gave a look full of sweetness, addressing her father, yet staring directly at the duke. "Papa, how can I refuse him if I have not yet been asked?"

The duke stared in disbelief at her outrageous implication. "I beg your pardon?"

"I cannot simply lie to everyone," Madeline stated as if speaking to a small child.

"Now, now, my dear . . ." began Lord Maxwell, stunned into rising from his chair. It would not do for his daughter to anger the already irritated duke. "Be reasonable."

Madeline sauntered to the tea cart and calmly poured herself a cup of tea, confident that the duke would do what she wanted. "I must be asked before I can refuse, Your Grace." She posed prettily with a delicate china teacup in her hand, fluttering her eyelashes with just the right amount of innocence.

The duke muttered something under his breath. "Let me understand this, Lady Madeline. You wish for me to propose marriage to you now, so that you can refuse me honestly?"

"Yes." She used the full force of her baby blue eyes to appeal to him. "Is that too much to ask?"

The clock on the mantel ticked rather loudly, echoing the silence of the elegant library. Madeline watched the tense emotions play across his face. He did not know what to make of her. Nevertheless, she knew him to be a gentleman. She waited patiently.

"Will you marry me, Lady Madeline?" The words were harsh, his voice like ice.

She set down the teacup, fluttered her long lashes again, and spoke with soft earnestness. "Thank you, Your Grace. You do me a great honor, but I fear that I cannot accept your proposal in good faith, although our families dearly wish for us to marry. To state it quite simply, I am in love with another. I hope you are not too disappointed. Please consider me your friend. I could not bear for anyone to believe that there were any ill feelings between us. Now if you will please excuse me, I must return to our guests. Good evening, Your Grace. Papa." Lady Madeline turned and glided from the library, leaving the two men standing there quite speechless.

* * *

"How did she take it?" Lily Sherwood asked, handing the Duke of Woodborough a crystal glass filled with the finest bourbon his money could buy.

"Thank you." He kissed her cheek as he gratefully accepted the drink from her. "She handled it better than I expected. Lord Maxwell actually seemed to take it harder than she did. But then again, he has to live with her and her disappointment. Poor old man." He shook his head grimly as he sipped his bourbon.

Lily gave a little laugh. "Well, as I said earlier, all of London is under the impression that you are going to marry this girl. You've been buried out at Ridge Haven and Summerfields since Christmas and have ignored all the talk about you and her." Lily's dark eyes sparkled with a seductive gleam. "You have to admit, it was rather an ingenious plan. She even had your father's consent. You can't blame the girl for trying."

With her silky black hair, clear white skin, supple body, and long legs, Lily Sherwood had once been an acclaimed ballerina. But she was over thirty years old now and well past the time when she could dance for a living. The duke met her six years ago after one of her performances at the theater. He had been taken by her stunning beauty and quiet manner. So much so that he set her up in an elegant house in a fine neighborhood and provided very well for her, an arrangement of which she did not take advantage. They had a good relationship and they enjoyed each other's company immensely, both in and out of the bedroom.

"I'm going back to Ridge Haven tomorrow. I need

to get out of London." He laid down on his back, settling into the comfortable pillow-strewn sofa.

"But you only arrived a few days ago." She brushed her hand along his arm. "We've hardly seen each other."

He groaned at the prospect of remaining in the city. He could not stomach another Season of greedy women vying for his attention. The first Season he had participated in during his early twenties had soured him on the whole marriage business. It wouldn't matter if he were a miserable miser with a hump and one eye, as long as he was the Duke of Woodborough and had money, women would seek him out to be his wife. Since his father's death, his obligation to marry had been brought to light with more urgency, and he had steeled himself to participate in the coming Season. And once again, he found himself the object of acquisitiveness in women. The last straw had been that conniving Madeline Maxwell and her mother. The entire situation left him with a sordid feeling. Imagine the gall of that girl in demanding that he propose so that she could refuse him to save face in circumstances of her own creation! At least the matter was done now. Marriage! It turned females into crazed creatures and turned him off the entire thought of it. Oh, he knew marrying well was his duty, and he had every intention of fulfilling that duty, but for some strange reason he needed to know that he was wanted for something more than just his title and wealth.

"I know. But I cannot abide all these marriage-hungry mothers, throwing their dreary daughters at me. It's appalling. I spent most of the evening outside to get away from the matchmakers." His hands set her long hair free from its knot atop her head, sending it cascading in dark silky waves around them.

She made mocking *tsk, tsk* sounds as she teased him. "Poor baby. Women falling at your feet. All men should have such troubles." Her sheer negligee barely covered her as she stretched her lithe dancer's body on top of him.

He laughed with ease and kissed her, but inwardly he wished Lily understood what he meant. He wanted something special. Something different from anything he had yet to find. And not for the first time this evening, an image of Caroline Armstrong flashed through his mind.

"You have to marry, and once you do, all these women will leave you alone. Or so one would think." Her long fingers caressed the masculine line of his jaw. "You're too handsome by far, Alex."

He took Lily's hand in his and kissed her fingers one by one. It seemed throughout his childhood he was reminded that he would inherit the highly vaunted title of Duke of Woodborough one day. To that end, he never knew if he was valued for himself or for his title.

"Just get married. Just get married. Carry on the family name. Have sons. Pass on the title. That is all I have heard my whole life. It was my father's dying wish to me last summer, and it was my father who began all this nonsense with the Maxwells in the first place, all the while knowing that I had no desire to marry that spoiled, vain, little twit. Now it seems that every female of my acquaintance has taken it upon herself to see that I get married."

"So marry someone," Lily suggested, placing feathery kisses along his jawline until she encountered his ear, where she began to nibble delicately, which she knew from years of experience that he adored.

"Do you think I haven't thought about doing that? But I cannot marry just anyone."

She began to undo the buttons of his finely starched, white shirt. "Men do it all the time. Choose some biddable young girl with a pretty face, a good family, and a large dowry, and marry her," she said somewhat sarcastically.

He playfully swatted her bottom. "I don't wish to marry someone simply because she has the proper pedigree. These empty-headed girls only want me for my title and my money. They don't want to know me. Who I really am. I need something more from a wife. I want to marry . . ." His voice trailed off as he thought of a green-eyed beauty who did not wish to marry.

Lily suddenly stilled her movements, her heartbeat increasing its pace. "You're actually looking for a love match, aren't you?"

He caught her hands in his. "Now that you mention it, I suppose I am." With a brooding look, he formed into words the thoughts that had been buried within him for years. "I've seen too many marriages turn out badly, full of bitterness and anger. I want a marriage similar to the one my parents shared. They truly loved each other and were genuinely happy together. Why should I have to settle for less to fulfill an ancestral obligation? I want to marry someone I actually wish to spend my time with. Someone intelligent and passionate. Not one of these mindless girls on the marriage mart."

Lily blinked, her dark eyes wide. He had never talked of his feelings about marriage to her before.

Being a realist, she knew he could never marry her, a common dancer from the East End slums of London, nor had she expected it of him. She clearly understood that a duke had to marry. It was his familial duty. However, she cherished the idea that one day he might love her. She wouldn't care if he married some dim-witted society girl like Madeline Maxwell. A girl like that could never make him happy, which is precisely why she didn't mind. He could keep his little society wife and still love Lily. She had loved this man for five years and, if she knew nothing else, she knew without a doubt that if he married for love then it would be over between them. "What if you don't find that someone?" she asked in a breathless whisper.

He smiled seductively and tugged at the silken ties of her negligee, revealing her creamy white breasts. "Then I'll remain a bachelor all my life."

Lily placed her mouth on his and kissed him with an eager need, and he pulled her against his aroused body, blocking all thoughts of marriage from their minds.

CHAPTER 4

The Fairchild townhouse was awash with fresh flowers the morning after the Maxwells' ball. While Olivia, Emma, and Caroline sat sipping chocolate in the pale yellow morning room and discussing the night's events, bouquet after bouquet had been arriving for Emma with cards enclosed from suitors announcing their intentions to call upon her.

No flowers had come for Caroline.

"I do wish you had felt better last night," Emma said with a note of sadness in her voice. At seventeen, Emma had a pretty face, an impish disposition, and laughing hazel eyes. She was proud of the hearts she had won at her very first ball. "Half of these flowers should rightfully be yours, Caroline. You never gave any of the gentlemen a chance really."

"I just wasn't feeling well," Caroline said with forced cheerfulness as she refilled her cup with chocolate. "There will be other balls and I will dazzle all the men there." She curled up on the comfortable, chintz-covered sofa.

Olivia shook her head with a frown, clearly

disappointed by Caroline's lack of admirers. She had expected her beautiful granddaughter to be a success. "I am afraid the damage may already be done, Caroline. I told you that your first appearance of the Season would be the most important. First impressions are the most lasting, my dear, and you were acting quite old-maidish last night. Gentlemen do not find that very attractive. You won't get a husband acting that way."

That was the whole point, Caroline thought to herself.

"Isn't it astonishing that Madeline Maxwell refused the Duke of Woodborough's proposal?" Emma changed the subject with ease. "They say the duke was so dejected that he left the ball early."

Caroline's head turned sharply in her sister's direction. "The Duke of Woodborough isn't going to marry Madeline Maxwell?" she asked, aware that her voice sounded unusually high and that her heart began to beat faster.

"No! The engagement is off! Lady Madeline refused his offer. It was all anyone was talking about," Emma gushed, her face alive with the excitement of sharing such scandalous information. "How could you not have heard?"

"I'm not sure," Caroline murmured, realizing she had been too lost in her own thoughts of standing on the balcony in the arms of the duke to notice anything else last night. If Alexander Woodward was not marrying Madeline and he was kissing Caroline, what did that mean? He certainly didn't seem dejected! Recalling his dark eyes looking at her, teasing her in the moonlight, the duke seemed very self-assured. In fact, he was a little full of himself. No, he was not acting the least bit dejected.

"She's a very foolish girl if you ask me," Olivia added pragmatically. "But then she takes after her mother. I was never fond of Ellie Maxwell."

Fraser, the Fairchild butler, entered the morning room carrying an extravagant arrangement of gardenias in an elegant crystal bowl. The sweet fragrance of the delicate, white blooms filled the air.

Immediately Emma ran to look at the card, giggling. "Oh, they're simply lovely! I wonder who sent them?"

"You must have made quite an impression on someone, my dear. They are most exquisite. And quite costly," Olivia observed as Fraser placed the arrangement on the mahogany end table next to a smaller bouquet of pink rose buds.

As Emma took the small white envelope in her hands, a curious expression came over her face. "These flowers are not for me . . ." She turned to smile at her sister. "They're for Caroline."

Caroline's face registered her astonishment as she glanced quickly between her sister and grandmother. She certainly had not encouraged anyone last night! "Who could have sent me flowers?" she wondered aloud.

"They were delivered by a servant of the Duke of Woodborough," Fraser stated dramatically, knowing it was not every day that a duke sent flowers. Then he discretely left the room.

"The Duke of Woodborough? Caroline!" Olivia's voice was filled with wonder as she abruptly rose from her chair. "When did you meet the Duke of Woodborough?"

"I . . . I didn't . . . That is . . . I didn't learn who

he was until afterward," Caroline stammered, a warm flush rising on her cheeks. "We only spoke for a moment."

"Well, give her the card, Emma," Olivia urged eagerly.

Emma rushed to Caroline, pressing the envelope into her hand. "Hurry and read it! I'm simply dying to know what it says!"

With shaking hands, Caroline opened the crisp white envelope sealed with the duke's family crest in dark blue wax. Why was Alexander Woodward sending her flowers? What could he possibly have to say to her? Her heart racing, she silently read the brief message written in bold masculine strokes.

> *My Dear Miss Armstrong,*
> *I felt compelled to thank you for such delightful conversation last evening. The gardenias remind me of you. I hope you will permit me the honor of calling upon you tomorrow afternoon.*
> *Alexander Woodward*

Caroline read the note a second time in disbelief. The words seemed to blur before her eyes. *Why on earth would he call on me?* Her heart filled with a mounting sense of unease. The duke knew that she was discouraging suitors and yet he still sent her flowers. Was he doing this to deliberately put her in an awkward situation? What was he up to?

Then there was that kiss. That kiss! Her cheeks reddened yet again at the memory of his lips on hers. His hands. His eyes.

He was not marrying Madeline Maxwell.

"Well . . . What does it say?" Emma asked impatiently,

standing on tiptoe, trying to peer over Caroline's shoulder to read the note.

"Read it, Caroline," Olivia demanded, eager to know what the duke had to say to her granddaughter.

Hesitantly, Caroline read the note aloud. When she was finished, she looked up at her speechless grandmother and sister.

Olivia sat down helplessly in her chair. After a moment, her eyes narrowed suspiciously. "A conversation? He sent you these expensive flowers to thank you for a conversation? What on earth did you say to the man, Caroline?"

"We spoke but for a moment," she answered vaguely.

Emma squealed in delight. "He's going to call on you! Here we thought you were ill and not enjoying yourself last night. Then you go and catch the Duke of Woodborough, without telling anyone. And pretending as if you didn't know! When did you speak with him?"

"Yes, when?" Olivia asked, her sharp eyes watching Caroline.

"Truly . . . It was nothing," Caroline stated slowly, for Emma's enthusiasm was making her nervous. "After dancing, I had a headache so I went outside for some air. He was already on the balcony. We spoke for a moment or two. I wasn't even aware he was the Duke of Woodborough at the time."

"'The gardenias remind me of you,'" Emma mused dreamily, holding the note in her hands. "That sounds very romantic. Whatever did you talk about?"

"Nothing special." Caroline felt uncomfortable discussing her encounter with the duke. What could she say? That she confessed her secret plan to him? She certainly could not tell them that she had kissed him passionately. And enjoyed it.

"Well, this is a pleasant surprise. I can't believe you didn't mention any of this last night, Caroline," Olivia said, regaining some composure while absently smoothing her silver hair. "Apparently the duke is quite taken with you."

Emma giggled, her hazel eyes dancing. "Mary Ellen Talbot pointed him out to me once last night, and he's devastatingly handsome. All the girls were mooning over him. I can't wait to tell Aunt Jane and Uncle Kit! The Duke of Woodborough and Caroline! It's too good to be true!"

"That's exactly it, Emma," Caroline exclaimed. "It is too good to be true. Why would a duke possibly be interested in me? I'm not the duchess type. He'd be wasting his time." She could not become involved with the duke, no matter what his intentions. It was impossible for her to become involved with anyone! Yet she had no idea how to explain that to her grandmother. She took a big gulp of air and blurted out, "I refuse to see him when he calls tomorrow."

"Nonsense!" Olivia said in a tone that brooked no argument. "We will just have to see what the duke has to say for himself. It can't hurt to speak with the man. Besides, we can hardly refuse to receive him, Caroline. He is a duke, after all."

That was exactly what Caroline was afraid of.

The next afternoon Alexander Woodward, the seventh Duke of Woodborough, was seated in the drawing room of Olivia Fairchild. Although he was usually put off by society matrons who were only interested in getting him to marry their daughters, Alex found himself liking Olivia right away. He admired her honesty and warmth, as well as her no-nonsense approach to his calling upon her grand-daughter. She was not at all intimidated by the fact that he was a duke, as most people were. After all the polite questions about his family, their health, and his health, Olivia finally asked the question to which he knew she really wanted the answer.

"So is it true that the Maxwell girl turned you down?" Olivia watched him carefully, her blue eyes peering at him.

Alex answered with caution, aware that a gentle-man must never disparage a lady in any manner. "It seems that way."

Olivia harrumphed skeptically. "I don't believe you. There is no way that spoiled little thing would have refused your proposal. You saw right through her plans, because you're intelligent. You weren't going to be railroaded into that marriage. And you are only saying that she turned you down to save her face." She smiled approvingly at him, satisfied with her analysis of the situation.

Maintaining a poker face, Alex stated calmly, "Madame, I don't know to what you are referring."

"A gentleman! I like that. You're much better off without her, young man. Madeline Maxwell, as pretty as she is, is spoiled, selfish, and vain. She would have made your life miserable." She nodded her head in approval of his actions.

Alex only smiled at her. "You are a very wise woman, Lady Fairchild."

She grinned at his compliment and smoothed her silvery hair with her hand. "Now to the point,"

Olivia said, her tone more serious. "What are your intentions with my Caroline?"

Alex sat quietly for a moment, unsure of what to say. Then he uttered quite clearly, "I want to marry her."

The words came from his mouth, yet he couldn't believe that he had said them aloud. He didn't even know what he was doing there getting grilled by the elderly countess, except that he could not help himself. Unable to stop thinking about Caroline, he didn't even stay the night at Lily's as he usually did. Restless and preoccupied with thoughts of their rather passionate encounter, he spent the next day finding out everything he could about her. Gaining knowledge of her unusual background, he laughed to himself as he heard some descriptions of her as being "a bluestocking" or a "trifle odd" and knew that Caroline would be pleased to learn that her little plan was working quite well after just one night. He remembered her on the balcony with the silvery moonlight spilling all around her, making her hair shimmer and her white satin gown glisten. She looked like a pensive little angel. She had been beautiful, witty, and surprisingly intelligent. He called on her today because he simply had to see her again. To see if she was truly as wonderful as he remembered her to be when he held her in his arms.

Marriage had not entered his mind. Well, not quite, anyway.

Now that he had said it aloud, marrying Caroline Armstrong seemed most appealing. Although he had only met her once, he sensed something about her that set her apart from the other women he knew. She was different, special somehow, and he was drawn to her. He had the oddest sensation that she belonged to him. Odder still was the feeling that she knew it as well. There was definitely something between them that night. They conversed easily enough and laughed together. He had also never had such a strong physical reaction to a woman before. However, he could not tell her grandmother that.

"Why do you want to marry her?" Olivia asked, full of curiosity. "You've only just met her."

"Upon meeting her at the ball, I found Caroline to be a very intelligent, charming, and beautiful young lady. I enjoyed her company immensely," he managed to say after a long silence. "I also have to marry. It is my duty as the Duke of Woodborough."

"Hmmm . . ." Olivia pondered this, again watching him with her sharp eyes. "So you want her to be your duchess?"

"Is that so surprising to you?"

"Frankly, yes," she said with candor. "Caroline and her sister, Emma, were not raised as ladies." She paused before stating, "I am sure you've heard about the terrible scandal concerning my daughter, Katherine."

Alex could sense that this was a painful subject for her, but he shook his head slightly, encouraging her to explain. Of course, he had heard the rumors but had never really paid much attention to the infamous story of Katherine Fairchild before; now he wanted to learn the truth about Caroline's family from its most reliable source.

Olivia gave him a look, as if trying to make up her mind about him, and then she began resolutely. "When Katherine was seventeen she was engaged to be married to Lord Montgomery, a handsome young man from a fine family, whom we had chosen for her. We did not know that she had already fallen in love with Richard Armstrong. Richard had been our son Kit's tutor. Richard was poor but from a decent enough family in Kent. My husband, Edward, and I tried to reason with Katherine, but she was young and foolish. One night the two of them simply ran off together. Their elopement caused such a dreadful scandal that Edward disowned her, cutting her off from the family completely. That was a terrible time for us." Olivia paused to dab her teary eyes with a lace handkerchief and continued with a slight sniffle. "So Katherine and Richard settled in the country, where he taught at the university in Shrewsbury, and they lived very simply. Katherine died of consumption many years ago, but it was not until Richard himself died last October that I was finally able to meet my granddaughters and bring them to live with me. Richard had been very ill, and Caroline had been supporting the family, working at the university. She was about to take a position as a governess when I arrived on their doorstep. Obviously the girls were not raised to be a part of our society, although I must say they were very well educated. They have only recently learned the finer points of proper etiquette for their coming-out. It could be quite daunting for Caroline to fill the role of duchess." Olivia glanced at him meaningfully.

"That means nothing to me. Caroline is different from any other lady of my acquaintance, and that is why I find her so attractive. She is bright and witty and versed in many languages. I have no doubt that she is more than capable of learning anything she needs to learn to be a duchess. Her background is irrelevant." Alex paused to add, "I also think that she is the most beautiful woman I have ever seen."

Olivia was speechless, yet beaming with pride at his praise of Caroline.

"Do I have your permission to call upon her, Lady Fairchild?" Alex asked.

"Why yes, of course. Now I will have her come down to see you."

"Would you allow me a moment of privacy with her, Lady Fairchild?" He knew it was improper, but he also knew that she was impressed with him.

She gave him a long look as she summed him up. "Your intentions are quite honorable, and I would not mind having you for a grandson-in-law," she stated with a grin. "I will allow it this one time."

A few moments later, Caroline came to the drawing room alone. She stood hesitantly in the doorway, and Alex suppressed the urge to laugh. Despite her attempt to appear otherwise, she was even more beautiful than he remembered. Her pale skin was flawless, her cheeks suffused lightly with color; her golden hair was pulled tightly back from her face and topped with a severe black mobcap; and her deep green eyes were almost hidden behind the thick, dark spectacles that perched absurdly on the tip of her little nose. Dressed in a dull black gown that had to be at least two decades behind the current fashion, with wide sleeves and a loosely fitted bodice that seemed to swallow her petite body completely, she looked ridiculous. Still, desire flickered within him at the mere sight of her, fueled by the memory of her in his arms. He extended his hand to her.

"I'm happy to see you again, Caroline." As he touched her hand, he was again struck by the powerful attraction between them. It was as if a jolt of some unexplainable force went through him and all he wanted to do was pull her into his arms and kiss her.

Caroline merely nodded her head in answer to his greeting, while he held her hand, unable to pull her gaze away from him. They simply stood there and stared at each other. Alex came to his senses and led Caroline to a chair. He released her hand in the hope that he would be able to speak again.

She, however, managed a fierce whisper. "What on earth are you doing here?"

He laughed and smiled at her. "Not quite the greeting I was hoping for, but to answer your question, I wanted to see you again." His eyes moved over her.

"And whatever possessed you to send me flowers?" she asked irritably.

"I wanted to apologize to you. We parted so abruptly the other night and I didn't want you to think that I was taking advantage of you or the—"

"It's best if we forget what happened that night," she interrupted him, looking away.

Standing in front of her, Alex lifted her chin with his index finger so she was forced to look up and face him again. Gently removing the hideous spectacles from her face, he felt her tremble. He asked very softly, looking into her eyes, "I don't think I can forget about it, Caroline. Can you?" He brushed his finger across her lips, as he held her chin. Her sharp intake of breath answered his question more eloquently than words. Tempted to kiss her then and there, but thinking better of it, he stepped back from her and said in a conspiratorial whisper, "It won't work."

"What won't work?" she asked breathlessly.

"Your little spinster disguise." He tossed the spectacles back to her and was pleased by her quick agility in catching them. "It won't work."

"That's only because you know my plan." She did not don the spectacles again, however, but fiddled with them in her palm. "I had no idea you were the Duke of Woodborough the other night."

"I figured as much. But does your knowing who I am change what happened between us?"

She gave him a sharp look and changed the subject. "I thought you were supposed to marry Lady Madeline."

He sighed heavily and directed his gaze at her. "This is very ungentlemanly of me to say, but I would prefer to be honest with you. I never had any intention of marrying Madeline Maxwell."

"But everyone said that you—"

"No," Alex interrupted her, "Madeline led everyone to believe that I was going to propose to her, when I never indicated anything of the sort."

"Oh," she murmured, her green eyes wide. "So what are you doing here?"

There was a long pause as his little plan took its final shape in his mind. "I've been considering our secrets, and I thought we might be able to help each other."

"What do you mean?"

"Well, I've been thinking. Since neither of us wishes to marry at the moment, for whatever reasons . . ." He glanced at her meaningfully. "And since everyone expects us to get married, I thought that maybe we could let everyone assume we are going to marry each other and then the pressure would be off both of us."

Caroline stared at him, a puzzled expression on her face. "What are you saying?"

"What I'm saying is that both of us are presently under some pressure from our families to marry someone soon, correct?"

"Yes."

"And neither of us particularly wishes to marry for the time being, correct?"

"Yes . . ." Caroline's green eyes were riveted to him.

"Here comes the part where we can help each other out a bit. We like each other and can be friends, can't we?" he asked, luring her in.

She nodded at him, her beautiful face looking intent.

"Well, if everyone thought you were engaged to me, you wouldn't have to attend the rest of the parties and balls pretending to be a dull spinster to ward off unwanted suitors. On the other hand, it would also work to my benefit, for if everyone thought I was engaged to you, I would be free of matchmaking mothers and other female maneuverings, *à la* Madeline Maxwell. If she could so readily lead the *ton* into thinking that I was about to propose, why couldn't I do the same thing to my own advantage? Why not let everyone assume that you and I are going to be engaged, and then we could do what we like and enjoy ourselves instead of hiding on dark balconies? It could work out very nicely for us and buy us both some time. What do you think?"

"I think you are positively mad."

Alex laughed at her astonished expression. "You're a smart girl, Caroline. Think about it." He smiled mischievously. "It could work."

Her delicate brow furrowed. "We pretend to be courting and then betrothed? Fooling everyone?"

"Yes, more or less."

"But wouldn't our families expect us to marry each other eventually?" she asked.

"We wouldn't have to worry about that for months. We could start slowly, being seen together at parties and balls. The gossip would start and everyone would know I was courting you. Eventually, we could announce an engagement, which we could make as long or as short a time as we wanted. Then we could break off amicably, declaring that we discovered that we do not suit one another well, and part as dear friends. What do you think?" When she didn't respond, he perceptively added, "I know you are waiting for someone, Caroline . . . You can end our arrangement whenever you wish."

Their eyes locked for some minutes. His heart pounded.

"We don't even know each other," she said at last.

"I disagree. I think we already know each other better than most people do. We can certainly converse easily enough, and I appreciate your wit and intelligence. I believe we can be good friends and enjoy each other's company." He arched one black eyebrow as he stared at her. "And we can get to know each other better in the meantime." He grinned playfully, and she laughed a little. Feeling he was making a good case, he continued, "We wouldn't be hurting anyone. It only concerns the two of us, and no one has to know about it. It would be our little secret."

She glanced uncertainly toward him, her gorgeous eyes wide.

Alex smiled at her. He couldn't help but smile at her. She was so incredibly beautiful. As he watched the play of emotions across her face, he knew he was slowly winning her over, and it made him irrationally happy to think that she would agree to his little plan. A part of him still wondered what the hell he was doing here and just what he was getting himself into, knowing only that he wanted this woman more than any woman he had met in his life and this was the only way he could think of to get her. He was also supremely confident that he could make her forget this other man, whoever he was, and he could marry her. "Well?" he prompted her suggestively.

She sat still, staring at him, her face serious. "You know that I cannot marry you and that this pretense would be only for our mutual convenience?"

"Of course."

"I can end this arrangement whenever I wish?"

"Yes," he agreed, still smiling into her green eyes.

Unable to resist his smile, she grinned back at him. "I cannot believe that I'm saying this, but I will agree to this unusual arrangement with you."

"I knew you were an intelligent young lady." He leaned closer to her, inhaling the sweet scent of her, and murmured, "Shall we seal our new secret with another kiss?"

"Oh no." She shook her head violently. "We will have no more of that. If you want me to agree to this, then you have to agree there will be no more kissing."

"But you want to kiss me," he laughed. He knew she did. He just wanted to tempt her.

"No kisses or no deal." Her sensuous mouth was set in a line of determination.

"Deal." He agreed, and smiled at the look of surprise on her face.

CHAPTER 5

The afternoon following the duke's visit to Caroline, Lady Weatherby celebrated her seventy-first birthday by having an intimate tea with forty of her closest friends and family. As the guests assembled in the main salon of her townhouse, Lady Weatherby sat like a benevolent queen holding court, where she welcomed everyone with a smile and commanded them to have refreshments. She was a kindly woman who loved parties and gossips. Olivia Fairchild was her dearest friend. While the older women in this gathering of females sat in chairs and sofas near their hostess, the younger girls congregated in the small side parlor.

Caroline and Emma were by now acquainted with most of the girls there and greeted the friends they had made during the pre-Season activities, and they were introduced to those individuals they had not met before. There was much kissing, hugging, and complimenting of pretty pastel dresses. With her outgoing ways, friendly manner, and easy sense of humor, Emma was a particular favorite among the girls. On the other hand, Caroline, who had not been able to participate wholeheartedly in the discussion of beaux and needed to keep herself as unobtrusive as possible, had kept a low profile at social functions, and because of this the other girls perceived her as rather bookish and shy.

The first ball of the Season was the main topic of conversation, and the room was soon filled with girlish chatter and laughter.

Emma, in her element, asked animatedly, "Did anyone else dance with Arthur Kingston? He is simply detestable. At the end of our waltz, I had to practically peel him off me!"

"Well, he spilled punch all over my new, white gloves. The ones I got in Paris! They're completely ruined," wailed Betsy Warring, a plump blonde with a wide mouth.

Mary Ellen Talbot confided in a heated whisper, "My brother warned me to stay away from him, because he's rather fast."

As talk of the repulsive Arthur Kingston escalated, Lucy Greenville, a slim girl with reddish hair and an impudent nose, whispered urgently to Madeline Maxwell, "She's here!"

"Who?" asked Madeline, somewhat puzzled, idly twirling a blue silk ribbon that was tied in her yellow hair. A little bored when she was not dominating the topic of conversation, she wondered if one of the girls would be spirited enough to question her about her break with the duke or if she would have to bring it up herself.

"The one I told you about," Lucy explained with impatience. "The one on the balcony."

Instantly alert, Madeline lowered her voice and glanced suspiciously around the crowded room. "Are you sure?"

Lucy spoke in a dramatic whisper. "I was just introduced to her, and I'm sure."

"Who is she?" Madeline demanded.

Nonchalantly, Lucy picked up her teacup and murmured, "Don't look now, but she's sitting by the window, wearing the light green dress."

Of course, Madeline looked immediately and was surprised at what she saw. She had met Caroline Armstrong at an afternoon tea two weeks ago and instantly dismissed her as a little nobody from the country, even though her grandfather had been, and now her uncle was, the current Earl of Glenwood. Caroline struck her as somewhat different, shy, and academic, not a girl she would want to bring into her close circle of intimate friends, like Lucy. She didn't take Caroline seriously then and subsequently paid her little attention.

Now she regarded her with a critical eye. Madeline noticed Caroline's curling golden hair, highlighted by the sunlight filtering through the window behind her, and her pretty face with clear, smooth skin. Her pale green tea gown was filled out nicely, and the color accentuated the green in her eyes. Madeline at once felt threatened, a feeling with which she was very unfamiliar.

Was this really the girl that Lucy saw holding hands with the duke on the balcony of her house the night of the ball? It didn't make sense though. The duke could have only just met her, so how could they be familiar enough to be holding hands? Besides, he couldn't possibly be interested in a boring girl like Caroline Armstrong! Madeline had no recollection of seeing Caroline that night, but then again she was too preoccupied pretending to be in love with Oliver Parkridge to notice anything else. However, Madeline vividly recalled when Lucy Greenville told her that she had seen a very pretty girl on the balcony with the Duke of Woodborough, holding hands and speaking rather intimately.

Madeline whispered incredulously, "Caroline Armstrong?"

Lucy nodded her head in affirmation.

"You're positive?"

"Positive."

Madeline stared directly at Caroline. Caroline glanced up and stared back. For a moment, they regarded each other warily, then Madeline made her move.

There was a slight lull in the conversation, and Madeline inquired rather loudly, "I don't recall seeing you dance at the ball, Caroline. Where did you keep yourself all night?"

The other girls glanced from Madeline to Caroline, wondering why the popular Madeline would show any interest at all in the decidedly unpopular Caroline Armstrong.

"I wasn't feeling very well and spent most of the evening with my grandmother." Caroline looked directly at Madeline, her gaze unwavering.

"Didn't you dance with anyone special or perhaps go for a walk with someone?" Madeline's words dripped with false sweetness, her blue eyes wide with innocence, daring Caroline to answer. "Surely you didn't spend the entire evening sitting with your grandmother, a pretty girl like you?"

The other girls sensed the undercurrent of tension between Caroline and Madeline, and everyone was waiting for Caroline to answer.

"Of course I danced," she responded airily. "I danced with Edward Winslow and even Arthur Kingston."

"Madeline, is it true that you turned down the Duke of Woodborough?" Emma interrupted demurely, casually smoothing the ruffles of her yellow muslin dress.

Madeline turned her icy gaze toward Emma while Emma stared indifferently back at her. As she scrutinized Emma's silky chestnut hair, flashing hazel eyes, and pretty face, Madeline realized that she had completely underestimated the Armstrong sisters. A mistake she would not repeat. She had been expecting this question all afternoon and as yet, no one had been brave enough to ask her about it directly. Madeline knew that everyone had learned of her break with the duke on the night of the ball, but not even her closest friends had heard her prepared speech of why she turned him down. *Well, now is as good a time as any,* Madeline thought to herself, begrudgingly grateful to Emma Armstrong for getting the subject out in the open.

She stood up, with her hands on her hips, and smiled conspiratorially at the room, as if letting them in on a special secret, and whispered dramatically, "It's true. *I* turned *him* down!"

There was a collective gasp, and with a sense of excitement, the girls realized they were finally going to hear what they had been waiting for all afternoon.

"Oh, but why, Madeline?" asked Betsy Warring, truly amazed that anyone could possibly say no to the handsome and charming duke.

"How could you?" marveled Elizabeth Dishington, her black curls bouncing as she shook her head in disbelief.

"I'm simply not in love with him." Madeline paused for effect, as if that fact alone explained everything. Just as she had rehearsed in front of her mirror for the past two days, she continued, "The duke was crushed, absolutely crushed, when I told him that I couldn't possibly marry anyone I wasn't in love with. He confessed—"

"How could you not be in love with *him?*" interrupted Mary Ellen, dreamily.

"Because I'm not!" Madeline snapped, stamping her foot and glaring at Mary Ellen for interrupting her performance. "So . . ." She clasped her hands together against her chest as if in anguish. "He confessed that he was desperately in love with me and couldn't I please learn to love him a little? He pleaded with me to be his duchess. I simply shook my head and told him that I was sorry." Madeline shook her head woefully. "I explained that even though his parents and my own dear family wished it of us and all of London expected it of us, I could not in good faith marry him, because . . ." She again paused for suspenseful effect, sighing delicately.

The girls waited expectantly for her to finish. Every eye in the room was riveted to Madeline's revelation.

"Because . . . Because I am hopelessly in love with another!" Madeline finished her little speech with a flourish of her hands, and satisfied with the girls' reaction, she reclined gracefully on the sofa, as she was showered with frantic questions.

"Oh Madeline!"

"In love with whom?"

"Who is he?"

Madeline dissolved into excited giggles and exclaimed blissfully, "Oliver Parkridge! Our engagement will be announced this weekend!"

The girls' attention was instantly diverted from Madeline's refusal of the Duke of Woodborough to her engagement to Oliver Parkridge, which was exactly what Madeline had planned.

* * *

Caroline glanced at Emma, wondering if she accepted Madeline's fabricated story as easily as the other girls did. Was it just because Caroline knew the truth that she could see through Madeline's false and staged performance? She didn't think so. Madeline seemed to truly believe the story she told, which is what made her so convincing to the others, she supposed.

Emma raised an eyebrow sardonically, and Caroline nodded. Her sister knew exactly what was going on.

It was a relief to Caroline that the remainder of the afternoon continued without any further remarks from Madeline. She had a feeling Madeline's sudden interest in her had to do with her visit from the duke, although she wasn't sure how she could even know about it. Caroline herself was still struggling to take in the enormity of the situation.

Somehow, she had agreed to form a secret alliance with the dashing Duke of Woodborough.

The idea was quite outrageous. At first, she had been stunned by his proposal that they pretend to be courting to dissuade any other overtures of marriage. It was scandalous. But the more she thought about it, the more it made sense, in a crazy sort of way.

It would help her get through this Season at least, without becoming entangled in a courtship that had no future. Her grandmother had been so positive that Caroline would make a brilliant match and undo the disgrace that Katherine had caused with her elopement. Caroline feared any gentleman becoming interested in her, because she had no idea how to extricate herself from a courtship without telling her grandmother the truth. That Caroline could never do. The last thing she wished to do was to cause another scandal and embarrass her grandmother. She simply could not marry anyone. However, the expectations of marriage from Olivia, who had been so good to her and Emma, were a constant source of worry. So she had devised a plan to discourage suitors by acting extremely intellectual and dull and being a terrific bluestocking. It made her feel depressed.

Although, sometimes it seemed that she had been depressed for a long time. Since her mother died. Since Stephen left. Since her father died. The entire burden had been upon Caroline to support the family during her father's lengthy illness. She had taken over some of her father's work at the university, through the help of his friends. They had kindly allowed Caroline to do research for some of the professors and rewrite some articles. She was an excellent proofreader, and they had relied upon her talents. After he died last fall, she had secured a position as a governess to a family in Sussex. She was still searching for a position for Emma when the grandmother she hadn't known existed rescued them. She did not have to work as a governess. She no longer had to worry about money. She was now a lady of leisure. Yet her problems were still there.

The duke's secret arrangement offered her a slight reprieve. For a little while, she could enjoy her new life and all it had to offer, but only for a little while. Then she and the duke would break off and end their supposed courtship and she would be expected to marry once again. Maybe by then she would have another solution. In the meantime, she and Alex would help each other. She didn't want to marry him, and he didn't want to marry her. It was perfect. As he said, they could be good friends. Although she had to institute the no-kissing rule. There was no need to get involved that way! She had to admit she was tempted though. Alex had something about him that drew her to him. She couldn't explain it, but the feeling was almost hypnotic.

At the end of Lady Weatherby's party, while they were saying their farewells, Caroline, Emma, and Olivia happened to be following behind Lady Maxwell and Madeline as they made their way to the carriages out front.

At that moment Lady Weatherby's high-pitched voice rang out, "Olivia, dear, I forgot to ask you, was that the Duke of Woodborough's carriage I saw in front of your house yesterday afternoon?"

Her blue skirts swirling, Madeline whipped around to stare at them, her eyes wide in astonishment, as did Lady Maxwell, her sour and pinched face looking ridiculously surprised.

Olivia smiled and responded matter-of-factly, betraying nothing, as if the Duke of Woodborough visited her on a regular basis. "Why, yes, it was! Such a charming young man. He was just paying me a friendly call."

Madeline's hard blue eyes raked over Caroline, an undisguised look of malice on her pretty face. Caroline was quite taken aback by the unbridled hostility that emanated from the petite blonde. It left her with the uneasy feeling that by becoming involved with the duke, however innocently on her part, she had somehow made an enemy of Madeline Maxwell.

CHAPTER 6

Although not quite as large an event as the Maxwells' ball the previous week, there were still a considerable number of people in attendance at Lord and Lady Talbot's, for they were well known for their lavish entertaining, and each of their affairs was looked forward to with great anticipation. The opening dance at the Talbots' ball that night was not the traditional quadrille, but a waltz, and the chattering voices in the ballroom hushed in astonishment as Alexander Woodward, the handsome and elusive Duke of Woodborough, escorted the little known Caroline Armstrong out to the dance floor.

The duke looked more striking than usual in his tailored black superfine evening clothes and crisp white shirt, which set off the clean lines of his incredibly handsome face. His dark black hair gleamed. He was impossibly masculine and had a very commanding presence. Caroline was stunning in a low-cut jade green silk gown that cinched in her narrow waist with a wide green bow in the back. Her honey-gold hair had been piled into soft ringlets on the top of her head and held together with pale jade ribbons that cascaded down her back.

The hushed crowd stared openly at the handsome couple on the dance floor, and even the most cynical socialite was intrigued by this latest development. The gossips were still wagging their tongues over Madeline Maxwell's outrageous rejection of the duke only last week and then her sudden announcement at Lady Howard's dinner party of her engagement to Oliver Parkridge.

Now this strange occurrence!

Everyone knew that the duke rarely attended Season balls, and it was rarer still for him to actually dance at one. Now he was dancing with Caroline Armstrong. Was this simply to put on a brave face after Madeline Maxwell spurned him? Or was this a new romance?

And here was the late Earl of Glenwood's lovely granddaughter, the product of that scandalous tutor elopement and the one all the young men were calling a bluestocking, on the arm of the most sought-after bachelor in London. What was one to make of this? It was too intriguing!

All eyes discretely turned to watch Lady Madeline's reaction to the duke's very public display of attention to the Armstrong girl. What they saw was Madeline Maxwell, looking as pretty and feminine as ever with her yellow curls perfectly arranged and wearing a baby blue Worth gown, clinging rapturously to the arm of Oliver Parkridge, seemingly oblivious to the duke's presence in the room.

Betsy Warring whispered frantically to Mary Ellen Talbot, "Why is the duke dancing with Caroline Armstrong?" She tugged self-consciously at the too-tight fit of her lemon satin gown and wished desperately that she were the one dancing in the arms of the handsome duke with everyone watching.

"I haven't the faintest idea! He never dances with anyone. Oh, I just don't understand how Madeline could have refused him." She shook her head in disbelief. "She must be blind. Will you look at him?" Mary Ellen sighed, her big brown eyes gazing longingly at the duke.

"Who would have guessed that the duke would show interest in her of all people? She just appeared out of nowhere," wondered Betsy, as she turned her rather wide nose up in the air with a disdainful sniff. "I heard that she was quite tedious at the Maxwells' ball."

"Well, she seems nice enough, just a little shy. Her sister, Emma, is great fun, though. I think my brother, John, is sweet on her," Mary Ellen whispered to the girls as they continued to watch the couple at the center of the ballroom.

After her dance with the duke, the *ton*'s interest in Caroline increased. There had to be something special about the older Armstrong sister if the Duke of Woodborough danced with her. Surely Arthur Kingston's reports of her being a stuffy country bore must have been exaggerated. The gentlemen all flocked to the shy beauty. Caroline's dance card filled up quickly, and she danced with so many partners that night that she could not recall any of their names the next day.

Alex stood aside, watching her dance, never taking his eyes off her, an enigmatic smile on his face. By dancing with Caroline, he had set her apart from the other girls, which is exactly what he intended. Now aware of her sheltered childhood, the loss of both her parents, and how she supported her family, Alex felt that she needed this special time for herself, to enjoy being young and beautiful. She deserved it after all she had been through. It was surprising how happy it made him to see her laughing and smiling.

When he recalled how sad she looked on the balcony that night and compared it to her glowing face on the dance floor now, he was amazed at the difference in her. It would be criminal to have such a beautiful girl hide herself and pretend to be uninterested in life when she deserved to be admired and the center of attention. There was a sadness about her. She was hiding something, and he was determined to find out what it was. Watching her glide across the room in graceful, fluid movements, he actually felt proud of her.

"What's all this about you and the Armstrong chit?" a familiar voice asked.

Lord Peter Forester grinned at Alex. He was a handsome man, almost as tall as Alex, with sandy blond hair and laughing eyes. The two men had been friends since childhood, and Peter knew that there had to be a very important reason for Alex to put in an appearance at a second Season ball within a week. Peter was more than a little intrigued by his friend's current behavior.

"What are you doing here?" Alex countered. Peter detested the social season almost as much as he did.

"I was going to ask you the same," Peter responded. "But you didn't answer my first question."

"Shouldn't you be dancing with your fiancée?"

Peter grinned knowingly. "Another artful dodge. But to answer your question, my darling Victoria is chatting with her friends at the moment. More to the point, what are you doing here?"

"I am simply enjoying the Season," Alex answered casually, feigning innocence.

"This isn't your thing at all, Alex. You haven't attended a ball in years. Only a week ago you were complaining to me of matchmakers and giddy girls throwing themselves at you. I do recall you saying that after you straightened out the Maxwell situation, you were returning to the peace and quiet of Ridge Haven. What gives, my friend?"

Alex hesitated, not sure how to answer, his eyes following Caroline moving across the ballroom.

Observing that Alex had not taken his eyes off the young lady in question, Peter concluded, "Then it must have something to do with the lovely Miss Armstrong everyone is suddenly buzzing about."

"Maybe it does."

"Word is she's a bluestocking."

A slight smile played across Alex's face. "Not true."

Without another word, Lord Forester handed Alex his drink, maneuvered agilely across the crowded ballroom, and managed to catch Caroline just as a dance ended. Leave it to Peter to take matters into his own hands. Alex watched in amusement as Caroline smiled at his friend in acceptance of his invitation to dance and moved elegantly with Peter on the dance floor. Peter must have said something that charmed her, because her laughter brightened her eyes, and her smile was captivating. She was truly breathtaking and was the most beautiful woman in the room. The jade-colored gown she was wearing accented the green in her eyes, and her golden hair framed her delicate face prettily. When the dance ended, Peter bowed smoothly to her and made his way back to Alex.

"I now understand completely why you are here," Peter commented evenly, taking his drink from Alex's hand.

"I thought you might," was Alex's only response.

"It seems you have finally been caught, my friend. And by a most lovely trap."

"It seems that way," Alex admitted.

Continuing to watch Caroline, Alex didn't mind when she danced with young Henry Whiting or Lord Marshall, or even his best friend, but he most definitely minded when Lord Kingston claimed her for a dance. Kingston was a notorious rake and treated women carelessly. The man clutched her too closely, and the lecherous look on Kingston's face alone would have made Alex want to strangle him.

Ignoring Peter's smug expression, Alex quickly made his way to the dancing couple and tapped Kingston, none too gently, on the shoulder as he overheard the man whispering to Caroline, "Are you sure you are the same girl I danced with last week?"

"I believe the lady has saved this dance for me," Alex interrupted.

Smiling in relief, Caroline yanked herself free from Kingston's clinging hands and gratefully slipped into Alex's arms. "Of course, Your Grace. How silly of me to have forgotten that I promised this dance to you! Please excuse me, Lord Kingston."

Leaving the slick man standing there alone and irritated, Alex expertly waltzed Caroline away.

"Oh, thank you!" she exclaimed. "I wasn't sure how to extricate myself from his grip without being too rude."

He held her close as he guided her across the floor in time to the music, marveling at how perfectly she fit in his arms. "You could always cough in his face again."

"I was thinking just that!" she laughed.

He looked down at her, again struck by her beauty. "You met Lord Forester."

Her eyes sparked with interest. "I did, indeed."

"He's an old friend of mine."

"So he mentioned."

"Did he mention anything else?"

"Just that he was one of your oldest and dearest friends and that if I wanted to know any of your secrets I only had to ask him."

"And did you ask him?"

"Of course!"

His eyebrows rose. "Did you learn anything?"

She frowned in disappointment. "No. He said that there were too many interesting stories to tell, but he promised to enlighten me another time."

Alex laughed, and then gazed into her emerald eyes. "So tell me, Caroline, who can I ask to learn your secrets?"

Her eyes shuttered. Glancing away, she said, "Oh, I don't have any secrets."

"Don't you though?" He knew there was something she was keeping from him. He sensed an invisible wall go up around her.

She smiled brightly at him. "Do you mind if we

rest for a while? I'm exhausted, and these new slippers are pinching my toes."

"Of course." There wasn't a woman he could think of that would admit that her feet hurt while dancing with the Duke of Woodborough. *She is refreshingly different,* he thought to himself, as he escorted her to an unoccupied settee and then brought her some cool punch.

The Duke of Woodborough's attentive behavior to Caroline Armstrong was not lost on the gossips, who were observing them avidly. A low buzz of conversation rose in volume as they watched the pair in question conclude their second dance together and then retire to a secluded spot. Why, the duke was positively hovering over her!

Lady Weatherby, in her typically direct manner, asked Olivia Fairchild, "What is the duke doing with your granddaughter? He has danced with her twice this evening! It's almost scandalous. Now look. He's sitting rather cozily with her over there in the corner."

Olivia responded in a light tone, "Well, Martha, it is quite obvious that he is taking an interest in her." Pleased beyond words with Caroline's actions this evening, Olivia thought the change in her granddaughter was remarkable. The duke seemed to have worked magic on her, for she no longer sat miserably in a corner but laughed and chatted readily with everyone.

"An interest!" snorted Lady Weatherby, her thin face showing disbelief. "Why, he's shown more interest in your granddaughter this evening than he ever did to that Maxwell chit he was supposed to be engaged to!"

That last comment was overheard by Lady Madeline herself. Surreptitiously Madeline turned her head so she, too, could see the duke, a smile on his handsome face, sitting with the older Armstrong sister. It enraged her to think that Lady Weatherby's remark was accurate. The duke had never danced with her twice in one evening, had never sat alone and talked with her, or even brought her a glass of punch! The truth was quite obvious now. Caroline Armstrong had deliberately stolen the duke away from her, forcing Madeline to throw herself at the dull Oliver Parkridge to save her face. How she hated Caroline Armstrong! Who did she think she was? And the faithless duke! How dare he cast her aside so carelessly! It was unbearable. Glaring at the couple lounging together, Madeline made a silent vow that she would find some way to make Caroline Armstrong pay for humiliating her.

Intuitively sensing her gaze, Caroline glanced up and caught Madeline Maxwell staring at her. The two girls looked at each other for a long moment. At last, Madeline shrugged her delicate shoulders, sauntered over to Oliver Parkridge, placed a tiny hand on his arm, and whispered in his ear. A smile spread across Oliver's face as he escorted Madeline to the dining room.

Caroline shuddered from the blatant hostility she felt from Madeline once again. "I think Madeline Maxwell despises me," she said to Alex in a hushed tone.

"Why would she? If she hates anyone, it's me."

"I have a feeling that she thinks you broke off with her for me."

"That's ridiculous. There was never anything between us to break off from, except in her own imagination."

"That may very well be, but I don't think she sees it that way."

"I wouldn't worry about her," Alex laughed, but Caroline could not shake the distinctly foreboding feeling that Madeline had just given her.

CHAPTER 7

Caroline spent the Season attending balls, supper parties, and theatrical productions in the company of the Duke of Woodborough, and the fact that Alexander Woodward was courting Miss Armstrong was obvious to everyone. Their secret arrangement was working well for Caroline. With the duke escorting her about, there were no offers from other gentlemen for her to dissuade, and since she knew that Alex did not want to marry her any more than she wanted to marry him, she felt very comfortable in their relationship. Alex would occasionally wink at her and cryptically refer to their little agreement, but he never suggested that there was anything more between them than allowing them both to escape unwanted attention.

Yet a true friendship was growing between them. Sharing a love of books and poetry bonded them together and gave them a foundation upon which to build their common interests, as Caroline freely exhibited her vast knowledge of the arts with Alex's enthusiastic approval. Matching their wits with lively discussions regarding politics or historical points became a regular pastime. To Caroline's great delight, she found she adored the theater as much as Alex did. At the various parties and balls, they discovered their love of dancing, and they danced quite well together, becoming particularly skilled at the schottische.

Reflecting on how wonderful it was to be herself when she was with Alex, she was aware that she didn't have to pretend she was someone she was not. Alex genuinely appreciated her intelligence and actually seemed proud of her academic accomplishments. Surprisingly she found that she was having the time of her life.

Meanwhile, Emma had fallen in love with Lord John Talbot, a handsome young man with a quiet and serious manner. The possible match surprised everyone, but it seemed that the two opposite personalities were attracted to each other. Olivia was quite pleased that her granddaughters had made such fine matches during their first Season. Nothing was officially settled yet, of course, but she was sure that within the year she would have two weddings to plan!

As the days passed in a frenzy of social activity and the Season drew to a close, Alex was required to return to his country estate to attend to business matters, and he invited her entire family to join him at Summerfields. Olivia accepted his invitation with elation, for she was eager to visit with Alex's mother and further the blossoming relationship between him and Caroline. In Olivia's eyes, some quiet time spent at Alex's ancestral home, away from the hustle and bustle of London, would help the situation along nicely.

However, Emma was so distraught at being dragged away to the country when she was being courted by John Talbot that Olivia compromised by remaining in London a week longer with Emma.

Since Uncle Kit had business to attend to at Fairview Hall, he, Aunt Jane, and Teddy would join them at Summerfields a week later also. Caroline and the duke departed as scheduled, with Caroline's lady's maid, Bonnie, acting as chaperone.

Now that the Season was over, Caroline thought that she and Alex should probably end their secret arrangement, but she enjoyed his company so much she couldn't bring herself to mention it when Alex didn't. By now he almost seemed as if he were a member of her family. Strangely enough, she was intrigued by the idea of visiting Alex's home and meeting his family.

Traveling to Summerfields was a two-day journey by carriage. For most of the trip, Alex rode his prized black stallion alongside his elegantly appointed, black lacquered carriage, the doors emblazoned in gold with the Woodborough coat of arms, in which Caroline sat with Bonnie, while the second carriage carried the duke's servants and all the luggage.

Because they were due to arrive at Summerfields later that afternoon of the second day, Caroline was dressed in her best traveling suit of light brown linen, trimmed with wide cream ribbon edging on the short fitted jacket and the long pleated skirt. Her cream silk blouse had a high-necked collar with small pearl buttons down the front. The matching brown bonnet with tiny embroidered flowers in the crown was perched jauntily on her head.

After they stopped for a quick lunch, the August skies rained down. As they left the small inn where they ate, Caroline barely made it to the carriage before the deluge began. She had just settled herself against the seat and looked up. It was not Bonnie in her usual position across from Caroline, but Alex.

"Where's Bonnie?" she asked.

Alex grinned at her in such a way to cause her heart to skip a little beat. "She's in the other carriage. I thought I'd ride with you." Glancing out of the rain-splattered window and settling back into the comfortable seat, he remarked, "We should still make it to Summerfields tonight, if this rain lets up."

As she covertly eyed his shiny black Hessian boots, tan breeches, and crisp white shirt covered with a black broadcloth jacket, she could smell the clean scent of him, mingled with rain-swept earth and fresh air. His sensual lips and the masculine lines of his face and jaw were striking, made even more so because he was clean shaven. His dark black hair was dampened by the rain, and the bright blue of his eyes added to his handsome appearance. His presence overwhelmed the small space due to his tall and muscular frame, and Caroline immediately felt more physically aware of him than she had since the day they made their secret arrangement. It suddenly occurred to her that it was the first time they had been completely alone since then. She had always been completely at ease with him. Now, confined in a small area for an indeterminate length of time alone with him, her senses were heightened. She felt her pulse racing at the intimate atmosphere and nervously fiddled with the slim brown ribbons of her bonnet.

"Oh, I don't mind traveling," she responded with a breathlessness that surprised her. "Probably because I've done so little of it. Aside from London, I've never been anywhere interesting."

"We will just have to see that you get to go abroad sometime," he said with a wide smile, revealing his straight white teeth.

"How I would love to!"

"Where would you like to go?" he asked with interest.

Her eyes sparkled with excitement. "Now you've asked my favorite question. There are too many places to choose among. If I had to make a short list, I would say France, Germany, Italy, Spain, Russia, India, Egypt, Greece, and China, and of course, North and South America."

He laughed. "And that's the short list?"

"I've only read about them in books. I would love to go around the world and see absolutely everything!" She sighed, her eyes full of longing. "Where have you traveled?"

"I've had the usual trips to the continent when I was younger. Paris. Madrid. Rome."

"Was it wonderful?"

"Yes. It's an eye-opening experience to see how other people live, to hear different languages and see unusual customs, to try new foods and learn about different religions."

"I want to see everything someday."

"Perhaps you will be able to. For now though you'll have to content yourself with this beautiful English countryside."

"It is pretty," she agreed readily with a glance out the window. "So tell me about your home. What is Summerfields like?"

"It defies description."

She gave him a puzzled look. "What does that mean?"

Alex smiled mysteriously. "It's a place you really have to see to believe."

"So you are just going to keep me in suspense then?" she asked.

He nodded his head.

She sighed in resignation and played with the small pearl buttons on her cream-colored gloves.

She had learned enough about Alex to know that he could not be goaded or cajoled into doing something he didn't want to do. If he wanted to keep Summerfields a mystery to her until they arrived, then that is the way it would be.

"Have you enjoyed the Season?" he asked lightly, watching her with hooded eyes.

She gave him a warm smile. "I've never had so much fun in my life. Thank you for making that possible."

"It was my pleasure." He paused for a moment. "So our little arrangement has worked well for you?"

She nodded her head. "Yes. I've had the most wonderful time, with no one asking to marry me." She glanced over at him, thinking he was startlingly handsome. "And has it worked well for you?"

"Perfectly. This was the best time I ever had during a Season. Not a single mother is throwing her impossible daughter at me, and everyone thinks I'm bringing you home to be inspected by my mother."

"Just what does your mother think about this?" Caroline asked, suddenly more aware of the awkward position she would be in upon meeting his mother.

His voice was casual. "Oh, I've written her all about your family, for she was acquainted with your grandmother. Undoubtedly, she still expects your sister and grandmother to be arriving with us, since I didn't send her a message of our change in plans. But she thinks that it's simply a visit from the family of her dear old friend, whom I happened to befriend in London."

His explanation seemed plausible enough. She asked, "What is she like?"

"My mother?" Alex rolled his eyes, as a slight smile tugged the corners of his mouth. "She's a character. Very dramatic. And she can talk a blue streak."

Caroline smiled at his description, trying to imagine the woman who bore such an incredibly handsome and masculine son. Then her thoughts turned serious. "Is it terrible of us to fool everyone this way?" she asked, a look of concern on her face.

"We're not deliberately fooling anyone, Caroline. They are jumping to conclusions, which is their own fault. Have we ever mentioned marriage to anyone? No. Therefore, we have not lied. We can't help what people think, even if they are promoting our needs."

"Yes, but what about my grandmother and your mother? Isn't this unfair to them? My grandmother is under the distinct impression that we are going to marry."

"I'm sure they'll be disappointed, but they'll recover."

"Still . . ." She hesitated, feeling a conflicted sense of remorse. "It doesn't seem quite right."

"Are you saying that you're ready to end our arrangement?" He gazed at her intently, and she was unnerved by the look in his blue eyes.

She sensed something had changed between them since they left London. For one thing, he looked at her differently. It caused a strange fluttering in her stomach. "The Season has ended, so maybe we should end it too."

"We put no time limits on our arrangement. We can continue it as long as we wish. Or not."

Flustered by his careless attitude, when she herself so unreasonably wanted it to continue, even though it was not quite right, she stammered, "No . . . I don't want to end it. I . . . I like spending time with you. It's just that it seems, well, dishonest."

"To a certain extent," he reasoned calmly. "We're

only good friends helping each other out." He gave her a conspiratorial smile.

A smile that suddenly made her stomach flip and then tie itself in knots. He made the arrangement sound so easy and convincing; he defied the logic that she was usually adept at defining. "So you say," she admitted grudgingly.

"Do you want your grandmother to pressure you into a marriage again?"

"Of course not."

"Can you think of another solution?"

"No."

"Well, then," he said as he lifted his arms in casual mock surrender, a look of feigned helplessness on his face, "what else can we do?"

There was no winning an argument with this man. He had a way of twisting the meanings of things to his own advantage. Returning a rueful grin to his look of innocence, she shook her head in exasperation. "What else can we do?" She repeated his own question.

A companionable silence filled the carriage. Caroline leaned her head against the window and watched little drops of rain trickle down the glass. What would have happened if she had not agreed to Alex's arrangement? Would she have escaped the pressures of the social Season without arousing her grandmother's suspicion? It was pure speculation, because now she would never know. In essence, all the arrangement with Alex was giving her was a little more time. For she would be in the same position again when it ended, simply because as a woman she was expected to marry. Her grandmother would recover from her disappointment with the failed engagement to the duke and then promptly insist that Caroline marry someone else. And Caroline knew that she could never marry anyone else. Not after what had happened between her and Stephen that day. Not after what they had done. The shameful memory caused her head to throb.

The rhythmic sway of the carriage and the steady patter of the rain made her sleepy. The bed at the inn last night had not been very comfortable, and consequently she had not slept well. Barely keeping her eyes open, she stifled a yawn. Thinking it might be rude to fall asleep with Alex sitting across from her, she struggled to stay awake.

Alex watched Caroline as she attempted to keep from dozing off. "Who are you waiting for, Caroline?" Alex's deep voice penetrated the silence.

Startled, she turned to him, her eyes blinking, instantly awake. "What do you mean?"

"Who are you waiting for? Pining for? Who is the reason you won't marry anyone else?" The sound of his voice was gentle, his eyes steady on her.

"Why?" A slight note of panic tinged her voice as she sat up straighter. "Why do you want to know?"

A look came over Caroline's finely wrought features that Alex had never seen before. He had refrained from bringing up this sensitive subject for weeks. Did she have any feelings for him at all? Or was she still in love with this mystery person? "Because we've grown to be friends and I care about you. I thought it might help you to talk about him."

"I don't ever talk about him." Her voice quavered, and she looked away.

"Why not?" His eyes never left her, willing her to answer.

There was a prolonged pause before she answered

him, as if she were weighing the decision. "Because it's a secret."

His brows furrowed. "Who said it had to be a secret?"

"He did."

"And you agreed?"

She nodded her head slightly.

"From whom does it need to be a secret?"

"From everyone."

"Why?"

There was another protracted silence. Only the sounds of the swaying carriage, the patter of the rain, and the splashing of the wheels over the muddy road could be heard. She stared out the window, and Alex was beginning to think that she wouldn't answer him.

Then she barely whispered, "My father didn't want me to be with him."

Well, that was the first thing she said that made any sense to him and provided him with a somewhat reasonable explanation for her secrecy. "I see. A student from the university. Is he still back where you lived, in Shrewsbury?"

She shook her head.

Whatever happened was obviously painful for her to share, and he felt somewhat callous for urging her to talk about it. Nonetheless, he continued his line of questioning. Now that she finally opened up, he could not stop. "When did he go away?"

"Two years ago."

"I take it he said he would come back for you?"

Again, she nodded. The delicate movement of her head caused his heart to constrict in his chest. She aroused such deep emotions in him. "Where did he go?"

"America."

"America?" he said with considerable surprise. "That country has been at war for years!"

She continued to stare out the window, a faraway expression on her perfect face, her mouth a thin line. "He went there to fight for the Confederacy."

"To fight?" His eyebrows rose inquiringly. "Then he's not English?"

"No, he's from Virginia."

"Ah. I see, a southerner. From what you've told me about your father, I think I can guess why he disapproved of him. Have you received word from him? The war ended last April, you know."

Abruptly she turned to face him, her voice tight with emotion, her chin quivering slightly. "Yes, I know the war is over, and no, I haven't heard from him. I don't know where he is. I don't know if he is alive or dead or if his home is still standing. I don't know anything except that I promised to wait for him to return to me. And I promised not to tell anyone." The sudden explosion of words was filled with sorrow as well as anger and bitterness.

"I'm sorry, Caroline," Alex whispered. With a clearer image of what had happened between her and her sweetheart, he assumed that she was simply cherishing a romantic love for her missing soldier, who apparently had forgotten all about her or had been killed in the war. Alex felt an unfamiliar twinge of jealousy at the depth of her emotions for this person and was a bit relieved that she had not heard from him in two years.

"Why not just explain this to your grandmother? I'm sure she would understand why you don't wish to marry now," he suggested kindly.

"It's more complicated than that," Caroline managed to choke out.

"How long are you supposed to wait for him?"

"I don't know." Her voice was thin and full of tension.

Alex could tell by the pained expression on her face that he should stop questioning her, but he could not help himself. He had to know. "What if he doesn't come back for you? Are you supposed to wait forever?"

Finally looking him directly in the eyes, Caroline stared wordlessly. That look conveyed more anguish than she could ever have stated in words, and it twisted his heart. Her eyes brimmed with tears, and he felt cruel for asking her that question. He wanted to take all the sorrow and pain from her and bring joy and light to her gorgeous green eyes. It angered him that this American boy left her waiting for him like this. On impulse, Alex moved across to the opposite seat to sit beside her. He pulled her into his arms, allowing her to rest her head on his shoulder.

Caroline began to relax as he held her, and her tears ceased. He sensed immediately when she fell asleep, because her whole body seemed to melt against him. Placing a gentle kiss on the top of her head, he held her close as she slept. The faint scent of lavender enveloped him, and she felt warm and soft in his arms. She seemed so fragile and haunted when she spoke about her sweetheart, and he felt an overwhelming sense of protectiveness for her. It was unbearable to think of her being hurt in any way, especially by another man.

He wondered how serious her feelings for the American soldier were, holding a hope that they were simply a girlish infatuation. He easily understood how the boy could have fallen in love with Caroline and why he would make her promise to wait for him. She was just the kind of girl any soldier dreamed of coming home to.

His feelings for her bewildered him. He had never felt this all-consuming need to be with another person. Caroline was intelligent, warm, thoughtful, funny, and beautiful. Yes, he was physically attracted to her. So much so that no other woman even appealed to him anymore. Yet there were more feelings involved than that. He could actually envision a life with Caroline: waking next to her each morning, sitting across the dinner table from her, holding her close all night, having her by his side at social events, creating a home with her, raising a family with her, growing old with her.

Without even trying, Caroline had made it impossible for him to imagine life without her.

He had been on his best behavior with her all through the Season. He had been a perfect gentleman, suppressing his desires to touch her, to hold her, and to kiss her. He acted almost as a brother would. Now that she was comfortable being friends with him and he would have some time to be alone with her at Summerfields, he would do more than just escort her to parties. He would make her forget this American soldier. He would romance her. He would win her over by making a full-out assault on her heart.

The Lion's Paw Inn, a traditional English tavern, was dark, smoky, and filled with noisy patrons eating from pewter plates piled high with food and drinking ale in tall cups at worn wooden tables and benches scattered around the large, low-ceilinged room. There was a strong fire blazing in the hearth, and the odor of roasting beef permeated the air. A sudden hush fell over the room as all eyes turned to see the finely dressed nobleman carrying a beautiful lady in his arms. It was a peculiar sight, indeed.

"Why are we here?" Caroline asked sleepily, her eyes blinking.

"We're fairly close to Summerfields, but the storm has worsened, and now it's too dark and the roads too muddy to go any farther. We'll stop here for the night and continue tomorrow," Alex explained as he carried her effortlessly through the crowded inn.

Blushing at the curious looks from the villagers, Caroline whispered emphatically, "You can put me down now."

Alex grinned teasingly, looking into her eyes. "I rather like carrying you. You weigh nothing at all."

"I can walk, you know," she protested.

"Oh, I don't mind." Enjoying her embarrassment and not wanting to let her go, he followed the innkeeper up the narrow wooden staircase with Caroline in his arms.

"'Tis this way, Your Grace," the plump and balding innkeeper informed them as they reached the upper landing and continued down the hallway. They stopped in front of a door, which he indicated was for Caroline. "Your room is right across the hall. The two rooms at the end of the hallway are for your servants. 'Tis an honor to have you here. Anything else we can do for you, Your Grace?"

"Please send up a tray of food for the lady. I'll be down directly for my own meal. Thank you."

Alex entered the small, clean room, kicking the door closed behind them and carrying her to the narrow, quilt-covered bed near the window.

He just stood there, holding her over the bed, staring into her fathomless green eyes. God, how he wanted her. The feel of her in his arms left him longing for more. He could almost taste the exquisite feel of her on his lips. She was so close, yet so out of reach. The image of her lying on the pillow, her long golden hair tumbling around her naked shoulders, her arms outstretched to him in invitation, presented itself in his mind, and for a moment, he could not breathe. How would she react to his kiss? If he kissed her now in the privacy of this little room as he yearned to do, could he stop at just a kiss? He did not think so. In fact, he knew he could not.

The minutes ticked by slowly as he stood there, holding her in his arms, gazing into her eyes. His face was so close to hers that he could feel the heat of her breath on his cheek, the rapid beating of her heart.

After some time, he laid her gently on the bed and placed a velvety kiss on her cheek, his lips lingering ever so slightly over her mouth. "Good night, Caroline," he whispered in a husky voice. "I'll see you in the morning."

He then left the room, closing the door quietly behind him to see Bonnie standing in the hallway with a disapproving look on her round freckled face.

A long breath of air escaped her as Caroline fell back against the pillows. The sudden tension between them was palpable, and her face reddened, imagining what could have happened if he had kissed her lips. The fact that she longed for him to do just that left her trembling. His broad chest had felt warm and hard as he held her tightly against him. Even though she had protested his carrying her, it was mere pretense, because it was expected of her. She had, in fact, enjoyed the feel of his body close to her own. He made her feel strangely safe and protected, yet at the same time terribly vulnerable. She had been the one to institute the no-kissing rule at the onset of their secret arrangement, and here she was hoping that he would break it!

Alex.

What were these feelings she had for him? She wanted him to kiss her and touch her, and that was frightening. It was certainly nothing like what she had felt for Stephen Bennett. This felt dangerous somehow. There was no reason to continue this charade with Alex any longer. The Season had ended and so should their arrangement. Then why was she on her way to Summerfields to meet his family?

Why had she told him about Stephen?

Stephen.

There had been so little time to think about him during the past few months. It used to be that all she ever thought about was Stephen. He used to haunt her dreams. Now it was becoming a little more difficult to recall the soft, lazy sound of his voice or the handsomeness of his boyish face. She could still remember the bright blond of his hair and the warmth in his brown eyes, although the memories became hazier as each month went by. Sometimes all that had taken place between them seemed very far away, as if it were a strange dream. Caroline could almost make herself believe that none of it had ever happened.

But it had. Of that there was no doubt. What she had done with Stephen was wrong in more ways than she could name. The lies to her father alone would haunt her forever. Of course, she had never intended for it to happen that way, for it to end the way it did, in shameful secrecy. At the time she had loved Stephen desperately and would have done anything for him. And she had. She had given him all of herself. No man could have her now. Her whole life was changed because she had loved Stephen Bennett.

And now he was gone.

Oh, Stephen. Where are you?

The pouring rain outside her window reminded her of the day she met Stephen. She stood, wrapping the quilt from the bed around her like a shawl to keep warm, and walked to the window. She pressed her forehead against the cool glass of the small window and sighed. It was impossible to believe that Stephen had ever been with her when he was so incredibly far away now.

Turning away from the window, Caroline opened her reticule and removed a small leather pouch in which she kept the only letter she had received from Stephen after he left. She unfolded the slightly yellowed page carefully, her fingers caressing the familiar handwriting. She read the words softly to herself, even though she had the entire letter memorized by heart years ago. She always tried to picture him and where he was when he wrote it, but even that was becoming harder to do.

September 21, 1863

My Dearest Carrie,

I finally arrived in Virginia yesterday. I miss you terribly, my darling, and I thought of nothing else but your beautiful face during the long journey home.

Although my parents are furious with me, I enlisted in the Confederate Army today and should be joining my regiment within the week. I am anxious to engage in battle. The sooner the war is over and the South is free, the sooner you will be able to join me here. I can easily picture us living happily at

Willow Hill together. You will love it here, Carrie.
It is beautiful and peaceful.

The day this war is over, I will be on the first ship
back to England for you. Knowing that you are hon-
oring your promise to keep our secret, my dearest
Carrie, is the only way I can bear this separation.
Always remember how much I love you and that you
belong to me and no other.

Forever Yours,
Stephen

Those words haunted her every day. No, she
could never forget that she belonged to Stephen
and Stephen alone. He had made sure of that
before he left.

CHAPTER 8

Their arrival at Summerfields the next afternoon was heralded by a tremendous thunderstorm. However, the dramatic thunder and lightning display only enhanced the impressiveness of the estate. Seeming as if it were torn from a page out of a picture book of fairy tales, Summerfields Castle was constructed of gray limestone bricks and boasted two pairs of matching round towers with pointed roofs on the four corners of the square-shaped main building. Brightly colored pennants emblazoned with the Woodborough family crest whipped in the wind from their posts atop the four towers. There were crenellated parapets along the top walls as well as stone machicolations below them, while the many delicate mullioned windows displayed pretty cinquefoils in the window tracery. The crumbled remains of an old stone gatehouse were still standing, and their carriage even passed through an ancient portcullis. Dark green ivy, intertwined with climbing roses in hues of pinks and reds, covered the stone archway of the entrance. The only articles missing to complete the fairy tale effect were a moat and a drawbridge, but still Caroline could easily imagine knights in armor walking along the turrets.

"You didn't tell me that you lived in a castle," she said breathlessly, her eyes wide as she peered through the window of the carriage staring at the extraordinary rain-swept citadel in front of them.

"I told you it defied description."

"You could have just said 'castle.'" Caroline laughed, giving him a scolding glance. "I think I would have understood."

Alex merely smiled at her.

What seemed like an army of liveried servants efficiently ran Summerfields, and in a matter of moments, they had Caroline and Alex out of the carriage and the heavy downpour and into the surprisingly warm entry hall. A massive curving stone staircase covered in thick red carpet dramatically dominated the hallway, which was lit by elaborate wrought iron sconces holding beeswax candles along the gray limestone walls.

"It's a little overdone, don't you think?" Alex asked her wryly, one eyebrow raised in question.

"It does rather take one's breath away," Caroline responded, still taking in the grandeur of the place. "It feels like a storybook castle."

"That was my great-grandfather's intention when he had this place rebuilt. At one time it was actually a functioning defensive castle, but now it's simply decorative. Although I suppose we could put it to good use if we needed to defend ourselves in a pinch," he added with a laugh. "It's been in my family since the second Duke of Woodborough acquired it."

"Excuse me, Your Grace," began a neat-looking gentleman, about forty years old and wearing the

Woodborough livery. "Your mother has requested that you visit her immediately upon your arrival."

"I've no doubt she did, Harrison. Thank you. We'll go right up to her. Come along, Caroline, and meet my mother."

"Oh, but I look a frightful mess, Alex," Caroline protested, indicating her rumpled brown linen traveling suit and her rain-dampened hair. It wouldn't do to meet the Dowager Duchess looking like this!

"You look as lovely as always," he consoled her as he took her hand in his and ushered her up the curving stone staircase.

Caroline could only follow along helplessly as they walked down a narrow and dimly lit corridor lined in more deep red carpeting. The stone walls were adorned with massive oil paintings in ornate gilt frames barely visible in the flickering candlelight. Finally, they stopped before a pair of huge, intricately carved wooden doors.

"Do you recall what I told you about my mother?" he asked in a hushed whisper.

"She's very talkative?"

"That's an understatement, but I'll try to get it over with quickly. Remember, I warned you." Alex flashed her a quick and devastating smile, knocked briefly, and opened the heavy double doors.

If Summerfields is a true castle, thought Caroline, *then this woman is certainly its queen.*

Alex's mother, the Dowager Duchess, Elizabeth Gwyneth Ellsworth Woodward, reclined elegantly in her large canopy bed, which was festooned with pink damask curtains held in place with heavy gold corded tassels and surrounded by pink satin pillows and coverlets. In fact, the whole room was pink and extremely feminine; from the soft pink-flowered wall tapestries, to the thick dusty rose carpet, to the pale pink damask window drapes that matched the curtains on the bed, to the many bouquets of varying shades of pink and red roses in delicate Irish crystal vases that were artfully placed on nearly every tabletop surface in the room. The heavy scent of roses and a rose perfume permeated the air, while several elaborate and highly polished silver candelabras glowed with wax candles. A blazing fire burned brightly in the stone fireplace.

The room was amazing in its luxury, but the centerpiece of it all was Elizabeth Woodward herself, resting among the feather pillows. A strikingly beautiful woman with delicate features, she had fair skin and soft black hair, without a trace of gray, even though she had to be in her fifties. She had an impish smile that must have led men on a merry chase in her younger days. Wearing a white silk bed jacket embroidered with tiny pink rosebuds, she had swept her dark hair elegantly atop her head, and her quick blue eyes were already taking stock of Caroline. Caroline imagined that she was probably quite stunning in her youth and deduced that Alex's good looks definitely came from her.

"My darling boy, come and give your poor mother a kiss! I've been waiting days and days to see you. Was the trip dreadful with all this rain?" Not waiting for answers, she held out her hand as if granting favors. "You get handsomer every day, Alex. Now introduce me to the late Earl of Glenwood's granddaughter who I've heard so much about." Elizabeth's words were uttered in a breathless rush, her voice airy and girlish.

Grinning, Alex placed an affectionate kiss on her cheek. "Mother, this is Miss Caroline Armstrong.

Caroline, this is my mother, the Duchess of Woodborough. Lady Fairchild and Caroline's younger sister, Emma, will be joining us in a few days, as they had some matters to attend to in London first."

Elizabeth's eyes turned away from her son toward Caroline. "Well, come closer so I can get a better look at you, my darling," she commanded in a sweet voice.

Caroline stepped forward to greet her. "Good afternoon, Your Grace," she said politely, suddenly thinking that despite her first impression, there really was nothing fragile about this woman.

"So you are Katherine Fairchild's daughter. Oh my, but you're a pretty little thing, aren't you? You certainly take after your mother. Poor Katherine. I felt so dreadful when I heard that she died. Please accept my sincerest condolences. I remember her as such a sweet girl. Was she happy, do you think?"

"I beg your pardon?" Caroline was not sure what Elizabeth Woodward was asking and was somewhat taken aback at the unexpected mention of her mother's death.

"Mother . . ." Alex's voice had a warning tone to it, which Elizabeth blithely ignored.

"Was she happy with her decision to run off with her brother's tutor? It took such courage for her to do what she did. I don't know if I would have been brave enough to give up everything for the one I loved. Luckily, my true love happened to be the duke, and I didn't have to give up anything at all! But an elopement! Now that is romantic! Ah . . . I did so want to have a romantic elopement. But I couldn't have lived with myself if I hadn't had *the* most celebrated wedding of the decade. Which I *did*! It was perfectly lovely! Everyone talked about it for months. We had it right here at the castle. But still, all these years I couldn't help thinking about young Katherine Fairchild afterward. She was so young and he was so poor. How did it turn out in the end? It was so outrageously romantic, don't you think? Yet so tragic too. But that's what adds to the romance, I suppose. Nothing can be truly romantic unless there's a little tragedy thrown in as well. I've been curious to know how it all turned out, but there was no way for me to know, since the earl cut her out of his life and no one could even mention Katherine's name in his presence. And poor Olivia. It simply devastated her. I just know I would be tormented if my only daughter ran off and I couldn't see her anymore. But I never did have a daughter, even though I wanted one desperately. Every woman needs a daughter . . . But I had just my two handsome boys, Alexander and Charles." She turned to look at Alex. "You won't run off on me, will you, darling?" Not waiting for a reply, she turned back to Caroline. "So was she happy, your mother?"

Not quite sure how to respond to this vivacious and very romantic lady, Caroline glanced toward Alex for guidance, but he only shrugged his shoulders helplessly. It was unsettling to have her family's embarrassing scandal spoken of so casually. While she was growing up it was never mentioned, and even now her grandmother refused to speak of it. "Well . . . she and my father did love each other very much—" she began.

"Oh, I knew it!" Elizabeth interrupted dreamily. "I knew true love would triumph! Although sometimes it doesn't. I am so happy to hear that Katherine's great risk was successful in the end. I'm thrilled to have you visit me. The product of such a grand love. And your sister too! When will everyone arrive? I am so eager to see Olivia again. She and I have such a lot to talk about—"

"Mother." Alex broke off Elizabeth's speech without apology. "Caroline is very weary from traveling. She needs to rest from our journey, but I'm sure she would love to come and spend some time with you tomorrow. Let me show her to her room now, and I'll be back to visit with you for a while."

"Oh, yes, of course. Please forgive me, darling. I was just so excited to meet you, Caroline. Go and relax, my dear, and come visit me in the morning and we'll have a good long chat. Some nice girl talk." She gave Caroline a knowing look, nodding her head in Alex's direction. "But go. Go. Don't let me keep you any longer." She waved her hand dismissively, a cheerful smile on her face.

"Thank you, Your Grace. I would be honored to visit with you tomorrow," Caroline replied before Alex escorted her from the room.

"I am sorry, Caroline. Please forgive my mother," Alex whispered as he closed the doors behind them. "Like this castle, she can be a bit much."

"Well, I can't say that you didn't warn me." She breathed at last. They began walking down the red-carpeted corridor and ascended a spiraling stone staircase.

"As you can tell she's very excited to have you here. I'm not in the habit of bringing female guests to visit my mother, you know. And she hasn't had many visitors at all since my father passed away."

"Please don't think me rude, but why is she bedridden? She doesn't look ill. In fact, she seems perfectly healthy."

"Because she is perfectly healthy."

"Then why—"

"You're looking for a logical answer, Caroline. And when you are dealing with my mother, you'll find that there is no logic." They had stopped at the top of the stairs and opened a heavy oak door. "Well, here is your room."

She was about to question him again, but her breath was taken away by the sight in front of her. It was a tower room, with stone walls covered in thick, colorful tapestries, depicting Regency couples dancing in romantic garden settings. A massive stone fireplace dominated the room, while a blazing fire roared within it. Several oriental rugs covered the stone floor. A large flamboyantly carved canopy bed stood in the center, draped with purple velvet curtains trimmed with long gold fringe. Dozens of crimson and gold satin heart-shaped pillows covered the bed. More purple and violet velvet drapes lined with red satin and tied with golden tassels enveloped the windows. Two ostentatious, standing gilt-framed mirrors adorned with fat golden cherubs flanked the heavy, oak armoire. The room was a garish nightmare. Caroline had never seen anything like it.

"So? What do you think?" Alex asked with a skeptical smile.

Caroline thought longingly of her tasteful blue toile room at Fairview Hall, her elegant cream-colored bedroom at the townhouse in London, and even the plain, little whitewashed room she had shared with Emma at Lilac Cottage back in Shrewsbury, and answered softly, trying to be positive, "Well . . . I've never stayed in a round room before."

Alex laughed at her stunned expression. "It looks like a brothel."

"I wouldn't know," Caroline said dryly, shaking her head, a slight gleam in her eyes, "but I'll take your word for it."

Alex laughed again. "The whole house looks like this. My great-grandfather was a bit eccentric in his tastes, and then my mother took over. As you can see, her tastes lean toward the dramatic."

"Perhaps it is a little overdone," she conceded politely.

"A little? It's God awful! And it's all right for you to say so. It tells me you have good taste. Anyway, this room can be freezing in the winter, but you'll be comfortable enough for now."

She grinned. "I'm sure I'll be fine. I can pretend I'm the heroine in some sort of gothic novel."

"This is the place to do it," he commented sardonically.

Bonnie entered the room behind them. "I've already unpacked your things, Miss Caroline, and ordered some tea and a hot bath for you."

"Thank you, Bonnie," Caroline said gratefully, at once realizing how tired she was.

"I'll stop by later and take you on a little tour of Summerfields before dinner. How does that sound?" Alex suggested.

"That sounds wonderful."

"I'll see you at seven o'clock then." Alex turned and left them.

"Oh, Miss Caroline, isn't this the most beautiful place you've ever seen? I feel like I'm in a make-believe story my granny used to tell me about a princess in a castle." Bonnie sighed, her freckled face round with awe.

Caroline held back her laughter. "This place certainly defies description."

* * *

Alex returned to his mother's suite after leaving Caroline. He sat uncomfortably upon a small, pink love seat across from her bed, his strong muscular form seeming impossibly out of place in the extremely feminine surroundings. "Well, what did you think of her?"

Elizabeth gave her son an encouraging smile. "Alex, she is just lovely. Truly, my darling."

"I think so," he agreed softly. He had known immediately that his mother would like Caroline. Who wouldn't? She was perfect. He grinned with pride.

"When are you going to propose? I can give you my emerald ring, if you like. You should ask her in the little gazebo by the river. It's so pretty there—"

"Mother, I'll take care of it in my own time in my own way." His tone was quite clear. The timing on this would be critical. He had to make sure that Caroline was ready, and he didn't want to overwhelm her. Their conversation in the carriage yesterday confirmed his suspicions that she was still mooning over her sweetheart. He would need more time to woo her away from his memory. The thought of the American boy who stole her heart caused a strong pang of jealousy to course through him. But he was a man who was used to getting what he wanted.

And he wanted Caroline.

He had held himself in check all Season, not betraying his intentions toward her and behaving in a brotherly manner. However, the carriage ride alone with her yesterday changed everything. He felt he had finally broken through that invisible wall that she hid behind. She had finally confided in him, and her tears had touched something deep within him. He had never felt this way about anyone before. Then he had held her in his arms as she slept. He had come so very close to kissing her at the inn the night before. With her sleepy green eyes looking up at him and her soft lips parted in invitation, he knew that she had wanted him to kiss her. It took all his self-control to set her down and leave the room.

Yes, Caroline was quite irresistible to him, but he had to tread carefully with her.

Elizabeth pouted. "Oh, you're no fun, Alex. You know how I've been longing to plan your wedding."

Of course he knew it. It was all he'd heard for the past ten years. The last thing he wanted to do was discuss wedding plans with her. He deftly changed the subject to another of her favorite topics. "Have you heard from Charles?"

"I received a letter from him only yesterday," she answered brightly. "He should arrive within the week, once he gets to London. I'll be so happy to have both my boys home again." She frowned slightly. "I'm not sure if I'm up to having so many guests, Alex. I haven't entertained since your father passed away."

"Maybe it would be good for you, Mother," Alex suggested, "to see people again. It's time for you to end your mourning." He had hoped that the prospect of his engagement and upcoming wedding would tempt her out of her self-imposed confinement and mourning.

Elizabeth, a far-off look in her blue eyes, whispered softly, "Yes. Maybe. I don't know . . ."

Alex kissed her cheek. "I know." He straightened up, turning to go. "I'll see you in the morning. You can spend some time with Caroline then."

Elizabeth brightened at the prospect. "That will be nice. We can talk about the wedding!"

"No," he warned her, shaking his head. That would certainly scare off Caroline. "No wedding talk, Mother. If you ever want to see me married, don't say a word to Caroline about a wedding yet. I mean it. Not until I mention it first. Agreed?"

"Oh, all right." She folded her arms across her chest in silent objection, but Alex paid no attention to her.

"Good night, Mother."

"Good night, darling." Elizabeth waved lightly as her son left the room.

Later that evening Alex gave Caroline a tour of Summerfields. She followed him up hidden stone staircases, peeked out from small lancet windows, strolled along the parapets in the mist, and marveled at polished suits of armor standing proudly on display. Each room they visited was just as garishly and ornately furnished as the last, which was an endless source of amusement to both of them.

Instead of dining in the elaborate and formal dining hall, Alex chose to have an intimate supper in the small parlor off the main hallway. Seated at a gleaming cherrywood table in overstuffed leather armchairs before the fireplace, they dined by candlelight on roast partridge with rosemary potatoes, sautéed greens with candied almonds, and peach tartlets in heavy cream.

"Did you spend your childhood here at Summerfields?" Caroline asked while sipping red wine from a crystal glass.

"Just summers mostly. The rest of the year we

spent at our more traditional estate, Ridge Haven. My father didn't particularly care for this place at all, but he conceded because my mother loved it so much. Living here as a boy was fantastic though. My brother and I had many great adventures together up in the towers," Alex explained, his face lighting up at the fond memories.

"I can imagine you would! This is a perfect place for a child's imagination to run wild." Caroline tried to picture Alex as a small dark-haired boy climbing the stairs to the tower, a mischievous grin on his handsome little face. The image made her smile.

"Yes, it was. I can't complain about my childhood. My parents were very good to us."

She glanced across the table. "What did your mother say about me?"

Alex smiled at her, and his eyes crinkled at the corners. "She thinks you are lovely, is thrilled that you're here, and can't wait for us to get married. She has my proposal to you all planned out."

"Oh, Alex!" Caroline cried in dismay. "We can't do this. It's too mean to mislead her about our marriage like this. Especially in her condition."

"She has no condition. There's nothing wrong with her," he stated flatly, shaking his head.

"Then may I please ask why she's in bed?"

"My mother's temperament has always leaned toward the dramatic, and my father simply indulged her in whatever she wanted to do. Theirs was an unusually loving marriage, and when he died last year, she was completely devastated. And in keeping with her flair for melodrama, she took to her bed in a grand fashion. She hasn't left Summerfields since the funeral, rarely entertains, and won't listen to reason."

"That's so sad."

"I think eventually she'll snap out of it, when the romance of it wears off. I thought maybe your visit, along with your family, might do the trick and force her out of her self-confinement, if only to be a good hostess. My brother and I have tried many times to lure her out of the house."

"What is your brother like?" she asked. He had revealed very little about his family during the Season, and she was curious.

"I would say Charles is a bit of a playboy."

"Oh?" Caroline was intrigued. "I've never met a playboy."

Alex leaned back in his chair, looking relaxed and at home. "I suppose I shouldn't paint such a picture of him. Charles just isn't very serious. He enjoys himself thoroughly and tends to be more romantic, like our mother."

"And you're not?"

"I'm not what?"

"Romantic."

He leaned his head toward her, his blue eyes twinkling devilishly, flashing her a devastating smile. "Why do you ask?"

"Just curious." She turned her attention to her plate, finding it difficult to breathe when he looked at her that way. Her heart pounded.

His gaze lingered over her, and he said casually, "Let's just say I'm more on the practical side than either my mother or my brother."

"I see," she said, still trying to catch her breath from the look he had given her. It had sent tingles down her spine. "Where is Charles now?"

"He's on his way here from Paris. Where I am sure he keeps a bevy of beautiful women on pins and needles waiting for him. He usually leaves a trail of broken hearts wherever he goes."

"And what about you?" Caroline couldn't help asking. She couldn't quite picture him in the role of heartbreaker, but then again she wasn't sure.

Alex looked at her intently, his eyes glinting. "Oh, I've left my share of broken hearts. But nothing to match Charles."

The looks Alex was casting in her direction caused an odd sinking sensation in her stomach. When she agreed to come to Summerfields she hadn't realized that she would be spending so much time alone in Alex's company. Certainly they had not been alone together at all during the Season, and she just assumed that would be the case at Summerfields. It wasn't that she particularly minded being alone with him. It was more the peculiar sensation that he aroused in her when they were alone. She only knew that these fluttery feelings in her stomach were a little more than disconcerting.

After dinner Alex then acquainted Caroline with the very small Summerfields library, which possessed a few tall shelves lined with some dusty old tomes that appeared not to have been touched in years.

"There aren't many books here since neither of my parents were the literary types, as you can see." He waved his hand indicating the sparse shelves. "But I have acquired quite a large collection over the years, and my library at Ridge Haven is much more extensive. I'll have to take you there someday. I have a few books that I think you would enjoy reading."

"That would be lovely," she uttered, and then found herself covering her mouth to stifle a yawn at the same moment.

He noticed it at once and gave her a sympathetic look. "I'm sorry. You're exhausted and I've kept you up too late. You should probably retire to your room now and get some sleep," he suggested with a smile.

She nodded. "I think I will. It's been a very long day. Any advice before I see your mother again tomorrow?"

"You can interrupt her, you know. You almost have to interrupt to get a word in," he quipped.

She rolled her eyes and laughed. "I meant, what if she asks about our wedding?"

"Tell her you don't think it's proper to discuss it before I have officially proposed." He winked at her.

Caroline ruefully shook her head, turning away and opening the arched door. "Well . . . good night." She stood hesitantly at the entrance of the library, one hand on the heavy iron doorknob, and tilted her face to look up at him. "Alex . . ." she began slowly.

He watched her expectantly. "Yes?"

For some reason she needed him to know that she appreciated his friendship. "It . . . wasn't easy for me to talk about, but thank you for allowing me to confide in you while we were in the carriage yesterday. I did feel a little better afterward."

Walking over to where she stood, he took her small hand in his. "I'm glad I could be there for you. You can confide anything in me, Caroline. I hope you consider me your friend."

She simply nodded again, because words inexplicably escaped her, and looking up at him, her eyes locked with his. His hand was warm and felt good holding hers. It felt perfect. He was standing so close she could smell the clean scent of him, the starch in his shirt. She could see the fine shadow of new whiskers along his jawline. She could almost feel the length of his body against hers. If she moved just a fraction of an inch forward, their bodies would be touching. Terrified, she held herself perfectly still, gazing up at him. Then, as if reading his mind, she *knew*. She knew he was going to kiss her. And she also knew, with the utmost certainty, that she was going to let him kiss her. There was that endless moment, suspended in time, when they both knew without saying a word exactly what was going to happen. Her breath caught in anticipation as he captured her face with both his hands, leaned into her, and placed a delicate kiss on her lips. His mouth was soft, and his breath was hot on her cheek. She closed her eyes. Caroline couldn't breathe for all the sensations pulsing through her veins. He was warm and soft and hard all at once. It was a sweet kiss, a tender kiss.

His sensual lips pressed into hers with more urgency, more need. Then it seemed to set off a spark, and it became a kiss that made her feel wanted, desired. It was a demanding kiss. Her heart dropped into her belly, and her legs weakened. Oh, she should not be kissing him! This should not be happening.

And as if he sensed her split second of hesitation, his arms wrapped around her and pulled her against him. His mouth came down upon hers with a swift surety, and she found herself returning his kiss with the same intensity. His tongue entered the sweetness of her mouth, and their kiss deepened. Sliding his hands up her back, he pulled her closer against his chest as her arms encircled his shoulders. She could feel the rapid pounding of his heart against her breasts, and a tingling sensation began to form low in her belly. She felt light-headed and dizzy. Her fingers splayed through the dark hair at the nape of his neck and traced paths down his neck. All she could do was kiss him, stunned by the realization that she had longed for this to happen. Again. She had been waiting for this to happen again since the night they met. But why? Why were they kissing like this? They were just friends. Didn't he just say so? Oh, it was so wrong to be kissing him this way, yet she could not help herself. She wanted it to go on and on and on.

Hearing footsteps moving down the corridor brought them both back to reality. One of the servants could easily discover them, especially with the door wide open. Alex reluctantly released her. Caroline looked up at him with a shy smile, her breathing rapid and her cheeks scarlet. She could see the longing and desire in his eyes, and it astonished her.

"Go to your room quickly," he whispered in a hoarse voice. "Or you and I are in very big trouble."

She fled then, scurrying down the hall and up the stone staircase to her round and garish tower room.

CHAPTER 9

Bright sunshine filtered through the mullion windows in Elizabeth Woodward's pink bedroom the next morning as Caroline sat on a delicately carved cherrywood chair with pink damask cushions, sipping hot tea from a paper-thin porcelain teacup. She wore a butter yellow dress with fancy, white lace edging, her golden hair held back with white and yellow ribbons. While trying to give the impression that she was listening to Alex's mother, her mind kept reliving the kiss he had given her in the library the night before.

She barely slept all night for thinking of it. Kissing Alex left her weak and breathless and longing for more. It terrified her. What did it all mean? How had she let this happen to her? Again. Something crazy happened to her when he was near because she had wanted him to kiss her that way. And how could she be sitting here in front of his mother and imagining his lips on hers and his hands caressing her back, pressing her closer to him . . . It really shouldn't happen again.

She had to be stronger somehow and resist him.

". . . and we released ten white doves! It was perfectly beautiful. Everyone still talks about it." Elizabeth was again propped up in her bed by many pillows and wearing a sumptuous pink bed jacket, her black hair swept elegantly into a knot atop her refined head. "I honestly don't think there has been a wedding to compare with it since. Although Mary Worth-Biddle's wedding to the Duke of Ashcroft ten years ago came close in style, the emotional impact was missing. They just weren't in love with each other. Whereas John and I were mad about each other. Weddings are great fun! I cannot wait to begin planning yours!" Elizabeth actually paused for a moment, her hand over her mouth, realizing she said something she shouldn't have.

Brought back from her memories of Alex's kisses to the present by the sudden silence, Caroline was startled. Mortified to be caught not listening, she worried that the Dowager Duchess had just asked her a question and was unsure how to respond. "Excuse me?"

With an angelic smile, Elizabeth apologized. "I'm sorry, my dear. I shouldn't mention such things to you yet. I promised Alex I wouldn't talk of weddings to you. Please forgive me."

"Of course, Your Grace." It was a relief that she wasn't expected to give a response!

"You are a dear, Caroline." She smoothed the pink bedcovers over her lap and leaned back against the pillows once more. "So. Tell me now, just between us girls, what do you think of my Alex? You must admit he's a very handsome man."

"Yes, he is quite handsome," Caroline nodded her head in agreement, somewhat embarrassed at confessing this point to his mother. Even though

Alex *was* the most handsome man she had ever met. Without a doubt.

"Alex never tells me anything, so I'm relying on you, Caroline. I'm simply dying to know. How did the two of you meet? Was it love at first sight? I want to hear all the pretty details," Elizabeth cooed.

Inwardly Caroline squirmed. What was she to say? It was all a pretense. She and Alex were not in love, and they were not getting married. She couldn't possibly explain that they were just friends and that they could never marry. How could she giggle girl-ishly with his mother over the raptures of their first meeting? She wasn't comfortable having these kinds of feminine conversations, especially with Alex's mother! She and her own mother had never talked this way, nor did she talk like this with her grandmother. This was more Emma's style. It was too personal and fraught with the lies she would have to tell. However, common sense told her that the closer she came to telling the truth, the better. "We met at Lord and Lady Maxwell's ball at the opening of the Season."

"And did you dance together?" Elizabeth cajoled, her look inquisitive.

"No . . . We just talked for a little while."

"Where? In a secluded corner? On a garden path?"

Caroline smiled in spite of herself, catching Eliza-beth's mood. "No. On a balcony."

Elizabeth nodded her head in approval. "Was there moonlight?"

"Yes."

Elizabeth asked with anticipation, "And . . . did he kiss you?"

Oh, did he kiss me, Caroline recalled. *He took me in his*

*arms and kissed me as I had never been kissed before. And
he kissed me again last night!* But that little tidbit was not
to be shared. Instead she said, "He sent me flowers
the next day and asked if he could call on me."

"He should have kissed you!" she said emphatically, yet she was intrigued. "Alex actually sent you
flowers? What kind?"

"Gardenias." Caroline remembered the amazed
expressions of her grandmother and Emma at the
flowers from the duke and how secretly thrilled she
was to receive them.

"Oh, how lovely!" Elizabeth clapped her hands
like a child getting an unexpected present. "That's
so unlike my Alex. Imagine a romantically extravagant gesture like that! You must have really caught
his eye, Caroline. He never does anything remotely
romantic. He's much too serious, or so I've always
thought. Even as a little boy he was serious. Now my
Charles, on the other hand, he probably sends flowers to a different lady every day! But not Alex. No,
no. I am very surprised but so pleased with him!
Were you thrilled to have him court you?"

Caroline nodded, wishing she were anywhere but
there.

"So are you the reason that Madeline Maxwell
was fit to be tied?"

Caroline's mouth opened in surprise. "You know
about Madeline Maxwell?"

"Darling, of course! I may be hidden away in my
castle, but not a bit of gossip do I miss. My friends
write me daily with all the news. A little late, but I
do hear everything eventually. My John and Lord
Maxwell were friends, and they always thought it
would be a good match between Madeline and
Alex, although I personally disagreed. Besides, I

had so many inquiries from my close friends wondering about an engagement between Alex and Madeline Maxwell that even I began to wonder if it were true! I finally cornered Alex and asked him straight out if he was going to propose to Lady Madeline, and he said, with quite an attitude mind you, that he wasn't interested in marrying anyone at the present, thank you very much, and left the room in a huff. The next thing I heard was that Madeline Maxwell was marrying Oliver Parkridge, and suddenly Alex's name was linked with yours! I thought it positively intriguing! Naturally, I deduced that Alex met you and instantly fell head over heels in love. Which is just too perfect for him! Imagine, my dignified and serious son falling in love at first sight!"

"Oh, I don't think it was love at first sight—" Caroline protested in panic, hastily setting down her teacup.

"Of course it was!" Elizabeth interrupted. "Don't you see? It couldn't be any other way with Alex. He's too sedate and controlled and used to having everything his own way. He needs to be shaken up a little. Which is exactly what you've done. I knew as soon as he wrote that he was bringing you here to meet me that you had to be someone very, very special to him. You are just what he needs. You swept him off his feet."

"No, I didn't." Caroline was appalled at the thought. Elizabeth was creating a fantastical love story out of their façade of a courtship.

"Have you ever looked in a mirror, my dearest girl? You are very beautiful. Alex cannot take his eyes off you."

Feeling overwhelmed and full of guilt at their lies,

she murmured, "We haven't discussed marriage. I'm nothing special to him really."

"But you are, Caroline, you are indeed! He's always had this ridiculous notion that women were interested in him only for his title and money. But I've told him many times, to no avail, that with the way he looks, women would fall at his feet if he were a mere pauper. He didn't believe me and brooded about it. He wouldn't attend Season parties or discuss marriage, even when his father insisted that he marry. But you, Caroline, he saw something special in you. Why do you think he brought you here? Alex has never brought any woman home to meet me. I know he wants to get my blessing before proposing to you. Oh, yes, you have caught my son most definitely, and I for one could not be happier about it!" She clapped her hands again like a giddy schoolgirl.

Caroline's heart began to pound erratically at the Dowager Duchess's enthusiasm over this nonexistent situation.

"And if this isn't proof that he's going to marry you, I don't know what is." Elizabeth's voice dropped to a dramatic whisper, and in a show of confidentiality, she stated, "I've also heard that he has even given up Lily Sherwood."

Caroline stared at her blankly.

"Lily Sherwood, his London mistress," she stated as if Caroline should know. "Alex gave her up. Broke it off. Ended the affair."

Caroline sat in stunned silence, thinking she hadn't heard Elizabeth correctly. Not having given the issue much thought before, she was somewhat surprised to learn that Alex had a mistress, although she was aware that most gentlemen of his class did and everyone accepted it as a matter of course. She wasn't completely naïve, having picked up a few things during her London Season, scandalous as the topic was. She hadn't thought of Alex in that context before, but now she was deeply curious. Alex and another woman? A mistress? What was she like? Was she beautiful? Where did he keep her? She felt a little twinge of jealousy at the thought, and that confounded her as well. Did Alex truly give up his mistress and for what reason?

"I have very reliable sources, my dear. He gave up his mistress all right. In June." When she spoke, her words came out in rapid succession. "I know we shouldn't be discussing these things, and please don't tell your grandmother. Olivia is very proper and would probably be quite cross with me if she knew I was chatting about mistresses with you. But I have always been of the opinion that ladies should be aware of these situations. Honestly, we find out about it sooner or later anyway! A woman has precious little resources in this life, and information is absolutely vital. As much as the men would like to keep us women in ignorance of their little peccadilloes, I believe forewarned is forearmed. I make it my business to know what is going on. Of course, Alex would just die of mortification if he knew that his mother knew all about that part of his life, so I play ignorant and let him hold on to that little illusion. However, it is a fact that most gentlemen do keep that other sort of woman. Although my darling John swore to me that he never did. But they think we should just accept it and not speak of such things. Well, I disagree. Wives have a right to know what's going on and put a stop to it, if they are so inclined. Now Alex is very handsome and well . . . unattached, so of course he would have a mistress.

As his future wife, you have a perfect right to know these things." She gave Caroline a knowing look.

Their little chat had wandered so far from what was considered polite and socially acceptable conversation that Caroline remained utterly speechless.

"Oh dear. I can tell by the look on your face that I have shocked and embarrassed you. You're so very shy. Forgive me, please. There I go again, talking too much! I promised Alex I wouldn't talk about your marriage until he formally proposed to you. It's so silly really. You know why you're here. But I suppose he has his reasons."

At that moment Alex entered the room, his male presence instantly smothering the intimate conversation. Caroline and Elizabeth looked awkwardly at each other.

"I've come to rescue Caroline," he announced with a gallant flair, a teasing smile on his handsome face. His blue eyes darted from his mother's to Caroline's expression, trying to read the situation.

Elizabeth frowned, irritated by his remark and his untimely interruption. "Don't be mean, Alex. We were having a perfectly lovely time together. Weren't we, dear?" She turned to Caroline to confirm her statement.

"Perfectly lovely," Caroline echoed woodenly, feeling like a hypocrite.

Alex attempted to discern the somewhat dazed expression on Caroline's face, worried what his mother might have said to her. "Just the same, I promised to show Caroline the estate this afternoon."

Caroline knew he had not promised her any such thing but was so grateful for his presenting her with an opportunity to escape that she nodded enthusiastically.

"Oh yes, I had quite forgotten. I hope I didn't keep you waiting."

"Not at all," he said with a charming smile. "But I do have a meeting with my estate manager later today, so we should get started."

"Don't let me keep you two." Elizabeth gave them a knowing look. "Come and kiss me good-bye, Caroline."

Caroline dutifully placed a kiss on the older woman's cheek, feeling a pang of guilt for participating in this charade. Under normal circumstances she might have liked talking with Alex's mother. But this situation was too fraught with secrets, and she felt uncomfortable talking with her about anything. "Thank you for a lovely afternoon, Your Grace."

"No, I must thank you. It's been ages since I've had a good girlish chat. I'm looking forward to having your family here also. Come and kiss me good-bye as well, Alex."

In the safety of the corridor, Caroline released a heavy sigh as they continued to walk downstairs. "Thank you for rescuing me."

"I had a feeling you might need some help. Was it that bad?"

"No, but she's created quite a love story about us, Alex. It's all she talks about. Romances. Engagements. Weddings. She is going to be completely devastated when we don't marry."

"Oh, don't worry about that. I'll handle my mother."

She stopped suddenly, placing a hand on his arm and looking him directly in his eyes. "Alex, I think this is getting out of hand now. We are deliberately misleading everyone. And we're going to hurt and disappoint our families terribly. This has already gone too far. We need to end it now."

He looked down at her, unable to decide which was her most beautiful feature. Sometimes he thought it was her expressive green eyes. Or her elegant little nose. Or her full pink lips. Or the slight dimple in her left cheek when she smiled. Maybe it was the worried little frown she wore at the moment. All he wanted to do was make her happy. "Leave everything to me, Caroline."

"But she thinks we're in love, Alex. She's beginning to make wedding plans. Which will only get worse when my grandmother arrives. Isn't that letting this go too far?"

Actually it was part of Alex's alternate plan. If he couldn't convince Caroline to give up her foolish devotion to that American, he would just allow his mother and her grandmother to arrange the wedding until it was too late for Caroline to refuse him.

"Don't worry, Caroline. I'll take care of everything. And we won't disappoint anyone. I promise."

CHAPTER 10

"I've told you, horses don't like me," Caroline warned as they walked through the well-maintained stables of Summerfields.

Upon discovering that Caroline did not know how to ride a horse, Alex was determined to teach her. He couldn't think of a more enjoyable way to spend the day than giving her a riding lesson.

Caroline, however, was miserable.

"What's not to like?" Alex asked light-heartedly, eyeing her pretty ensemble and the even prettier package it contained. She was wearing a chocolate brown velvet riding habit stitched with black velvet piping and smart black leather boots. A tall, brown top hat was perched on her head, with a long filmy veil cascading down the back. "Everyone knows how to ride. Really, Caroline, I expected you to have more adventure in you."

"You weren't a witness to the first time I tried to ride and sprained my ankle. My Uncle Kit and Emma couldn't stop laughing when I fell in the mud," she muttered.

"I must say I'm not a bit surprised to hear that

about Emma, but your uncle too? That was not well done of him." He made a slight, mocking *tsk, tsk* sound, as if he were shocked at her uncle's behavior. "You must have been quite a sight though." He chuckled at the thought.

She gave him a disdainful look and ignored his laughter. "I'm not overly fond of animals. Especially large ones."

"Now why is that?"

"I suppose because I was bitten on the hand by a huge dog when I was five years old. Dogs are unpredictable and they make me nervous. Horses are even bigger versions of dogs."

"They are nothing alike! Your uncle just didn't find the right mount for you. Now, here's Penny. She's the sweetest mare you'll ever meet," Alex said, leading a large, but gentle-eyed horse out to the ring. The mare was a soft, silvery gray and not too intimidating looking. He noticed that Caroline followed reluctantly behind them.

"She is pretty," Caroline grudgingly admitted. "But Penny is the wrong name for her. It's a good name for a coppery-colored horse, but she's gray," she pointed out. "We should change her name to Dove."

He laughed at her, knowing that she was stalling for time. "In case you are under the impression that you are having your lesson upon an erroneously named animal, I must inform you that Penny is the diminutive for Penelope."

"Oh." Her tone was crestfallen. "Then I suppose I have to ride her after all."

He smiled sympathetically at the dejected tone of her voice but sensed her anxiety. "Penny won't hurt you. I'll just walk you both around the ring very slowly. Here, step up," Alex commanded as he held out a hand to her.

With great trepidation Caroline placed her elegantly booted foot in the stirrup and pushed herself up on the saddle with all the force she could muster. Apparently too much force, because she went hurtling off the other side, landing with a sharp cry and a heavy thud in the dirt.

"Caroline!" Alex called, his heart in his mouth. He raced around the horse to find Caroline lying on the ground. If anything happened to her, he would never forgive himself. Kneeling beside her, he tenderly felt for any broken bones. "Are you all right?"

"I think so," she murmured shakily.

"You're sure? No broken bones?" His eyes scanned her small frame, assuring himself that she was all right. He gently helped her to rise.

She gave a rueful smile and took hold of his hand. "Just wounded pride and probably some bruises."

"I think you just got the wind knocked out of you." She had propelled herself over the horse with a force that was surprising for someone of her small size. Now that he knew she was quite all right, he relaxed a little. "Why did you throw yourself over?" he asked playfully, trying to suppress his laughter at the thought of her sailing over the horse.

"I didn't throw myself over! I was simply trying to get on!" Caroline said heatedly, hastily brushing the dirt and dust off her habit and picking up her little velvet top hat, which had been knocked off during her fall.

"Well, it looked like you were trying to get off," he teased, finally giving in to his laughter.

"That's it," Caroline declared as she began to walk, none too steadily, from the ring. "I'm through riding horses." She slammed the hat back on her head in an effort to regain some dignity, the dusty veil trailing behind.

"You haven't even ridden yet," he pointed out, still laughing at her. He liked the way she looked with her green eyes flashing and her hat perched crookedly on her head.

"You're even worse than my uncle," Caroline sniffed, walking away with an injured air.

Alex hurried after her, still laughing. "Wait, Caroline . . . I'm sorry. I shouldn't have laughed at you."

"I'm just not horse-riding material."

"I have an idea." He actually liked this idea better than the first.

"No. I'm finished," she said emphatically as she continued to march with indignation toward the stable.

Alex caught her by the arm and spun her around to face him, his eyes sparkling. "You can ride with me."

"Oh no!"

"I didn't expect you to be a typical *female* and be afraid," he challenged with a smirk.

Caroline stared angrily back at him. He could see the turmoil in her eyes, torn between her fear of riding a horse and her desire to prove to him that she was not afraid. She was beautiful even when she was angry and scared. Hands on her hips, she jutted out her chin defiantly and took a deep breath. "Fine. I'll ride with you."

"That's my girl."

Before she could utter another protest, Alex had her seated in front of him atop his large black stallion.

She held on to him for dear life as they galloped across the fields. Completely terrified, she clutched him frantically, with her head pressed against his chest and her eyes squeezed shut, certain that she would go sailing off the stampeding animal and end up crashing to the ground. The unfamiliar rhythm of the horse jostled her body so that she barely noticed Alex's muscular arm wrapped around her waist, holding her securely.

"I won't let you fall," he whispered to reassure her.

When she realized that she had not gone flying off the stallion as she first feared, she relaxed bit by bit, as she grew accustomed to the movements of the animal. She even managed to open her eyes. They galloped past lush green hills and flower-filled meadows and large oak and maple trees, full with the verdant foliage of late summer. Sheep and cow pastures lined by stone fences and tall, dense woods filled the distance. The sky was overcast, and the breeze was cool and crisp, with a hint of autumn in the air.

Caroline began to rest against his broad chest, because his arm held her so securely that she no longer felt as if she would pitch over the side. Enjoying the feel of the wind on her face, she tilted her head up. Her long hair, already loosened from its pins during her fall from Penny, had completely escaped from her velvet top hat, which was long gone, and it now swept around them in golden waves. She breathed deeply of the fresh, cool air and leaned into his warm body, wondering how the feel of him could be so very muscular and hard, yet warm and inviting at the same time. His clean male scent made her think of kissing him again, and that startled her.

In silence, they rode across the Summerfields estate and along the narrow, winding river that divided the expanse of property in half. Alex turned the stallion around when they crested the top of a small ridge, and they glanced back at the house. From that vantage point Summerfields truly looked like a little fairy tale castle.

"It looks perfect from here," Caroline sighed.

"That's because we can't see the inside," he answered dryly.

She laughed as they headed back home, but they didn't speak again. She was impressed with how his long, powerful legs could control the horse so easily. A nudge here, a touch there. A flick of his wrist with the reins and the animal moved where he wanted it to. Alex was a very skilled rider, and she felt safe with him.

And there was something very intimate about riding with him, sitting pressed closely against his body, feeling his breath on the back of her neck, having his arm tightly across her waist, that took her breath away. Her heart was beating faster, but she wasn't sure if it was from the thrill of riding or from being in such close contact with Alex. It was all rather puzzling.

They had been at Summerfields for almost a week now, and still Grandmother, Emma, Aunt Jane, and Uncle Kit had not arrived from London. Neither had Alex's brother, Charles. This situation made Caroline uneasy, for there was no real chaperone for them. Although Bonnie was technically her chaperone, she wasn't a very practiced one. She was having a little romance with one of the young footmen at Summerfields and was too preoccupied with him to pay any attention to Caroline. The most she gave were disapproving frowns. Since the Dowager Duchess never left her room, she and

Alex were spending a great deal of time together unaccompanied. Back in London that probably wouldn't have mattered to her, because they had shared such an easygoing and casual friendship.

But since their trip to Summerfields, she detected a very different feeling from him. There was an intensity about him that she couldn't quite define but could tell only increased after they kissed in the library that first night. Caroline felt him watching her closely, and she would often catch him staring at her when he thought she was unaware. Alex didn't seem to be acting brotherly anymore. She couldn't put her finger on it, but she sensed something. Being alone so much was creating a tension between them, and she wished her family would arrive soon to relieve some of it. She also suspected that Olivia did not know that the Dowager Duchess was bedridden and would certainly not approve of the current semi-unchaperoned situation, but there was very little Caroline could do to remedy it now. Especially while she sat pressed against him on a horse!

When they finally returned to the stables, Alex reined in his horse and dismounted. He reached up to Caroline, his strong hands spanning her small waist, and easily lifted her to the ground. His hands lingered longer than necessary at her waist, and they stared at each other. As always, she had to look up at him because he was so much taller than she was. *Oh, but he is so handsome,* she thought. His aristocratic nose. The lean line of his jaw. Those sensual lips. The crystal blue of his eyes, fringed with thick black lashes. There was a look in them at the moment that Caroline could not read. It was slightly vulnerable, and she was not sure what that meant. She continued to stand there, his hands upon her, unable to move.

He abruptly let go of her, patted the stallion, and handed the reigns to the stable boy, and he and Caroline walked slowly through the gardens back to the castle.

"There! You mounted a horse and managed to stay on for more than a minute!" he congratulated her teasingly. "You did very well."

"Thank you. Now I can brag to Emma and my Uncle Kit that I have actually ridden a horse. They won't believe it!" she said, her voice somewhat breathless.

"You lost your little top hat."

"I know." She laughed and removed her gloves, attempting to smooth her tousled hair with her hands. "But I was too terrified at the time to care."

"We'll have to get you a new one." He grinned. "So what did you think?"

"It was nice," she admitted with a little laugh. "Once I relaxed."

As they continued down the limestone path into the garden, they walked through a more secluded area surrounded by tall, well-manicured hedges and flowering rose bushes. Alex casually took her hand in his. "I'm happy you enjoyed the ride."

"I'm amazed that I did." She was also amazed at how natural it felt to hold his hand this way.

He glanced down at her as they continued to walk. "Do you think you might like to try to ride on your own sometime?"

"I don't know . . . I feel safe with you." She glanced up at him, then confessed hesitantly, "And I think I would prefer riding with you better."

Alex stopped and stared at her for a silent moment,

his blue eyes glinting with an unspoken desire, his dark brows furrowing. Instantly the comfortable mood vanished, turning serious, consequential. He suddenly swung her into his arms and without giving her time to react to his intent, he kissed her. Hard. She did not protest, but responded eagerly to his impassioned overture. His lips moved hungrily against her mouth, and she simply yielded to him. In one seamless movement they went from talking to kissing heatedly. The silkiness of her loosened hair beckoned him to entwine his fingers among the golden tresses, and then he cupped her face in his hands, breathing deeply of her scent. Parting her lips with his warm tongue, he entered her mouth, and his whole body tensed with the sensation of it. His hands caressed the length of her back, luxuriating in the lush velvet-covered curves of her body, and cupped the rounded flesh of her bottom, pressing her ever closer to him. She gasped into his mouth at this new intimacy, a strange buzzing and thrumming within her.

In the next moment he carefully lowered her to the ground and eased himself over her as she lay upon the grass. There in the gardens of Summerfields, behind the tall leafy hedges and next to the white rose bushes, the Duke of Woodborough lay in the grass with Caroline. She looked at him above her, the clean lines of his face, the smile lines around his mouth. He resumed his kiss. And it was happening again, this strange, compelling attraction between them. She knew it was wrong, but Caroline, for the life of her, was unable, and admittedly unwilling, to put a stop to it. In fact, she had been waiting for this for months, haunted by the memory of that first kiss on the balcony and further enticed by their recent kiss in the library. It was unstoppable. So she surrendered to the force of it, closing her eyes.

Time seem suspended, endless. They could have been kissing for hours or mere minutes. It was of no importance. All that mattered was the press of his lips on hers. The brush of warm skin against skin. The caress of his breath on her cheek. His murmured words tumbled tenderly around her. Sweet. Beautiful. Perfect. She couldn't speak, couldn't think, couldn't breathe. She simply clung to him as he kissed the delicate skin of her throat, her neck.

It was when the cool air brushed her skin that she realized that he was unbuttoning the front of her riding habit. An alarming thought that she should definitely stop him now flashed through her passion-fogged brain, but she only continued to twirl her tongue in his mouth and arch forward to allow him easier access to her breasts. Hands. His exquisite hands were everywhere, inside and outside of her clothes, his fingers so warm they burned where they touched the skin of her naked breasts. His hands, at once so strong and powerful, now were tender and gentle. It felt as if she were drowning in his kisses. Swirling. Sinking. Smoldering. It was incredible. Endless. His tongue. His lips. His skin. More. Her body was aching from the amazing sensations he created within her. Unconsciously, she pulled him closer to her, pressing herself against the length of his hard, muscled body and melting into him, as a strange feeling of urgency and an increasing desire overwhelmed her so that she couldn't think clearly. She was aware though, as if watching herself from far away, that she was kissing him fervently as his hands roamed her body, while her own fingers were entwined in the thick dark hair covering his head.

Caroline heard him mutter an oath, and in that same instant she could breathe again because he suddenly released her. As if in a trance, she gazed up at him. He was breathing heavily, coming up for air, staring at her with his piercing blue eyes. The pained expression in his face concerned her. There was a vulnerability in his eyes. What had just happened? Why was he looking at her like that? Why had he stopped kissing her? The kiss that had begun so unexpectedly had ended far too soon. She had wanted much more from him, and the reality of that fact left her shaking.

Alex caressed her cheek with his fingers, lightly brushing against her flushed skin. As he looked down upon her he knew he had been very close to completely losing control. He had been with her constantly since the Season started and had been so very careful with her. Granted, it was easier then, because they had never been alone together. But after traveling together for two days and spending time alone with each other without having a real chaperone, he was stretched to the limit. The breaking point had been the horse ride when he held her so closely. The passion and the tension between them was now undeniable and his desire for her too great. She looked so beautiful laying in the grass beneath him, looking up at him beneath thick dark lashes, her green eyes warm with desire, her lips full and kiss-swollen. She had been so responsive and passionate, he hardened at the mere thought of her. Having her here at Summerfields, he meant only to woo her gently with sweet kisses and romantic gestures. Yet those sweet kisses instantly turned into a passionate fusion that could quite easily spin out of his control. Nothing was going according to his plan. He couldn't continue to take advantage of her this way, and yet he couldn't stop himself either. Which made for a very dangerous situation. He wanted her and wanted her to know it.

And there was only one way he could have a woman like her.

"Marry me, Caroline," he whispered huskily, his lips brushing against her cheek, his voice ragged.

He felt her freeze in his arms, her green eyes wide with shock.

"Honestly. Forget our secret arrangement and marry me for real." His gaze was steady, reading the stunned expression on her face. He knew he had spoken too soon, but he wanted her more than he had ever wanted anything in his life, and he couldn't keep playing this little game, pretending that he didn't want her. And she deserved better than this. They were lying out in the open in the grass! If this wasn't proof that things were getting out of hand, he didn't know what was.

"But why?" she managed to choke out, her voice high and sharp.

"Why?" Alex looked at her with complete disbelief. He asked her to marry him and she asked why! "What do you think almost happened here just now? I can't kiss you like this again and promise that I'll be able to stop before I compromise you."

Caroline closed her eyes for a moment. Her dark lashes fluttered against her pale cheeks, then she opened her eyes to look at him. His body was completely covering her, his face inches from hers. "We're not supposed to be kissing anyway. That wasn't a part of our deal."

"But you like kissing me. Admit it."

She simply ignored him. "Let's end it then," she said. "The Season is over. It's gone too far. We should have ended it in London. I don't even know why I'm here with you in the first place."

"You're here because I want you here." Yes, he wanted her here. With him. Always. God, how he wanted her.

"So I'll leave," she said in an unsteady voice.

"I don't want you to leave, Caroline. I want you to marry me."

"So is it all about what you want, then?" she blurted out heatedly, trying to push him off her.

"After the way you just kissed me, you know it's what you want too." Alex's voice was calm, but he wanted to scream at her. He felt terrible that he had handled the situation so badly. This was not how he intended to propose to her. She deserved a more romantic and classic approach. But it couldn't be helped now.

Tears threatened behind her luminous eyes, and she looked away. "You know why I can't."

"No. No, I don't know why." How could she still be thinking about that boy and respond to Alex's kisses the way she just did? What kind of hold did that American have over her? "I'm the one here with you now, Caroline. Holding you. Kissing you. And he's two years and thousands of miles away."

"Don't!" she gasped, squirming beneath him.

"I want you to forget him. Marry me."

"I can't."

He took her face in his hands and held her gently, holding her still and forcing her to look at him. Couldn't she see how much he wanted her? Was the girl that naïve? He was the Duke of Woodborough, for God's sake! He was the most sought-after bach-

elor in London, with women throwing themselves at
his feet. He could have any woman he wanted, and
any one of them would jump at his offer of marriage. And here he was, inexplicably lying in the
grass, pleading with this little green-eyed beauty to
marry him. How had it come to this? "Yes, you can,
Caroline."

She shoved him, blinking back hot tears of anger
and frustration. He rolled to his side, releasing her.
She hastily sat up and concentrated on her clothes,
adjusting her cotton chemise and tugging the
brown velvet closed over her breasts. Her fingers
were shaking so badly she could barely fasten the
buttons on the front of her riding habit. Alex
reached over to assist her, but she slapped his
hands away. He simply wanted to pull her into his
arms and hold her until she stopped trembling.
He hadn't meant to upset her. Why couldn't she
just say yes?

"You can't wait for him forever," he warned.

She didn't respond, but gave all her attention to
the velvet-covered buttons.

"If your American didn't exist, would you want
to marry me?" he questioned her, somewhat
harshly.

Her fingers stilled on the last button. She stared
at him mutely and did not answer his question. She
attempted to stand.

"Caroline," he cried, grabbing her hand and
pulling her back down toward him. "Answer me."

"Let me go." She wrenched her hand away from
him and managed to remain standing.

He stood up and grabbed fast her arm, holding
her to him. He had to know the truth now. "Are
you still in love with him?"

She didn't respond.

"Are you?" he demanded.

"I don't know," she muttered edgily.

He looked at her intently, his blue eyes determined. "Then marry me." He watched an unreadable expression come over her face. There was something that removed her from him. That invisible wall surrounded her again.

"I cannot marry you, Alex."

There was mounting impatience in his voice. "He's on the other side of the world, Caroline. You don't even think you love him anymore. What is there to stop you from marrying me?"

She glared at him, her arms folded across her chest. "You have no idea what you are talking about!"

Frustrated with the turn of events and at the obvious impasse between them, he voiced between clenched teeth, "He hasn't written to you. He's not coming back. He's forgotten all about you by now."

Her other hand flew out and stung his cheek with a smart crack. Alex didn't even flinch, just continued to stare at her. She snapped her hand back in remorse and covered her mouth with it as she gasped in surprise. He let go of her other arm.

She murmured, "I'm sorry."

It was a cruel comment and he should not have said it. It was simply another example of how he lost any sense of reason around her. "I deserved that."

She only stared at him in silence.

Still he continued. Nothing she said made sense. She could not possibly have told him everything, the whole story. Some essential element was being withheld from him. "Don't you think I deserve an explanation at least? Why can't you marry me?"

"Because I can't."

He needed a real reason. A reason he could understand and make sense of. He needed something real from her. "Because why?" he persisted.

"I just can't!" she cried. She turned and fled from him. He let her go and watched her race along the limestone path back to the castle.

CHAPTER 11

After entering her garish round room, Caroline flung herself on the purple velvet bed and covered her face with her shaking hands. Overcome by a sense of panic, she jumped up again and began pacing in front of the fireplace. The golden cherubs decorating the ornate room seemed to be laughing at her.

What had just happened out there in the garden?

Alex had asked her to marry him! That changed everything. She had to leave Summerfields immediately. She had to get away. She could not marry Alex. He asked if she still loved Stephen.

Of course she still loved Stephen. *Didn't she?* She should still love him, shouldn't she? It had been so long she wasn't sure anymore. That caused her to stop pacing for a moment.

She wasn't sure anymore.

An image of his boyish face, pale blond hair, and warm brown eyes was drawn in her memory. It was hazy, the edges blurred and faded, replaced by the more vivid picture of a tall, handsome man with jet black hair and laughing blue eyes. Lean, hard muscles. Long legs. Warm hands. A quick smile and melting kisses.

She tried again to concentrate on Stephen. She sat on the crimson velvet divan and wrapped her arms around her knees.

Did she still love him? At one point she thought she did.

Two years ago Stephen Bennett had turned her world upside down, but Stephen's kisses never inspired the wildly erotic impulses that surged through her when Alex kissed her. When Alex kissed her she wanted more from him than just kisses. She wanted all of him. That feeling terrified her. She was thankful Alex had the good sense to stop things when he did.

With Stephen she had always been the reasonable one, the one to say no. That fateful summer it was she who put a stop to their kissing when things seemed to be getting out of hand, and things always seemed to be getting out of hand with Stephen. Yet she remained virtuous. That is, until that last day. When things had gotten so far out of hand that she cringed to think about it. The day that Stephen left, he had taken more than just her innocence.

If Stephen Bennett didn't exist, her life would be completely different. She would not have had to keep secrets from her family. She would have gone to London eagerly, without a sense of dread. She would have enjoyed the Season freely and flirted and danced, without fearing an attachment. She would not have had to make this arrangement with the duke.

Now here was Alex, stirring such tumultuous emotions in her. Kissing her. Holding her. Making her want things she couldn't have. A home. A family of her own. A future filled with happiness. With him. And it could be so easy. It could all be hers.

If only Stephen Bennett didn't exist . . .

But he did exist.

The day she met Stephen was one of those cold, dreary winter days when it seemed the rain would never stop and the very dampness soaked into one's bones until it seemed one could not get warm enough. The ground was oversaturated, with puddles and veritable streams springing up everywhere, making it difficult to walk on the mud-covered pathways. Caroline had to bring some papers that she had finished proofreading to her father at the university. Drenched from the downpour on her short walk to the campus, she slowly trudged up the staircase of the main building and was just reaching the second-floor landing when a young man came racing down the upper flight of stairs. He quickly rounded the corner and collided forcefully with her. For a split second Caroline knew with a sickening certainty that she was about to plummet backward, down the stairs she had just climbed, when the young man instinctively grabbed hold of her. He pulled her toward him in a rough motion while Caroline clutched frantically at him, knocking him off balance and causing the two of them to fall in an awkward heap on the second-floor landing. The surprise and force of their collision, as well as the terrifying realization that they each could have plunged down the hard stone steps together, left them mutually breathless and stunned.

When he managed to sit up, the young man spoke first. "I beg your pardon, miss. Are you hurt at all? I should have taken more care where I was going. Please accept my sincerest apologies."

Now acutely aware that she was sitting on a stranger's lap, Caroline tried to rise, but her rain-dampened woolen skirt made moving her legs a somewhat difficult task.

After he extricated them both from a compromising position and stood up, he helped Caroline to her feet. "I'm terribly sorry. I'm afraid I was in a hurry and not paying attention. Are you all right, miss? Miss . . . ?"

Caroline, now tentatively standing again, answered, "Miss Armstrong." She attempted to adjust her twisted skirt.

"Are you sure I haven't hurt you, Miss Armstrong?"

"I'm fine."

"Please forgive my clumsy behavior. I wish we could have met under better circumstances. I am Stephen Bennett."

Although already twenty years old, Caroline had had little contact with the opposite sex, and this particular gentleman's presence overwhelmed her. While sneaking a glance at his light blond hair and appealing smile, she bent down to gather her books and papers. She could feel the slight sting of a heated blush on her cheeks as she murmured, "Well, if you will please excuse me, sir."

"Why, you must be Richard Armstrong's daughter! He's my Latin tutor," Stephen declared, while eyeing her slender and shapely form.

She was flustered by the intensity of his gaze and looked away as she answered. "Yes, he's my father. I was on my way to see him."

"Isn't that amazing? I was just leaving his class when I ran into you. Quite literally!" He laughed and ran his hand through his blond hair. "May I escort you to his room? To be sure you are safe? I do feel responsible for almost sending you to your peril at the bottom of the stairs." He grinned sheepishly.

"I suppose that would be all right," she agreed, noticing his unusual accent. "You're not English, are you?"

"No. I'm American. From Virginia. But please don't hold that against me." He flashed her a winning smile. "May I, Miss Armstrong?" he asked, his arm extended toward her.

Hesitantly, Caroline took his arm as he led her up the third flight of stairs and down the corridor to her father's classroom. Stephen opened the door into the recently emptied room and announced, "Mr. Armstrong, I have just had the great pleasure of running into your lovely daughter."

"Good afternoon, Papa," Caroline smiled with some trepidation in her father's direction and placed the papers on his desk.

"Pray tell, Mr. Bennett. How did you manage to meet my Caroline?" Richard questioned. Although there was a definite familial resemblance between Richard Armstrong and his daughter, his hair had grayed prematurely and his face showed lines that made him look much older than his forty-five years.

"I just collided with her on the staircase. Although it was not entirely my fault, sir. You see, part of the blame belongs to Miss Armstrong. It seems I lost my balance when presented with the nearness of her beauty," Stephen complimented her, a charming smile on his face.

Caroline felt her face flush anew as she wondered why this young man should go on so about her. Her heart was beating so loudly she almost missed hearing his next remark.

"Mr. Armstrong, would you please grant me the privilege of calling on your daughter?"

Caroline caught her breath but wasn't sure if she was hoping her father would answer yes or no.

Richard glanced between the two of them. "While not my best student, Mr. Bennett, you are certainly not my worst. I don't believe that I have any objections to you, but it must be Caroline's decision."

His brown eyes gleaming, Stephen smiled engagingly at her. "Well, Miss Armstrong, do I have your permission to call?" Then he added with a laugh, "I give you my word that I will not allow you to fall down any stairs."

Caroline was speechless. She had not been searching for a suitor but had simply come to bring her father's papers. After tramping through the pouring rain, she had planned to go straight home and sit in front of the fire with a good book and a cup of hot tea. She was not prepared for this handsome man who wanted to call on her. Besides, she looked frightful! Her only decent winter dress, the navy blue wool with matching overcoat, was damp and spotted with mud, and her hair was wet and straggling from her bonnet. Deeply flattered and amazed that he showed such interest in her, she didn't quite know what to say.

So she said, "Yes."

That was the beginning of everything. One little yes had led to so many yeses. And so many secrets.

* * *

The first time Stephen came to Lilac Cottage to call on Caroline, he took her for a walk along Langton Lake. On the shore of the lake was an ancient oak tree with huge gnarled roots pushing out of the ground. The thick intertwined roots formed a natural sort of bench, creating a cozy seating area with a view of the tranquil lake and the soft green hills surrounding it.

Caroline and Stephen sat there in silence, admiring the shimmering reflections on the blue water. Finally he said, "I'm surprised I haven't run into you before, Miss Armstrong. Do you come to the campus often?"

"I assist my father with his work, so sometimes I visit his classroom. I help recopy, edit, and proofread the essays and articles on Latin and Greek literature that he is writing. It's fascinating," she answered, proud of the fact that she was able to work with her father.

Eyebrows raised, he remarked with a derisive laugh, "That sounds very tedious for a girl. All the pretty girls I know tend to study art or music. Or sewing."

For all her intelligence, Caroline was completely inexperienced in dealing with the opposite sex, and this handsome young man's approval was suddenly very important to her. With his careless comment, he made her feel terribly unfeminine. She had never flirted or acted the coquette in her life and was unsure of herself in his presence. Usually proud of her academic accomplishments, although aware that educated women were generally frowned upon by the male population, Caroline intuitively sensed

Stephen's unease and disapproval, and she felt the need to soothe his fears that she was not a bookish bluestocking. She wanted him to like her. Her voice was apologetic as she downplayed her role in her father's work. "My father believes that men and women should be educated equally, so he taught my sister and me everything he would have taught us if we were his sons. Now I act as his secretary. Sometimes I study art and music as well. And I can sew too."

"Behind all that schooling I could tell you were a proper young lady!" He smiled at her in relief. "I think your father is an excellent teacher. One of the best I've had."

"Thank you." She beamed at his compliment of her father. She was proud of him and how he raised her and Emma. She surprised herself by saying, "He hasn't been the same since my mother died."

"It must be terrible to lose your mother," he remarked kindly.

She nodded. "Yes. Yes, it is." She glanced away, wishing to change the subject. "Tell me about Virginia, Mr. Bennett."

He sighed a little and leaned back against the tree-root bench. "My family has a plantation called Willow Hill. We own twenty hundred acres and about three hundred slaves. We grow rice and a little cotton, but tobacco is our main crop. We have the biggest tobacco plantation in six counties."

Caroline inwardly cringed when he mentioned having slaves and had to bite her tongue to keep it in her mouth. She had read extensively about the war in America. Slavery was an appalling and archaic institution, and she believed the northern states were right to want to free the slaves, but instinctively she kept her thoughts to herself, sensing they would offend him. "Why is it called Willow Hill?" she managed to ask.

"Because there's a long winding drive lined with giant willow trees leading up to the house. The house itself is a beautiful building with six white columns in the front, resting on the crest of a low hill. In the summer we have lawn parties and barbecues with friends and relatives visiting all the time. In the winter we always have skating parties on the river and a grand holiday ball. It is absolutely perfect there. One day it will be all mine." His smile was one of satisfaction.

"It sounds wonderful," Caroline remarked. She could listen to his soft, almost musical way of talking for hours. His voice was lazy, easy, and so different from the clipped, brisk English she was used to hearing. His accent fascinated her. "Why did you ever come to school in England?"

"My mother is English, like you." He smiled at her. "She always wanted me to be educated here, although it didn't make a difference to me where I went to school. I'm afraid I'm not much of a student. Just ask your father."

Caroline nodded her head, giving him a sheepish look. "He mentioned that."

Stephen laughed good-naturedly and continued, "As I said, my mother had her heart set on my being educated in England. When I was seventeen the war started. Even though everyone said the war would only last a couple of weeks, my father was terrified he would lose me, his only son. So my parents shipped me off to my Aunt Helen's house in London to keep me from joining the Confederate

Army. And here I am, still safe in England two years later."

"Do you wish you were there? Fighting, I mean?"

His eyes narrowed, and a far-off look came over him. "Every day I think I should be there. Defending my land and my home. My parents won't hear of my coming home. And yet all of my friends are with the army . . . My best friend was killed in Antietam the first year of the war. I feel like the worst kind of coward, hiding over here."

"But you're not," she said, not really knowing what to say to him. It was difficult to imagine being in his situation.

An engaging smile replaced the serious and determined look, and he said rather lightheartedly, "Don't be sorry for me. There are definite advantages to being safe in England watching the sun set on a lake with a beautiful girl." Then he added, "And you are very beautiful, Miss Armstrong."

She smiled shyly. "Thank you."

"May I kiss you?"

Although surprised by his inappropriate request, Caroline gazed upon his handsome face, his bright blond hair shining in the sunlight, and mutely nodded her head in acquiescence. If truth be told, she wouldn't object to being kissed by him. She was curious about kissing. Emma had been kissed lots of times but refused to give her older sister any details, stating that Caroline would just have to stop being so serious and find out for herself someday. Although it seemed rather serious to her now.

He inched closer to her, but as soon as his lips touched hers, she pulled back, and before she could stop herself she began to giggle nervously.

His brows furrowed, Stephen asked, "What's wrong?"

"Nothing," Caroline whispered, biting her tongue in an attempt to control the helpless laughter bubbling inside her and half-hoping that he wouldn't kiss her again. But he did. And the giggles commenced anew. She simply could not suppress them. The whole idea of kissing him sent her into spasms of nervous laughter.

"Miss Armstrong," Stephen, his brown eyes flashing, stated in a tone that one would use when scolding a child. "I'm going to kiss you until you *stop* laughing." Putting his hands on either side of her face, he gently pulled her toward him. "Haven't you ever been kissed before?"

"No." Her answer was barely a whisper, and she could feel the heat of a blush creeping up her cheeks.

"So I would have the honor of giving you your first kiss then?" His voice was gentle and his eyes kind.

Embarrassed beyond words, she simply nodded her head.

"May I call you Caroline?"

"Yes."

"Then you must call me Stephen."

Again she nodded her head in agreement.

"I think I shall call you Carrie."

She looked into his brown eyes, noticing they were flecked with tiny bits of gold and hazel. No one had ever called her Carrie before, and it seemed strange to have him refer to her that way, especially in that languid way he had of speaking.

"Do you want me to kiss you?" he asked.

She shrugged her shoulders, neither a yes nor a no.

Stephen leaned over and very lightly placed a kiss on her forehead.

Caroline closed her eyes in anticipation.

And then he placed another little kiss on the tip of her nose. Encouraged by her lack of nervous giggles, he kissed her cheek and inched along unhurriedly until he reached her mouth. Then he pressed his lips against hers.

His lips were warm and soft, and Caroline was just beginning to get accustomed to the feel of them, when it was suddenly over. Not sure if she was more disappointed than relieved, she opened her eyes to see Stephen's smiling face.

"Don't look so serious, Carrie. Kissing is supposed to be fun," he teased. He brushed a stray lock of her golden hair from her eyes and asked, "Was it so awful?"

She smiled at him, feeling very inexperienced and uncertain. "No . . . It was rather nice."

"You just need a little more practice, that's all." He took her hand in his and squeezed reassuringly.

"You've had a lot of practice, I suppose?" The question leaped from her mouth before she could stop it. She wanted to know the answer, of course, but realized it wasn't proper for her to ask such a thing.

With a sly grin, he answered, "Maybe. But a true gentleman doesn't kiss and tell." He smoothed a ruffle on the sleeve of her dark green dress.

"Have you kissed many girls in Virginia?"

"There are many beautiful girls in Virginia, Carrie, but none as beautiful as you," he answered. "Come along. I'll walk you home before it gets too dark."

As the weeks passed, Stephen visited Lilac

Cottage often. Emma teased her for finally having a beau of her own, and Sally Rogers, their house-keeper, lectured her often, although not as often as she had to lecture Emma, on the proper con-duct with a gentleman. Meanwhile Caroline spent less time in her father's study and more time baking Stephen's favorite treats and sewing hand-kerchiefs embroidered with his initials.

Stephen became an irresistible force to her. He was cheerful and engaging, and he lavished her with attention. She enjoyed spending time with him, al-though he was not the literary type and found books, poetry, history, and any of the subjects that interested Caroline boring. However, she instinc-tively avoided the topics that displeased him and tried to be what he wanted her to be. In return, he was charming and attentive.

They attended the Spring Festival, danced at the May Day celebration, had picnics in the wildflower meadow, and afterward he and Caroline would always walk by Langton Lake, where he would give her more kissing lessons. To her immense relief she no longer giggled during these romantic inter-ludes and believed herself quite accomplished at this newfound art.

As spring turned to summer, it was obvious that the relationship between them was growing serious.

"Do you have genuine feelings for Stephen Ben-nett, Caroline?" Richard Armstrong asked one evening after supper.

"What do you mean, Papa?" she asked as she washed the dirty plates in the kitchen basin. It was Sally's night off and had been Emma's turn to clean up, but she had begged a favor from

Caroline and had just left to go out walking with her latest beau.

"Oh, he's charming enough, of course, but not right for you. A girl of your background and intelligence deserves a man she can converse with on her own level. Discuss poetry, philosophy, art, history. Stephen is not that man. He's just a farmer. I expected you to be more discriminating."

"I admit that he's not academic, Papa," Caroline responded, puzzled at her father's disapproving tone. Although part of her had to grudgingly admit that it irritated her that she could not quote a line of poetry or make a historical reference without a bored frown from Stephen. He knew of tobacco farming and how to run a plantation, and that was about it. But he said the prettiest things to her, she mused as she efficiently dried the plates with a clean cloth and placed them in the small cupboard.

"I want better for you than Stephen Bennett."

"You don't seem so concerned about Emma and Ned Cooper," she contested matter-of-factly. "His family owns a farm." After covering the table with a cheerful chintz tablecloth, she quickly smoothed out the wrinkles with her hand.

"Emma is different. She's not serious about that boy." Richard's voice grew more agitated.

Caroline began sweeping the wooden floorboards with long, even strokes. "Well, she might be serious about some farmer one day."

"Yes, but not a farmer from Virginia!"

She paused, resting her hands on the broom handle, and looked at her father. "Stephen's family owns a plantation. The largest in six counties. The Bennetts are very successful, Papa."

"Yes, but at what price, Caroline? Stephen is a slave owner, for heaven's sake! He will make his riches off slave labor! He stands for everything we disagree with! He's not the right man for you," Richard stated with a worried look on his face.

"It's not as bad as all that. His family has been involved in slavery for so long that it has become a part of their culture and they don't know any better," she justified softly, not meeting her father's eyes. "But the war might change all that."

Richard suddenly slammed his fist down upon the table. "Caroline, you are being a fool! Blinded by his charm! Before you know it you'll end up in Virginia married to a slave owner, and I will not have it! You must not see him again!" His face turned a mottled red and his voice shook with anger and unspoken fear. "I insist that you obey me in this matter!"

Caroline flinched at her father's words as the broom dropped from her hands and clattered to the floor. He had never called her a fool! She couldn't recall a time when he had raised his voice to her, or to anyone else. It was so out of character for him that she was quite taken aback. As she stared at her father, he suddenly looked very old and frail. His gray hair and gaunt figure gave him the appearance of a man much older than his forty-five years. The watery blue eyes in his heavily shadowed face seemed frightened.

He was truly distraught over her relationship with Stephen Bennett.

Caroline had never seen him this upset or angry with her. Not even when she was thirteen and had accidentally spilled an entire bottle of ink on his expensive leather-bound edition of Plato's *Republic*, which had been a special gift from his uncle when he was eighteen. Despondent over what she had done, she had tried to wipe off the ink, creating a worse mess. He had been very angry, but he never yelled at her, although she was not allowed to work in his study again for days.

Looking at him now, she was confounded. And a little afraid. "Do you really mean that, Papa?"

"I think I know what's best for you." There was a definitive note of authority in his trembling voice. "I forbid you to see him."

How could she possibly give up Stephen?

Yet how could she disobey her father?

She stared at him, remembering all the wonderful hours she had enjoyed learning at his side, as he patiently answered her myriad of questions, faithfully encouraged her thirst for knowledge, and readily inspired her when she made mistakes. When she was eight years old he had a miniature desk made to match his so she could work beside him in his cramped little study. He delighted in her quick wit and challenged her to excel in all she did. He had always been proud of her. In return, she had adored him and believed him to be the smartest man in the world. She knew that she was his pride and joy.

He had never demanded anything of her before.

She could not bear to be foolish in his eyes. She would rather die than disappoint him in any way.

Sighing, she patted his thin shoulder in an effort to soothe him and responded inevitably, "All right, Papa. If it upsets you this much, I promise I won't see Stephen Bennett anymore." But even as she uttered the words, she wondered how she would ever fulfill them.

"That's my smart girl. You'll see in the end that I'm right about this," Richard said as he breathed a little more calmly.

After a sleepless night, Caroline rose early the next morning and packed a picnic basket to surprise Stephen with lunch between his classes. He was overjoyed to see her, declaring her an angel, and suggested they sit in the shade of an elm tree. It was a warm afternoon, and the bright blue June sky was cloudless. The air was perfumed with roses, and fat bumblebees droned loudly around them. Stephen reclined on the blanket, and Caroline sat beside him.

As they ate the freshly baked bread and sharp cheddar cheese from the basket, Caroline finally just blurted out, "I can't see you anymore, Stephen. My father doesn't think it's a good idea."

"What are you saying, Carrie?" he asked with alarm, raising himself up on one elbow, his brown eyes puzzled.

She whispered, "My father doesn't think we should be together."

"But why?"

She stared mutely at him. She had to obey her father's wishes.

"I'm aware that I'm not as academic as he'd wish, but I thought he liked me," he said.

"That's not it, Stephen. He does like you," she insisted, lamenting the fact that his family owned slaves. Why did it have to be so difficult? Why couldn't she have fallen in love with someone more suitable? How could she please both men?

Stephen's face became clouded with worry.

"Why then? I'm a decent fellow, from a good and very wealthy family."

Unsure how to tell him, she answered in a lighter tone than she felt. "It's just that you're American . . . and . . . you own slaves . . . and I think he's afraid that you'll whisk me away to Virginia with you."

"Well then. He's right to be afraid," he said, reaching for her hand.

The impact of his words sunk in, and she looked at him searchingly.

"Don't you know that I'm in love with you, Carrie?" He kissed her fingers, which were clutched tightly in his hand.

Her heart flipped over. "Stephen . . . I . . ." She tried to say something. She wasn't sure what.

"Shh." He put a finger to her lips. "You don't have to say anything. I know that you love me too. Don't you?" he questioned her with a heart-melting smile, his blond hair glinting in the sunlight.

Caroline nodded her head in agreement, unable to resist him. Her heart was pounding. He loved her! And she loved him! It was too wretched that her father disapproved of him.

Stephen gazed at her. "You're so sweet and shy. That's what I love best about you." He kissed her cheek.

She smiled indulgently at him.

Then his expression turned serious. "There's something that I have wanted to tell you, Carrie."

"What is it?"

"I've made up my mind to finally join the Confederate Army. I've booked passage on a ship that sails to Virginia in August."

Her heart began to pound rapidly as the meaning

of his words sunk in. He was leaving her. *He was leaving her.*

He became more impassioned as he spoke. "I'm twenty-one years old now and I can't hide in England anymore. I never should have left in the first place. If I stay here much longer I will miss the war entirely and never be able to show my face in Virginia again. All my friends are fighting. My parents won't be able to stop me once I'm already there. I'm a man and I have to fight for my home. You do understand that, don't you, Carrie?"

She nodded her head. "Yes, I see." But she didn't. How could he just say he loved her and then say that he was leaving her? It didn't make sense. How could he be leaving? Yet it magically solved her problem with her father. She certainly couldn't see Stephen if he were on the other side of the Atlantic Ocean.

"We have less than two months to be together before I leave. Surely, you can't refuse to see me now."

Of course, she couldn't.

Caught between the two most important men in her life, Caroline wanted to obey her father yet still wanted to be with Stephen for the little time they had left together. It was impossible to please them both. So she gave in to her lovestruck heart and began to meet Stephen in secret at the unused caretaker's cottage on a nearby estate. They met frequently, and both took great precautions to not be seen there together. The guilt she felt at deceiving her father tore at her, but she reasoned that it was only for a short time and then Stephen would be gone. With all of her academic intellect she had never imagined herself being overruled by her emotions. The studious and reliable Caroline Armstrong was in love.

Fearing that when Stephen left she would never see him again, imagining that he would be killed or wounded or that he would forget about her completely, Caroline savored each and every minute with him, caught up in the romance and drama of their situation. Stephen vowed to come back when the war was over to marry her and take her back to Virginia with him, and Caroline hoped that by then her father would have softened his views of the Bennett family. When Stephen returned, her father would finally see that he really loved her.

The last day they spent together was etched in her memory so deeply, she could never be rid of the feelings it evoked. Stephen had been so insistent, so persuasive, so earnest, that she could not deny him anything he asked. And he asked everything of her that day. Distraught at his leaving, she could do nothing but give in to his every wish.

"Promise me you won't tell anyone," he demanded, holding her warm body close to his and showering her face with his kisses.

"I promise," she whispered. Heated tears streamed down her cheeks, and she choked back a sob. Of course she promised not to tell, for whom *could* she tell? Certainly not her father. She had no choice but to keep this promise. She couldn't bear to think about it. What she was promising. What it really meant. What it would mean if anyone found out.

And it was too hot. Insufferably hot. The August sun burned down without a single cloud in the sky to break its intensity, and they sweltered inside the small wooden cabin. The air was thick and heavy, and it was difficult to breathe. The oppressiveness of the heat and the closeness of his body made her feel she was suffocating. Her hastily rebuttoned pink gingham dress, the one she had worn just for him because it was her prettiest summer dress, clung to her sweat-dampened skin, and her long golden curls hung limply down her back. Tiny rivulets of sweat trickled down between her breasts, tracing the path where his hands had been. The salty taste of tears, mingled with his kisses, filled her mouth. She felt very lethargic, almost sleepy, for the steamy stillness of the day had a dreamlike quality to it, seeming even more unreal in the aftermath of what they had just done.

"Promise me you'll wait until I come back," he insisted again, holding her body tightly, urging her to look at him.

"I promise," she murmured once more. Looking into his chocolate brown eyes, she tried to block out the images of what had just happened in that cabin. In that bed. Her body felt it could not support her weight. Her legs were shaky and weak. Her stomach constricted into knots, and the stuffy room swayed dizzily around her. Everything blurred. She closed her eyes.

"This will be our secret." His voice, usually lazy and teasing, was now filled with an urgent, almost desperate, plea.

She nodded her head obediently, not seeing him.

"Look at me, Carrie." Stephen's hands cupped either side of her face.

Slowly she opened her eyes. He was leaving her now, yet she could not take in that fact. Instead, she was fascinated by the way his light blond hair clung to his damp head and little beads of perspiration dribbled down the side of his face. Her eyes followed the path of each tiny drop, one after the other, as they raced erratically down the smooth skin of his neck, disappearing beneath the open collar of his shirt. Disappearing from sight. Just as he would.

"When I come back, I will make everything right again. You'll see. It will all work out the way we want it to. I promise."

She nodded her head, unable to control her silent tears, but noticing every little pore of his sweat-soaked skin and feeling as if she were watching herself from far, far away. This was happening not to her, but to some other girl. Some other girl was standing there being held by him. Being kissed by him. Being left by him. How could he leave her now? What would she do? What if he never came back? She wanted to scream at the top of her lungs, but she knew if she began to scream that she would never stop.

While his fingers wrapped tightly around her upper arms, he continued to kiss her face, her hair, her cheeks, her lips, her neck, as if he were memorizing every detail of her face. "Tell me you love me," he whispered into her ear, his lips pressing against her damp hair, his warm breath increasing the heat around her.

"I love you," she responded faintly, wishing he would let go of her so she could catch her breath for a minute. The scent of him was overpowering. She was drowning in a steaming sea of skin and sweat and salty tears. There wasn't enough air. If only there were a cool breeze. A puff of air. Anything.

"You're mine now, Carrie." Stephen kissed her

mouth again, deeply this time, as if he were branding her as his once more.

Then he was gone, for America and the war, leaving her alone with their secret.

A month after he left, one letter arrived from him and then no more. She had written him three or four times a week, letters addressed to his family's estate in Virginia. At first her letters were full of longing and love, and then, as she received no further word from him, they became questioning, and then, thinking perhaps she had written something to offend him, apologetic in tone. There was still no reply. Wracked with worry she even wrote to his parents, with no response. Not knowing what to think, she finally ceased her correspondence all together, waiting to hear from him.

The days and weeks and months slipped by without a word.

CHAPTER 12

Summerfields Castle
August 1865

When Caroline did not appear for their usual supper in the side parlor that evening, Alex, determined to see her one way or another, knocked quietly on her bedroom door later that night after the rest of the house had retired. He had been thinking of her all day. He knew he had made a mess of things and wanted to put them to rights. Just how he was going to do that he wasn't quite sure.

"What are you doing here?" she asked nervously, her eyes darting into the hallway to see if anyone was there.

"I need to speak with you." It was completely unsuitable for Alex to be in her room like this, while she was dressed only in her nightgown, and he knew it. But he stepped in the room and closed the door softly behind him anyway. He noticed that she had recently bathed, for her hair was still damp and fell in loose curls down the back of her simple, white cotton nightgown. The scent of the French lavender soap she used wafted over to him, and he resisted the urge to reach out and touch her. "I had a feeling you wouldn't come to me, so I had to come to you. Do you mind?"

She shook her head imperceptibly, and there was an awkward silence. Caroline nervously walked to stand in front of the fireplace. It had been a cool day, with a touch of autumn in the air, and it was proving to be an even cooler evening. She stood warming herself by the fire, her arms folded across her chest, her back to him.

Alex stood a few feet away, watching her intently. "I'm sorry," he said, breaking the silence between them.

"You should be."

The force of her words surprised him. He felt the sting of her anger and knew he deserved it. He never should have taken such liberties with her that afternoon. He had her down on the ground with her dress undone and half her body exposed, for heaven's sake! He seemed to lose all sense of good judgment in her presence. Not that she wasn't a perfectly willing participant, which thrilled him to no end, but still there was no excuse for it. "I apologize for my behavior in the garden today. It was unforgivable of me to take advantage of you in such a way."

She nodded her head in quiet acceptance of his apology.

"Caroline, I never meant for any of this to get so out of hand."

She turned to face him with an accusatory look, her green eyes flashing. "I thought you understood. You knew I was waiting for someone else. When we made our arrangement you told me that you didn't want to get married either, which is not what you said this afternoon."

"You're right," he admitted with a sigh. "It wasn't fair of me to change the rules like that. We made a deal that we would help each other escape marriages, and here I am asking you to enter into one with me."

"Why are you changing the rules now?" Her tone was sharp, and she kept her arms tightly clasped across her chest.

He walked to where she was standing and placed his hands on her slender shoulders, looking directly into her eyes, his voice soft. "Why do you think, Caroline? Why do you think I've been spending all this time with you?"

"Because we're helping each other."

He looked at her with a wry smile, one eyebrow raised. "I think I can keep myself from marrying some silly little society chit without any assistance from you."

She shook her head, puzzled by his comment. "I don't understand then."

His blue eyes regarded her intently. "I want to marry you, Caroline. I have from the moment I met you."

She shook his hands from her shoulders and took a step back. There was a long silence as she pressed her fingertips to her temples. Her voice was very clear, almost icy, when she finally spoke. "So this was all a game to you, then? To trick me?"

"No, no. It's not like that . . ." he protested. This state of affairs had turned into a complicated tangle of intentions. He knew he was to blame. It had seemed like a good idea at the time, to lead her along, make her forget about her absent sweetheart, and then suggest that they marry in earnest. It could have worked out perfectly, but he hadn't expected such resistance from her. Now he was at a loss. "I didn't mean to deceive you. Honestly. You were so set against marrying anyone. I just wanted more time with you, hoping you'd give up on this other man and maybe change your mind about marrying me."

Now Caroline covered her face with her small hands and sighed deeply. She lowered her hands and looked at him again. The hopeless expression on her face twisted his gut. "I cannot marry you, Alex. I thought you understood that," she stated in a weary voice. "I'm not good enough for you. You deserve someone better than I am. This whole situation is impossible. As soon as my grandmother arrives, I shall tell her that there will be no marriage and that I wish to return to Fairview Hall. Our arrangement is over. We shouldn't have made it in the first place. And if I ever gave you the impression that I expected you to marry me, I'm sorry."

"Caroline, you don't have to apologize to me. I'm a part of all of this too. And there's no need for you to leave when your family arrives. I want you to stay."

Another long sigh escaped her, and she shook her head. "There's no reason for me to stay."

He closed the small distance between them and, again, placed his hands upon her shoulders. "Of course there is. I find it hard to believe that you can kiss me as you have and not have feelings for me. You have to acknowledge that there is something between us. I feel it, so you must feel it too. Admit it."

Caroline looked away with a noncommittal shrug.

"You still love him that much?" he asked, watching her expression carefully. He held his breath waiting for an answer.

She avoided his eyes and folded her arms across

her chest again, a defensive gesture that was not lost on Alex. "Please go now. I don't wish to discuss him with you." She tried to pull away from him, but he would not let her.

"Well, I do." He lifted her chin with his hand, urging her to face him. "Look at me, Caroline, and tell me that you are still in love with this American boy that you haven't seen or heard from in more than two years. I don't believe that you are. Not after the way you have kissed me. But if you can honestly look me in the eyes and tell me you still love him, I will not trouble you again." His blue eyes pierced hers, as if willing her to give him the answer he wanted to hear. As he uttered the words, he wondered if he really could just let her go if it came down to that.

She closed her eyes. He could see that she was scared. "Just go, Alex."

"Look at me, Caroline," he urged, squeezing her chin lightly. "Open your eyes and look at me."

Her lids fluttered open to face him. They stared at each other in silence. He looked into the emerald depths of her eyes for an answer, a sign of what she was feeling. He could hear her breathing softly and could feel the delicate pulse in her throat as he held her small chin. The fire sparked and crackled in the grate. His own heart thundered in his chest, waiting. The minutes ticked by.

"Tell me the truth." His voice was an urgent whisper.

"Alex, please don't do this . . ." she said faintly. Her eyes pleaded with him.

Alex sensed her uncertainty and her avoidance of an answer, and he knew. "You can't say it."

She shook her head but would not meet his eyes. His smile was victorious. "You can't say it. You don't love him," he stated with relief, wrapping his arms around her and pulling her against his chest, kissing the top of her head, inhaling the clean scent of her. He was filled with elation that she didn't love her American soldier. But then why would she refuse his proposal of marriage? *How did she feel about him?* He pulled her back to see the expression on her face. "So why—"

For reasons he would never understand, Caroline leaned forward on her bare tiptoes and gently touched her lips to his face, placing the lightest of kisses on his cheek.

Astonished, Alex stood motionless, feeling as if his slightest movement would cause her to flee. He gazed at her silently.

She pressed hushed, feathery kisses across his cheek, inching slowly closer to his mouth. When she finally touched his lips, lightly, her sweet breath brushing across his warm skin, the sensation sent hot shivers between the two of them.

Alex could barely breathe, but he let her explore. His body immediately hardened in response to her interest. His entire being throbbed in anticipation.

She pressed her lips to his. They were warm and soft, seeking and insistent. Wanting. Her arms slowly made their way around his shoulders, and she placed her slender body against the length of him. A spark ignited between them, and unable to do anything else, he eased closer, leaned into her, his mouth opening to invite her in. Her warm tongue found his, and she made a provocative little sound in her throat that nearly drove him mad.

Although surprised by her sudden overture, Alex returned her kiss, feeling the heat rise swiftly between them. She was warm and pliant in his hands, and he knew intuitively that he would meet no resistance from her if he carried her to the bed. And he did just that, lifting her effortlessly off her feet, the heat from her body permeating through the gauzy cotton of her nightgown, revealing that she wore nothing underneath. His blood pounding in his veins, he lost himself in her kiss, the fragrance of lavender surrounding him. Carrying her to the purple velvet bed, his lips never losing contact with hers, he laid her down gently on the velvet pillows, his hard, taut body covering hers completely in one fluid movement. He sunk his fingers into the silky mass of her hair, pulling her face closer as his tongue delved into the succulent recesses of her mouth. He could kiss her forever and never tire of it. She was so beautiful, so perfect, so inviting, he couldn't get enough of her. He had never felt this deep connection to a woman before. As if she belonged to him and him alone. It terrified him and compelled him at the same time. He simply had to have her. His hand brushed the length of her shoulder and dipped lower to stroke the softness of her breasts, cupping the fleshy fullness of her through the thin cotton material. Slowly, gently, he unfastened the ties that held the simple gown in place, revealing the creamy whiteness of her skin. She was all softness and scent. He wanted to bury himself in her. He began at the sensitive skin of her throat, her neck, her shoulders, moving lower and lower. Kissing. Nibbling. Licking. Tasting her. Feeling her skin, her breasts. A soft cry of delight escaped her as his tongue circled delicately around one pale pink nipple. Teasing. Tantalizing. Tempting her with the promise of more.

Inflamed by the feel of his mouth on her breasts, her movements became bolder, more provocative. She fervently ran her fingers down his long back, arching toward the male hardness of his body and wanting more from him. Discovering the small buttons of his white shirt, she impatiently tugged them apart, spreading it wide open. Her slender hands splayed across his finely muscled chest, absorbing the heat from his skin, while her mouth burned a sensual path across his chest. She was devouring him little by little, bit by bit. She pressed herself against him ardently, hungry for something only he could give her.

And he knew exactly what she wanted.

His hand slid lower, below her hips, below her belly. She was still covered by her nightgown, and his hand delicately brushed across her, and then down the inside of her smooth thighs. He felt her trembling and knew she was aching for him. Just as he was aching for her. She was not pulling away, not freezing up. She was lost, and Alex knew it. It aroused him wildly that she would give herself to him this way. *But what was she thinking?* He knew this was dangerous, a game no longer, and that he should stop before it went any further, before there was no turning back. While his body shook with desires needing to be fulfilled, his mind—his calm, cool mind—reasoned that he should not take advantage of her this way. Although she clearly initiated the first move, this was not the right time. She just refused his offer of marriage because of her feelings for another man and then she made overtures to him. How could she know how she felt about Alex? Did she even know what she was doing?

Ah, but he couldn't resist the exquisite feel of her. She was so warm and sweet and willing. He had wanted her and waited for her for months, and now he had her beneath him in bed. And eager for him. She was so caught up in the passion of the moment, he could easily make her his. If he did this now, then she would have to marry him. Even so, deep in his heart, he knew it was not the right thing to do. He didn't want her that way.

He moved over her, claiming her mouth with his once again. Her mouth was hot and sweet. He kissed her hard, and then drew back panting, resting his forehead on hers.

"Caroline. Caroline. You're killing me," he breathed huskily in her ear.

"What is it?" she gasped, looking at him with concern, her green eyes dark and heavy lidded with passion, her hair tumbling around her beautiful face.

He kissed her tenderly on the cheek, resting his head on his elbow, his taut body stretched alongside of hers, trying to slow the rapid pounding of his blood, his heart. It took every ounce of his willpower to put an end to this erotic little encounter. As well as a moment of doubting his sanity. But there was too much at stake with her. He had to end this. Even if it killed him. "The next time this happens, I swear to you that we are not stopping." He gently pulled the ties of her nightgown together, covering her tempting body from his sight.

"Stopping?" she questioned in confusion. "Why?"

"Because, my love, I don't want it to be this way between us. I feel like I've pressured you when you are confused and torn about someone else. You don't really know what you feel for me. And I can't take advantage of you like this. However tempting you may be at the moment." He grinned wolfishly at her and kissed the tip of her nose. Then his expression turned serious. "Besides, you would hate me tomorrow if I made love to you tonight."

A chance Alex was not willing to take. He lovingly

kissed her cheek, feeling the silky softness of her skin and inhaling deeply of her sweet, flowery scent.

"Oh," she managed to say in a throaty whisper.

He smiled in understanding and again touched her face with his hand. "Don't think that I don't want you right now, Caroline. Honestly, I am not rejecting you. Just this particular situation."

She blinked in response, not sure what to say to that.

He gave her an enticing grin that made her shiver and whispered in her ear, "But we're not finished yet, you and I. This is just the beginning." He kissed her again and got off the bed, pulling the covers over her protectively. "Go to sleep, my love," he whispered before he left, closing the door behind him.

Caroline was mortified and stared uncomprehendingly at the ceiling. Feelings of shame, regret, disappointment, and pent-up desires that had found no release flooded her being. Tears threatened but would not come. *What had she just done?* Her cheeks burned scarlet at her reckless, and exceedingly immodest, behavior. How would she feel tomorrow if he *had* made love to her tonight? Cringing at the mere thought, she closed her eyes. In spite of these feelings, she was still able to discern that he might very well be right. Thank God, Alex had some sense, because she certainly didn't possess any. What was wrong with her to act like that? She threw herself at him and invited him to take liberties with her. She didn't understand the wild feelings that possessed her when she was with

Alex. Such an incredible attraction. Suddenly, his merest look or touch ignited something within her.

Now Alex wanted to marry her. She had gotten herself involved in a situation that was headed for disaster. Marriage! She couldn't marry Alex! All she had wanted to do was escape the pressures of the Season, she hoped buying herself a little more time until Stephen Bennett came back for her and she could better explain to her grandmother what had happened. In hindsight, involving herself in Alex's scheme probably wasn't the wisest of decisions, but it seemed reasonable at the time. She hadn't meant to hurt anyone. Now the lines between truth and fiction somehow had become terribly blurred.

Now she looked back on the Season with a new perspective. Alex truly wanted to marry her from the start. He was actually courting her, actually wanted to marry her. Which is why it was probably so easy for everyone in the *ton* to believe that the Duke of Woodborough was courting Caroline Armstrong, the little nobody from the country, for marriage.

Because it was true!

But why? Why would Alex want to marry her? She wasn't of the real nobility and claimed a scandalous background. She had not been raised to be a duchess nor had she any desire to be one. He knew she was waiting for someone else. Why was he doing this to her? He was ruining everything when she had thought she was safe with him. How was she to extricate herself from this mess now? Everyone believed they were going to marry, including Alex.

Apparently the only one who wasn't aware of the impending marriage was Caroline herself.

But what were these feelings she had for him? These feelings that made her lose all sense of logic and reason? She had just thrown herself at him, for heaven's sake! *"No, I can't marry you, Alex, but please come to my bed."* It was shameful and disgraceful behavior. What did he think of her now? How could she possibly face him again? She groaned inwardly at the thought.

Suddenly, she remembered what his mother had said to her the other day. That Alex had never brought a lady home to meet her before. That he was usually so controlled and dignified and serious. That he had fallen head over heels in love with Caroline. That he had given up his London mistress.

Could Alex really be in love with me?

The thought was terrifying and caused her heart to flip over in her chest.

He honestly wanted to marry her. She should be flattered. Any girl in her right mind would jump at the chance to marry him. But then, Caroline wasn't in her right mind and hadn't been since the day she met Stephen Bennett. Tonight in her room had been the perfect opportunity for her to tell Alex the truth and explain to him why she couldn't marry him, but she couldn't bring herself to say the words out loud. Instead, she just seemed to dig herself deeper into deception.

Alex asked if she still loved Stephen Bennett, and she couldn't look into his eyes and say the words. She simply could not.

But she did love Stephen.

Don't I?

Again she asked herself that question. It had been so long since she had seen Stephen that she wasn't sure anymore. It was difficult to even draw an image of Stephen in her mind with Alex standing so close to her. Alex's physical presence easily overshadowed any memory she had of Stephen. But, in any case, she could not consider Alex's proposal.

Caroline turned her head and pressed her heated cheeks into the cool pillow, shutting her eyes tightly in an attempt to block out the buzzing thoughts in her mind.

Sleep did not come to her easily that night.

Alex wandered the darkened paths in the garden, smoking a cigar and hoping the cool night air would clear his throbbing head and aching body. He rarely smoked, but he needed it tonight. Especially after that little interlude with Caroline. He had gone to her room simply to talk to her, to discover where he stood with her, and to apologize for his crude behavior toward her that afternoon. He hadn't expected to end up in her bed. Although, she had been quite astonishing. Warm. Sensual. Responsive. Eager. Passionate. Engaging. Everything he had imagined her to be and more. And she had been completely willing. He could have bedded her easily, and then, once compromised, she would have had no choice but to marry him.

But he couldn't do it.

It had taken every ounce of his self-control to end it when he did. As painful and as torturous as it was, he knew he made the right decision. He didn't want to force Caroline's hand in this, because for some reason he needed her to *want* to marry him. He was being ridiculous, losing his heart and his head over her in this way.

He was in love with her.

Alex smoked the cigar, the tip glowing red in the darkness, slowly pondering the thought.

He was in love with Caroline Armstrong.

There was no doubt about it. It had come about so naturally that he wasn't even sure exactly when or why it happened. Was it that moonlit night on the balcony when he first kissed her? Or the afternoon she agreed to his now ridiculous plan? Was it because of the way she tilted her head and looked up at him through the thick lashes of her deep green eyes when she was teasing him? Or because of the way she fit so perfectly in his arms when they danced? Was it the sweet sound of her laughter? Her quick wit and intelligence? Her incredibly beautiful face? The lush curves of her body? Or was it the knowing way she smiled at him from across a crowded room in understanding of what he was thinking before he even had to say it? What was it about her that set her miles apart from any woman he had ever met? What was it about her that made him want her so intensely?

It was all of her. It was simply Caroline.

How ironic that he was in love with the one woman in all of London who was not interested in marrying him! No, that wasn't quite right, he amended. He couldn't say that she was not interested in him. When she kissed him earlier, she had been very, very interested . . .

Now the question was, how could he make her forget about the American? How could he compete with a memory? A ghost love? It was almost impossible. He didn't even know the man's name! But she was with him now, and Alex wouldn't let her go so easily. He would make her forget that soldier.

Determinedly throwing the stub of the cigar on the slate path, he crushed it with the heel of his black boot and went back inside the castle.

CHAPTER 13

The events of last night were still fresh in her mind when Caroline awoke somewhat groggily at noon the next day. Her head was pounding as she sat up against the satin pillows. The last thing she remembered was tossing and turning while the faint hint of dawn tinted the sky. She was surprised to find that she had actually slept at all.

"I peeked in a few times this morning and you were still sound asleep, Miss Caroline," Bonnie said as she placed a breakfast tray laden with warm muffins and tea on the side table next to Caroline's bed. "It's so unlike you to sleep this late that I thought maybe you weren't feeling well, so I didn't want to disturb you. I thought you might want a little something to eat."

"Thank you, Bonnie. I guess I didn't realize how tired I was from my riding lesson yesterday. I had a dreadful headache last night that kept me up rather late," she answered as she gratefully sipped her warm tea and watched as Bonnie laid out a pale turquoise and white striped dress for her to wear.

Mentally reliving what happened in her room last

night in her very own bed, she cringed. She had thrown herself at Alex, and quite shamelessly too. How could she ever face him again? That thought, among others, had kept her up all night.

Caroline laid her head back down on the soft pillows and watched the warm afternoon sunlight spill across the purple bed. It seemed too bright, too cheerful, the exact opposite of her current mood. Her situation seemed no better in the light of day than it had in the darkness of the previous evening.

Couldn't I just stay here all day and not face him?

The thought was definitely tempting, but she would have to confront him sooner or later. It would be too cowardly of her to hide, and he would know. Alex always seemed to know what she was thinking. It was strange the effect that he had on her senses.

Oh, the unexplainable sensations Alex caused her to feel! She had been willing, and quite eager, for him to take her last night. Little butterflies fluttered in her stomach at the memory of his kisses. It had been that way from the moment they first kissed on the balcony at the Maxwells' ball to their kiss in the garden grass yesterday afternoon. Then last night! She all but melted into him! It was as if she had no control over herself whatsoever.

Stephen had never caused her to feel these strong physical urges that left her weak and breathless as Alex did. Nervousness and awkwardness were the dominant feelings she recalled when she had been with Stephen. With him she had always felt as if she were trying her best to please him. Yes, she thought with some surprise, maybe she had been trying too hard to hold on to Stephen by doing anything to please him while stifling her true self in small ways so as not to displease him.

Oddly enough, from the very beginning she had always just been herself with Alex. Even though he was a duke and intimidating to most people, she hadn't tried to make an impression on him. Alex made her feel comfortable, so it was easy to be herself.

She recalled Alex's forthright question to her last night and how she could not answer him. She could not look in Alex's eyes and say that she loved Stephen. So much had changed since she had seen Stephen that it was difficult to say. There was still no word from him. She didn't miss him any longer. What could she even remember about him?

Caroline's thoughts swirled in a heavy fog around her as she washed her face and dressed mechanically. At least Bonnie had the good sense to notice her somber mood and refrained from her usual chatter. Caroline sat patiently while Bonnie combed out her hair and pinned it elegantly upon her head.

As Bonnie busily straightened up the wardrobe, Caroline stared out the small lancet window of her tower room, gazing upon the green fields and hills in the distance. The other question Alex asked troubled her.

If Stephen didn't exist, would she want to marry Alex?

The answer was yes.

She had not allowed herself to contemplate marriage to Alex during the Season, although now the thought tempted her. It was heady enough being escorted about by such an eligible bachelor! He would make a wonderful husband to some other woman. But not her. Ever.

A desperate thought occurred to her just then.

No one knew what had happened between her and Stephen Bennett two years ago, so why should she have to tell anyone? It was obvious now that he was never coming back for her as he promised, and maybe she needed to face that fact. The newspapers claimed there had been hundreds upon hundreds of casualties in the bloody battles of the War Between the States. Realistically, Stephen could very well be one of those killed. He had not been a trained soldier when he enlisted and was very inexperienced. If he were alive, surely he would have found some way to contact her after two years. That is, if he wanted to. No. Stephen was never coming back for her. Ever. So why should anyone have to know about what happened the day he left? She had promised Stephen she would keep it a secret, and she had.

Why couldn't she just keep it a secret forever?
Why should she suffer the rest of her life waiting in vain for him to return to her?

A heavy knock on her bedroom door so startled her that she jumped. Bonnie hastened to answer it; as Alex stepped inside, Caroline gave a nod to her, and Bonnie, with a disapproving look, discreetly left the room. Grateful that she was dressed prettily and not still lying in bed, Caroline looked nervously at Alex. As always, she was struck by how handsome he was. Tall and fit, jet black hair, a ruggedly chiseled jaw, sky blue eyes, and that engaging smile all added up to a stunning male presence.

"Good morning," he stated softly, his eyes searching hers for a sign that things were all right between them.

Her cheeks warmed as he looked at her, recalling in graphic detail how she had ached for him to touch her body only a few hours ago. "Good morning."

"I learned that Bonnie had just brought up a tray for you, and I wanted to make sure you were not feeling unwell. But I see that you are looking as beautiful as ever."

He smiled warmly at her, and she melted at the way his eyes crinkled at the corners when he grinned. Apparently facing him was not as humiliating as she would have imagined. "I simply overslept. I'm feeling fine, thank you." She hesitated before beginning, "Alex . . . I need to ap—"

He interrupted her. "I would like to apologize for my ungentlemanly behavior toward you, yet again. It seems I lose all sense of reason when I kiss you, Caroline. I hope you can forgive me. You have my word that I will not put you in such a position again."

She looked into his blue eyes and understood the considerate escape he offered her. He knew very well that she alone initiated last night's impassioned encounter in her bed, while he had been the one with the resolve and the decency to end it before it went too far. Yet here he was begging her pardon in order to spare her the indignity when she had been on the verge of apologizing for her shameless conduct.

"Alex, I know that you—"

He interrupted her again, not allowing her to finish. "I also wanted to let you know that your grandmother and the rest of your family have just arrived. Harrison is taking them to their rooms now."

"They're here? Now?" Caroline paled in panic. The one day when she simply wanted to hide in her room and sort through her tumultuous emotions, she had to face her grandmother and pretend that all was well. For the past week she had been praying for them to arrive to break the tension between her and Alex, and now that they had finally arrived, she wished fervently that they had not.

"Caroline!" Emma's squeal of pure delight echoed down the corridor before she came bouncing into the room. "Oh, Caroline, this is a *real* castle!" She ran past Alex and threw her arms around Caroline.

Caroline hugged her sister as she continued to stare over Emma's shoulder at Alex, all the words unsaid between them hanging in the air.

Dinner that evening was a grand affair as Kit and Jane Fairchild, Olivia, Emma, Caroline, and Alex all gathered in the formal dining room. The Dowager Duchess actually left her room to join the family, too excited to stay in seclusion any longer.

"Isn't it wonderful to have your granddaughters with you? And to have two such beauties! You must have had your hands full this Season!" Elizabeth stated.

Olivia concurred, "It was wonderful, if I do say so. We worked very hard getting the girls prepared for their debut, didn't we, Jane?"

Aunt Jane, a pretty woman with dark eyes, said, "Oh, but it was fun too! And worth every minute!"

"I did miss the Season this year." Elizabeth's voice steadily increased its pace as she spoke. "I haven't seen my friends or entertained at all since I lost John. It feels wonderful to have company again! I apologize for not having anything planned for you. I simply wasn't thinking. However, I will host some parties and send invitations around to everyone in the area. Oh, I have the loveliest idea! We could have a picnic by the river! We should still have some warm days left before the weather turns too cool. Charles will have arrived by then . . ."

As Elizabeth prattled on, Caroline glanced toward Emma to see her sister's reaction to the duchess. Emma raised an eyebrow and tried to suppress a smile. Chatterbox Emma had finally met her match in the loquacious Dowager Duchess.

"Wouldn't that be a grand idea?" Elizabeth finally paused breathlessly, her eyes sparkling with excitement.

"It's a lovely suggestion," Aunt Jane answered. "I'm sure we would all enjoy a picnic. Especially Teddy!"

"Your son will love it," Elizabeth agreed. "Then it's all settled. So tell me now. I know how Caroline did this Season . . ." She glanced knowingly at Caroline and Alex. "But now I want to hear all about our darling Emma."

Uncle Kit laughed, his green eyes remarkably similar to Caroline's. "There's a lot to hear about our darling Emma."

Elizabeth grinned in excitement. "Pray tell, is it true that Lord Talbot set his cap for you?"

"He and quite a few others," said Aunt Jane.

Emma beamed, her hazel eyes alight with pride, eager to discuss her successful Season. "I've had three offers!"

"Three! My dear, that's a coup! Who are they from? Have you decided?" Elizabeth questioned.

"Well, there's John Talbot, of course. Lord Gardner. And the Earl of Ledgemont."

Elizabeth clapped her hands. "An earl! That's simply wonderful. But your heart's set on Lord Talbot, isn't it?"

"I don't think Emma's heart could settle for just one!" Alex said in a teasing tone, broadly winking at her.

Emma tossed him a superior glance, as if to say

men knew very little about anything important. It was a struggle for her not to stick her tongue out at him. Only the presence of the Dowager Duchess kept her tongue in its place. Her hazel eyes sparkled, and she stated coolly, "In fact, I haven't made up my mind yet who I'm going to choose."

Surprised, Caroline asked, "But what about John? I thought things were all but settled between you when we left London."

"He hasn't been as attentive as he should be," Emma sniffed with an injured air.

"It seems John Talbot went riding with Margaret Essex last week," Olivia explained calmly with a knowing glance around the table.

Alex teased, "A little of your own medicine, eh, Emma?"

Emma rolled her eyes at Alex. "So I went riding with the Earl of Ledgemont."

"If you really care for him, don't play games, Emma," Caroline chided.

"No, no. Emma's right!" Elizabeth interjected. "It doesn't do to let a man get too complacent. It's a good thing you left the city, Emma. You've shown him that you won't wait around for him if he's going to traipse about with other girls. A little time away from you should teach him a lesson."

"I'm sure it will," Alex added dryly.

Elizabeth ignored him. "Men are very predictable creatures. I just know he'll come crawling back to you, begging to be in your favor again."

"If I even want him then," Emma stated, with a toss of her head.

"That's right, dear—" Elizabeth was interrupted by a voice booming in the hallway.

"Where is everyone to welcome me home?"

"It's Charles!" Elizabeth cried.

Alex rose from his seat. "It seems my brother has arrived."

A handsome young man with bright blue eyes, dark brown hair, and a beguiling smile entered the room carrying an armful of packages. He had the tall look of the Woodward family, and he definitely had their charm.

As Elizabeth made the introductions, she presented Caroline last. "And this is your future sister-in-law."

"So I made it in time for the wedding then?" Charles asked with a grin.

The next few weeks were such a whirlwind of activity that Caroline barely had a moment to herself. Gone were the intimate dinners that she had shared with Alex. Gone were their companionable walks in the gardens. Gone were their peaceful afternoons in the library. The castle became a veritable center of social interaction with the news that the Dowager Duchess had ceased her confinement and had begun entertaining again.

Caroline was amazed at the response to Elizabeth's invitations. The rounds of calls from the gentry of the surrounding estates were endless. As special guests of the duke, Caroline and Emma's company was much sought after.

Meanwhile, Charles Woodward had captivated them with his playful and lighthearted humor. He flirted shamelessly with Caroline and Emma, and even Olivia. He was lively and full of fun and taught them new parlor games. With all the parties and picnics, dances and dinners, there was never a dull moment.

In some respects, Caroline was relieved to be immersed in social activities. The prospect of being alone with Alex made her too uncomfortable now, knowing that he really wanted their marriage to take place. He would catch her eye now and then as if trying to say something, but she would simply turn away. They hadn't spoken a private word to each other since that one morning in her bedroom. Grateful for the distraction of their families, Caroline planned activities with Elizabeth and Olivia each morning; attended teas, picnics, and lunches each afternoon; and went to dinners, parties, and dances each evening, before she collapsed, exhausted, into bed every night.

It was only then, alone in the darkness of her garish tower room, that she would indulge herself in imagining what her life would be like if she married Alex. Although she knew it could never be . . . A small flicker of hope allowed her to dream of him and all that would be possible if her life had not been forever altered by Stephen Bennett.

Her attraction to Alex was undeniable. The way he held her. The way he kissed her. The way he looked at her. It was almost magical. But there was so much more to it than that. She loved his laughter and the way he challenged her to try new things. She loved his intelligence and his thoughtfulness. She loved talking to him. She loved how he treated her family. She loved how he kissed her. But she dared not let herself love him. That was too dangerous.

What worried her now was how all of this would end. She overheard Elizabeth and her grandmother already compiling a guest list that morning. Alex told her not to worry, but how could she not? Now she had the suspicion that Alex would do nothing to stop the marriage.

If Alex didn't end their "engagement," what would happen then? Would she be swept up in the wedding plans without a means to stop it? She wished she had simply told the truth from the beginning. To her father. Her sister. Her grandmother. Alex. But she had been too afraid. Too ashamed. Too cowardly. At the time she had no idea it would evolve into such a mess. Now it was too late. They expected her to marry Alex, and without telling them the truth she had no reason to refuse him. But she could not bring herself to tell them the truth. She could not possibly marry Alex.

Or could she?

A single thought continued to tempt her.

I could keep Stephen Bennett a secret forever.

No one knew about him. So how could they possibly find out? Only if Stephen came back. And the truth was, Stephen Bennett was never coming back for her. It was obvious now. She had to face that fact. He was most likely dead. And their little secret could be buried with him.

Could she do it? Could she marry Alex?

It would make everyone happy. Alex. His mother. Her grandmother. She was so proud that her grand-daughter was marrying a duke. She seemed to think it made up for Katherine's mistakes. How Caroline wished she could grant that wish for her! But no one would understand why she would refuse Alex, and there would be explanations expected from her. It would be so much easier to simply go along with everyone and marry Alex.

If only she could . . .

It was well after midnight when she heard a light tapping on her door. By the light of the fire she climbed from her warm bed and padded softly across the floor of the circular room. Assuming it was another one of Emma's midnight visits to discuss her love letter from John Talbot, she opened the door expecting to see her sister, but it was not Emma who stood there.

It was Alex.

CHAPTER 14

"I was hoping you were still up. May I come in?" he asked quietly.

Nervously she nodded, thinking he looked more handsome than ever. He entered and closed the door behind him. She tried not to imagine what her grandmother would say if she knew that Alex was in her bedchamber, alone, with Caroline dressed only in her thin nightgown. Again. The memory of the last time Alex was in her bedroom at night flickered through her mind, making her uneasy.

"You couldn't sleep either?" he said to her.

Caroline shook her head.

"I apologize for coming to your room like this, but I haven't been able to see you alone, and I needed to talk to you privately," he explained.

"It's all right." It was odd how she had been craving his presence all evening. Here he was, as if he read her mind.

"We need to talk," he said, kneeling before the fireplace and adding more wood to the flames.

She followed him and waited until he turned to her. The words tumbled from her mouth hurriedly.

"We have to end it, Alex. I overheard my grand-mother and your mother discussing a guest list for our wedding today. This has gone too far."

"Not if we get married," he suggested practically. His expression was serious.

She shook her head and began to protest. "Alex, please—"

"Caroline, he's not here with you now. I am." He held out his hand to her and she took it, lowering herself to the thick carpet to sit beside him in front of the fire.

They stared at each other.

"It's not that simple, Alex." Tears of frustration stung behind her eyes.

Alex pulled her to him gently and wrapped his arms around her. Her small body pressed against him, and she rested her head on his chest, listening to the steady beating of his heart. They sat that way for some minutes. His hand held hers, his thumb gently stroking her palm. She breathed in the male scent of him. Something spicy, manly. How strange that she should feel so at home in his arms. It felt so good, so comforting when he held her. His arms were powerful but gentle, his hands strong and warm. Nothing wrong, nothing bad could ever happen to her in his arms. She felt completely re-laxed and at ease with him.

"Just forget him and marry me, Caroline," he whispered again, pressing his lips against the top of her head. "It would be so easy. We could be happy together. Don't you think so?"

She nodded her head in agreement. *Very happy,* she thought. She felt so cherished. So safe. If only . . .

"Then say yes," he urged charmingly, trying to win her over.

"I'm not good enough for you, Alex."

He placed his hands on her shoulders and turned her to face him. There was a hard glint in his blue eyes. "Why do you keep saying that?" he questioned in frustration. "So your father was just a tutor and not a lord and you were raised in a little country cottage and not a manor house. None of that matters to me. Only you do. Let me be the judge of who or what is good enough for me."

"Oh, Alex, you are making this so difficult for me."

He grinned with satisfaction. "Good."

She stared at him, her eyes serious, wishing he would understand her without having to say the words. She scooted back from him, giving them a little distance. "I can't marry you, don't you see?"

"No, I don't see. Enlighten me." He folded his arms across his chest.

Caroline hesitated, her heart pounding in fear, her stomach in a knot. "I . . . I haven't told you the truth." Now was the time to tell him, but how? How could she say the words aloud? What would he think of her? She clenched her hands together and took a shaky breath. "You deserve to marry someone . . . more . . . more worthy of you." She looked at him pleadingly, hoping he would understand her meaning without her actually having to say the words outright. "Someone . . . someone who doesn't belong to someone else already."

There was an awkward silence before Alex said softly, "Oh, I think I see now." He paused for a moment, his eyes shuttered, unreadable. "You and the American . . ."

The words left unsaid hung palpably in the air around them.

The slight nod of affirmation Caroline gave him

was almost imperceptible since she was unable to face him, her embarrassment and humiliation too acute, her cheeks burning with mortification, wondering the price she paid for confessing such a ruinous secret to him.

"You believe that you can't marry me because you are not a virgin?"

Caroline cringed at the bluntness of his words. Did he think her disgraceful? A loose, immoral woman? What else was he to think, especially after she threw herself at him that night? He must be disgusted with her. Alex certainly wouldn't consider marrying her knowing that she had been with another man. She was not good enough for him. She hesitantly raised her face to his, and her breath caught in her chest at the compassion she saw within his eyes.

"That doesn't matter to me, Caroline," he whispered tenderly as he cradled her face in his hands. "I would never hold that against you. Believe me, you are more worthy to be my wife than any of the so-called noble women in London who have been in and out of more beds than you can possibly imagine. Because you, Caroline, are nothing like those supposedly well-bred women. You are still the same honest, intelligent, kind, and beautiful woman you were before you told me this."

As he spoke those words, she was unable to hold back the tears that had threatened earlier, tears of thankfulness, relief, frustration, regret, sorrow. She was genuinely touched by him. Her past did not matter to him. He thought she was still good enough for him. "But you're a duke, Alex. I'm just the ruined daughter of a poor tutor. No one would accept me as your duchess."

His blue eyes intent on hers, he said, "They would have to accept you, simply because I wish it and you would be my wife. Besides, you are the granddaughter of an earl, and that holds some weight." He placed a tender kiss on her forehead. "And you are not ruined, Caroline, simply because you gave yourself to a boy you loved. I can't honestly say that I'm not disappointed that I would not be the first man to be with you . . . But there is no reason that I would cast blame on you for that or think any less of you. Since you never told anyone, who would even know? But it wouldn't matter to me even if everyone did know."

Overcome by the tenderness and forgiveness in his tone, she could not help the hot tears that spilled anew down her shame-reddened cheeks. "Oh, Alex. I am not worthy of you."

He gently brushed her tears away with his fingers and sighed. "Don't ever say that."

"But I'm already taken—" she began.

"No. No, you're not. He left you and has been gone for years. Are you supposed to wait forever for him to return? Put your life on hold indefinitely, with no word from him? Is that fair to you?"

She sniffled and shrugged her shoulders, amazed that once again he had voiced her own thoughts.

"Caroline, answer me this," Alex said. "If nothing had ever happened with your American, would you honestly want to marry me now?"

Could she erase Stephen Bennett from her mind forever? Forget all that happened between them? Disregard what they did? Could she give herself to Alex? "Yes," she murmured, knowing she already had.

"Then let's forget it ever happened. Forget he ever existed. I'll help you forget. I love you, Caroline. It doesn't matter to me where you came from or what you have done in the past. I've loved you from the moment I first set eyes on you, looking like a beautiful silver angel shimmering in the moonlight. I've done nothing but dream about you for months. Tell me you feel what's between us." His gaze bored into her. She could not look away. "Tell me I'm not imagining this connection. Tell me you feel it too."

She nodded her head, wiping distractedly at the tears, and admitted, "I feel it."

"Then do me the honor of marrying me, Caroline."

Caroline was suspended in disbelief. Alex still wanted her, even knowing that she had been with Stephen. He loved her, dreamed about her. It was unbelievable. No one would ever have to know the truth, because Stephen was never coming back for her. She could do this. With one little word she could have all that she ever dreamed of. After a long moment of looking into his deep blue eyes, she hesitantly reached out for a chance at happiness with him and whispered in a faint breath, "Yes."

"Yes" was all she had time to say before his mouth enveloped hers in a searing and possessive kiss that instantly erased every coherent thought from her mind, except returning that kiss with all the power within her. She gave herself to him, surrendering to his loving assault. He was branding her, and she knew it, his mouth burning and relentless as the kiss grew in intensity. Their hot mouths were invaded by stroking tongues, heated breaths mingling together against fevered cheeks. He was drinking in every ounce, every breath of her, and Caroline desperately yearned to give him just that. Her very being. All of her. Alex was doing exactly what he said, making her forget everything. Obliterating her past with the present. She wanted to forget the past. Now was all that mattered. Now. They were starting over. They were just beginning.

They were devouring each other.

He kissed her face, her eyelids, her cheeks, the tip of her nose, the corners of her mouth, dipping down to the delicate skin of her throat, leaving his mark, his brand, on her everywhere.

His fingers caressed and massaged her back in long sweeping motions, pressing her petite body closer to his, sliding purposefully up her spine to the graceful arch of her neck, then threading loosely through the silky curls of her honey-colored hair. Her own hands clung to his broad shoulders, holding on for dear life. She gasped aloud as his mouth claimed hers once again in a deep and penetrating kiss that left her dizzy and faint. When Alex finally came up for air, the sound of his voice broke through the passionate haze that enveloped her.

"I swore to you that the next time we kissed like this, we wouldn't stop. And we're not," he said, his voice thick with emotion. With an effortless and fluid movement he lifted her from the floor and swept her up into his strong arms. "Not this time."

Alex laid her on the purple velvet bedspread and lay down beside the length of her, his eyes reflecting his intentions. His lips covered hers once more, and his tongue entered her mouth with more tenderness than before. Tracing a path down the front of her nightgown, his hands cupped one soft breast and then the other through the thin, white cotton. Caroline shivered as he unfastened every tiny button, slowly one by one, kissing each newly uncovered patch of silky white skin until her bare breasts were completely exposed. Then he slid the material over her shoulders. He pulled away and looked at her meaningfully.

"We're definitely not stopping," he asserted, on some level offering her one last chance to escape the inevitable.

"Definitely . . . not . . . stopping . . ." she echoed breathlessly, looking into the darkened blue of his eyes. Just the mere thought of ceasing the exquisite feel of his mouth on hers was too desolate an option to contemplate at this point. All she could think of was that he still wanted her. That was all that mattered. Alex wanted her. And she wanted him. It was really happening this time, and there was no stopping it now. Impatiently, she wrapped her arms around his neck and pulled his handsome face toward her. She brushed her lips along the beginning of stubble growth on his jawline, marveling at the roughness of him. She kissed the corners of his mouth.

Aroused by her response, Alex placed hot, fervent kisses on her lips, her cheeks, her neck, along her shoulders, across her chest, until he began licking the rounded tip of one small, pink nipple and then the other, his tongue swirling around each point in tiny, lazy circles. Caroline gasped in pleasure at the tantalizing sensation he caused. Inflamed, she arched up and pulled at his shirt. Alex easily lifted the garment over his head, flinging it across the room.

Caroline ran her mouth across the warm expanse of his chest, delighting in the texture of his skin and the male scent that surrounded him. Pressing her breasts against his bare chest, she could sense the searing heat between their flesh and melted into him. Her mind was unable to focus on anything except the feel of him. The heat of his skin.

The firm potency of the corded muscles in his arms that held her. The strength of his long legs that were intertwined so intimately with hers. The feel of his fingers running through her tousled hair. The compelling taste of his mouth covering hers. The sensation of his tongue on her breasts. She wanted to absorb him into every inch of her body. She wanted to breathe him in.

Alex rolled onto his back, pulling Caroline on top of him. Her golden hair tumbling in waves around her, she was only half dressed, with her nightgown falling seductively from her shoulders as she brazenly straddled him. She felt wanton and relished the power that position entailed. Stroking her hands across his broad chest, she once again rained hot kisses upon his already smoldering skin, lavishing the same attention upon his nipples that he had showered upon hers, leisurely making her way down across his taut stomach to the waistband of his trousers. As she placed her small hand over the large bulge of material that was straining with his desire for her, she paused with uncertainty and glanced up at him.

"Unfasten them," he growled low in his throat, his eyes heavy lidded and dark.

Nervously her slim fingers fumbled with the ties until she had set him free. His pants quickly joined his shirt somewhere in the darkness of the room. Amazed at the rigid contour and smooth silkiness of his male body, she fondled him in an awkwardly arousing manner, then brushed her lips across the soft tip of him. Alex groaned with pleasure, and she smiled at him. When he could take no more of her teasing, he reached for her hungrily. His mouth took hers, and they fell back among the velvet pillows, their bodies intertwined.

"Ah, Caroline, you are so beautiful," he whispered huskily in her ear. "I've never seen anyone more beautiful than you are. Everything about you."

Time was suspended indefinitely as flickering light illuminated the darkness that surrounded them. A surge of emotions so strong she could not speak washed through her, and she kissed him, clung to him, pressed herself against his hard body. By now her nightgown was bunched up around her hips, revealing her bare legs. His hands glided up her smooth thighs to the special juncture between them. Her sharp intake of breath did not dissuade him from his task. His skilled fingers nestled among the soft thatch of dark hair and the moist folds that lay hidden beneath and began to stroke in little, languorous circles near her most sensitive core. Caroline whimpered with wanting, not quite knowing what she was seeking. But he knew. And Alex continued his flawless ministrations upon her body, stroking her, massaging her, caressing her, pressing her, moving her. Adoring her. Worshipping her. Loving her. Giving her more and more. More than she knew existed. More than she knew was possible. He whispered honeyed words into her ear, seductive, sinful, provocative words in hushed murmurs, melting her. Caroline found herself drowning in the exquisite sensation, enveloped in it, consumed by it, and then suddenly, amazingly, astonishingly, it washed over her in a cascade of pleasure so pure it bordered on the sublime. She soared upward to the stars, shattering into a million little pieces, and floated breathlessly back to earth, crying his name over and over in the darkness.

Not giving her a moment to recover, Alex breathed, "I want you."

He deftly eased himself between her thighs and pressed himself into her, aching with the desire to possess her completely, to feel her surrounding him. She was warm and slick and ready for him. Accepting him hungrily, she could not get enough of him.

"Oh, Alex," she sighed in daze of pleasure. "Alex." His name was a wish that came true.

The intense feeling of his body moving in and out of hers was both sensual and seductive, making her feel incredibly feminine. The deeper he moved inside of her the more she felt she was part of him, that she belonged to him and him alone. He was her world. She was surrounded by him, covered by him, possessed by him. There was no one else in the universe but the two of them, naked upon soft velvet in a high castle tower.

She arched up to meet each of his thrusts, matching his every movement, which became more and more urgent, more forceful. His body was slick with sweat as he strained his muscles above her, and she ran her fingers in a silken path down his back and then clung to him desperately as he moved above her, possessing her, claiming her as his own. Panting heavily, he groaned her name as he reached his peak, and was suddenly still, overcome with the powerful emotions that washed over him, clasping her warm body to him tightly, never wanting to let her go.

In the soft flickering firelight of the tower room, kiss after kiss inflamed their desire for each other until they were both eager for more. There was no shyness, no inhibitions between them. In a daze of pleasure and sensation, their naked bodies entangled on the purple velvet-covered bed and they lost themselves in each other again and again during the long, dark night.

Before the first pale glow of sunrise peered over the horizon, Alex wrapped Caroline in his arms, lovingly stroking her golden hair, her head resting on his chest. He found it hard to believe that he was still in her bed and was ridiculously happy that she had finally agreed to marry him. What was the hold this woman had over his heart? She had no idea that she could turn his world upside down with just one glance from her deep green eyes. "What are you thinking?" he asked her.

"I'm glad you didn't stop."

Alex laughed and kissed her in agreement. "Me too."

"That was not what I imagined it would be like at all . . ." She sighed softly.

"And just what did you imagine?"

"Well . . ." Her cheeks flushed. "I just didn't think it could ever be so wonderful." She grinned shyly at him, snuggling deeper into his embrace. "Or that I would want to stay like this forever."

"That can easily be arranged." Placing another kiss upon her cheek, he continued, "But unfortunately not today. I should leave before I'm discovered here. Imagine how the household would be scandalized to find me in your bed?"

Caroline's green eyes sparkled mischievously. "What do you think they would say if they found us like this?"

He grinned and pulled her closer, settling back into the velvet pillows and sighing with contentment. "Hmmm. First off, I think your grandmother would be absolutely outraged and would have me horsewhipped on the spot. And rightly so, I would imagine. Your uncle and aunt would be mortified. While Emma, on the other hand, would be secretly fascinated by it all and wishing something so dramatic would happen to her. My brother, no doubt, would congratulate me heartily. And my poor mother would be quite horrified by my ungentlemanly behavior and faint straight away."

Caroline laughed at his colorful descriptions. "I think you're right about the others, but I don't think your mother would really mind. She's very open about such things."

Alex was shocked. "My mother? What do you mean?"

Caroline explained matter-of-factly, "She's more worldly than you give her credit for, and more understanding. She knows about these things."

"What in heaven's name did you two talk about?" He wondered just what their conversation had entailed and was a little worried at the possibilities.

"Many things," she said with an enigmatic smile.

"Well, you have been given the wrong impression of my mother. She's a very proper and old-fashioned lady."

"But she has very modern ideas," Caroline asserted. "She even knows about your mistress." Her hand covered her mouth a second too late.

"What did you say?" Alex asked in utter disbelief, his eyes wide. He didn't know which shocked him more, Caroline knowing he had a mistress or his mother knowing.

"Nothing," she mumbled, hiding her face.

"Caroline," he said with an edgy voice, "What did you and my mother talk about?"

"She told me that you had a mistress but that you gave her up recently."

"Oh, she did, did she?" His eyes narrowed.

Caroline nodded. Alex could see on her face the internal war she was waging and that her curiosity finally won when she asked, "Is it true?"

"That I have a mistress or that I gave her up?" he countered.

"Both."

"Why are you so interested?"

"Because your mother told me that a wife should know about these things—"

"My mother—" he broke off in exasperation.

". . . and I just thought that if we're to be married . . . that . . . I . . . ." Caroline stammered helplessly.

"Already being a demanding wife, are you?"

"No, no," Caroline protested, flustered and embarrassed. "It's just that I was curious. I've never known anyone with a mistress before."

"You've probably known more than you realized," Alex said ruefully. "But if you feel you must know, the answer to both questions is yes. And that's all I'm going to say on the subject."

"Oh," was all she could respond.

He then lifted her chin to look at her. His tone grew serious. "We can't help who we've known or what we have done before we met, Caroline. We both have pasts. I'll forget about yours and you can forget about mine. We are going to be married. The present and the future are ours. We belong only to each other. We're together now, and no one comes between us. Agreed?"

"Yes," she consented easily. She kissed him, and he smiled at her.

"Now my little nosy body, I'll see you later." He couldn't resist one last kiss before he crept silently from her room.

CHAPTER 15

London, England
October 1865

"Why that's perfectly lovely news, Lady Weatherby! I'm so relieved that the duke has recovered from his broken heart and found another who loves him." Madeline Maxwell Parkridge gave a bright smile to Lady Weatherby, but inside she seethed, determined that the guests at her dinner party would not discover her true feelings about the upcoming wedding of the Duke of Woodborough to Caroline Armstrong.

Lady Ellie Maxwell sniffed disdainfully, her thin nose in the air. "I'm rather surprised he's marrying someone so beneath him socially. A duke should choose a bride with more care."

"Well, her grandfather was the Earl of Glenwood, you know, so she has some noble blood in her. And she is a sweet thing," Lady Weatherby said after taking a bite of her roasted lamb. "The word is that it's a true love match. The duke is quite smitten with her and dotes on her every whim. Who would have imagined the serious and proper duke acting in such a lovesick fashion!"

"I can only hope he's as happy in his marriage as I am in mine," Madeline declared with false sweetness, giving her head a flirtatious toss.

From the head of the table, Oliver Parkridge cleared his throat pointedly, and Madeline shot him a quick and furious glance, silently berating him. He responded with a sardonic grin and continued eating.

Unaware of the silent interchange around her, Lady Weatherby continued to ramble. "Well, I spoke with Lady Fairchild only this morning, and she informed me that the invitations will be sent out this week. She is beside herself with happiness over Caroline's success. And Elizabeth Woodward is so thrilled that she left her beloved castle for the first time since her husband passed away. She's planning a wedding for them that will outdo even her own illustrious wedding. They have the three finest seamstresses in London designing the bridal gown as we speak."

"Well, it couldn't be lovelier than your wedding to Oliver, now could it, Madeline?" Ellie said soothingly to her daughter. She turned toward the others. "Madeline was the most beautiful bride."

Madeline responded with a thin smile, batting her eyelashes in Oliver's direction. He ignored her.

Recently returned from her honeymoon in Paris, Madeline was completely incensed over the news of Alexander Woodward's engagement to Caroline Armstrong. Madeline should be the one marrying him and becoming the new Duchess of Woodborough. It should be her wedding that was the talk of London, not Caroline's!

She asked in a cheery voice, "Would anyone care for more wine?" *I certainly would*, Madeline thought to herself. Automatically, she fell into her role as the perfect hostess to the fifteen or so invited guests seated around her elegantly set table.

However, marriage to Oliver Parkridge did not exactly agree with her. As the new Lady Parkridge, Madeline spent his money freely on whatever caught her fancy, entertained with lavishness in their stylish home, and did all the fashionable things that were expected of young wives of the nobility, but at a very high price.

The more Madeline thought about it, the more incensed she became. What good was it to be married to Oliver Parkridge when she was clearly meant to be a duchess? All Oliver wanted to do was paw at her with his clammy hands. In fact, the intimacies of marriage had come as quite a shock to her. Oliver's relentless groping of her and his wet, sloppy kisses left her feeling cold. Before they were married, of course, she had allowed him a few liberties to entice him to propose so quickly, but her marital duties were something else all together.

Their wedding had been a heavenly affair, but their honeymoon in Paris had been the most wretched three weeks of Madeline's life.

First, how did anyone understand those babbling Frenchmen? To have been tutored in French year after year while being praised for her flawless pronunciation for it to be of no use at all in Paris was really too maddening! She hadn't understood a single word anyone said to her. Then there were those haughty Parisian women who seemed to be looking down their sophisticated noses at her, as if she were some sort of country bumpkin! Could there be a greater disappointment than to see all the most stylish little shops filled with the most exquisite and frightfully expensive things only to have her new husband deny her anything she wanted to purchase? It was intolerable! She cried daily with the disenchantment of it all.

On top of all that, she had to perform her wifely duties for a man, she realized too late, whom she didn't particularly like. It was agonizing to endure each evening in Oliver's bed, with his groaning and sweating on top of her while he selfishly used her body for his own purposes. The whole experience was too humiliating for words! Why any woman wanted to have a honeymoon was beyond her comprehension. To her complete despair, Oliver seemed to take immense pleasure in her perfect little body. On the third night of her honeymoon she feigned illness to escape his advances, and she learned in a rather degrading manner that her new husband was not as easily manipulated as she first presumed him to be.

"You're not ill, my dear wife," he said with deceptive sweetness. "There's nothing wrong with you, except that you are spoiled rotten. You haven't stopped whining since we arrived in Paris. Coming here was your idea, if I remember correctly. In fact, you insisted upon it. 'Everyone who is anyone goes to Paris,' you claimed. And pretty, pampered, overindulged Madeline has to have her way in all things. But having your way doesn't always work out, does it, sweetheart? Nothing is as you thought, is it?"

Madeline's blue eyes flashed with rage at the truth of his harsh words, and she lashed out at him. "Marriage to you certainly isn't what I expected. Let's just say you weren't my first choice."

Oliver's voice crackled with anger. "Do you think I didn't realize you were never in love with me? That it was only an act? I know perfectly well that you only married me to save yourself from public humiliation after throwing yourself at the Duke of Woodborough. He didn't want you, Madeline. But for some reason, I did. Now you're not a duchess, and I have you. I'll admit I'm disappointed that you're not as passionate as you are pretty, but you're my wife now and you don't get to have your way in all things anymore. You'll do as I say from now on." His usually kind face darkened as he scowled at her.

"You can't make me do anything," she sneered at him, hating him for seeing through her façade and making her act so ugly and shrewish while her pretty pouting no longer had any effect on him. He was a different person from the one she had expected to marry.

"If you want any money, any money at all, for your precious clothes, for things for the house, for entertaining, for anything, you'll get in this bed with me and pretend to enjoy it. Or you'll not get so much as a shilling from me when we get back to London," he threatened in a low voice, his scowl dark.

Enraged, it dawned on her that he, not she, was in control of their marriage. She had made a terrible, terrible mistake in marrying him. She had grossly underestimated him. Her voice was a shrill scream, "I hate you, Oliver Parkridge."

"I don't care," he answered in an icy tone as he shoved her down on the bed.

By the time they returned to London their marriage was irrevocably sealed in bitterness and disappointment on both their parts. Madeline used his title and his money, and in return Oliver used her body. In public, Madeline fawned over her husband, giving no hint to outsiders that all was not perfect in her marriage. In private, she made no pretense of her hatred for him.

And it was all Caroline Armstrong's fault, Madeline decided. If it had not been for that conniving country nobody, the duke certainly would have married her. There was not a doubt in her mind about that. Caroline Armstrong was the only reason the duke had turned away from her, forcing Madeline to rush blindly into a disastrous marriage with Oliver Parkridge. Madeline knew instinctively that Alexander Woodward would have made her happy and that she would not have minded performing her wifely duties for a duke.

Madeline continued to force herself to smile as the conversation about the duke's wedding continued. She glanced around and caught her mother's eyes. Ellie smiled at her benevolently. Madeline looked away, feeling betrayed. Her mother should have prepared her better for marriage. Especially for a husband who used her with such ruthlessness. She saw her father sitting across the table, and Albert nodded at her. Still nursing a righteous anger at her father for not forcing the duke to marry her, she turned her face away. Lucy Greenville, her closest friend, was talking animatedly to Lady Weatherby about the grand wedding. Indeed, all of her guests were discussing the duke or Caroline Armstrong or their wedding. It was enough to make Madeline scream.

Oliver, her husband, sat across the table from her. Looking at him now, he seemed like such a nice, even-tempered gentleman. With his dark brown hair and chocolate-colored eyes, straight nose and neatly trimmed whiskers, he was even rather handsome. But she hated him more than she imagined possible. Who would ever guess that he could be so perverted and cruel? Madeline drank another glass of wine, having learned early on that it would make more bearable what Oliver would do to her later.

How had she come to this?

She was Lady Madeline Maxwell, the prettiest, the most fashionable, the most popular girl in London. She was the blond-haired, blue-eyed golden girl. She always got what she wanted. But she had not wanted this. This was definitely not supposed to happen to her. She was supposed to have married spectacularly and led a grand life of prestige and wealth. She was supposed to have married the Duke of Woodborough.

I hate you, Caroline Armstrong. You have stolen the life I should have had and ruined what I have left. I hate you. I hate you. I hate you. I will find a way to make you pay for what you have done to me, Madeline vowed silently to herself.

She smiled sweetly at her guests and drank more red wine.

CHAPTER 16

Shrewsbury, England
November 1865

It was damp and cold in Shrewsbury the day Sally
Rogers read the engraved wedding invitation with
tears of pride in her eyes. Her round, wrinkled face
beamed with satisfaction. Her Caroline was marrying a fancy duke! She had known that everything
would work out well for her, but a duke! Well now,
that was something special, indeed. It was much
better than Caroline marrying that no-good American boy, Stephen Bennett. From the minute she
met him, Sally knew that he wasn't right for Caroline. She helped raise both Armstrong girls from
babies and understood them better than anybody,
and she always knew what was best for Caroline.

As she slowly pulled herself up from the chair
and achingly stood up, she wished the misery in her
back would allow her to journey to London for the
wedding. How proud she would be to see Caroline
married off in style! But she could not bear the

pain traveling would cause her. She knew Caroline and Emma would understand.

For more than twenty years she had worked for Katherine and Richard Armstrong, and she grew to love them as her own family. Why, Caroline and Emma had her heart from the moment they were born! And didn't she help deliver both of them? Those girls were more her own than their grandmother's. She had been with the Armstrongs since they were first married, when Richard hired her temporarily to help his wife learn to cook and clean their tiny cottage. But after Caroline was born, Katherine refused to do without Sally's help. So Sally stayed on with the family and took care of the girls after Katherine died.

But it was right that they go to live in the elegant house with their real family, Sally thought to herself as she shuffled through the kitchen of Lilac Cottage. She had continued to reside there after Olivia Fairchild took the girls to live with her. Olivia Fairchild had offered to have Sally come to live at Fairview Hall, but she could never fit in with those fancy types. Sally knew her place, and she belonged in Shrewsbury, not in a grand manor house with all its high-class rules and proprieties. Instead, Olivia had bought Lilac Cottage for Sally, in gratitude for taking such good care of her daughter and granddaughters throughout the years.

Yes, things had turned out just fine. She knew Caroline's mother would have been happy with this turn of events. For Sally had kept her promise to Katherine.

The promise she made the night that Katherine died, just before she had finally succumbed to the consumption that ravaged her. Sally had sat beside

Katherine late that night, cooling her fevered body with damp cloths. An exhausted Richard had finally gone to sleep in his cramped little study. It was then that Katherine opened her eyes and grabbed Sally's hand with her own weak one.

"I've been thinking," Katherine whispered faintly, although it was an effort for her to do even that.

"What is it?" Sally asked tenderly.

"I want so much for my girls . . ." Katherine struggled to suppress a deep rasping cough. "I worry about them." The coughing overtook her.

Katherine Fairchild Armstrong's once renowned beauty was now faded. Her honey-gold hair was streaked with gray and silver, and her creamy complexion was ashen and creased with lines of worry and sadness. Her arresting green eyes no longer sparkled with merriment but were dull and lifeless, sunken into her gaunt face.

"You don't need to worry a fig about those girls," Sally said when her coughing subsided. "They'll be just fine."

"I'm dying, Sally. When I'm gone, what will become of them? Sometimes I wish they had been born boys. Their lives would be so much easier. Men have all the freedom. Men can go and make their future in life. But that's not true for women. I think I was too selfish in running off with Richard. I should have listened to my father. I never thought of the consequences for my children. I haven't been a very good mother—" Katherine coughed as hot tears spilled down her fevered cheeks.

"Nonsense. You're a wonderful mother. You mustn't ever wish not to have had those two beautiful girls," Sally whispered, calmly wiping Katherine's cheeks and forehead with a damp cloth.

"Don't ever . . . tell Richard," Katherine sputtered between coughing fits that wracked her emaciated body. "But I . . . I want my family to take care of the girls. They would have a much better life at Fairview if my father would take them in."

It was the only time that Sally had ever heard Katherine speak with regret for the lifestyle she sacrificed to marry Richard Armstrong, the love of her life.

"I want my daughters to have more . . . than . . . this," she managed in a rasping whisper, indicating the tiny cottage and the life it contained. "What will happen to them, Sally? It would never occur to Richard to think of their futures. Caroline is already twelve. In a few years, she'll be old enough. My daughter can't marry some common villager."

"Drink this." Sally poured some cool water between Katherine's cracked lips.

"Promise me, Sally. Promise me . . . You will make sure that the girls get to my parents." Katherine's glassy green eyes pleaded with her.

"I promise. Don't you worry. I'll make sure those girls are taken care of," Sally vowed, failing to hold back her own tears.

Katherine nodded her head slowly, her eyes closing. "Thank you," she whispered in relief.

True to her word and unbeknownst to Richard, Sally wrote a letter to Katherine's parents informing them of her death and stating that it was Katherine's dying wish that Olivia and Edward Fairchild raise her daughters. Sally watched in silent frustration as Richard turned down the offer from his in-laws, declaring that he would rather raise them himself. But when Richard Armstrong died eight years later, Sally contacted the Fairchilds yet again, making them aware that their granddaughters were left destitute orphans. By then the old earl had died also, and of course Olivia Fairchild practically flew to Lilac Cottage to claim Caroline and Emma.

Yes, Sally felt satisfied that she had fulfilled Katherine's wishes in taking care of the girls. Only good things would happen to them now. Katherine would also have been pleased with how well Sally had protected Caroline. Even Richard would have been pleased, had he known.

Sally opened a small wooden box with some letters inside. She picked them up and leafed through the many envelopes addressed to *Miss Caroline Armstrong, Lilac Cottage, Shrewsbury, England*. They were all unopened, of course. She was hardly a spy! She would never read someone's private letters, but she clearly had to take them. Wasn't it her responsibility to keep Caroline from making the terrible mistake of running off with that American boy? She belonged right here in England like the good English girl she was!

Sally chuckled a little to herself. Caroline hadn't suspected that she had intercepted all of her correspondence. It certainly came in handy to have a cousin who delivered the post! Her eyes fell across the address on another envelope written in a girlish hand, *Mr. Stephen Bennett, Willow Hill, Richmond, Virginia*. Not only had Sally kept the letters that Stephen had written to Caroline, but she had also taken the letters that Caroline had written to him.

She sighed heavily, recalling how sad and withdrawn Caroline had become when she received not a word from Stephen. Sally hadn't meant to hurt the dear girl, just protect her. And didn't it turn out fine? Caroline was going to be a duchess and live like a queen instead of traipsing off to the wilds of a God-forsaken country with that no-good boy!

That Stephen Bennett! He had a charming smile, but she couldn't trust him as far as she could throw him. He didn't fool Sally. He had wicked designs on Caroline right from the beginning.

No, Sally did right by poor Caroline.

Sometimes she wondered if she shouldn't just toss all the letters into the fire. But she reasoned that one day when Caroline was happily married, Sally would send her the letters and Caroline would laugh and thank her for saving her from a terrible fate in America! Yes, Sally thought, she would hold on to these letters for a while longer. Especially since new ones were still arriving.

CHAPTER 17

November 1865
London, England

"I've never seen such a crowd," Emma exclaimed as she peeked out the window of the carriage at the throngs of people gathered outside the cathedral.

It was a surprisingly sunny November morning, and London's elite was already seated inside the massive cathedral, while what seemed like the rest of the city had flocked to the surrounding streets to witness the society wedding of the decade any way they could.

"It's not every day that a duke gets married," Kit Fairchild, the Earl of Glenwood commented. "Especially to my niece." Uncle Kit smiled fondly at Caroline, who sat across from him in the carriage. "You look so much like my sister it takes my breath away. She would be so happy for you."

Caroline held back tears at the thought of her mother.

"You make a beautiful bride, Caroline," Aunt Jane whispered.

"Thank you," she murmured, glancing out the window. Her heart began racing as soon as she saw the cathedral. She breathed nervously, unable to quell the persistent feeling that she was making a dreadful mistake. But it was too late to back out now. Not with all these people watching and everyone expecting her to be wed.

For the past weeks she had simply allowed herself to be swept up in the enthusiasm of planning her wedding and had not given much thought about what she was actually doing. It all seemed to happen extremely fast. From the moment she said yes to Alex, it was all out of her hands. Everyone was so happy about their engagement that it was difficult for her not to be. And she *was* happy. But now, on the actual day she was to speak her vows, great misgivings pricked her conscience.

"It's so exciting!" Emma said as she squeezed Caroline's gloved hand in hers.

Uncle Kit ushered them from the carriage, through the hordes of people and into the cathedral. Inside, hundreds of invited guests sat in the polished wooden pews waiting for the ceremony to begin. Aunt Jane and Emma carefully arranged Caroline's white silk wedding gown and its fifteen-foot train. The pale pink roses of her bouquet were gathered from the Dowager Duchess's greenhouse and matched the baby roses that crowned her hair and held her filmy white veil in place. As bridal attendants, Emma and Aunt Jane wore pale pink satin gowns and carried bouquets of light pink roses as well. Teddy, Jane and Kit's son, was outfitted in a miniature gray morning suit and clutched a white satin pillow that held her golden wedding band with all the importance his five-year-old person could muster.

"It's time, Caroline." Uncle Kit held out his arm

and she followed him, as the organist began playing a fanfare.

A hush fell over the guests as they waited expectantly for the bride. Teddy wobbled precariously down the red carpet, the satin pillow held close to his chest for fear of dropping the precious ring. Aunt Jane gracefully followed behind him. Emma, the maid of honor, her face beaming, sailed down the aisle, taking her place next to Charles Woodward at the alter. Caroline could just see Alexander standing at his side, looking handsome and elegant in his gray morning suit.

Holding her uncle's arm, Caroline somehow managed to walk down the aisle without tripping over her gown. She carefully made her way to the altar, her heart pounding with trepidation. The trip seemed endless as the music echoed sedately through the cathedral and the scent of countless rose bouquets and burning candles permeated the air. The sea of faces surrounding her, blurry from the morning sunlight spilling in from the tall, stained glass windows, was cast with colorful shadows.

What was she thinking? She shouldn't be doing this! How could she possibly believe that she could marry the Duke of Woodborough? It was arrogant and reckless of her. She didn't know which thought terrified her more: fleeing the cathedral now and renouncing everything or actually staying and vowing to spend the rest of her life with this man. However, her uncle's hold on her arm kept her in the cathedral, and she suddenly found herself trembling at the altar.

The archbishop waited regally, his formal robes flowing about him. "Who gives this woman in marriage?" His voice echoed deeply throughout the nave.

"I do, Your Grace. Her uncle." Kit lifted her veil and kissed her on the cheek and took his place in the pew beside Olivia, who was dabbing her teary eyes with a lace handkerchief. Caroline held her own tears in check and, taking a deep breath, looked up at her future husband.

Alex was smiling at her, his blue eyes sparkling. He clasped her small hand in his, squeezing lightly for comfort. "You're so beautiful," he whispered before the archbishop began the ceremony.

Alex's voice rang out strong and clear as he spoke his vows. Caroline stared fixedly at him while she whispered her vows to love, honor, and obey. Teddy came forward unsteadily, after a little prompting from Emma, to hand over the wedding band. Alex took Caroline's hand and placed the small golden ring on her finger. Then she signed the marriage certificate with a trembling hand. The archbishop declared them man and wife, and Alex wrapped her in a passionate embrace that left no doubt in the minds of anyone in the cathedral of his feelings for his new bride and reminded Caroline of just why she consented to marry him in the first place.

Breathless after their kiss, Caroline was given over to more congratulatory hugs from her family. It was all quite unreal. She was now Alex's wife.

Olivia, still teary, hugged her. "My dear, I couldn't be happier for you. I know your parents would be too."

"Thank you, Grandmother," Caroline said, suddenly longing for her mother and father. What would they think of their daughter marrying a duke? Oddly enough, she wouldn't even be here now if they were still alive.

"Caroline, you're a real duchess!" Emma exclaimed.

Aunt Jane and Uncle Kit kissed her affectionately, and after kneeling down to his height, Caroline received a little bear hug from Teddy.

"Did I do all right?" he asked her, a serious expression on his baby face.

"You did an excellent job, Teddy. No one could have done it better," she proclaimed, and was rewarded with a luminous smile from him.

Charles kissed Caroline's cheek and said with a grin, "Now I have a little sister to tease!"

"And I finally have a daughter!" Elizabeth declared, wrapping Caroline in a warm embrace. "Now I only need grandchildren!"

"One thing at a time, Mother," Alex chided her. "Let's attend our reception first, shall we?" A traditional wedding breakfast was planned for special guests at the Fairchild townhouse. He offered Caroline his arm, and they began the recessional up the aisle.

As they reached the main doors of the cathedral and entered into the bright November morning, Caroline blinked rapidly from the brilliant sunshine after the dim interior of the church. Among the masses of people gathered on the steps to watch the duke and his new duchess ride away in their fancy carriage, something familiar called to her. An odd, tingling sensation bubbled within her, causing her to turn to the right. The sunlight glared fiercely, and she squinted her eyes to see who it was. From the blurry sea of faces in the crowd, one stood out.

He had bright blond hair and deep brown eyes. Eyes that knew her. Eyes that haunted her. Eyes that were full of pain and angry recriminations.

Stephen Bennett.

The entire world began to tilt and spin violently

around her, and the ground suddenly seemed to rise up. Her vision focused down to a tiny pinpoint of light and then went completely black.

Caroline's unexpected halt and sharp intake of breath caused Alex to turn to her. A collective gasp erupted from the onlooking crowd as the Duke of Woodborough managed to catch his new bride in his arms just as she fainted.

When Caroline awoke she was reclining on a cushioned seat with her head resting in Alex's lap as their carriage made its way through the busy London thoroughfares toward the Fairchild townhouse.

"The thought of being my wife was too much for you?" he teased her with a rueful smile when her eyelids fluttered open. He caressed her face gently with his fingers.

Caroline blinked in confusion, trying to recall what had happened. Hazy images flickered through her mind. The cathedral. Alex whispering, "I do." Signing her name with a shaking hand. Alex kissing her. Congratulations and hugs. Blinding sunlight. Hundreds of faces.

And Stephen Bennett's.

Her stomach lurched, and she thought she might be sick. She closed her eyes tightly.

Stephen.

It couldn't have been him, she reasoned to herself. It had to be her mind playing tricks on her, surely. It was a simple case of nervous stress. He couldn't possibly be in London on the very day of her wedding to Alex! It was too much of a coincidence. She had to be seeing things.

Yet it was his blond hair glinting in the sunlight

that had first caught her eye. She would know those brown eyes anywhere, for hadn't she looked into them thousands of times? Those brown eyes pleaded desperately with her today. In just the flicker of an instant, she read the longing, the questioning, the anger in them. Then everything went black.

Her head throbbed as panic welled up inside, and she again felt the need to be sick.

Alex, his voice laced with concern, asked, "Caroline, are you all right?" Her face was ashen, and he feared she would pass out again.

Opening her eyes once more, she saw Alex looking at her worriedly, the anxiety plain on his face. She nodded her head with great effort and whispered, "I assume I fainted?"

"In front of hundreds of people, my love. It was quite a spectacle. Luckily, I caught you before you hit the ground."

"Thank you," she murmured. "I don't think I have ever fainted before."

"Well, let's not make a habit out of it, shall we?" He grinned at her.

Caroline managed a weak smile and tried to sit up.

"Rest a little longer," Alex urged her. "The color is just returning to your face now."

She put her head back down gratefully and sighed.

He gazed at her, smoothing the hair from her face. "What happened? Why did you faint, Caroline?"

She hesitated in answering. "I'm not entirely sure."

He raised an eyebrow. "Regrets?"

"No regrets."

"Nervous about being my wife?"

"No." Caroline smiled reassuringly at him. "I suppose I was just nervous about the day. So many people and the excitement of everything. It was a little overwhelming." *Which was partly true,* she thought, as the vision of Stephen receded. Talking to Alex had calmed her into believing she simply imagined him.

Alex nodded in understanding, continuing to smooth her hair with his hand. Then a slight chuckle escaped him.

"Why are you laughing?"

"I was just thinking. I'm afraid you caused some gossip today. Brides fainting on their wedding day leads people to speculate about timing."

She looked at him, obviously puzzled. "Timing?"

"You can bet the gossips will be counting the months very carefully until the birth of our first child."

"The months until . . ." Realization began to dawn. "You mean they think that I'm going to have a baby?"

He feigned innocence. "What else could be the matter?"

"But I'm not!" she cried.

"I know that, but if you were, you wouldn't be the first bride who had to rush to the altar. They'll find out the truth eventually, so nothing to worry about really." He smiled at her. "You gave the crowd quite a show."

She laughed contritely. "I suppose I did."

The carriage came to a halt, and Alex helped her rise. "You're looking better now. I was worried about you."

"I'm fine," she stated, making herself believe it was true.

"You lost your veil when you fainted."

"Did I?" She hadn't noticed, but reached up to smooth her tousled hair.

He looked lovingly at her, and her heart skipped a beat. "We'll get you another one. Are you ready for your wedding breakfast, my fainting little wife?"

"Yes, my gallant husband," she said with a smile, and she gratefully took his arm.

CHAPTER 18

London, England
December 1865

The Duke and Duchess of Woodborough were the guests of honor at Lady Weatherby's holiday party, and half the *ton* was coming to her townhouse to see their first social appearance together as husband and wife since their return from their honeymoon. Alex would have preferred to journey to Ridge Haven rather than remain in London. He was eager to share the home he loved with Caroline and wished to spend their first Christmas together there. But Emma's betrothal to John Talbot was finally going to be announced at the Talbots' annual Holiday Ball the following week, and he and Caroline did not have the heart to disappoint her by not attending.

"Do you think I would actually miss the announcement that you finally snared poor John Talbot?" Alex teased Emma as they rode in the Woodborough carriage on their way to Lady Weatherby's house.

"What can I say?" Emma retorted lightly. "We

Armstrong women are skilled at snaring men. Isn't that so, Caroline?"

Caroline laughed, glancing at Alex. "Speak for yourself, Emma. I'd have to say that Alex did the snaring in our relationship." She smoothed the deep rose velvet of her favorite new gown. It had long sleeves that came to points at her wrists, a high collar with a plunging neckline, a matching rose-colored cape, and small muff trimmed in white fur. It was the perfect ensemble to wear on a chilly December evening. Alex had the gown made especially for her at a small boutique in Paris, and she loved it.

"I'm afraid I have to side with Emma on this one, Caroline." Alex gave his wife a seductive smile. She returned the same look to him, much to his delight.

Emma tossed her head coquettishly, her eyes twinkling. "Don't underestimate your own powers, Caroline."

"You're right, Emma," Alex agreed with a laugh.

Lady Weatherby's party was a mad crush of people congratulating the newly married couple. The duke and duchess were the toast of London, and everyone was eager to greet them.

Even Madeline Maxwell, now Lady Parkridge, congratulated them. Wearing her signature blue gown trimmed with white lace, Madeline maintained her appearance of a fragile china doll. Caroline idly wondered how many baby blue gowns Madeline had in her possession.

With her blue eyes wide, Madeline smiled up at Alex. "Your wedding was lovely, Your Grace. I do hope you enjoyed your trip abroad."

"Thank you, Lady Parkridge. We had a splendid time," Alex answered casually.

"And Caroline! My, my. Marriage seems to agree with you! You certainly look very well fed!" Madeline gushed with sickening sweetness.

"Thank you, Madeline," Caroline answered dryly, knowing that Madeline was attempting an insult, and returned a false smile. "I can only hope that you're as happy in *your* marriage as I am in *mine.*"

"Oh, I am," Madeline answered in a singsong voice. "But now I simply must introduce you both to someone very special."

Alex whispered for only Caroline to hear, "Nice retort, my love."

She grinned conspiratorially at him. "I thought so."

He placed a loving kiss on her forehead. Gazing at her husband, Caroline did not notice the young man who walked to Madeline's side.

Madeline, looking like the cat that ate the canary, said pointedly to Alex, "I would like you to meet Lord Parkridge's cousin from America. The Duke of Woodborough, may I present Mr. Stephen Bennett."

Caroline froze in horrid fascination as Alex politely shook hands with Stephen Bennett. Oliver Parkridge's cousin! Madeline's husband was Stephen's cousin! Stephen was here! In this very room. With her. And Alex. *This couldn't be happening.* The blood rushed to her head, and she felt violently ill. She literally willed herself not to faint.

"It's a pleasure to meet you, Mr. Bennett." Alex greeted the younger man with his natural good grace.

Stephen gave a grim smile. "I've heard a lot about you."

"Caroline," Madeline cooed, "You must meet my husband's cousin. The Duchess of Woodborough. Mr. Stephen Bennett."

A mask of a smile touched her lips, and Caroline

mumbled, "How do you do, Mr. Bennett?" Filled with dread and a sickening feeling of nausea, she wondered if Stephen would betray her. He took her gloved hand in his and brought it to his lips. Her heart seemed to stop beating altogether.

"It is my pleasure to make your acquaintance, duchess." Stephen placed a sarcastic emphasis on the title of duchess, but no one seemed to notice except Caroline. They just assumed he was a typical American, ignorant of the correct use of English titles. His brown eyes bored into her, and he did not release her hand.

"Stephen, did you know that Caroline was just recently married?" Madeline asked, looking keenly at both of them.

"So I have learned," he answered, not taking his eyes off Caroline. His hand gripped her fingers. Tugging at her hand, Caroline looked at him with beseeching eyes, and finally he let go of her.

At that moment Lord Peter Forester called Alex over to him. After excusing himself, Alex joined his friend, leaving Caroline alone with Madeline and Stephen. Giving a quick and silent prayer of thanks to Lord Forester, Caroline wished desperately she were anywhere but where she was at the present moment.

"Stephen attended the university in Shrewsbury, Caroline. Isn't that the little backward village you are from?" Madeline asked with a sly smile.

Caroline nodded her head, avoiding Stephen's eyes.

"Didn't your father do some kind of work at the university, Caroline?" Madeline prodded, her sharp eyes glittering.

Caroline lifted her chin defensively at the mention of her father. "He taught Latin there."

"Of course he did. But surely the two of you must have met before!" Madeline gushed ingeniously. "Stephen seems to think he remembers you. Don't you, Stephen?"

Caroline held her breath, praying he wouldn't say anything. How much had he told Madeline about them? She waited tensely, thankful that Alex was momentarily engaged in a lively conversation behind her.

Stephen continued to stare at Caroline. There was silent accusation in his eyes, although his voice still held that lazy, familiar charm. "I might have seen you once or twice upon occasion with your father."

Making an effort to explain to him what had led her to be there, she said, "My father passed away last year, and I came to London to live with my grandmother."

Compassion flickered across his face. "Please accept my condolences on the death of your father. I respected him greatly."

"Thank you, Mr. Bennett," she replied woodenly, afraid she would cry at the many meanings his words implied. Changing the subject, she asked, "Were you in the war in America?" It was amazing how calm her voice sounded while making polite conversation when inside she was screaming.

"Yes, I fought in the war, and I'm greatly relieved that it is finally over." He looked at her meaningfully. "I was wounded and quite ill for some months. It made me wonder why I gave up the safety of England in the first place."

She blocked out the images she had of Stephen hurt and in pain that had tortured her for two years. He was explaining to her as well. "Your home and family . . . Are they well?" He had often described Willow Hill to her in detail. Was she still the same girl who had dreamed of living there with him?

"We came through the war relatively unscathed compared to most of the homes in the area. We were very fortunate."

"I'm relieved to hear that," she murmured.

At that moment Mary Ellen Talbot, Elizabeth Dishington, and Betsy Warring suddenly descended upon her. Now that she was the Duchess of Woodborough, Caroline was more sought after socially than she had ever been as plain Miss Armstrong, and she had never been more grateful for the timely distraction these girls provided.

"Caroline! Welcome back!" Mary Ellen squealed as she embraced Caroline. Mary Ellen was exceptionally cordial to her now that John and Emma's engagement was imminent. She would now be sister-in-law to a duchess.

Madeline begrudgingly introduced Stephen to the others.

"Your dress is just divine!" cooed Betsy, while tugging at the bodice of her own ill-fitting pink gown. "It's from Paris, isn't it?"

"You must tell us all about your honeymoon!" Elizabeth Dishington giggled.

"Yes, do tell," encouraged Madeline coolly.

Before Caroline could utter a single word, Stephen excused himself from the group of young ladies. "It was a pleasure to meet you, duchess. I hope to see you again very soon." He squeezed her hand before he turned away.

Sighing with relief, Caroline forced herself to regale the girls with tales of her honeymoon trip to France and Italy.

* * *

Madeline lingered with the girls, more to see the effect of Oliver's cousin on Caroline than to hear about her honeymoon. Caroline's shocked expression when she recognized Stephen Bennett was too priceless for words! But then she acted so calmly, almost as if she were just meeting him for the first time. Madeline resentfully gave her credit for that.

It was really a shame that the duke had to be called away so abruptly, even before she had a chance to mention that Stephen had lived in Shrewsbury. Oh, but she did want to see Caroline Armstrong squirm! If only Stephen had given her more information . . . She was positive that something had happened between the two of them but wasn't sure exactly what. Stephen had been too tight-lipped. If only she could prove that they were lovers or at least hint at it enough to torment Caroline.

Madeline had been completely uninterested in Oliver's cousin when he arrived in November. She had sat at her elegant dinner table with her false hostess smile and glared at Oliver, while Stephen told boring stories about some war in Virginia or someplace equally countrified. Madeline thought he was handsome enough with his blond hair and big brown eyes, but he was an American, and therefore a nobody in her opinion, so she paid no attention to him. Then Lady Forester mentioned the Duke of Woodborough's upcoming wedding and how romantic that he was marrying Caroline Armstrong. Madeline hadn't thought anything of it at the time, but after the talk of the duke's wedding, Stephen never uttered another word. After their guests left, Stephen had called Madeline aside.

"Could you please tell me about this Caroline Armstrong who's marrying a duke?"

Instantly alert, Madeline's blue eyes narrowed sharply. "Why do you want to know about her?"

With a faraway look in his brown eyes he said, "I knew a Caroline Armstrong while I was at the university in Shrewsbury, and I wondered if she were the same person."

Regarding him with a keen look, Madeline chose her words carefully. "She is from some little country village. I don't remember where. Her mother's father was the Earl of Glenwood, but she ran off and married a poor man. It was quite a scandal at the time. When her parents died, Caroline went to live with her grandmother. It shocked everyone when the duke showed any interest in her. She's very plain, dull, and bookish, but somehow she snared the duke."

His brown eyes clouded. "I see."

"Is she the same girl you knew?"

"I think she might very well be. Although the Caroline I knew was quite beautiful, and certainly not dull," he replied, lost in thought.

No one's fool, Madeline quickly deduced that they must be the same person, and if she continued to play her cards right she might just learn some very worthwhile information. *Wasn't it wonderful that Oliver had a cousin?* Fluttering her eyelashes and placing her hand on his shoulders in false concern, she sweetly asked Stephen, "Was this Caroline your sweetheart?"

Flustered, he stammered hurriedly, "Uh . . . No . . . no. I just knew of her through her father. Thank you, Madeline."

"You're welcome, dearest Stephen. Any time I can be of help, you only have to ask me." She smiled prettily at him but continued to watch him closely from then on. Madeline, for once, was thankful she had married Oliver Parkridge and not some other lord. His boring American cousin could prove to be very useful, indeed, in causing trouble for Caroline Armstrong. So when Lady Weatherby announced that her holiday party would be to honor the newly married duke and duchess, Madeline simply had to bring Stephen Bennett and Caroline Armstrong together to see what happened. There was definitely something between them, and she would give anything to know just what!

Now here was Caroline acting calm and unruffled, happily married to the Duke of Woodborough with all the girls fawning all over her and her new Parisian gown. It enraged Madeline.

Caroline avoided Stephen whenever possible throughout the remainder of the evening. But she felt his eyes following her everywhere. She stayed close to Alex, because she didn't believe that Stephen would attempt to speak to her while she was with the duke. Her mind still could not accept what was happening. That Stephen was there. In this very room. After all this time. After she married the duke. After she was happily married.

Stephen Bennett was back.

It was her worst nightmare since she had agreed to marry Alex.

Although on some level it was a relief to know that he was safe and had not died in America and that his family and home were safe as well. She had worried for them and tried to picture what it would be like to live in Virginia. It had been so long since she had thought of him and so much had happened to her in the meantime that she wasn't sure what she felt for him anymore.

She just knew that Alex couldn't find out.

Oh, Stephen, she silently pleaded with him, *please, please don't say anything. Don't cause trouble for me.*

She turned to look at her husband and as always was struck by how handsome he was. He was tall and muscular and looked very elegant in his black tuxedo. He was clean shaven as always. His strong jaw and aquiline nose gave him a classic look, and his blue eyes stood out. She was proud to be with him and noticed the covetous glances she was given by other women. Why was he with her? Some little nobody from the country. She didn't feel deserving of him. More so now that Stephen was standing in the room with them.

She squeezed Alex's hand tightly, wondering how one little secret could unsuspectingly turn into something so terribly unspeakable . . .

Emma walked over and whispered anxiously in her ear, "Caroline, do you know that Stephen Bennett is here?"

Nodding a quick yes, Caroline stepped closer to Emma.

Emma continued breathlessly, "I just ran into with him while talking to Madeline Maxwell—I mean Parkridge. Did he speak to you?"

"Yes. A little while ago."

"How strange he should be here," Emma mused, staring across the room at the very subject of their conversation. She turned back to her sister, concern in her voice. "Are you all right? I mean, seeing him again after all this time?"

"I'm fine, Emma," Caroline lied, thinking she was about to shatter into a thousand little pieces. "Don't worry about me."

"You're sure then?" She patted Caroline's arm reassuringly. "Imagine seeing Stephen Bennett in London!"

The evening seemed to last an eternity to Caroline. She managed to make polite conversation, replying for the hundredth time that, yes, she had a wonderful time on her honeymoon trip. Smiling brightly through a veil of taut nerves, she hoped no one could sense how she was feeling. Especially Alex.

In the security of their bedroom later that night, she made love to him with an almost desperate fervency. As if it were their last time together.

CHAPTER 19

It was late the next afternoon when Stephen Bennett knocked on the front door of the Woodward townhouse in Mayfair. He had timed his arrival well, although quite unknowingly, for the duke had left earlier in the day to attend to business matters, the Dowager Duchess was shopping, and Charles Woodward was out riding in Hyde Park with his latest love interest, Lady Violet Ashton.

Caroline was at home alone.

With a disapproving frown from Harrison, the butler, Stephen had been ushered into the main parlor and was waiting uncertainly for Caroline to appear. The parlor was dimly lit, with dark green striped wallpaper and dark green velvet drapes adorning the tall windows. A fire burned in the hearth to lend some warmth to the dreary and cold December afternoon.

After a sleepless night of worrying, Caroline was sick with the news that Stephen Bennett was in her house and was tempted to have Harrison inform him that she was not at home. But what was to prevent him from calling on her tomorrow or the next day? It was inevitable that he would attempt to see her, but she hadn't expected him quite so soon. She reasoned that she had to confront him at some point, and now was as good a time as any. At least Alex was out and would not return until supper. So she requested some tea be sent to the parlor, smoothed her lavender day dress with the white piping that Alex had said made her eyes look very green, took a deep breath, and went downstairs to face Stephen Bennett after two years.

"I wasn't sure if you would see me," Stephen whispered to Caroline as she stood in the doorway.

Caroline hesitated a moment before deciding to close the parlor door. It wouldn't do for her to be alone in a room with a male guest with the door closed, but she did not want the servants to overhear their conversation either.

"Of course I would see you," she answered as he took her hand and kissed it tenderly. Too shocked to take in Stephen's appearance the night before, she regarded him carefully now. Except for the shallow scar that stretched from his right eyebrow to the top of his forehead, he still looked the same as she remembered. He was wearing a new black wool suit, his blond hair was neatly combed, and his face was cleanly shaven. His brown eyes were warm and gazed at her with steady intent.

"You're still the most beautiful girl I've ever seen, Carrie. You haven't changed a bit." A boyish smile swept his face as he looked upon her.

"Thank you," she murmured, melting at the force of his smile. "Please have a seat." How strange to hear him call her Carrie again! No one had ever called her that except Stephen. All the feelings that she had ever had for him welled painfully to the surface. "I was quite surprised to see you last night."

He sat on an elegantly carved chair, while she sat upon the sofa and poured tea with a trembling hand from the china pot.

His voice was low but full of meaning. "You do know why I am here?"

She nodded her head, not meeting his eyes, her heart pounding. Of course she knew why he was here. It was their little secret. But would he make demands upon her now? How would she ever explain this to Alex?

"Does he know about me?"

"No, not quite." Caroline shook her head. "Not everything."

"What are we going to do about this, Carrie?" He stood up and walked to the fireplace, turning his back to her.

"I don't know," she managed to say in a tight whisper. Her hand shook so terribly that she spilled the tea. She set the pot down with a clatter and glanced toward him apprehensively.

"Why didn't you ever answer my letters?" he demanded angrily, spinning around to face her.

Her chin went up defensively. "Why didn't *I* . . . ?" she challenged. "Why didn't *you* answer any of *my* letters?"

"What do you mean?" He stared at her in utter disbelief.

"The letters I wrote to you. Every week. I sent them all to Willow Hill, just as you told me."

He shook his head. "I never received any letters from you, Carrie."

"I only received one letter from you. Only the one," she stated softly, recalling every word he had written to her and how many times she had read them over and over to herself. *Knowing that you are honoring your promise to keep our little secret, my dearest Carrie, is the only way I can bear this separation. Always remember how much I love you and that you belong to me and no other.*

"It broke my heart when I didn't hear from you. But I kept sending letters until two months ago, when I wrote that I was coming back for you." Stephen added pointedly, "Apparently you didn't receive that one either. You were too busy marrying a duke." He couldn't conceal the note of sarcasm in his lazy voice.

Caroline chose to ignore it. "You truly wrote to me, Stephen?"

"Of course I did. Writing to you was the only thing that helped me get through that bloody war."

"And I wrote to you. Honestly. I was devastated when I didn't receive any more letters from you, after that first one. I thought you'd forgotten all about me."

"I could never forget about you, Carrie. I waited every day for a letter from you. The hope that each day might be the one that would bring a letter from you was what motivated me to get up each morning and continue fighting. When no letters came, all I could think was that something terrible had happened to you and that I needed to get back to you."

He had written to her after all. He had not forgotten about her as she had assumed. The knowledge filled her with sadness, remorse, and a painful feeling she couldn't quite identify. "But if you wrote to me and I wrote to you, what happened to all our letters? Where are they?"

Stephen looked as baffled as she did. "I don't know. It makes no sense."

A silence enveloped them. Stephen moved to sit beside her on the sofa. He touched her cheek and asked, "How could you marry him, Carrie? Why didn't you wait for me?"

"I did wait," she explained to him. "I know it doesn't appear that way, but you must believe me. After my father died, things became so terribly complicated. My grandmother came for me and Emma, and she took us to live with her. We were suddenly in a different world, and they planned for us to have a Season and find suitable husbands. No one knew about you. I didn't even know where you were or if you wanted me anymore or if you were still alive. I had to do something, so I pretended to be a bluestocking so no one would want to marry me."

Stephen nodded as an understanding dawned. "That explains the puzzling comments I heard about you being dull and boring."

"Yes, but then Alex came along and everyone expected me to marry him. I didn't know what to do. I hadn't heard from you in so long. Everything that had happened between us that day seemed so unreal, so far away. I almost believed that it never happened at all. I didn't think you were ever coming back for me. So I . . . married him."

He sighed wearily. "You have to tell him the truth." He placed a kiss on her forehead. "You were mine first. You belong to me."

"But I'm his duchess now . . ." Caroline wavered. "We were married last month. Everyone was there. Including you." Her green eyes sought his, and she gently traced the length of the scar on his forehead with her finger.

He reached up and took her hand in his. "Yes, I was there. I had just arrived in London and was on my way to Shrewsbury to see you. I was at my cousin's house when I learned about your wedding the night before. I had to see for myself if you were really the girl that everyone was talking about. I knew you recognized me when you fainted." He squeezed her hand. "Do you know what it's been like for me these past few weeks knowing that you were with *him* as *his* wife?"

Caroline began to cry. Out of fear. Out of sorrow. Out of shame. Her life was completely ruined. She had single-handedly destroyed everything. She never should have married Alex. How could she have been so selfish and foolish? What made her think she could get away with something like this? How would she ever explain this to Alex? Her grandmother?

"Please don't cry, Carrie. The last memory I have of you, you were crying, and it just about killed me." He dabbed at her tears with his handkerchief and kissed her cheek. "You have to tell him though."

"Tell him what?" she choked. "How can I possibly explain this?" Alex's face haunted her. Her heart was breaking. Too many secrets. Too many lies. She would rather die than face everyone with the truth now.

"If you won't tell him, I will." Stephen leaned closer and began kissing her tear-stained face. "Do you love him, Carrie?" There was an urgency, a desperateness in his voice.

Feeling as if he were smothering her, Caroline tried to pull away but only managed to sink further into the sofa cushions with him above her. Stephen wrapped his arms around her, pinning her down.

His mouth covered hers, and his tongue forced its way into her mouth. Memories of the last afternoon they spent together sprang unbidden into her head, and she fought him. She did not want this, did not want him touching her. His hand pawed at the front of her dress, and she wanted to scream but could not find her voice. Panic welled frantically within her, and she placed both hands against his chest and pushed as hard as she could. He resisted her attempts to free herself, gripping her more tightly. Breathing heavily, she struggled beneath him as he forced her farther down. The buttons of his black coat caught in her curls, and some of her hair ripped painfully from her head as she pushed against him.

"Stop!" she cried out. "Stephen, please don't!"

"Get your hands off my wife!"

Alex had entered the room and was standing before them.

After returning home earlier than he expected, Alex was surprised when Harrison informed him that Caroline was alone in the parlor with an unfamiliar gentleman. Finding the parlor door closed puzzled him even more. But when he opened the door to see Caroline on the sofa with another man in the throes of a somewhat compromising position, he was stunned. Further shocking him was the fact that he recognized the man in question. He had been introduced to him at Lady Weatherby's party only the night before. An American. Alex had shook his hand while Caroline had stood coolly beside him. Something triggered in his memory, and suddenly it was all very clear to him. This was Caroline's American soldier. The one she was

waiting for. Now that American had the effrontery
to be in Alex's house with his arms around Alex's
wife. A fury stronger than he had ever felt before
spread like lightning through his veins. He wanted
to kill the man touching Caroline and was amazed
by his own self-control. Some instinct held him
back. For now.

Caroline's face was ashen, her hair tousled, and
she had the good grace to look mortified. But Alex
could also tell that she had been crying, and it was
obvious that she had been struggling with the man.
Which made him even angrier.

"I said, get your hands off my wife." His voice was like
sharply edged steel, carrying an implied threat, and
his eyes turned a piercing ice blue.

Stephen glanced at Caroline's terrified face and
then back at the duke. He reluctantly released her
and stood up, facing Alex. He readjusted his coat
and squared his shoulders. His eyes flashing, he
took a deep breath and spoke quite clearly.

"I'm afraid there has been a misunderstanding.
Caroline is *my* wife."

The air fairly crackled with tension as Caroline
sat frozen in place on the sofa, too horrified to
move. She stared at the two men who each claimed
her as his wife. They stood in sharp contrast to each
other, Stephen's boyish blond fairness against
Alex's tall, dark masculinity. They were both livid,
and she was the cause.

"What did you say?" Alex's voice cut like a knife
through the taut silence. His disbelief was overwhelming.

Stephen ran his hand nervously through his blond
hair and ignored Caroline's appalled expression. He

cleared his throat. "I said that Carrie is *my* wife. We were married in Shrewsbury over two years ago."

At first Alex's anger had been directed totally at Stephen, but now the full force of his wrath was aimed at Caroline, and his blue eyes locked with hers in shock. "Is this true?"

Finally able to find her voice, she began desperately, "Alex, can I explain to—"

"Is it true, Caroline? Yes or no? Are you married to this man?" His words whipped across the room, his jaw clenched with rage. Could it be possible? Images raced through his mind. Caroline asserting that she could not marry him. Her constant refusals of his proposals. She had been so reluctant to marry him. She'd fainted on their wedding day. Now the pieces were falling into place.

Her green eyes wide, she whispered so softly that it was barely audible, "Yes."

He stared at her for a long moment, not saying a word, as if trying to see something that was not there. Trying to take in the meaning of what was said. He closed his eyes briefly, then shook his head. When he opened them again, they were shuttered and unreadable, with no hint of warmth.

His voice was harsh and full of anger. "Get out, Caroline. Get your things and leave. I don't ever want to see you here again." He turned to Stephen and said icily, "Take her then, and get the hell out of my house."

Without a backward glance at Caroline, Alex turned toward the door.

Caroline leaped up to follow him. "Alex, wait, please . . ."

As he left the room the parlor door slammed soundly behind him.

* * *

Stephen grabbed Caroline by the arm, preventing her from following Alex. He was relieved it was over. The duke had released her. She was his again. "Let him go, Carrie. It's better this way. He knows the truth. Pack some things and come with me now. We can leave right away. There's a ship sailing for Virginia in the morning."

"Let go of me. I need to talk to him. I have to explain—"

Stephen spun her around to face him, gripping her by both shoulders and shaking her determinedly. "Explain what, Carrie? That you're my wife? That I married you first?" he shouted. "It's not going to change anything now. It's over. He doesn't want you anymore. You belong to me."

"Let go of me!" she shrieked. Frantic, she kicked Stephen's shin with her high-laced boot and broke free of his grip. She raced to the door, flinging it open, and flew down the hallway, arriving at the front door just in time to see Alex's carriage drive away.

Stephen followed her. Caroline stood staring at the empty London street. He placed a hand on her delicate shoulder. "He knows the truth now and no longer wants you. Come with me to America," he whispered. "Everything will be all right." It had to be. He had loved her for so long and had dreamed of her for years. He never imagined that she would marry someone else while he was away. Now all he wanted to do was whisk her away to Virginia and keep her with him always. He knew if he could just get her out of this house, he could have her.

She stared blankly at him. "Please go away." Her voice sounded hollow.

"How can you say that?" He nervously ran his hand through his blond hair.

"Please go. I need to be alone for a while."

"Everything will be fine, Carrie. We can leave in the morning. You'll be happy in Virginia with me. You'll see."

"I am not leaving with you tomorrow, Stephen." Her words were hard, final.

Surprised by her reaction, Stephen protested. "Of course you are. You are my wife, and you can't stay here with him anymore."

"But no one knows that I'm your wife. They believe I am Alex's wife. I cannot simply walk away from my family. I cannot just leave without explaining to Alex what happened. He deserves that much from me at least. This will publicly humiliate him. Can you imagine what everyone will say? The Duke of Woodborough has married a married woman!" Caroline shook her head sorrowfully, tears welling up once again. "I have done a terrible thing. I need to explain to my grandmother, and Emma, and Alex's family as well. This is going to devastate them. I have misled everyone I love. I cannot run away now when I have to face the consequences."

Stephen avoided her beautiful green eyes, which were full of shame and desperation. He hated to see her this way. "I'm sorry, Carrie. You are right, of course. It's just that I want us to be happy again. Like we were back in Shrewsbury. When it was just you and me. We will be happy again. I promise you that." He sighed and kissed her cheek, ignoring how she stiffened. He wanted her with him as soon as possible. He wanted to hold her in his arms again. "But take some time to explain to your family and say your good-byes. We can leave together next week, the day after Christmas."

Caroline barely nodded her head.

"Will you be staying at your grandmother's until then?" he asked.

"What do you mean?"

"You're *my* wife, Carrie. He knows now. Obviously you can't continue to stay here with him as *his* wife. So I assume you'll go to your grandmother's house tonight?" The thought of Caroline spending another night in the duke's bed was more than he could bear.

She nodded her head stiffly. "I suppose you're right."

"Then I'll call for you at your grandmother's house the day after Christmas. That's one whole week. Plenty of time to get your affairs in order. You must know, Carrie, that your leaving will cause a scandal for him no matter what. But if you slip away with me quietly, you can make it look as though you're simply leaving him, and no one will have to know that you were already married. You can spare him that, at least." He looked at her sharply then. "But one week is all the time I am willing to give you to settle everything between you. If you're not ready to go then, I will announce to all of London that you married the duke under false pretenses. That will be much uglier for him than his wife's running off. Do you understand me?" He could not help the threatening undertone that crept into his voice.

Once again, Caroline only nodded.

"That's my good girl." Stephen kissed her, brushing his hand along her jawline. "Until next week, Mrs. Bennett," he whispered in her ear before he left.

CHAPTER 20

Caroline turned woodenly and made her way upstairs, avoiding the curious stares from the servants. Her eyes were surprisingly vacant of tears, and she was terrified. She had never been so frightened in her whole life. Not when her mother died. Not when her father died. Not when Stephen left her. Not when she married Alex. This was a whole new kind of fear. This fear wrapped itself around her like an ice cold snake from her head to her toes, squeezing and squeezing until she felt she couldn't breathe, gasping for breath, and then it squeezed some more.

Oh, Alex!

What must he think of her now? Did he think she planned this and deliberately lied to him? Did he hate her? She certainly couldn't blame him if he did. She hated herself for being foolish enough to think she could even marry him in the first place, knowing full well she was already Stephen's wife.

Then there was her family.

Her grandmother would be completely devastated by this news. She would never be able to hold

her head up again. Her granddaughter's marriage
to the duke was just a sham. It was another embarrassing family scandal. Caroline was more like
Katherine than anyone realized. Foolish and reckless. Poor Emma. The scandal would probably ruin
her engagement to Lord Talbot, and she would
never be able to live down the notoriety of her
sister's false marriage. Uncle Kit and Aunt Jane
would be humiliated also. The Dowager Duchess
would be so hurt and disappointed. Caroline had
single-handedly brought shame and ruin upon two
fine families.

Everything she had with Alex was destroyed.

He had turned her world upside down and had
given her more than she ever realized she wanted.
He had loved her for herself, for who she was. He
made her smile, made her laugh, made her think.
What they shared was so special. One look from
him still made her heart race. Simply thinking of
their lovemaking sent shivers down her body.
Surely that was special. Somehow she knew that last
night would be their last time together, and she had
savored every second of their closeness. Now she
would never have that again. Now when she knew
how much she loved him.

And she had been the one to hurt him.

She was Stephen's wife. She was Mrs. Bennett and
was obligated to follow her husband to his home in
America. To live on a tobacco plantation with a man
she didn't even love anymore. She didn't want to
leave with Stephen, but that did not matter. She was
his wife. He had come back for her, and she had no
choice. They would leave for America next week.

She had one week left to explain to Alex somehow. She had to face him and explain as best she

could. She couldn't leave without seeing him again. She needed to see him. To say she was sorry and that she loved him and that she never meant to hurt him.

Pacing nervously back and forth in her bedroom, she decided not to pack and go to her grand-mother's house, no matter what Stephen said. She would at least give the appearance that things were normal between them for as long as she could. Hiding at her grandmother's would certainly raise eyebrows. Besides, she needed privacy with Alex. No, she would wait for Alex to come home that night and attempt to explain everything to him then. She would let him decide how they should inform everyone of this horrible situation before she left for America.

It was after nine o'clock that evening and Alex still had not returned home when there was a gentle knock on her bedroom door. Not waiting for an answer, the Dowager Duchess breezed in, look-ing lovely in a midnight blue silk gown that made her fair skin seem younger than it was. Her dark hair was swept up on her head in an elegant knot, and the scent of roses enveloped her.

"Charles is at the theater with Violet Ashton. The servants are acting strangely, and Harrison won't say a word. Alex didn't return for dinner, and you're up here in your room alone. My darling, I simply must know, did you and Alex have a lover's quarrel?"

Caroline was curled up on an overstuffed chair covered in a bright floral chintz fabric, a strained expression on her face. "Yes," she answered. "I suppose you could say that."

"Oh then, darling, you are dressed all wrong!" Elizabeth's eyes glittered with enthusiasm. "A lover's quarrel can be so romantic when you kiss and make up. You need to be all pretty and soft when he comes home, so he finds you irresistible and forgives you anything. Now confess to me, darling, what did you do? Did you spend too much money?" Elizabeth asked sympathetically as she opened the doors of Caroline's closet and expertly began searching through the extensive wardrobe for something beautiful for her daughter-in-law to wear. She pulled out a pink lace peignoir set.

"No. It's not about money," Caroline answered as Elizabeth emerged from the closet. If only her trouble with Alex were about something so ordinary. That icy snake of fear curled around her stomach again, and she clutched her hands across her waist. For once Caroline was grateful for her mother-in-law's chatty nature. It made it easier now to not have to explain anything.

"Well, I'm sure it's nothing that can't be fixed. Although you do look very distressed, dear. But these things happen in a marriage. Lord knows, John and I had our share of arguments! Here, put this on, darling, and some sweet perfume. Something very feminine. So he can't resist you." She helped Caroline undo the buttons of the lavender day dress and slip into the pink peignoir set as she continued talking. "Don't ever go to bed angry with each other. That's the first rule of a good marriage. Even if you have to stay up all night! Just say you are sorry, even if it is his fault, because then he will feel so contrite that he will apologize too. Before you know it you're both kissing and you've forgotten all about your silly, little quarrel. But if it is his fault, it's good to let him suffer a little bit, but not too much. If you punish a man too much, there's no telling how he will react. You need to make him squirm just enough to teach him a lesson, and I'm sure Alex needs to be taught a lesson. All men do at some point. But still it would be good for you to be a little sad and pretty when he comes home, smelling sweet and acting demure. It never fails. There. You look lovely now. Let's loosen your hair a little. Let it fall around your shoulders. That's it. Men can't resist long, beautiful hair."

The tears sprang unbidden to Caroline's eyes, and she could not stop them. How terrible it was to have this kind and caring woman give her marital advice when she had lied to her and was not even legally wed to her son! She was not Alex's wife. She was Mrs. Stephen Bennett and had to move to Virginia next week to be with her lawful husband. Away from her family and friends. Away from the life in London she had grown to love.

Away from Alex.

That hurt more than all the rest. She could easily give up everything if she could still be with Alex. Nothing else mattered. But it was all lost to her now. She couldn't have Alex, because she had never really been his in the first place.

"Oh, darling, you mustn't cry!" Elizabeth exclaimed with dismay. "You'll make your eyes all red and puffy, not at all attractive. It's only your first lover's quarrel. It is nothing really. This is just the first of many, believe me." Attempting to calm Caroline, Elizabeth smoothed her golden hair gently with her hand and dabbed at her tears with a lacy handkerchief. "Alex mustn't come home and find you this way. It's too much. A woman must use her charms to win a quarrel. Only use your tears as a very last resort. Only if all else fails or if it's to get something you desperately want. Use your tears sparingly, my dear, or they lose all effect. Men can't abide constantly weeping wives. You cannot cry over your first quarrel, although it is rather touching. What happened, darling? Tell me. Was Alex casting eyes at another woman?"

At that question, Caroline sobbed hysterically. The irony of the situation was too much. Elizabeth should be consoling her son, not her! Alex did absolutely nothing wrong. He was the injured party. He had only loved her and wanted to give her everything. She was the one who had lied. She had ruined his life. The disgrace of it all and losing Alex forever was just too dreadful. Tears fell helplessly down her cheeks.

"Oh my. This is serious, isn't it." Elizabeth's concern showed on her face. She embraced Caroline in a motherly way. "If I know anything at all, my dear, it's that my son loves you deeply, Caroline, and that you make him very happy. I'm sure he will forgive you anything. You're his wife and he will always stand by you."

Caroline's sobs increased their intensity at Elizabeth's kind words.

Elizabeth's expression grew somber, and she handed Caroline another handkerchief. "I'm going to have more hot tea sent up to you, and I think you should go to sleep. I'm sure Alex will be home soon, my darling."

* * *

But Alex did not come home that night. Or the next two nights. And Caroline had no answers to give to the unspoken questions in the eyes of his mother, his brother, and the servants. She had pleaded illness in her written regrets to the dinner parties to which she and Alex had been invited and were now obviously not going to attend. Declining all visitors, she kept to her rooms and waited for Alex to return. She had been spared a visit from her grandmother so far, but her sister stopped by on the third day demanding some answers.

Emma bustled into Caroline's suite of rooms late that afternoon smartly attired in a crisp green plaid day dress with a matching bonnet that sported a jaunty black feather. "I'm hearing some terrible rumors, Caroline. What in heaven's name is going on? You and Alex have not attended a single gathering since Lady Weatherby's party."

"Alex and I have had a misunderstanding, that's all," Caroline lied, using the same excuse she had given his mother. Unable to help herself, she asked, "What have you heard?"

"Well," Emma hesitated, "are you sure you want to hear?"

"Yes," she answered reluctantly. Caroline knew she deserved whatever rumors were circulating about them, but Alex did not. Hoping they weren't too horrible, she sat upon the blue-striped damask chair in her sitting room. Emma was seated on its twin across from her.

"I coaxed John into telling me," Emma explained grimly. "He spoke to Alex at White's last night. Alex was very drunk and gambling heavily, which is quite unlike him and concerned John. He told John to mind his own business and to be wary of the Armstrong women." Emma sniffed indignantly at that last remark. "Alex has apparently been spending his days drinking and gambling at White's."

"And . . . his nights?" Caroline hated to ask, but she had to know the truth. Female intuition told her where Alex was each night. She just needed it confirmed.

"I had to do quite a bit of wheedling to get this last bit of information out of John. But he finally told me, although not in so many words." She glanced at Caroline and then just said it. "Alex has taken up with his mistress again."

"Oh." Closing her eyes, Caroline fought a surge of nausea at the thought of Alex with Lily Sherwood. Although she had no right to be upset with him for turning to another woman when she was married to another man. Still, it stung. What they had shared was so special that it hurt to know that he was now intimate with another.

Emma continued, "I've heard from Betsy Warring that you threw Alex out of the house. I've heard from Lucy Greenville that Alex is tired of you already and regrets marrying a little nobody from the country. Who knows how many other rumors are flying around that everyone is too polite to tell me." Emma sighed and then posed the question she was dreading. "I hate to ask, but does this have anything to do with Stephen Bennett being in town?"

Caroline hesitated before answering guiltily, "Yes."

"Oh Caroline! Please tell me that you're not still in love with Stephen Bennett!" Emma's voice was laced with scorn.

"It is very complicated," Caroline choked out

miserably. How would she ever be able to explain any of this to her family?

Losing all patience, Emma snapped caustically, "What is complicated about it? You are married to a duke, for heaven's sake! And a very handsome and charming one at that, one who worships the ground you walk on! Do you know how many girls would trade places with you? Forget about Stephen Bennett!" The black feather on her bonnet bounced with each outraged toss of her head, punctuating her angry words with a flourish.

"Do you think I don't know that?" Caroline retorted, full of frustration. "I would give anything not to be in the position I'm in right now! But you don't know what you are talking about, and this is something I have to take care of myself!"

Emma stared at her sister. "I'm sorry. I shouldn't have spoken so harshly to you. I haven't the faintest idea what is going on between you and Alex. It's just that I don't want to see you do anything with Stephen Bennett that you may come to regret."

"It's all so complicated, and I wish I could explain more to you. Although I will soon. I apologize if my actions will cause you to be hurt in any way," Caroline said sadly.

Emma's sweet face registered her alarm. "You're frightening me, Caroline. What is going on?"

"I can't discuss it with you now. But I will soon, I promise. I just need some time. I desperately need to talk to Alex."

There were only four days left until Stephen would come for her. Only four days. Caroline simply had to see Alex. She had to explain to him. Time was running out, and she couldn't sit at home and wait for him any longer, especially when he was so obviously avoiding her. It was time for her to take control of the situation she had created. She had to go and find Alex herself, and she knew she didn't stand a chance of gaining entrance to White's. Besides, it was too public. There was only one other option. She turned to Emma, who had been staring at her fixedly. "Do you happen to know where his mistress lives by any chance?"

"Of course not!" Emma was aghast at the question when a more dreadful thought occurred to her. "You're not actually thinking of going to her house, are you?"

Caroline did not respond but stood determinedly.

"You couldn't possibly do such a thing!" Emma cried, her voice rising in pitch.

Caroline's mind raced ahead, and she made her way to the door. Elizabeth would know. Elizabeth knew everything about everyone and, more important, she would tell Caroline what she needed to know. "I have to speak with Alex's mother at once."

"Caroline, please don't do anything drastic," Emma begged, her hazel eyes slightly widened with panic. "Think of our reputations. My engagement to John is being announced tomorrow night at the Talbots' Holiday Ball. You and Alex will be there, won't you?"

"I hope so, but I honestly don't know. I'm sorry, Emma," Caroline apologized in advance to her sister, hugging her tightly, not knowing how all of this would end.

CHAPTER 21

Lady Madeline Parkridge smiled victoriously as Oliver, wearing only his silk dressing robe, entered her candlelit bedchamber.

It had been a most rewarding evening, and she congratulated herself proudly for a job well done. Even her unpleasant husband couldn't ruin her good spirits tonight. Her blue eyes glittered, and she continued smiling at her reflection in the mirror as Oliver kissed her neck eagerly and unfastened the buttons down the back of her blue gown and untied the ribbons of her wide crinoline. As was their nightly ritual, Madeline raised her arms obediently above her head and Oliver lifted her petite body out of the voluminous layers of fabric that had enveloped her and carried her to the bed, where he laid her upon the silk pillows, her yellow curls spilling around her smiling face.

If Oliver wondered at his wife's secretive smile, he knew better than to ask her about it. He accepted her mercurial moods without a second's thought and enjoyed her rare good favor whenever offered. He pulled the lace chemise from her smooth shoulders, fondling and kissing her perfectly shaped breasts, and he covered her naked body with his own.

At the start of their marriage, Madeline had been genuinely repulsed by her husband's sexual behavior, but over the months she had grown accustomed to what she now regarded as his nightly worship of her body. Even though she knew she dared not refuse him and she no longer attempted to evade his advances, not once did she ever touch or kiss him in return or speak a word in response to him. She simply lay beneath him, listening to his groans and grunts, and let him pleasure himself within her.

Although she hated to admit to herself, there were moments when she felt she could almost take her own pleasure in this peculiar act of marriage. It was an elusive feeling, however, and some nights she felt herself teetering on the brink of something wonderfully mysterious but could never quite reach wherever it was. Which left her strangely angry and disappointed when Oliver was finally through. She tried to determine what it was on those vague occasions when she fleetingly enjoyed her husband's naked body pressed against hers and came to the conclusion that it had something to do with her consumption of red wine. Which she had plenty of earlier that evening.

And what an evening it had been!

The Greenvilles had hosted a dinner party, and of course, Oliver's cousin Stephen Bennett tagged along with them. After a dessert of soggy English trifle and listening to Lucy Greenville's younger sister Annabel play a painfully long set on the pianoforte, Madeline managed to corner Stephen alone in the study. She didn't know which was more boring, Annabel's piano recital or listening to Stephen's tales of Virginia, but her perseverance paid off quite well. By feigning concern for his emotional well-being, Madeline gained Stephen Bennett's confidence so much that he finally confessed to her a secret more scandalous than she had even dared to hope for! Of course she had promised him total discretion with respect for his unusual predicament, which she promptly disregarded. Her mind raced to plan how to use this devastating information to her best advantage, and she practically floated home on a cloud of anticipation.

Madeline now had the power to completely ruin Caroline Armstrong's life!

Just the thought made her giddy with excitement, and she unconsciously reached up and stroked Oliver's bare back with her hands. Unaware of her husband's stunned stare, Madeline felt a thrill coursing through her veins and arched her back, pressing herself against him. The sensation was so enthralling it caused her to catch her breath.

Astonished by his wife's sudden response, Oliver brought his mouth down upon hers in a passionate kiss. His heart almost stopped as Madeline's mouth opened in invitation and her small tongue darted into his mouth. He kissed her greedily, savoring each moment his tongue intertwined with hers. An intense, heavy heat spread between their bodies.

Spurred by a feeling she couldn't name, Madeline needed to caress his back, and she pulled him closer, her fingers moving higher to thread into his soft brown hair. She felt him quiver at her touch as their kiss deepened. It was an odd sensation to want to touch him, but she reveled in his response to her. She kissed him hungrily, her mouth seeking something intangible, and again she sensed that awareness of pleasure just beyond her reach.

"Oliver . . . please . . ." she murmured, a faint plea for she knew not what.

He held Madeline tightly to him, fearing that releasing her would break the sudden spell she was under. Aroused beyond reason that his frozen little wife was actually displaying such ardent feeling, he whispered fervently in her ear, "What is it, Madeline, my little doll? What do you want? I'll give you anything . . . anything . . ."

Suddenly inflamed by a spark of desire she didn't know she possessed, Madeline's shapely legs slowly opened in silent proposal to him. Unexpectedly stimulated by Oliver's moan of pleasure as he rammed himself into her, she found herself rising up to meet each of his thrusts as forcefully as he gave them. She gripped him tightly, her long fingernails raking into the soft flesh of his back.

"Oh God, Madeline. I knew it could be like this for us . . . I knew it. Oh, Madeline, I love you. I have always loved you . . ." Oliver confessed in heated breaths as he continued to drive into her.

Gasping in amazement as Oliver finally admitted his love for her, it was then that Madeline realized that she had been playing her husband all wrong. Instinctively, she knew the balance of power had just shifted in their marriage, and in her favor. Simply by using her body she could now control him, manipulate him, arouse him. A thrill of power raced through her.

Now she could rule Oliver Parkridge *and* destroy Caroline Armstrong!

As that double realization dawned, Madeline screamed out in ecstasy as wave upon wave of pleasure at last washed over her petite body. She had finally found what she was searching for.

CHAPTER 22

It was just after midnight, and the heavy, gray clouds that had overshadowed London for days finally cleared to allow a bright full moon to shine down on the sleeping city. The typical dense fog was absent, leaving the darkness crystal clear. The cobbled streets were vacant, and an icy December chill imbued the night air with an eerie stillness, which echoed the dread in Caroline's heart. She swallowed her nervousness and peered cautiously out from the carriage. Dressed in a sumptuous gown of deep green velvet with black lace edging, she had allowed Elizabeth Woodward to arrange her hair in a loose cascade of honey-gold curls.

"You must look the part tonight. Beautiful. Sad. Serious. Dramatic," Elizabeth had asserted, helping Caroline into the full, black woolen cape that would shield her identity.

Not only had Elizabeth given her Lily Sherwood's address, but she also suggested that Caroline hire a carriage and wear a dark cloak so she would not be easily recognized, should anyone happen to see her. From her wide and varied sources, Elizabeth had discovered the truth of her son's nocturnal visits to his former mistress before Caroline learned of it from Emma and understood the desperateness of the situation. Eager to help Caroline put her marriage to rights, she volunteered the essential information with a heavy dose of womanly advice, all the while regarding Caroline's plight as a grand, romantic adventure, as an obstacle to true love that had to be overcome, as a challenge that had to be boldly confronted.

For Caroline it was a blessing to have such a supportive mother-in-law, even though she was positive that Elizabeth would not be so supportive if she were aware of the true reason Alex had left her.

"Go and bring him home where he belongs, my darling," Elizabeth counseled before Caroline departed in the hired coach. "I don't know what is happening between you two, but I know that he'll melt when he sees you again. You can fix whatever is wrong, I am sure of it. Be careful not to let anyone see you. Being caught at the home of your husband's mistress would not do at all! But a woman must do what she has to do to keep her husband. Now, off with you and good luck, my darling," Elizabeth whispered in expectation. She gave Caroline's hand a final squeeze of encouragement.

When the hired carriage stopped in front of the elegant stone house on a quiet lane just outside Belgrave Square, Caroline instructed the driver to wait for her, but she remained seated within. No longer swept up in Elizabeth's positive predictions and romantic allusions, but now alone in a cold, darkened carriage, the seriousness of the situation in which she had thoroughly immersed herself settled upon her like a shroud. She was about to knock on the door to the house of Alex's mistress.

Filled with trepidation, she wondered at the kind of reception she would receive from this unknown woman. Would she slam the door in her face? Would she be rude and insulting? Was Alex even inside? Would he listen to her if he were? Would he throw her out? What if, horror of horrors, she found them in the throes of a compromising position? She would rather die!

Shaking her head in misery, she sincerely reconsidered the whole venture.

Caroline knew nothing about Lily Sherwood but knew Alex quite well and therefore assumed that Miss Sherwood had to be incredibly beautiful and terribly sophisticated, which left her feeling inadequate and countrified. What would Alex have confided in this woman about her? Had he told her everything? Her heartbeat increased its pace and, not for the first time, she seriously contemplated asking the driver to take her back home. However, her desire to see Alex again, to explain and apologize to him in some fashion, far outweighed her imaginary fears of meeting his mistress and facing his wrath at her audaciousness in visiting her house.

Having nothing left to lose at this point, Caroline took a deep breath and left the safety and warmth of the carriage, her head covered by the woolen cloak. She hurriedly climbed the few front steps of the house, her black cape billowing around her, and knocked hesitantly upon the solid door. Tucking her hands into the folds of the cape, she waited and shivered, her nervous breath creating little clouds of moisture in the wintry air. After perhaps a minute, she knocked once again with more force.

There were candles lit inside the windows and smoke drifting from the chimney, which indicated that, indeed, someone was at home, although no one answered the door. She stood shivering in the darkness, berating herself for making another mistake by coming here.

You're a great fool, Caroline Armstrong, she scolded herself, *charging over to Alex's mistress's house in hopes of winning him back when you are married to another man!*

Losing her nerve completely and thinking better of her wild plan, she turned away feeling defeated and pondered how she would attempt to find Alex again, when the door unexpectedly opened, casting a path of warm light down the steps.

"Can I help you?"

Her heart in her mouth, Caroline slowly twisted around to face the lilting, almost musical voice from the house.

A stunning woman stood before her. A tall, slender body draped in a clingy white satin robe, trimmed with white fur at the cuffs, collar, and hem, posed informally in the doorway. The first thing Caroline noticed was the silky black hair that fell in a straight curtain to her waist and framed a face beautiful in its simplicity. Instinctively she knew that this woman knew how beautiful she looked and used it to her own advantage without compunction. And she got what she wanted because of it.

Completely intimidated, Caroline trembled, now not sure what to say, if she ever had been. Should she ask if Alex was there? Should she state her name first? Would this woman ask her to leave? Nervous and tense, and feeling like an utter fool, she simply stood there.

* * *

Lily Sherwood knew instantly who the young woman with the frightened eyes was. It could only be Alex's little wife. A mixture of emotions stirred within her. Jealousy. Rivalry. Anger for whatever it was that she had done to hurt Alex so terribly.

She had never seen Alex in such a state.

Six months ago when Alex ended their affair, he had been a complete gentleman about it. In fact, he had left Lily so well off that she had not needed to acquire another protector. Now financially independent, but still recovering from her futile love for him, she had not yet sought out the company of another man. But Lily Sherwood was no fool. She knew Alex was too much of a gentleman to ever come back to her, for he was madly in love with his young bride and would remain unfashionably faithful to her. It was just a matter of time before Lily felt strong enough to accept one of the many offers she had received from the wealthy noblemen. She had been the Duke of Woodborough's mistress, and that added quite a bit of cachet to her desirability as a mistress among London's men about town.

After she and Alex parted on the best of terms, and with no hysterics from her, for which she prided herself, Lily had not even seen him once. So it took her by complete surprise when he arrived on her doorstep three nights ago, drunk and miserable. Never had she seen him in such a pitiful state. Nor had he divulged any details about his obviously harrowing problems with his wife, only mumbling incoherently about lies and betrayal and deception. Lily could see that Alex was deeply wounded by whatever his wife had done. After being intimate with him for more than five years, she knew Alex very well, and this man was truly devastated by something. Lily could only guess what had happened. Intuition told her it had to be another man. What else could be so dreadfully wounding to a husband? Although she was gratified that Alex had come back to her, it broke her heart to see him so distraught. She had silently cursed the conniving little wench she pictured as his wife for hurting him so.

Now that same wife stood before her, hidden in her dark cloak. She was not at all what Lily had imagined her to be. Amazed that this little slip of a girl had such power over Alex, a ripple of sympathy for her washed over Lily. She looked so young and frightened. It must have taken a great deal of courage for her to come here tonight.

"He's not here yet, but you can come inside and wait if you like," Lily offered quickly, before she could change her mind. She saw the surprise register on the girl's face.

"Yes, thank you. I'm Caroline—" she began uneasily.

"Oh, I know who you are. Just as you know who I am. And we both know why you're here."

Caroline simply nodded, visibly grateful she need not explain.

"Please come in." Lily stepped aside, inviting Caroline into her house. The house that Alex had bought for her and where they had spent many blissful hours together. Before he was married, of course.

Taking a deep breath to steady herself, Caroline relaxed slightly, and due to the warmth of the room, she removed the hood of her cloak.

Now it was Lily's turn to be stunned. Looking at

Caroline in the light she could see that Alex's little wife was an exceptionally beautiful woman. Her long, golden hair glistened in the firelight, spilling around her in silken curls. She had perfect facial features: a small and straight nose, a sensual and alluring mouth, pale clear skin, and fathomless green eyes with surprisingly long, dark lashes. She was petite and graceful, and Lily just knew that beneath her velvet gown she had a perfect body. There was a simple aura of loveliness around her, a guilelessness that was difficult to define. She was definitely not your typical London debutante. Lily had assumed that Alex's wife would, of course, be pretty, if not beautiful, but there was something else about Caroline that Lily knew attracted men to her. Whatever it was, it had unquestionably caught Alex. If she could bottle that look and sell it, Lily would make a fortune.

"Can I get you something? A cup of tea, perhaps?" Lily suggested when she found her voice again. Then she added on impulse, "Or maybe you would prefer a glass of wine?"

"Thank you, but no."

"Well, he should be here soon. Hopefully he won't have had too much to drink tonight." Self-consciously Lily pulled the ties of her white satin robe tighter around her slender waist. It wasn't often she entertained guests in her home. Certainly not fine ladies at this late hour. And definitely not Alex's wife!

"Thank you for allowing me to wait," Caroline began uncertainly. "I suppose you're surprised to see me here."

"Frankly, yes." Lily sat down gracefully upon a small, cushioned divan, wondering what Alex's reaction would be when he arrived to find his little wife here waiting for him.

Caroline stammered, "Has he told you . . . about . . . about us?"

Lily responded with candor, calmly inspecting the red lacquer on her long fingernails. "Not in so many words. But he is quite devastated by whatever you did to him."

Caroline wrung her hands. "It's very complicated, and, unfortunately, all my fault. I just need to explain something to him. Then, I promise, I'll leave."

"You can stay as long as you need to," Lily offered with a careless shrug of her shoulders.

An awkward silence descended upon them. Suddenly Caroline wished she had asked for tea, for at least it would occupy them while they waited. She felt too silly to ask for it now. She removed her cloak entirely and falteringly sat herself on a small tapestry-covered chair and twisted the gloves in her lap. She uneasily glanced around the room. Why, it was lovely! Candles flickered cheerily in the sconces on the wall, a fire glowed warmly in the hearth, while beautiful and comfortable chairs and sofas were tastefully arranged around a thick oriental rug. The aroma of coffee, mingled with the clean scent of recently polished wood and a hint of a floral perfume, created a pleasant odor. A small Christmas tree stood in the corner, adorned with popcorn and cranberry garlands and tiny foil stars. The whole room was serene and inviting. Even cozy. Not quite sure what a "kept" woman's house would look like, she had envisioned a mistress's dwelling to be somewhat lurid and exotic. Oddly enough, the Dowager Duchess's decoration of Summerfields was more in keeping with her ideas of what the home of a mistress would be like. To her surprise, Alex's mistress had good taste.

Her heart hurt to think of Alex here with her. She felt the urge to cry but suppressed it. Now was not the time.

Now all there was to do was wait for Alex.

The ticking of the clock on the mantel seemed to echo through the room. It was close to half past twelve now. Minute after minute passed in strained stillness. The two women looked at each other in helpless, uncomfortable silence.

"You're very beautiful, Miss Sherwood. I can see why Alex would come to you," Caroline blurted out before she realized how terribly gauche she sounded.

Lily raised an elegant eyebrow, somewhat amused by the odd comment. "Thank you. I can say the same to you. He made a fine choice in a wife."

"Not quite," Caroline mumbled with slight sarcasm.

Once again, silence fell and the minutes ticked by. They avoided each other's eyes anxiously.

Suddenly the front door burst open and Alex's presence filled the room. He was disheveled and had the heavy shadow of a beard along his jaw. The unfocused look in his eyes was due to the many glasses of whiskey he had consumed earlier that evening. His tie was missing and his shirt collar was undone, while his gray wool topcoat was draped over his arm, obviously not having been worn on such a chilly night. There was a sheepish, lazy grin on his face until he saw Caroline sitting in the corner. His eyes became instantly alert and cold. Savagely, he muttered a vile curse and flung his coat across the room, knocking over a delicate china vase with a splintering crash. No one moved.

He tossed a brief and accusatory look at Lily, then stared at Caroline.

"I thought I made it clear that I didn't want to see you ever again."

Lily flinched at the tone of Alex's voice and the harshness of his words. "I think I shall allow you both some privacy," she murmured tactfully. When neither gave a response, she glanced at both Caroline and Alex and swept up the stairs to her bedroom.

Caroline rose to her feet and faced him with a brave squaring of her shoulders. "Please let me explain. I owe you at least that much." She took a hesitant step toward him, looking small in comparison to his towering, angry presence. She said a silent prayer that he would give her this chance.

"Get out." His words were harsh and flat, his body tense.

"Please, Alex. I'm begging you." Her hands were clasped in apprehension and in supplication. "Just listen to me first. Please."

CHAPTER 23

Alex stared at Caroline in disbelief. How dared she show her face here? It took every ounce of Alex's self-control not to turn and run from her. He had been such a complete fool over her. Caroline was no longer his wife, and in fact never was, nor had she really loved him. The man she truly loved, the one she had been secretly longing for all this time, had finally come back for her. She didn't want Alex anymore, so what was she doing here? Why hadn't she run away with her American soldier yet? Didn't she understand that he couldn't bear the sight of her? That just looking at her broke his heart? What was the little idiot thinking, coming here to Lily's of all places?

He heard her murmur softly, "I'm so sorry. I never meant for this to happen."

Alex sank heavily into the leather chair behind him and buried his face in his hands, expelling a breath of air in a long, low hiss. He could not look at her. "Ah, Caroline," he ground out in anguish from behind his hands. "Why didn't you just tell me the truth from the beginning? Why?"

Caroline rushed to him, kneeling on the floor at his feet, her dark green velvet dress pooling around her like the blossom of a huge flower. She placed her hands on his knees. "I'm sorry," she whispered quickly. "I wanted to tell you the truth so many times but was just too afraid. I didn't know what to do. I was so ashamed. Oh, Alex, I am such a fool."

He lowered his hands from his face and looked at her for a long time. She sat before him like an imploring angel. Wide green eyes reflecting the deep emerald hue of her gown. Delicate features shadowed softly by the candlelight. Glowing skin, lightly suffused with a flush of color. Loose golden curls glistening below her shoulders. Dainty hands resting on his knees. God, why did she have to be so beautiful? Why did just looking at her make him want to pull her into his arms and kiss her? Why did he love her so much? And after what she had done to him.

Grabbing her angrily by her shoulders, he shoved her back on the floor, knocking her legs out from under her until she was supine and he was lying on top of her. He leaned his full weight over her, his legs capturing hers on both sides, the strength of his body pinning her to the floor, his hands cradling her head, his face barely an inch from hers. His blue eyes flashed with ire, and he bitterly ground out the words between his clenched teeth, "Do you have any idea what you have done?"

He knew she was frightened of him. Her breathing increased, and her green eyes were wide with fear. She should be frightened. He felt like killing her. He laced his fingers through her hair, pulling too tightly upon the loose curls, forcing her face closer to his. He glared at her.

"Do you have any idea what you have done?" he repeated huskily. "Do you have any idea what this means? To me? To my family? Your family? The humiliation . . . The shame . . . Do you realize the extent of the scandal you have created and how many people it affects?" He shook her slightly, his fingers pressing into her shoulders, leaving impressions on the dark green velvet of her gown. "Do you?"

He watched her take a gulp of air and attempt to speak out, but he didn't give her a chance.

"And do you have any idea how much I love you? So much so that I'm ready to forgive your lying heart, steal you from your American husband, and run away with you."

Before she could react, he brought his lips down on hers with bruising force, kissing her savagely, with the intent to hurt her. His teeth cut her lip, and he briefly tasted blood. The rough stubble of his unshaven beard scratched and scraped the delicate skin of her face. He assaulted her with his tongue, capturing her, punishing her, burning her mouth and lips with his.

And Caroline returned his kiss as fiercely as he gave it. Suddenly he gentled and began kissing her softly, slowly, seductively. A familiar molten heat began to spread between them. His hands, no longer pinning her to the floor, moved across the length of her and caressed her. He continued to kiss her deeply, and she reached up to put her arms around him.

Abruptly he stopped and pulled her roughly to a sitting position, releasing her as if she had scalded him. Leaving her unbalanced, she quickly braced herself from falling backward by pressing the palms of her hands into the carpet behind her.

"Explain," he commanded, his voice hoarse. "Before I change my mind."

Still trembling, Caroline nervously sat up. She bent her knees and clasped her arms about them. Taking a shaky breath, she ran her hand across her face and absently smoothed her tousled hair. She began awkwardly to explain why she was already married to another man. "Well . . . we were . . . married . . . the day he left for America—"

"I don't know about you, but I need a drink," Alex interrupted, as he walked across the room and poured himself a straight whiskey from the crystal decanter on the mahogany sideboard. His hands trembled, from too much alcohol or too much emotion, he wasn't sure. He rubbed his throbbing temples with his fingers and exhaled the tension that wracked his entire body. He could not believe that she was actually here at Lily's. That he almost made a fool out of himself again by making love to her on the floor. God, but he wanted her. She had that effect on him, like a moth to a flame. Swigging down the drink in one gulp, he slammed the glass on the table with a resounding clink and poured a second.

How could she be married to another man?

He had been completely and utterly stunned since he had found her on the sofa with the American's arms around her. Since he had first met her, he had believed that Caroline was only nursing a girlish infatuation. That he could make her forget this young boy, whoever he was. That she would eventually fall in love with him. Now he dreaded that Caroline would say that she had never stopped loving Stephen Bennett.

How could I have known?

Good God! He had married a married woman!

All because he had kissed a sad and beautiful young woman one night and lost his heart to her. Because he had the most remarkable feeling that she belonged to him. That he belonged to her. And, more important, that they belonged to each other. He felt it in his soul that she had touched something deep within him that no one had ever seen before. And he fell more in love with her as the days passed. He had always liked a challenge and knew it would be one to get her to forsake her sweetheart, but he had always imagined the goal to be attainable. It never occurred to him that the reason she didn't want to marry him was because she was already married!

Why would she lie about something like that? How could she marry him, knowing full well that she was married to another? He had thought of nothing else since finding out the truth.

Why? Why? Why?

He had also had time the last few days to think about his own role in this awful situation, and he had to claim some responsibility for pressuring her so much. It pained him to think about it.

He downed his second drink in one fluid movement and quickly poured a third. With glass in hand, he joined Caroline on the thick carpet in front of the fire. The anger had dissipated from his eyes and he looked at Caroline expectantly, somewhat calmer now that he had more whiskey to fortify him. "Go on. Before I change my mind."

She sat up a little straighter, but he could sense the nervousness in her posture. Her golden hair glistened in the firelight, and his breath caught at the sight of her. He fought off the desire to pull her into his arms and hold her, praying she had a good explanation for all this.

She took a deep breath and began. "Stephen was a student at the university where my father taught. He was from Virginia, but his family sent him here to keep him out of the war. I met him while assisting my father. I'd never really had . . . You see . . ." She paused. "I'd never had a beau before Stephen."

That surprised Alex, but he nodded his head.

"At first my father approved of Stephen, but then I think he was afraid that Stephen would take me to Virginia with him. He hated the fact that the Bennetts owned slaves. Then my father forbade me to see Stephen anymore. I tried to obey him and break off with Stephen. But Stephen was too insistent and I . . . I was too weak. When he told me that he was going home to America to fight for the Confederacy, I was terrified of losing him and couldn't bear the thought of his leaving. But he promised to come back for me when the war ended, and I promised to wait for him. He said that we would marry when he returned to England and he would take me to live in Virginia. I had no idea how I was going to explain this to my father, but I figured that I would reason with him when Stephen came back. So we began to meet in secret. It was difficult for me because I knew my father was very disappointed in me for loving Stephen, when I had always been his pride."

Caroline's soft voice was calm, almost detached, as if she told the story about someone other than herself. Alex watched her intently, scrutinizing her expressions and inflections, and waited for her to continue.

"I remember it was terribly hot and humid the day

Stephen left. The kind of day when everything sticks to you. We met in an unused cabin on a nearby estate, where we had met secretly a few times before. I was trying to be strong and not cry about his leaving. I was surprised that Stephen brought a friend with him. But he explained that his friend was a chaplain and could marry us that day so we wouldn't have to wait until he returned. I said I didn't want to be married that way, in secret, without my father or Emma with me, but Stephen was too persuasive and I couldn't seem to say no to him. The ceremony is a blur to me now. I can't even recall what was said, except 'I do.' We signed the license, and his friend left us. Then we were alone . . . and then Stephen . . ." Her voice trailed off, and she stared into the orange flames of the fire.

"And then Stephen what?" Alex prompted her, knowing in his gut what her response would be.

Caroline looked him in the eye knowingly, then glanced away. "He kept telling me it was okay, because now we were married and that's what married people do with each other. He said that this way he knew I would be his, that I would . . . belong to him forever. That then he couldn't lose me." She closed her eyes briefly as if the memory were painful. "But I knew we shouldn't have done it. After we . . . afterward . . . he made me promise not to tell anyone. Then he left." She turned to look at Alex with an almost defiant apology in her eyes. "And I waited for him to come back."

"Ah, Caroline," was all he said. Sordid and vivid images of her and Stephen together flashed unbidden in his mind. Images he most definitely did not want to see. He hated to think of Stephen Bennett, or any other man for that matter, touching her. The

picture she painted was so clear to him, probably
clearer to him than it was to her. He had such a different perspective of what had happened between
them than he had first imagined. It wasn't at all
what he thought. It was not some heroic soldier's
love story with a happy ending. Stephen Bennett
took advantage of Caroline, used her selfishly to
brand her as his own, and then callously abandoned her to an unknown fate. It was a tragedy, for
her and for him. Alex shook his head slightly, as if
to erase the undesirable imagery from his mind.

They sat in silence for some time. Alex, eager for
something to occupy himself with, added more kin-
dling to the fire. Caroline continued to sit and stare
at the flames, rocking gently back and forth.

"Didn't you write to each other?"

"I wrote to him every week, and yet I only received one letter from him in all that time. I
thought maybe the post was unreliable because of
the war, or perhaps he was badly wounded and
unable to write to me. I stopped writing after a year
with no response. I didn't know what happened to
him, if he even survived the war."

"You never told anyone? Not even Emma?" he
asked at last.

"No one."

"So why did you keep it a secret after your father
died? You could have told your grandmother that
you were married."

"I was too ashamed," she admitted. "I had lied to
my father. I had disobeyed him. I married against
his wishes, in secret, and knowing what I did would
devastate him. When he died a year later, no one
knew about Stephen. I couldn't suddenly explain to
everyone that I had been secretly married for a year

to a man my father disapproved of. By then, I still hadn't heard a word from Stephen. I didn't know where he was or if he were alive or dead. I was beginning to think I would never see him again. The marriage seemed unreal, like a hazy dream, as if it never happened. So what difference did it make to tell anyone? I could go live with my grandmother and not think about him anymore. But then she started planning my debut and settled a dowry on me. Everyone said I was sure to get a proposal right away. I didn't know what to do. They were trying to find a husband for me when I already had one. I thought if I could just get through the Season without attracting any attention, I could escape it all. So I came up with the plan of being dull and bookish. It seemed to be working. Then I met you." She paused in reflection. "You didn't want to get married either. I thought I was safe with you."

"Then I pressured you to marry me," he stated darkly, finishing the last of his whiskey.

"You. And my grandmother. And Emma. Then your mother. Everyone wanted me to marry you. Look at you." She gestured pointedly to him with her hand, a helpless expression on her face. "What possible excuse could I give to make anyone believe that I didn't want to marry *you?*"

He grimaced guiltily. But there was something he still didn't understand. "But how could you think you could marry me when you knew you were already married?"

Caroline hesitated. "I . . . I hadn't heard from Stephen for two years . . . and I reasoned that he must have forgotten all about me or died in the war. By then I didn't believe he was ever coming back for me. Since no one knew about him, it was easy to keep the whole thing a secret, which I promised him I would do anyway. My marriage to him, if you can even call it that, seemed as if it never really happened." She leaned into him, touching her hand to his shoulder. "I *wanted* to marry you, Alex. Every time you asked me was like torture. I wanted to be your wife and couldn't be. I told you I couldn't marry you. I wasn't lying to you, and I tried to tell you the truth, Alex, but I felt so ashamed. I knew that everyone would be very disappointed in me if they found out, especially Grandmother. At that point, it seemed foolish to throw my life away while waiting for a man who was obviously never coming back for me. So I did what everyone expected me to do. But I wanted it too, Alex. I wanted to marry you more than I have ever wanted anything in my life. I knew I would be happy with you. I could be myself with you. I didn't have to pretend that I wasn't intelligent, that I didn't like books, or that I knew nothing about history and art. You made me feel special, and I wanted to be with you."

"And so you married me, and he came back for you after all." Alex sighed heavily, feeling unbelievably sober and rubbing his temples with the pads of his thumbs to loosen the tension.

"He was at the cathedral," she confessed, "the day we married. I saw him in the crowd as we were leaving."

His movements stilled, and he stared at her as understanding dawned. "So that's why you fainted."

She nodded. "Oh, Alex, I'm so sorry. I never did this to hurt you."

"I'm sorry too. I tricked you into making that deal with me, thinking I could persuade you . . . I wanted to marry you from the start. If I hadn't pressured you, and had everyone else pressure you, if only I had believed you when you said you couldn't marry me, this wouldn't have happened."

"No. This is all my fault," she protested, shaking her head resolutely. "It's all mine. For an intelligent girl, I've made some very foolish choices. I should have told the truth from the start, beginning with my father."

"That night at Lady Weatherby's? Was that the first time you saw him?" Alex had been ridiculously happy that evening, just back from his honeymoon and so proud to escort his beautiful new wife. He recalled the American standing there, shaking Alex's hand. Nothing seemed out of the ordinary at the time.

"Yes. I hadn't seen him since I fainted at the cathedral. Even then, I was convinced that I had only imagined it. I had no idea he was Oliver Parkridge's cousin, and I was stunned to see him at Lady Weatherby's. I wasn't sure if he'd told anyone he knew me, but we both acted as if we didn't know each other. I panicked when he came to see me the next day at home. That's when you found us."

Alex's eyes were heavy and dark. The image of Caroline sprawled on the sofa with the American practically lying on top of her had tormented him every waking second until he thought he would go mad. He had drowned himself in fine liquor and hid himself at Lily's, unable to face Caroline and the entire mess. "I thought I could make you forget him."

"Oh, but you did," she whispered, a warm smile on her face, her eyes shining. "I could never have married you if I still loved him. I always wanted to be with you, Alex, even when I said I couldn't. I was meant to be your wife, not Stephen's. I don't know that I ever loved him at all really. I didn't know what love was until I met you. *You* are the only one I love."

Alex gazed into her green eyes, his heart pounding. "Say that again."

"I love you."

It was unbelievable. He had been waiting months to hear her say those words, dreamed of her saying she loved him. He had begun to think that she would never give up her first love. "Do you know that this is the first time that you have ever spoken those words to me?"

She nodded in understanding. "I think that I was afraid to. Afraid to admit that I loved you from the start."

"Why?"

"Because I knew that I couldn't truly belong to you . . ."

"You do belong to me. We belong to each other." Alex pulled her into his arms, holding her close, and he kissed her. Caroline's warmth and her scent seeped into him. The feel of her in his arms soothed an ache inside his heart that nothing else had ever come close to easing. "Oh, Caroline. Do you have any idea what you have done to my heart? My soul?"

"Only what you have done to mine." She tilted her head up so he could kiss her again. "I'm so sorry. Can you ever forgive me?"

How could he not forgive her? He loved this woman with all his being. "I don't know that I have much of a choice," he murmured ruefully. "I love you too."

"Oh, Alex, thank you. I don't deserve your forgiveness, but thank you." She kissed him, her hands caressing his face lovingly.

"What happens now?" he asked her.

Her expression clouded with fear. "Stephen is coming for me the day after Christmas. To take me back to Virginia with him. I don't want to go."

"You're not going," Alex said decisively, with a determined look. "I won't let you go. We'll think of something. I'll talk to my solicitor. There must be a legal way out of this awful mess. I promise that I will never let Stephen take you from me."

"I'm so afraid of what will happen," she whispered fervently, thankful that Alex still loved her, still wanted her, and hopeful that she could remain with him somehow. "How can you even love me after all of this?"

"I just do, Caroline. I just do." He pressed his lips against hers, holding her tightly. "Let me take you home now."

CHAPTER 24

Alex had gone upstairs for a short while and come down alone. Whatever he said to Lily Sherwood Caroline never did find out, but they left her house immediately in his carriage and said not a word to each other the entire ride home. As soon as they returned to the townhouse, however, Alex lifted her in his arms and carried her with purposeful strides through the dark and quiet house up to the privacy of their bedroom.

Alex's breathing was heavy as he lowered her to the bed, covering her petite body with his long, muscular one, while Caroline's own breath came in short gasps of anticipation of what he was going to do to her. It felt like an eternity had passed since they had been together.

He kissed her lazily, as if he had all the time in the world, but with a decidedly purposeful air about him. He was going to savor her, and she was glad of it.

His lips, his incredible sensual lips, pressed against her mouth, and he tasted faintly of whiskey. She breathed him in, his scent, his being, his maleness.

It excited her. She opened her mouth in invitation to him, sliding her tongue deep into his mouth to meet with his. They drank of each other. The feelings grew in intensity, increasing with their every movement. She reached for him, caressing the back of his neck, stroking her fingers through his soft black hair, pulling him closer and closer. She couldn't seem to get close enough to him. To show him just how much she loved him. How much she wanted to be with him.

A potent, languid heat flared and smoldered between them, belying the December chill outside, and Caroline, suddenly sweltering, struggled to remove her green velvet gown. Alex gently turned her over so she lay on her stomach, and lazily he unfastened each tiny velvet button on her back, his warm fingers sending intense pulses of heat through her skin, directly into her throbbing veins. Molten kisses descended along the length of her spine as he undid each velvet button, the hot breath from his mouth causing her to shiver. He slowly eased her out of the gown and the layers of lacy undergarments beneath. When she was finally free of the many confines of her clothes, he turned her back around to gaze upon her naked body, her golden hair spilling in silken waves around her.

"Nothing happened with me and Lily," he whispered thickly, his face close to her cheek, his blue eyes intent. "I only slept at her house at night."

She stared at him; his feelings for her were written openly on his handsome face. They were in the softness of his blue eyes as he gazed upon her. They were in the tender corners of his mouth, smiling at her. They were in the earnestness of his dark brows, as he nodded in confirmation of his words. This man loved her. And God, she loved him.

"Oh, Alex, thank you." Caroline wept. Tears spilled like a little fountain down the sides of her cheeks, dripping into her ears. The thought that he had been intimate with Lily this past week had tormented her. He was not married to her and it was within his rights, yet still . . . It touched her, thrilled her, that he had not forsaken her, when he so easily could have.

"I thought that would make you happy. Not cry."

"I am happy," she whispered chokingly.

"Then don't cry, my love." He tenderly kissed away her tears, licking a trail to her ears. "You have the most perfectly shaped little ears . . ."

She laughed in spite of herself. "I love you so much." There was nothing left to hide from anymore. He knew everything now. All her secrets. He still loved her. More important, he forgave her. It was all she ever wanted and more.

"I love you," he murmured in response, caressing her cheek, wiping a stray tear. "More than I thought was possible."

Her eyelids fluttered closed, and she drew him toward her.

Alex kissed her then, teasingly, temptingly, deliberately, as if he wanted to claim her once again as his own. His kisses scorched each part of her, and the rough stubble of his unshaven beard left tender burns across her smooth, white skin. Over and over, he rained kisses on her lips, face, cheeks, and neck. Drinking her in. Devouring her. She wanted him to bury himself in her.

Slowly traveling lower down her shoulders, he moved from kissing her breasts to kissing her stomach to kissing her hips. His tongue scalded a path down the length of her shapely body until he came to the delicate juncture between her thighs. His hot tongue licked her most intimate place, caressing her there, and Caroline shuddered with the pleasure of it. It lasted an eternity, his tongue swirling around her, teasing, tickling, pressing.

"Oh, Alex . . ." she murmured weakly, lost in the sensation, her fingers wrapped tightly in his dark hair. She felt complete abandonment. Complete surrender. Complete and utter bliss. Suddenly overcome, she cried out from an explosion of ecstasy.

Before she could even catch her breath, he spread her long legs and pushed himself inside her, with slow, deep thrusts, losing himself within her, over and over again, in a timeless rhythm. His mouth returned to hers, kissing her thoroughly, hungrily, as he continued to move over her, his pace quickening with the intensity of the feeling. She matched his every thrust, opening herself to more pleasure and the sensations built anew. His breathing was heavy, and she lost herself wholly in the sensation, until at last, they both called out each other's names.

"A package just arrived for you, my lady," Harrison informed a bleary-eyed Caroline the next morning.

Exhausted, both physically and emotionally from the trauma of the last few days, she rubbed her temples as the throbbing of a headache blossomed, and she fought off yet another wave of nausea. "Thank you, Harrison. You can bring it here to me." She sipped her weak tea, having skipped breakfast, too tired and tense to eat.

A bright and cheery Elizabeth entered the parlor, followed by somber Alex. The Dowager Duchess winked conspiratorially at Caroline, pleased that their little plan was successful in bringing Alex home.

Caroline offered Elizabeth a wan smile. Yes, Alex was home, but her troubles were far from over. Stephen Bennett was still coming to claim her.

"I'm off to do a little Christmas shopping this morning. Would anyone care to join me?" Elizabeth asked. She adjusted a pert bonnet upon her head.

"No," Alex and Caroline moaned in unison, both suffering the effects of a sleepless night, and in Alex's case, a little too much whiskey as well.

"It seems some people were up rather late last evening!" Elizabeth teased, as Caroline accepted a small parcel from Harrison. "Who is the package from?"

"It appears to be a gift from Sally Rogers. She was our housekeeper at Lilac Cottage. She practically raised Emma and me after our mother died," Caroline murmured absently, reading the familiar handwriting scrawled on the package wrapped in plain brown paper and string.

"I hope it's something nice," Elizabeth said, slipping into her fur-trimmed coat. "Don't forget we have Emma and John's engagement at the Talbots' ball this evening. It will be wonderful to have you both together again! We can say you have recovered from your 'illness,' Caroline. Get some rest, both of you, and I will see you later." Elizabeth smiled warmly at her son and daughter-in-law as she departed.

* * *

Grateful that his mother had left them alone, Alex pondered the peculiar situation in which he found himself. After his initial shock and fury had receded upon seeing Caroline on her knees before him at the home of his former mistress, some small semblance of sanity returned to him. There had to be a way out of this mess. He certainly would not let Caroline sail to America in two days with another man.

Another man.

Yet that man was her legal husband. His gut wrenched at the prospect of losing her forever. He would do anything in his power to prevent that from happening. Maybe an annulment was possible. Then he and Caroline could marry again, legally. He had already sent a message informing his solicitor to expect to see him this afternoon on a matter of the utmost urgency. If anyone could figure a way out of this mess, Geoffrey Claypool could.

The story Caroline told last night played repeatedly in his mind. Something about it did not fit, and a seed of an idea sprouted in his brain. If he could only find the proof, then his marriage could be saved and a terrible scandal avoided. Would his hunch prove correct or would it just give Caroline a false hope if he mentioned his theory to her?

A sudden gasp from Caroline caused Alex to turn to her. "What is it?" he asked, his brows furrowing in concern. Caroline held a sheet of paper in her trembling hands. She looked as if she'd seen a ghost. "Caroline, what is it?" he asked again.

She looked at him with a dazed expression on her face. "Sally didn't think I should marry him, so she kept them from me. She hid all of our letters," she whispered.

"What letters?" asked Alex. A feeling of unease crept over him.

Her eyes fell back to the wooden box in her lap. "My letters. Stephen's letters." She looked up at Alex again. "He did write to me, Alex. All this time I thought he didn't write to me, but he did." She stared at the small, plain box, which held the undeniable truth of her secret relationship with Stephen Bennett. She handed him the letter from Sally.

Alex took the letter from her and read it himself.

Dearest Caroline,

Now that you're happily married to the duke, I'm returning these letters to you as they are rightfully yours. I probably shouldn't have hidden them from you, but I only did what was best for you and tried to keep you safe. It was what your mama and papa would have wanted me to do. I know you made your dear mama proud, marrying as you did. Better than that no-account American boy. I thought you might find these letters amusing now.

Keep an eye on Emma. Make sure she marries as well as you did. You know I think of you as my own daughter and I hope you can find it in your heart to forgive me if this upsets you. Merry Christmas!

All my love,
Sally

Alex grew quiet, and they sat in awkward silence for some minutes. A troubled and heavy feeling settled into his chest. Was it only last night that Caroline whispered that she loved him for the first time, making his heart soar? Would reading Stephen's letters after all this time alter Caroline's feelings now? Would the letters from her legal husband cause her to fall back in love with him? Suddenly Caroline's declaration of love last night seemed unbelievable.

Sighing wearily, he stated in a clipped tone, "This changes things, I see. These letters from your husband."

"Should I read them?" She gazed helplessly at him, missing the fact that he had referred to Stephen as her husband.

"I don't know." The timbre of his voice was flat. He wanted her to fling them into the fire, declaring that they belonged to her past and did not matter. Suddenly Alex was afraid. Afraid that Stephen's written words would be too much of a temptation for her, that she would choose Stephen over him. The impulse to leave her alone with her past was too strong to ignore, for he could not stay and watch her read them. He stood abruptly and made his way toward the door, touching her lightly on the shoulder as he passed by her chair. "I think I will go out after all."

"Alex?" She reached for his hand, but it was too late.

He paused by the door. "Yes?"

She shook her head. "Nothing."

As he closed the door behind him, he watched Caroline take a deep breath and carefully open the first letter.

Close to an hour later, almost noon, Harrison entered the parlor where Caroline sat reading alone. "There are some visitors to see you, my lady."

"Please tell whomever it is that I am not at home." Caroline did not notice the worried look on the butler's face, since she did not look up from the letter she was reading. It was the last one in the box. The letters had transported her back to the little village of Shrewsbury and the terrible pain and guilt she had endured after Stephen had left her. Rereading her own words, as well as his, from a new perspective created a strange feeling inside her. She didn't know Stephen at all, had never truly known him. Her father had been right. He was not the man for her. How blind she had been. And so incredibly foolish.

Harrison cleared his throat loudly. "You have visitors, my lady."

"Mmm?" Caroline murmured distractedly, still reading.

"It's Lady Parkridge," Harrison said nervously, trying to maintain his usually calm demeanor and failing. "And she has a constable with her."

That caught Caroline's attention. Looking up, she stared at Harrison blankly for a moment. If Madeline were here, it could only portend bad news. And with a constable? Her heart began pounding rapidly in her chest. It suddenly occurred to her that she was home alone. She tried to recall where Alex had said he was going and remembered that he had left her rather coldly. "The duke hasn't returned yet?" she asked without much hope.

Harrison shook his head sympathetically. "No, my lady."

"Could you please try to send a message to my husband, Harrison? That I need him home as soon as possible."

"I'll send a footman to find him right away. About the visitors . . . Lady Parkridge seemed most determined to see you. I must say, the constable did not appear overly friendly. Is there some trouble, my lady?" Harrison looked genuinely concerned.

"There might very well be." Caroline closed the box with Stephen's letters, placing it on the small cherrywood table beside her, and stood up. Squaring her shoulders and brushing her hands across the front of her navy blue wool dress, she faced Harrison. "I assume they are not here on a social call, but have some tea sent in anyway. You may show them in now, Harrison. Thank you."

He nodded, somewhat worriedly, and left the room.

Caroline wrung her hands nervously as the throbbing of her earlier headache resumed with full force. She was light-headed and dizzy. There was a tightening in the back of her neck. It was noon, and she hadn't eaten since yesterday when Emma came to call. She had been so consumed with finding Alex at Lily Sherwood's house last night that she had not had supper. Indeed, she had been too worried and nauseated to eat much of anything in the days following Alex's discovery of her marriage to Stephen Bennett.

Why would Madeline come to see her with a constable? If this had something to do with her marriage to Stephen, then where was he? She wished, not for the first time, that Alex were home with her.

The door opened, and Madeline Parkridge sailed into the parlor looking as fresh and dainty as ever. Her yellow curls peeked out beneath a delicate, silver knit bonnet that matched her long, silver cloak. A white fur muff was clutched in her small hands. Her blue eyes sparkled and challenged Caroline silently. Behind her followed a tall and gangly officer of the peace, wearing a standard black hat and cape. His face was hard with a rather bulbous nose and ruddy cheeks.

The constable cleared his throat noisily and spoke with a deep, gravelly voice. "Good afternoon, Your Grace. I am Constable Harry Jones, and I'm afraid that I'm here on some very unpleasant business. I take it your husband is not at home?"

"I told you that the duke is *not* her husband!" Madeline snapped irritably at the man, her blue eyes flashing.

Caroline's heart sank at Madeline's remark, but she ignored her and managed to smile politely at the constable. "No, sir. I am afraid my husband went out earlier today, but I am expecting him momentarily. Please sit down. May I offer you some tea, Constable Jones?"

"No, thank you, Your Grace." He cleared his throat again, his large hands folded together behind his back. "Some very serious charges have been brought against you. I had hoped the duke would be at home to clear this up. Unfortunate thing this is. People don't go making charges against a duchess like yourself willy-nilly, but Lady Parkridge here insists she knows that you are not truly married to the duke. Says she has proof and all. With her being a lady of the nobility, I got to take her word."

"What about my word?" Caroline inquired softly, her eyes on the constable.

"Thing is, you're the one being charged, Your Grace. So your word don't count for much. Now if the duke was here—"

"Well, he's not, is he?" Madeline interrupted hotly. "Arrest her!"

Caroline's eyes widened in alarm. She couldn't breathe.

Constable Jones shifted his tall body uncomfortably on his feet, nervous at being in the middle of an argument between these two pretty noblewomen. One of them a duchess, no less. Lady Parkridge had offered him a handsome sum of money to accompany her on this little visit, and with it being almost Christmas he figured he could use the extra income to surprise his family with some special gifts, so he accepted her unusual offer. Lady Parkridge seemed a bit temperamental, but the money was too good to pass up. He assumed it was just some silly female misunderstanding and intended to clear the whole mess up quietly with the duke himself. Now he wasn't so sure. The duchess was very beautiful but quite frightened. He took note of the dark circles under her eyes. She didn't look like she had been resting with a clear conscience. Constable Jones possessed a strong sense of right and wrong. He looked sternly at the little duchess. "You know that it's a grave crime to be married to two different men at the same time, ma'am?"

Paralyzed with fear, Caroline stared at them. Caught. She was caught. Her secret was truly out now. Stephen must have told Madeline everything.

"Is it true that you were married to a Mr. Stephen Bennett of Richmond, Virginia, well over two years before you married the Duke of Woodborough in November?"

Madeline smiled viciously, waiting for Caroline's response. She finally had Caroline Armstrong where she wanted her!

"I thought . . ." Caroline stammered weakly. "It was . . . He—" She stopped. Maybe it would be better not to say anything until Alex was home. She pleaded with the officer wordlessly.

Constable Jones stared at her, his hard eyes intense. "Is it true?"

"Of course it's true!" Madeline interrupted with impatience, an unflattering scowl on her face. "I already informed you that her real husband, Stephen Bennett, told me of their marriage himself. He is my husband's cousin, so I know he is telling the truth. He and Caroline were married in Shrewsbury over two years ago, and then he went to fight against the slaves in America! Mr. Bennett doesn't want to cause any trouble, so he is going to try to take Caroline to Virginia before anyone finds out what really happened. This woman has played the duke for a fool and tricked all of London. How can she stand here and pretend to be the Duchess of Woodborough when she knows perfectly well that she is married to another man? She is a bigamist, for heaven's sake! She needs to be punished!" Madeline's voice reached a fevered pitch as she concluded her tirade.

"Lady Parkridge, please contain yourself!" Constable Jones looked down his bulbous nose at Madeline, somewhat taken aback by her outburst. He sensed there was something else altogether going on between these two women. However, the fact remained that a serious crime might very well have been committed and the little duchess was not protesting the accusations, which lent credibility to Lady Parkridge's charges. He had to bring her in for questioning.

Madeline sniffed indignantly, turning her pert little nose up in the air. "But I'm right, aren't I, Caroline?" She twirled her white fur muff carelessly, glaring at Caroline in triumph. "Aren't you really married to plain old Stephen Bennett and not the Duke of Woodborough?"

Caroline covered her face with her hands. How could she deny the truth? Every word Madeline said was true. She was a bigamist. She deserved whatever punishment she got.

Nervously clearing his throat, Constable Jones announced as gently as he could, "I'm afraid you'll have to come with me, ma'am. To stand before the magistrate."

It was all over now. She had made her bed, and now . . . Well, there was no escaping the consequences now. Accepting that her little secret had finally been revealed, she asked in a trembling voice, "Couldn't you please wait and discuss this when my husband comes home?"

"HE IS NOT YOUR HUSBAND!" Madeline shrieked at the top of her voice.

The constable turned to gape at her, but Madeline merely smiled at him.

"I'm afraid I can't wait, ma'am," he said, having the uncomfortable feeling he was arresting the wrong woman. But she was not the one paying him. "You'll have to come with me now."

"Where are you taking me?" Caroline asked worriedly.

"Where else do they take common criminals, you little bumpkin?" Madeline sneered with a satisfied gleam in her eyes. "To Newgate Prison."

CHAPTER 25

After spending a good part of the afternoon at White's having a whiskey or two to ease his lingering hangover and brooding over the love letters that Caroline had received, Alex realized he was not accomplishing anything just sitting there drinking. The letters were the least of his problems. There were more serious complications involved, and he didn't know if his heart could survive losing Caroline again. Not after she said she loved him.

It was quite unbelievable.

His wife was married to another man, who was planning to reclaim her, and God help him, Alex still loved her.

After leaving his club, he called upon his long-time solicitor, Geoffrey Claypool, Esquire, to learn his thoughts on the situation. At Mr. Claypool's orderly and comfortable office, they discussed Caroline's marriage to Stephen Bennett at great length. Alex explained as much as he knew. Mr. Claypool opined that an annulment might be viable, given the hurried and secretive circumstances of the marriage, as well as the fact that the young man in question had abandoned his new wife immediately after the ceremony. Mr. Claypool had many questions regarding that fateful day that only Caroline could answer, so Alex invited his solicitor to come by the house for dinner later to meet with her.

In the meantime, Alex decided that he and Caroline should act as if nothing were amiss to quell any rumors while obtaining an annulment as quickly and discreetly as possible. They would maintain appearances as usual and attend the Talbots' ball that evening. As for Stephen Bennett, Alex owed that gentleman a friendly visit. He stopped by the American's hotel but learned Mr. Bennett was out. That confrontation would have to wait.

The snow that had begun to fall earlier, covering the streets in a blanket of fine white powder, made traveling somewhat slow, and it took him longer to return home than he anticipated. When he finally arrived, his London townhouse was in a state of turmoil. His mother was wide-eyed and frantic, pacing back and forth, while Olivia Fairchild was seated on the sofa, sobbing and wringing her hands. Caroline was nowhere to be seen. He looked to Harrison for answers.

"What the devil's going on here? Where is Caroline?"

His usually staid butler was very upset. "They took her, Your Grace," Harrison mumbled with agitation.

Confused, Alex shook his head. "Who took her?"

"The constable and Lady Parkridge."

Alex knew that this did not bode well at all. "The constable and Lady Parkridge? Where?"

Harrison cleared his throat. "To Newgate Prison."

Newgate! Alex's heart froze in his chest. Caroline in Newgate Prison? Suddenly he knew. Somehow,

Madeline Parkridge had found out about Caroline's marriage to Stephen Bennett. So much for keeping everything a secret. He stared in disbelief at Harrison.

"We must get her out right away!" declared Olivia, panic stricken.

Alex answered emphatically, "Of course we'll get her out of there."

"I sent for Olivia as soon as I found that Caroline was gone," Elizabeth explained. The usually light girlish tone was absent from her voice. "We've had footmen searching for you all over the city, Alex. Why would they take our darling Caroline? What could she possibly have done wrong? What does Madeline Parkridge have to do with any of this?"

Charles Woodward burst into the room, his wool coat and top hat covered with snow, an expression of worry on his usually smiling face. "Alex, what in the hell's going on? One of the footman just told me that there is a great emergency and that Caroline's in danger!"

Alex simply stared at them all.

Harrison, his kindly eyes blinking back tears, said, "I should have tried harder to stop them. Lady Caroline looked very distressed when Lady Parkridge arrived. Since you were not at home, I was concerned for her welfare, and if you'll forgive me, I listened in on her conversation with the constable. I didn't want to say anything until you were here, Your Grace." He paused nervously, eyeing the Dowager Duchess and the Countess of Glenwood. "You can count on my discretion one hundred percent, of course. It seems that Lady Parkridge has charged your wife with bigamy. They took her to Newgate."

"Dear God in heaven!" Olivia exclaimed, her

hands pressed to her cheeks and her eyes wide in disbelief. "What does that mean?"

"Bigamy?" Elizabeth cried out in dismay. "Alex, what do you know of this?"

Wearily, Alex turned to his butler. "Thank you very much, Harrison. I appreciate your efforts, as I'm sure the duchess does. I know we can depend upon you to keep this matter very quiet. Could you please have Hubert ready my carriage with fresh horses immediately? Also, please send a footman around to Mr. Claypool's house with an urgent message for him to meet me at Newgate Prison just as soon as he can," Alex commanded quietly with a grim face.

Harrison expediently left the room.

"Alex, what is all this about?" Elizabeth demanded with impatience, her hands placed on her hips.

Alex looked resigned. "I was hoping to keep this quiet and settle it in private, but that's not a likely possibility at this point." He sighed heavily. "It seems Caroline was married in secret two years ago back in Shrewsbury to an American from Virginia, who happens to be Lord Parkridge's cousin. Which obviously makes her not legally my wife. He has finally returned for her. I only learned of the situation myself a few days ago. A fact that apparently had not escaped Madeline Parkridge. It now seems she has reported Caroline to the authorities."

"Oh my. Whatever did Caroline think she was doing?" asked Elizabeth.

"An American from Virginia . . ." Olivia echoed in complete bafflement, sinking down into an overstuffed armchair. "Why didn't she tell us about any of this?"

"She didn't want to disappoint you, as her mother did," said Alex quietly. Aware that this information was devastating to Olivia, he explained gently, offering a glimpse of hope. "I've just met with my solicitor, and an annulment may be possible. There are some details to work out first, and then Caroline and I can eventually marry again. However, we didn't anticipate Lady Parkridge becoming involved and having Caroline arrested. This seriously complicates things."

"I can't bear to think of Caroline in Newgate. Let's go get her out of there now and sort it all out later," Charles hastened them impatiently, turning toward the door.

"I'm going with you," Olivia declared, rising from the sofa and wiping her eyes.

"But tonight's the Talbots' ball and Emma and John's engagement," Elizabeth pointed out. "What will everyone say if we are not there?"

"She's right," Charles remarked. "It won't look good."

"Nothing looks good right now," grimaced Alex. His brow furrowed and his hands clenched. "But you have a valid point, Mother. Let's try to keep this as quiet as we possibly can. Olivia should go to the ball as planned. You too, Mother. Newgate is no place for either of you. Charles and I will bring Caroline home safely. You must go and try to keep up appearances. Tell everyone that Caroline is very ill or something of that sort. It doesn't matter what you tell them as long as they don't believe that she's been in Newgate."

Olivia began to cry again. "I hid myself shamefully from Katherine's scandal. I won't do it again. I know Caroline is a sensible girl and has a good explanation for all of this. I'm sure of it."

Elizabeth rose to the drama of the occasion. "Come now. Alex is right. We, at least, must attend the Talbots' ball to lay to rest any rumors, which, if I know Madeline, may very well have started already. We will put up a great front, all of us. Even Kit and Jane. No one would dare gainsay the Dowager Duchess of Woodborough, the Dowager Countess of Glenwood, and the Earl of Glenwood and his wife as well." She glanced at her own son with compassionate eyes. "Don't worry about us, Alex. We'll take care of everything here. Go bring Caroline home now. Good luck, my darling."

Newgate is a synonym for hell, Caroline declared to herself.

All afternoon she sat huddled on the filthy stone floor of a dank prison cell, for there was no bench or chair. In fact, there was no furniture of any kind, just some grimy straw scattered over the even grimier floor and some threadbare blankets for a pallet. The darkness of the place mercifully hid some of the filth from her eyes. She shuddered from both revulsion and the bitter cold.

The hasty trip to Newgate with Constable Jones was now a blur, but her entrance into the old prison was the most terrifying experience of her life. The haunting sounds and putrid smells were intensified by the appalling darkness. Inhuman voices, hysterical sobs, and crazed screams echoed along the damp stone walls, causing Caroline to shake with fright. If one was not mad upon entering Newgate, then one was certainly driven mad within. Led roughly to her cell by a fat, leering guard with thick, wet lips, she had stumbled, and he grabbed her arms tightly and tried to kiss her neck. Constable Jones slapped him over the head.

"Keep your fat hands off this one, Jerry, if you know what's good for you. She may or may not be a duke's wife. He don't know yet that his pretty little lady's been arrested. So when he comes charging down here to have her released, he won't take too kindly to her being mistreated in any way. He'll probably pay nicely for her though. Unless, of course, she has duped him. Then you can have her."

Jerry shoved Caroline into the small cell and slammed the gate shut, leaving her alone. She was thankful that Jerry was at least smart enough to heed the constable's advice, although his words made her shiver.

The rotting, fetid smells nauseated her at once, and she vomited in misery, tears in her eyes. Because of her empty stomach, Caroline continued to gag wretchedly for the first hour of being imprisoned. When she found her small lace handkerchief, which was scented with lavender, in the pocket of her blue wool dress she managed to hold it over her nose to ease the stench and calm the nausea, bringing her a little relief. The numbing cold of the icy stone floor had left her chilled to the bone, and every muscle in her body ached.

She lost track of time. She could have been there for hours or days. At one point, someone brought her a dirty tin plate laden with a kind of moldy gruel and a cup of cloudy water. She couldn't bring herself to touch it, let alone consume it. But she took some small satisfaction in kicking the offensive dishes across the muddy floor.

Caroline sat there, huddled with her arms around her knees, hugging her cloak close to her, shivering. She dared not guess at the scurrying and skittering of tiny paws around her and struggled to ignore the putrid odors saturating the dank air, as she tried to block out the gut-wrenching cries of the other prisoners.

She was only getting her due.

She had lied to her family and betrayed their trust.

She had lied to Alex, the man she loved with all her heart and soul. She had ruined everything, and she deserved every minute she sat there.

What a foolish little idiot she was to think she could ever get away with this! She should have told the truth from the beginning. She should never have married Alex. There was no one to blame but herself. She deserved to rot in this prison.

That thought made her gag again.

Oh, Alex!

Did he even know where she was? Would he come for her? She longed for him to do just that. Although she couldn't blame him if he didn't. He had forgiven her last night when they got home . . . He still loved her. Surely, he would find a way to release her.

A shrill scream from another cell caused the fine hairs on the back of her neck to stand on end. As it continued, she covered her ears with her hands to silence the pitiful, endless screeching.

Thoughts of Stephen and Madeline flitted through her mind. Did Stephen know that Madeline had her arrested? Was he looking for her? Why had Stephen told Madeline about their marriage in the first place? Why would Madeline go to the trouble of obtaining a constable? It was a sad victory to learn that her first instincts about Madeline Maxwell were correct. The woman hated her. At least now the feeling was mutual!

The awful screaming from the other cell suddenly ceased, and Caroline, thankfully, removed her trembling hands from her ears.

Grandmother and Emma. Aunt Jane and Uncle Kit. She could just imagine how they would react to learn that she was imprisoned for bigamy. For once she was grateful that her parents were not alive to see her now. They would be ashamed of her.

Too stunned and terrified to even cry, she sat there for hours, cold, numb, and in shock.

Alex and Charles raced through the bitter night as swiftly as they could, given the amount of snow on the streets, to the foul-smelling pit of a prison called Newgate. Alex had had only one glimpse of the rotten place many years ago, when he helped a friend in trouble, and his heart beat triple time as he imagined Caroline in there.

A discussion of sorts with the corpulent and dim-witted guard on duty informed them that Caroline could not be released until she had been brought before the magistrate, and seeing how it was almost Christmas, the magistrate would not be returning until after the holiday.

Shuddering at the thought of Caroline spending another second, let alone three more days, in that squalid hellhole, Alex was spurred to threaten the guard with dire consequences if his wife was not released immediately.

The fat guard had been there when Caroline was brought in and couldn't resist taunting the highfalutin duke. "Heard tell she's not really yer wife there, guv. But a nice and tasty morsel she is at that," he snickered.

Without hesitating an instant, Alex slammed his fist into the man's bloated face, feeling a great sense of satisfaction at the sound of cracking bone. The guard reeled back in pain, knocking his thick head soundly on the stone wall behind him. Alex was about to beat the offensive man to a bloody pulp, if not for Charles.

"Not the way to win the chap over, Alex," Charles advised rationally as he restrained his brother from raining more blows upon the dazed guard's head. "We need him on our side, remember?"

While Alex seethed beside him, Charles, in his usual charming and persuasive manner, calmed and bribed the injured guard with a small fortune and some not-so-thinly veiled threats on his life that convinced the man that the Duchess of Woodborough was being held unjustly and that he should release her into the duke's custody immediately.

After exacting their assurances that they would be held responsible if Caroline did not appear before the magistrate the day after Christmas, the obese guard, resentfully rubbing his sore jaw, then led the two brothers to the women's ward of the prison.

With the stub of an old candle he had purchased at an outrageous price from the fat guard, Alex was barely able to see Caroline through the bars and dim shadows. "Caroline!" he called. "Caroline, where are you?"

Her terrified voice responded in relief, "Alex? Oh thank God."

"Unlock the gate, my fine friend," Charles ordered the guard.

The sound of rusted metal scraping against the stone floor echoed through the chamber as the gate was slowly opened. Caroline's whisper of an apology was barely audible as Alex grabbed her to him, wrapping her in his heavy woolen cloak and lifting her securely in his arms.

"Let's go," he said to Charles, as he felt the shivers wracking Caroline's body.

CHAPTER 26

When they reached the exit of the prison, they met Geoffrey Claypool just as he was arriving. "They want her to stand before the magistrate after Christmas," Alex explained hurriedly to him. "But we convinced the guard to release her tonight."

"I see," answered the solicitor, not blinking an eye at seeing the Duke of Woodborough carrying his bedraggled duchess out of Newgate. "Your wife being imprisoned does complicate things somewhat."

For a man of small stature, Geoffrey Claypool had a very reassuring presence, with a head of thick black hair, a neatly clipped beard, a straight nose, and clear gray eyes. He was perfectly groomed and impeccably dressed. The only adornment to his otherwise sedate gray and black attire was a brightly colored tie, imprinted with flowers in vivid hues of yellow and orange. The effect was a bit startling.

Mr. Claypool spoke briefly to the guard and then turned his attention back to Alex and Charles. "Since you have posted more than a fair amount of bail already, I assured the nervous guard that the legalities would be observed and the duchess would be returning to see the magistrate at the appointed time. Shall we see the lady home now? I have my carriage just outside. The snow has stopped, and it seems to be clearing up."

Alex gave Charles a knowing look. Charles nodded his head in silent agreement. "I'll meet up with you at home, after I make a little stop." He flashed a reassuring smile to Caroline and hurried off into the night.

Alex and Caroline settled themselves in Geoffrey Claypool's large and comfortable carriage, which was furnished with heating pans and foot warmers. Small candle sconces were placed along the walls, giving off a dim light within.

Caroline was so grateful that Alex had come for her that she didn't protest when he insisted that she sit upon his lap but sank against his blessedly warm body. He covered her with a heavy carriage blanket, tucking it around them.

Relieved that she was merely suffering from cold and hunger and that no other terrible harm had befallen her, Alex promised to have her warmed up and fed a delicious meal as soon as they arrived home. As he wrapped his arms around her shoulders, he noticed how cold her ears were.

"Did you lose your hat?" he asked, rubbing his hands quickly up and down her arms in an effort to warm her. It was a silly thing, but she always seemed to lose her hat. Remarking on it broke some of the tension.

"I suppose so," she shivered through her chattering teeth, and he pulled her more tightly against him.

"Well, it seems you have gotten yourself into quite a tangled mess, my lady," the neatly groomed solicitor began, not bothering with obvious introductions. "I have some questions for you. But first, please take this . . ." He handed her a silver flask, indicating for her to drink from it. Accepting it with a shaking hand, Caroline took a small sip, felt the brandy burning her throat, and almost gagged.

Alex smiled at her fitful coughing. "Have another drink," he encouraged. "It will warm you up."

Hesitantly, Caroline swallowed a second mouthful of the burning liquid and surprisingly did begin to feel slightly warmer. She handed the flask back to Mr. Claypool. She could easily picture him wearing black robes and a long gray wig that all legal authorities were required to wear in court. If anyone could find a way out of this mess, she knew instinctively that he could.

Geoffrey Claypool stared at her with his intent gray eyes, his manner extremely professional. "The duke has told me all that he could, but there is some vital information pertinent to this case that only you can provide, my lady. Then I shall need to question Stephen Bennett as well. Let us start at the beginning, shall we? First of all, can you tell me the name of the person who married you and Mr. Bennett?"

Her head was spinning, but she tried to focus on the question. "I believe his name was Thomas . . . or Thomson. I don't remember exactly. He was a friend of Stephen's."

"Had you ever met this friend before?"

"No, I had just met him that day." She was amazed that he was able to jot down notes in the dim light while the carriage was bumping along the snowy street. His pencil moved with efficient speed across the page.

"Do you know where this person could be found?" he asked.

She shook her head doubtfully. "Maybe you could locate him through the university records?"

"Perhaps. Were you married in the Church of England?"

"No, in a cottage."

"Were there any other witnesses present at the time of the marriage?"

"No, it was just the three of us."

"That's good. Did Mr. Bennett give you a ring of any kind?"

"No, he didn't."

"And no banns were published, I take it?"

"No, there wasn't time." In fact, she did not even know they were marrying until five minutes before the ceremony.

"Why were you in such a hurry?" The little solicitor continued firing questions at her and scribbling on his tablet of paper.

"Stephen was leaving for America that day, to fight in the war."

"Why the need for secrecy?"

Caroline sighed. "My father did not approve of our marrying."

"I understand your father is no longer alive to support this statement?"

She nodded her head. "That is correct."

"How old were you at the time of the marriage?"

"I had just turned twenty."

Geoffrey Claypool paused a moment, his gray eyes darting quickly to Alex. "Forgive me, Your Grace. This next question is of a delicate nature, but the matter is integral to our case."

Alex gave a slight nod of assent, and the solicitor

directed his intense gaze back to Caroline. "Was the marriage consummated that day?"

Heat immediately suffused her cheeks with color as acute embarrassment washed over her like a wave on the sand. She closed her eyes.

Was the marriage consummated that day?

Recalling that sweltering afternoon with Stephen so long ago was unbearable. Misty images came to mind. The cramped wooden cabin. Scalding sunlight. Suffocating heat. Stephen, pressing her down on the hard little pallet, insisting that what they were doing was decent. His lazy voice whispering in her ear, pleading with her, over and over. "Carrie, Carrie, please don't cry. We're married. It's okay now. We won't tell anyone. Don't be afraid. I won't hurt you, I promise." She murmured yes. But then no. It wasn't supposed to be like that. She was unable to speak. Unable to stop him from what he was doing to her. He was holding her down, the heavy weight of his body controlling her movements. He was touching her, rubbing against her. His feverish kisses suffocating her. His eager boy hands tugging at the buttons of her pink gingham dress. A dress she was never able to wear again, so vividly did it bring back memories of that day. Of dirty pink gingham, damp and twisted, open to her waist and bunched up above her hips. Of hot, sweaty kisses and salty tears. Of Stephen's half-naked body, slick with perspiration, panting and groaning. Pushing against her, heaving over her, hurting her.

Everything had changed that day, in more ways than she could count.

Now, in front of Alex and a veritable stranger, she was expected to answer that complex question with one single word. Was the marriage consummated that day?

She opened her eyes and whispered, "Yes."

Under the blanket, Alex squeezed her hand in silent support. Although her affirmative answer was not news to him, she still could not meet his eyes.

Geoffrey Claypool continued in his businesslike manner, as if he asked these personal questions to women on a daily basis. "Was there a child resulting from this union?"

She shook her head in response. "No. None." She had thanked heaven for that bit of good fortune on more than one occasion. Alex's thumb caressed the palm of her hand in slow circles. Just his touch gave her strength.

"Did you sign a marriage license?"

Grateful to be on to less embarrassing questions, she answered with ease. "Yes. Stephen said it was a special license that his friend was able to obtain for us."

"Do you still have it in your possession?"

"Yes." She nodded her head.

"May I take a look at it when we arrive at the house?'

"Certainly."

"That's all for now, Your Grace. Thank you for being so cooperative." He organized his papers and returned them to the leather case.

Caroline leaned back against Alex, her head resting against his. He kissed her cheek lightly. She longed for nothing more than a hot bath and a soft bed.

"Do you think an annulment is possible, Geoffrey?" Alex asked, the tension in his voice evident.

The solicitor's expression was unreadable. "I don't like to presume, but I do think that we will be able to extricate ourselves from this matter. First, I would like to ascertain the legality of the marriage license itself. That could render an annulment a moot point."

Silence prevailed in the carriage after that comment as they made their way back to the Woodward townhouse.

When they arrived, Alex bundled Caroline in front of the fire in the study and ordered a veritable feast brought before her, although she was too tense to eat a thing and longed only for a hot bath. Bonnie was sent to their bedroom to retrieve the marriage certificate, which Caroline disclosed was hidden in a leather pouch packed at the bottom of her trunk. After Bonnie had given her the pouch and left the room, Caroline removed the thick papers inside. She unfolded one slowly. Handing it to Alex, she said, "This is it."

Alex looked over the document, noting that it was covered in intricately inked calligraphy, declaring it a Certificate of Marriage. Stamped with a wax seal and dated August 19, 1863, it was signed by Stephen Andrew Bennett and Caroline Olivia Armstrong, as well as another signature he could not decipher. It looked official enough to him. He passed the paper to Geoffrey Claypool, who examined it very carefully.

The solicitor glanced at Alex, then he looked toward Caroline. "Your Grace, this document is not a special license, nor is it a proper marriage license, failing to meet even the most standard clerical and legal requirements. The qualifications of the person who performed the ceremony are not listed. For all intents and purposes this license would not hold up in a court of law."

Stunned, Caroline gasped, "What does that mean?"

"It means, Your Grace, that this false document, in conjunction with the hasty and secretive ceremony performed with no legal authority or church sanctification, no parental consent, or reliable witnesses, makes your marriage to Mr. Stephen Bennett not valid. Which therefore makes your marriage to the duke quite legal."

Words escaped her, and Caroline stared blankly at the solicitor. Alex, however, his worried face breaking into an exultant grin, gathered her up in his arms.

"I believe that I shall allow you both a moment of privacy," the perceptive little man announced as he left them alone in the study.

"Do you know what this means?" Alex beamed. "It means that you are *my* wife and have always been my wife and no one else's." He cupped her face in his hands, his fingers laced through her hair, looking into her gorgeous green eyes.

"Oh, Alex, I'm your wife," she whispered with incredulity. "I love you so much." The relief was evident on her face.

"And I love you." He kissed her with infinite tenderness, holding her close to him. For almost a week he had been tortured by the belief that she was not his wife, when she had, in truth, been his all along. She always had been. He had come very close to losing her. If Caroline had not come for him at Lily's last night, he would still be drinking away his sorrows at White's and she would be leaving for Virginia with a man who was posing as her husband! His heart flipped over in his chest, and he longed to murder Stephen Bennett, clean and simple. He was suddenly aware that Caroline was crying. "What's wrong?" he asked.

She blinked at him, tears spilling down her cheeks. "It's everything. But it's relief mostly, I suppose. I feel terrible for hurting you," she said with a sniffle, wiping at her eyes and annoyed with herself for crying. "I'm just confused. I don't understand why Stephen would go to such lengths to make me believe that we were married when we weren't."

He sighed, his eyes flickering over her. "I'm not sure either. You'll have to ask him that question."

"He deliberately tricked me into signing a false marriage certificate."

"It might be that . . ." Alex paused before continuing. He could see it more clearly than she could. In fact, it was quite obvious to him. "It may very well be that he wanted you to believe that it was all right for you to be with him as his wife before he left for America."

She stared at him. She blinked.

He continued softly, "What I'm saying is, it just seems more than strange that there were no witnesses to the marriage, that there was no ring, that an unknown 'friend' of his performed the ceremony in haste, that he asked you to keep it a secret, and that *then* he coerced you into his bed. And left you afterward."

"Oh my God," she murmured, sitting up straighter on the sofa. "I am an idiot."

"No, you're not, Caroline."

"Yes. Yes, I am." She nodded her head. "You're right. What you said makes sense. It explains everything. All that summer Stephen had been wanting me to . . . asking me to . . ." Her eyes flew to his for the briefest instant. "I wouldn't do it. I couldn't. The day he left, I was so upset and I couldn't believe that we had just been married. I didn't want to, but I didn't know how to refuse him, and I just gave in. I thought he truly loved me. But when I look back now, I know that you are right, Alex."

"Caroline." He breathed her name, resting his forehead against her temple. "I'm sorry."

"I'm sorry, Alex. So sorry for all I've put you through."

"I'd go through all of it again if it meant that we would still be together."

"I love you."

"I can't tell you how happy I am to hear you say that, my beautiful wife." He spent several minutes just holding her close to his heart.

There was a soft knock on the door, and the Dowager Duchess, dressed in an exquisite gold and black silk ball gown, entered the study. "Mr. Claypool has just apprised me of the situation." She hugged Caroline. "My dear, I'm so relieved to see you home safely. We've been very concerned for your welfare. I did manage to convince your grandmother to go home to dress for the Talbots' ball. She was in quite a state of distress about you."

"So she knows what happened?" Caroline asked with trepidation.

"Yes, dear. I've just sent word to her that you have arrived home safely." Elizabeth patted her shoulder.

"Does Emma know? And Uncle Kit and Aunt Jane?"

"No. We thought it best to keep it from them unless absolutely necessary. But we are all attending the Talbots' ball to thwart any rumors," Elizabeth explained.

"Thank you. I don't know how any of you can forgive me for the shame I've brought upon you due to my own foolishness. I am truly sorry."

"We all make mistakes, my darling. I'm sure something can be done to undo this mess. Now, I'll excuse myself to finish dressing for the ball and leave you two alone." Elizabeth turned abruptly as the door flew open.

Charles Woodward burst into the room dragging Stephen Bennett by the arm, followed by Geoffrey Claypool.

"I found Mr. Bennett at his hotel and persuaded him to pay us a friendly little visit," Charles began to explain.

Alex leaped from the sofa in one swift movement and, before anyone could stop him, slammed his fist squarely into Stephen's jaw. Taken off guard, Stephen careened backward and tumbled to the floor as shrill screams issued from both Caroline and Elizabeth.

Charles quickly grabbed Alex to keep him from striking Stephen again. "I'll allow that you owed him that one, Alex, and probably more, but this is the second time tonight I've had to hold you off. Take it easy."

Alex stood aside, seething as Charles blocked his path. He wanted to kill the man. Geoffrey Claypool offered a hand to Stephen and helped him to his feet. Stephen's brown eyes flashed angrily at Alex, but it was to Caroline he turned. "I'd like to speak to you, Carrie." He gestured to the rest of the room. "Alone."

Glancing toward Caroline, Alex was torn between anger and apprehension. Caroline's face was pale, and the shadows under her eyes attested to her lack of sleep. She was close to exhaustion between the lack of food and the physical and emotional toll of the past week. Looking at her now, Alex wanted nothing more than to gather her in his arms, carry her to bed, and hold her close to him all night while she slept. "You have five minutes," Alex growled, glaring at Stephen, arms folded across his chest. "And I am not leaving."

Taking their cue, Geoffrey Claypool, Elizabeth, and Charles excused themselves at once.

Stephen rubbed his sore jaw, which was beginning to show the blossoming of an ugly bruise, and paced nervously, ignoring Alex's presence in the room. After a moment, he ran his hand through his blond hair and looked at Caroline. "Your lawyer told me that you now know that our marriage was not legal, Carrie. I am sorry. What I did to you is unforgivable. I won't even ask for your forgiveness, but I do want you to understand why I did it." His brown eyes pleaded with her as he stood awkwardly in the study with the Duke and Duchess of Woodborough. "Please believe me; I had every intention of coming back and marrying you properly. It was just that the thought of leaving you without marrying you was too risky for me. You were so young and beautiful; it was just a matter of time before someone would make you forget about me. I had to think of some way to keep you mine while I was gone, and at the last minute that was the solution I came up with. I knew your father didn't approve of me, but I thought if I allowed you to think that we were married, that would keep you safe until I could come back after the war and marry you in truth. I figured by then that your father might be willing to change his mind about me when he saw how much I loved you. I didn't know that the war would last as long as it did or that it would take me so long to return. I know you probably don't believe me, but I did write to you."

"I know you did," Caroline responded, a sad note in her voice. "I wrote to you too. Do you remember Sally?"

He nodded his head in affirmation. "She never did like me."

"She took our letters and hid them from me all this time and, oddly enough, just sent them back to me this morning. She thought she was protecting me from you. Now I see why she felt that way."

"I suppose it doesn't matter now," he sighed, his expression full of remorse. "Your brother-in-law also informed me that you spent the day in Newgate, for which I am sorry. It must have been unbearable. I'm sorry for telling Madeline about us. She seemed so kind and genuinely concerned with helping me. If I had any idea that she would want you in prison, I never would have confided in her. Why does she hate you so?"

"It seems that Madeline was under the impression that Alex was going to marry her, until he met me," she explained briefly. "Although I've always known that she hated me, it is shocking that she was capable of taking it so far."

"I'm sorry, Carrie." His voice was filled with sorrow, and he took a step toward her. He touched the sleeve of her dress.

Caroline flung her arm back, recoiling from his touch. Her eyes hardened. "You lied to me. You deliberately tricked me and took advantage of me before you left. What if you had gotten me with child? Did that possibility ever occur to you, Stephen? Do you have any idea what that would have been like for me? Alone with a baby and not even truly married, to face my family in shame? As it was, do you know what I went through while you were away? Wondering if I would ever see you again, if you had forgotten me, or if you were killed in battle . . . all the while wondering if I was still your secret wife. A secret that would destroy my father if he found out. And when he did pass away—" There was a slight catch in her voice. "When he did pass away, and my sister and I were left penniless, everyone's advice was for me to marry quickly—"

"Well, you certainly didn't waste any time marrying *him*," Stephen interrupted, gesturing with scorn toward Alex, "when you thought you were married to me!" He took a step closer to her, grabbing for her arm.

Alex watched the heated exchange with hooded eyes, steeling himself not to interfere, his jaw clenched in anger. This was Caroline's battle and she needed to fight for herself, although he longed to throw himself into the fray.

Caroline stood her ground with conviction, the hard look in her eyes daring him to advance farther. Stephen reluctantly withdrew his hand.

She continued with vehement rage. "I'm glad that I married him instead of wasting my life waiting for a schemer like you! When were you going to tell me that we were not legally married, Stephen? Only this morning I reread every letter you wrote to me, and that little fact seems to have slipped your mind completely. Did you think I would never find out the truth? Then, to come back here two years later to make me believe that we were still wed and attempt to steal me away from Alex! To cause me such pain and heartache, to threaten *me*, the woman you supposedly love, to force me to leave my true husband and family and run to America with you, when you *knew* I was legally married to Alex! How dare you, Stephen Bennett!" Her arm snapped out in a reflex action, and she slapped him across the face with all the strength she possessed. Her hand stung as she pulled it back to her side. She bit her tongue to stop the automatic apology that sprung to her lips.

Alex continued to observe the scene with an inscrutable expression on his face. Only the steady ticking of the ormolu clock on the mantel could be heard in the aftermath of her heated outburst. Standing like a stone statue, Stephen frowned, his brow furrowed in deep concentration. Caroline stood like a warrior princess, her delicate shoulders squared and her head high.

"My father was right about you," she denounced in a low voice. "How I wish I had listened to him and stayed away from you! You don't love me, Stephen. You never did. You couldn't possibly love me and treat me in such a manner. You don't even know what real love is. Neither did I . . . until I met Alex."

"I never meant to hurt you, Carrie," Stephen alleged, looking her in the eyes.

"Well, you did. And don't call me Carrie. I never liked that name."

Stephen sighed and ran his hand through his hair, a lost look in his eyes. "I am sorry. Nothing I've ever done was with the intention of hurting you."

Caroline glared at him. "While I don't mind for myself, I mind very much for what hurt your lies have caused to Alex and our families."

After a long pause, Stephen's voice was weak. "I

wish there was something I could do to make up for the misfortune I've caused."

Alex announced coldly, "You will appear before the magistrate with us and deny any marriage or involvement with Caroline."

Stephen nodded his head in agreement. "Yes, I will do that." All he could do now was to attempt to make up to Caroline the hurt he had inadvertently caused her.

"Then Mr. Bennett," Alex threatened unequivocally, "you can depart for America. Don't ever think of coming back here. Or I will personally have you thrown in jail for any number of charges." He stared at Stephen, and there was no misunderstanding his words.

Caroline announced clearly, "But first Stephen needs to come to the Talbots' ball with us."

"What?" Both Stephen and Alex questioned her in unison.

Caroline's green eyes flickered with spirit. "Yes, Stephen is coming to the ball with us. As a very dear friend of my father's from Shrewsbury to put to rest any rumors that Madeline may have started, which I've no doubt that she has. If we attend the ball, no one will believe that I was in Newgate this afternoon. If Stephen is with the Duke and Duchess of Woodborough, and with my grandmother, my uncle and aunt, and the Dowager Duchess in attendance, no one will believe anything Madeline might have told them." She looked toward her husband. "Lord knows there have been enough rumors about our marriage this past week, Alex. If we both appear as planned, and with Stephen, they will have nothing to gossip about."

Seeing the sense in her plan, Alex concurred

readily. "You will do this for her," he said to Stephen. He walked over to Caroline and placed his arm around her shoulders.

Stephen looked to Caroline with a somber expression clouding his boyish features. "I suppose I owe you at least that much."

"I suppose you do," Caroline retorted, taking Alex's hand in hers and squeezing tightly, absorbing the warmth of his skin pressed against hers. "I have one thing to do first."

She walked to the side table that held the plain brown box containing all the letters she and Stephen had written to each other. Taking the small wooden case in her hands and moving purposefully to the hearth, she emptied the entire contents into the fire. The letters quickly blazed into bright orange flames, curling into ashes while the sealing wax melted and sizzled from the heat.

Watching her, Alex could barely contain his pride and immense relief. It was as if Caroline had read his mind but was all the more precious, because she did it without any prompting from him. She had let Stephen go forever.

Caroline stood, turning her back on her bittersweet past burning in the fireplace, and brushed the dust off her hands. She glanced toward Alex, and their gazes met. She flashed him a weary smile. "Now, let's hurry."

CHAPTER 27

"Why, Madeline, what a beautiful necklace!" Betsy Warring exclaimed with an admiring glance.

"Isn't it exquisite?" Madeline Parkridge's small hand moved, quite consciously, to touch the sparkling diamonds that glittered around her neck. "Oliver just presented me with it." He had explained that it was an early Christmas present, but she had intuitively understood that, in fact, it was due to her unprecedented behavior in her bedroom the night before. Oliver had neither given her, nor allowed her to purchase herself, any jewelry whatsoever since they had been married, and she was elated to have the diamond necklace. She grinned in greedy delight at the prospect of all the pretty and expensive treasures she could have now that Oliver had opened his purse strings. Oh, if only she had realized how easy, and pleasurable, it would be to have Oliver in her power, she would have gone to his bed willingly in the first place!

She had arrived at the Talbots' ball in a state of high excitement and a little breathless. They were unusually late, due to her thanking Oliver properly for the necklace, and she worried that she would miss the announcement that the engagement of Emma Armstrong and John Talbot was called off due to the scandalous behavior of her sister, Caroline Armstrong Woodward, who was locked up in Newgate Prison! But it seemed that she had not missed a thing. Of course, she didn't know if anyone even knew of the events that had transpired at the Woodward townhouse that afternoon and wondered if word had leaked out somehow. But it seemed that it hadn't. So it was now up to her to spread the word.

The Talbots' annual Holiday Ball was now in full swing. The grand ballroom was festooned with garlands of ivy and holly, and a full orchestra played "Good King Wenceslas." Large Christmas wreaths adorned with bright red bows hung in the center of each of the symmetrically arched glass windows that lined the outside wall of the ballroom. A good-size evergreen tree decorated with small beeswax candles, glass ornaments, and red taffeta ribbons stood magnificently at the far end of the dance floor. The many elegantly attired guests crowded into the ballroom, laughing, chattering, and merrily partaking of the sumptuous food dishes and generous spirits in the adjoining dining room.

The thought that it was only a year ago that Madeline had waltzed so beautifully with the Duke of Woodborough in this very ballroom, and one and all had commented on how perfectly they looked together, echoed through her mind. That was when the duke had fallen in love with her and all her dreams of becoming his duchess seemed about to be fulfilled, until Caroline Armstrong appeared out of nowhere and ruined everything. But

Madeline would not let that fact spoil her present joyful mood.

Oh, and what a glorious day it had been! From the constable's agreeable nature to seeing Caroline carted off to prison, to Oliver presenting her with a diamond necklace, it was perfect. Now, this evening was the pièce de résistance: the traitorous Duke of Woodborough and both of those detestable Armstrong sisters would be publicly humiliated in this very ballroom!

Oliver returned to her side, whispering, "Your eyes are sparkling more than the diamonds."

Madeline fluttered her eyelashes prettily at her husband and favored him with a beaming smile. She smoothed the silk of her newest sky blue Worth evening dress with long sleeves and a low décolletage, and she glanced around the room in time to see Emma Armstrong, on the arm of Lord John Talbot, enter the main hallway. Emma looked pretty in her ivory gown embroidered with tiny violets, her chestnut hair cascading over her shoulders in long ringlets. Emma was obviously in love with John Talbot, a handsome young man with a reserved and dignified manner. Olivia Fairchild followed behind them with her son and daughter-in-law, Kit and Jane Fairchild. With all that happened today, Madeline was more than a little surprised that Emma and her entire family were in attendance, for she had not really expected to see them. Perhaps the Fairchilds had not yet learned of Caroline's disgrace. Madeline grinned smugly imagining their expressions of shock and shame when she let the news of Caroline's scandalous behavior be known to everyone present. Madeline's own husband stood next to her completely unaware of the bombshell she was about to drop.

Now the trick was for her to deliver the news innocently, as if it were common knowledge and not something that she alone was instigating. She had practiced affecting the proper tone with just the right amount of disdain and empathy in front of her cheval glass mirror all afternoon. A sympathetic expression for the Woodward family. A note of scorn for the Armstrongs. She would whisper first to Lady Weatherby, because she would spread the word faster than anyone else. "Isn't it just too awful about the poor, unsuspecting Duke of Woodborough being duped by that conniving Armstrong girl? Did you ever hear of such a thing?" A compassionate tear would appear in her eye, and then a look of surprise would come over her and, "You mean you haven't heard that Caroline Armstrong was arrested and taken to Newgate Prison this very afternoon for bigamy? I just happened to be walking by the Woodward house and saw the whole thing! How that poor family dares to hold its head up in public again, I don't know. But that's what comes of marrying beneath one's class." She would shake her head sadly at the tragedy. Lady Weatherby would tell Lady Talbot, and Madeline would tell her mother, and it would quickly be the complete and utter social ruin of Caroline and Emma Armstrong!

Madeline was so lost in her malicious thoughts that she almost missed seeing Elizabeth Woodward, the Dowager Duchess of Woodborough, arrive to be greeted warmly by Lord and Lady Talbot. She was followed by her younger son, the handsome Charles Woodward, and—Madeline could not believe her eyes—Stephen Bennett! How very odd! Why would Stephen Bennett, of all people, be attending the ball with the Woodward family? This development caused her pretty face to frown in puzzlement as she pondered its implications.

However, nothing prepared her for seeing the Duke of Woodborough himself, looking strikingly handsome and impeccably attired in black evening clothes, walk in the door with Caroline Armstrong on his arm. Caroline, wearing a stunning scarlet ball gown with small capped sleeves and long scarlet gloves, obviously from Paris. Caroline, looking beautiful and as if she hadn't a care in the world! Caroline, who should be rotting in Newgate Prison this very minute!

What had happened? How had Caroline escaped? Madeline had seen for herself the constable escorting the shamefaced hussy into his wagon only hours ago! But Caroline did not look the least like she spent any time in prison this afternoon. It was a pity no one had been on the street to witness the event, because it was doubtful that anyone would believe Madeline's story now. The duke certainly did not appear as if he just discovered that his wife was already married to another man. Especially when that man, Stephen Bennett, was chatting casually with his own brother. Madeline fumed and pouted in frustration.

Oliver leaned close and kissed her cheek, nuzzling her neck, and Madeline had to restrain herself from slapping him as she stared at the group across the room. She gained a reprieve as Oliver left to get her a glass of champagne, but she did not look away from the family by the entrance.

* * *

Emma rushed to Caroline's side. "I'm so relieved to see you here. I've been worried about you since I left your house yesterday afternoon, but it seems as though you and Alex worked everything out." Emma whispered with a pleased expression, but continued in a more hushed tone, "Why in the world is Stephen Bennett with you?"

"Answering that question at this moment would require more time and strength than I have at present, but I promise to explain it all to you tomorrow," Caroline responded as her sister gave her a quizzical look. "Just smile and act as if everything were normal."

"Isn't it?" Emma asked, her hazel eyes worried.

"Far from it," Caroline stated with a determined calm that she did not feel. "And the night has not yet begun."

Emma's perplexed gaze was overshadowed by their grandmother's presence. Olivia hugged Caroline to her tightly, half whispering, half scolding, "Do you have any idea how worried we have been over you? We shall have a long talk, miss, when this is all over."

"Yes, Grandmother," Caroline replied. If her grandmother had met her with disapproval Caroline was determined to be strong, but with that hug, her spirits lifted and gave her the courage to carry through with their plan. She smiled at her, saying thank you with her eyes. Then she carried forth with purpose.

Gliding over to Stephen, who was in polite conversation with Lord and Lady Talbot, she said, "Mr. Bennett, I believe your cousin is looking for you." She looked at him meaningfully.

Stephen excused himself from Lord and Lady Talbot and followed Caroline to Alex's side.

"Are you ready, Stephen?" she asked him. He nodded. "Then let's not waste any more time. She may have started already."

In unspoken agreement, the three of them made their way across the crowded ballroom toward Madeline Parkridge. No one in the room had any inkling of the drama that surrounded the outwardly calm demeanor of this unusual trio: the strikingly handsome duke, his beautiful wife, and the blond stranger from America.

Madeline saw them coming toward her and did not know what to make of it. Having the distinct feeling that it did not bode well for her plan to ruin Caroline, she suddenly felt the need for some protection, and her husband filled that position quite nicely. She began to inch her way to Oliver. He handed her a chilled flute of champagne, and she downed it in one fluid gulp, just as Caroline, Alex, and Stephen reached her.

"Good evening, Lord Parkridge. Lady Parkridge," Alex began in a cordial tone. His blue eyes flicked briefly over Madeline, then met Oliver's gaze. "Your American cousin just told us of the little joke he played on your wife and mine."

Oliver looked toward Madeline with puzzlement, to which she responded with a blank stare. With a half-hearted smile, he turned toward his cousin. "What's this, Stephen? You played a joke on Madeline and the duchess?"

"I'm afraid so, Oliver." Stephen laughed with a

false smile on his boyish face. "It wasn't very gentle-manly of me, but I say, you might find it humorous."

A discerning eye might have been able to sense the underlying tension between them, but Madeline only wondered why they appeared so full of mirth. These three people should not look so happy. After all, Caroline had played both of these men for fools and was even arrested for it, thanks to her own manipulations. Why would they be laughing together like old friends? It defied any logic she could comprehend.

"What do you know of this joke, Madeline?" Oliver asked, his face frowning with disapproval.

She fluttered her eyelashes. "I'm not quite sure, darling."

"Oh, you know all about it, Madeline," Caroline hinted in a singsong voice with a bright smile pasted on her face. "Remember your little visit to my house earlier today? It was really too terrible of Stephen to say what he did. But you did know that he and I knew each other years ago when he attended the university where my father taught, didn't you?"

"Stephen mentioned that to me. I believe he said that you two were more than just friends, Caroline." Madeline's voice was somewhat edgy as she glanced between her and Stephen.

Caroline gave an indulgent smile to Stephen and giggled to Madeline. "Isn't he just scandalous?"

"Please," Oliver added nervously, feeling like an outsider, "let me in on the joke."

No one noticed the hard nudge in the back that Alex gave to Stephen.

"Well," Stephen began with false jocularity, "I should apologize to Madeline first since I involved her in my deception, although I did cause quite a bit of trouble for Caroline, as well . . . But Caroline, being a terribly good sport, has forgiven me, as I'm sure you will too, Madeline."

"Go on," Oliver urged, glancing nervously at the Duke of Woodborough.

"Well, Caroline and I used to play jokes and little pranks on each other back in Shrewsbury. When I returned to England, I thought it might be fun to trick her, since I never paid her back for getting me into trouble with Professor Caruthers before I left. It seems she switched my last essay . . . So I needed to repay her somehow. I got the idea the night I arrived in London at your dinner party, Madeline, and heard everyone talking about Caroline's upcoming marriage to the duke. At the time, I wasn't quite sure if she was the same girl that I knew, but then I discovered that she was, indeed, my dear friend. Thinking it would be a great joke, little by little, I led Madeline to believe that I had married Caroline before she married the duke!" Stephen finished with a loud peal of laughter.

Caroline giggled. "Isn't that the most preposterous story you've ever heard?"

The duke gleefully slapped Stephen on the back in a gesture of camaraderie. "Yes, it's quite preposterous."

Madeline's baby blue eyes narrowed with suspicion. She didn't believe Stephen for an instant. Only last night at the Greenvilles' dinner party, he confided in her with heartbreaking sincerity that he had married Caroline two and a half years ago. Now he was recanting everything. "You mean it's not true?" she asked him.

Stephen continued to guffaw rather loudly. "Not a word of it!"

Oliver seemed lost and turned to Madeline for

confirmation. "I'm afraid I don't see the humor in all this."

"Neither do I," Madeline remarked dryly.

"I admit I found it difficult at first myself," the duke's icy blue eyes glittered menacingly at Oliver Parkridge.

"Oh, but it gets better," Stephen began to explain. "You see, Madeline believed me completely and brought a constable to arrest Caroline for bigamy this very afternoon!"

Oliver, not finding any of this amusing, stared at his wife in shock and anger. "You had Caroline arrested? How could you do such a thing, Madeline, even in jest?"

Madeline was nothing if not shrewd. Innately she sensed the tide had changed and readily assessed the new situation. She was not about to let herself be made to look the fool. Stephen was not telling the truth now, that she was sure of, and a clever act was being performed for her benefit alone. If the duke and Stephen Bennett were going to maintain that the whole incident was a simple joke, then she could not oppose them. It seemed that she would not be ruining Caroline Armstrong tonight after all. Fortuitously for Madeline, she had arrived at the ball late and had not had the time to spread her story of the false marriage and subsequent arrest. She would have looked very foolish now with the three of them on such friendly terms. In her opinion, Stephen and the duke were utter simpletons to be taken in by that conniving girl, but that was no longer her problem.

The contempt in Oliver's expression was enough to prompt her to change her position. She had just arrived at the point where she held all the cards in her marriage and she was not about to let that power slip through her pretty little fingers so quickly. She had to save herself now. "Well darling"—she gazed up at Oliver with her wide blue eyes—"how was I to know that it was a joke? I thought the poor duke had been tricked into a false marriage."

Oliver, now irate at the role his wife had in this sordid affair and fearful of angering the powerful duke, snapped, "You should have discussed this with me first. I could have told you the entire story was false. The duke is no fool, and obviously anything Stephen told you was not true. I don't understand how you could believe such a tale."

Stephen continued to laugh as he attempted to explain to his cousin. "Oliver, believe me, I had no idea that your wife would get so outraged that she would call a constable! I wasn't even sure that you believed me, Madeline! But to have innocent little Caroline taken off to Newgate! It's too funny!"

Caroline chimed in, "Luckily for me, the constable and I ran into Alex and Stephen after you left, Madeline. Stephen had already let Alex in on the joke, and when they explained everything to the constable, even he was laughing! I knew then that we had to fill you in Madeline, darling." She turned to Oliver with a mischievous gleam in her eye. "Your American cousin is really too much."

"Yes, it does seem that way," Oliver said with some skepticism as he frowned at his wife and his cousin.

Madeline began to giggle charmingly, playing along with them. "It is rather comical, don't you think, Oliver?" She batted her eyelashes at him. "It's amusing that I believed such a tale. Stephen, whatever made you do such a wicked thing?"

"I don't know. The idea just came to me when

everyone was talking about Caroline's wedding that first night I was in London." Stephen grinned impishly.

"Isn't it fortunate that I am not a gossipy sort of lady?" Madeline said with wide-eyed innocence.

The duke looked with pointed directness at Madeline and Oliver. "And is it not fortunate, as well, that I have such a good sense of humor about your wife and cousin's actions, Oliver? Can you imagine how ugly it would be if I were an unreasonable man? Or if the story of Caroline being married to Stephen weren't so utterly ridiculous? Some men might be very angry having such rumors spread about their wives. But then I know they are complete fabrications and the source was a silly prank played by a dear friend of my wife's. I know that no malice was intended, isn't that right, Stephen? Madeline?"

There was an unmistakable threat in the duke's words that was not missed by Oliver, or Madeline, for that matter. They understood that the very influential and powerful duke would be agreeable this one time, but any further remarks about his wife would not be tolerated with such good humor.

"Oh but, Alex, really! Who would believe such a nonsensical story?" Caroline asked him. He took her small, gloved hand in his, brought it to his lips, and kissed it elegantly. The possessive overture the duke made to his beautiful wife was not lost on the others.

"Who *would* believe such a story?" The duke stated more than asked the question, and looked directly at Madeline. "Surely you don't believe such drivel, Lady Parkridge? An intelligent and discerning lady as yourself?" He was making it quite clear that he would brook no further interference from her.

"Why, of course not!" Madeline protested prettily, waving her blue fan.

Stephen spoke up. "Please forgive me Madeline, dearest cousin. It was very ungentlemanly of me to involve you in such trickery."

Oliver Parkridge, a little unnerved by the duke's barely concealed threat, now directed some of his own anger at Stephen. Cousin or not, he ought not to have entangled his wife in an outrageous joke at the duke's expense. "You should be sorry, Stephen. Maybe these kinds of jests are humorous in America, but I can assure you that in England we don't find rumor and innuendo about one's wife amusing in the least."

"Quite right, Oliver." Stephen managed to look contrite, his eyes downcast.

"I suppose if Caroline can find it in her heart to forgive you, Stephen, then so can I," Madeline declared generously with a swish of her fan.

"Thank you for your forgiveness, Madeline. And you as well, Caroline." Stephen's apology was said softly to both women, but Madeline noticed that his eyes were on Caroline. "You know I never meant to hurt you."

Caroline waved her hand in the air and said breezily, "Of course you didn't. We know that, don't we, Alex?"

The duke simply nodded his head in agreement.

"Aren't you returning to Virginia soon, Stephen?" Oliver prompted his cousin, understanding the seriousness of the situation.

"Yes, the day after Christmas. Isn't that what you told us?" the duke said in a clipped voice.

Stephen nodded his head. "Yes. I will be glad to return to my plantation."

Elizabeth Dishington, her black curls bouncing and her dark eyes sparkling merrily, joined them. She thought that Oliver Parkridge's American cousin was handsome and mysterious and had been dreaming of dancing with him since they met at Lady Weatherby's party. She waved her dance card in the air. "Mr. Bennett, I believe you are my partner for this dance."

Stephen excused himself from the little group to partner Miss Dishington, leaving only the Woodwards and the Parkridges.

"Well, Caroline, I believe we should join your sister for the big announcement." He winked knowingly at Oliver and Madeline, for the announcement of John and Emma's engagement was supposed to be a surprise but was, in truth, common knowledge among the *ton*.

"Congratulations, Your Grace," Oliver offered affably. The relief that a possible disaster had been avoided was obvious on his face.

"Yes, congratulations," Madeline echoed woodenly, her eyes flickering scornfully over Caroline.

"Thank you," Caroline answered, ignoring Madeline's gaze.

"I hope you don't take my cousin's prank to heart, Your Grace," Oliver explained to Caroline. "He is an American and doesn't understand how society is here."

"I've forgotten about it already!" Caroline smiled benignly.

"You are very gracious. I apologize for my wife's behavior as well. It was not well done of her. I believe Madeline and I will take our leave early this evening," Oliver declared, an angry tone in his voice. He held tightly to Madeline's arm. "We have some things we need to discuss in private, don't we?" He turned to Madeline.

Madeline cringed inwardly, fearing that she had just ruined what had promised to be a very beneficial situation for her. She had never seen her husband look so angry. "Aren't we going to stay for the announcement, Oliver?"

"No, I don't believe we will. Madeline, please apologize to the duke and his wife." Oliver pushed her forward slightly.

Miserable at the turn of events, she muttered hastily, "Please forgive my actions."

Caroline and the duke nodded their heads graciously at Madeline, and she said her good-byes.

Madeline petulantly walked with Oliver, his hand pressing her arm too tightly as he ushered her out of the ballroom.

"You almost ruined us, Madeline," Oliver ground out between clenched teeth in a harsh whisper. "You are incredibly stupid. Do you have any idea what it would be like if the duke were truly angry with us for what you did to his wife? We would be ostracized socially, not able to show our faces. He could even ruin me financially if he chose to. Don't you so much as cast an unpleasant look in their direction, do you hear me?"

Madeline was about to protest when he reached around her neck and unclasped the beautiful diamond necklace that she had been showing off all evening.

Oliver hissed, "This goes back in the safe until I see some better behavior from you."

Madeline, stunned, stared at Oliver in disbelief as she followed him from the room.

Alex watched Lord and Lady Parkridge leave the ballroom and sighed in relief. Caroline's little plan actually worked, and a terrible scandal had been avoided. His eyes glanced at his beautiful wife. How she managed to pull herself together after the horrendous day she had endured and still look lovely and serene was a mystery to him. He knew she was completely exhausted. He pulled her closer to his side and placed an affectionate kiss on the top of her head.

She stared up at him. "I think it worked."

"I believe it did. Oliver looked very displeased with his wife. I don't think we'll have any more trouble from her."

"I hope not," she whispered wearily. "We still have to see the magistrate."

"That is a mere technicality now. You are my wife, not Stephen's. And soon he will be gone."

Caroline nodded her head. "Yes."

Alex held her hand firmly in his. "Let's go celebrate with Emma and John, and then I'm taking you home."

CHAPTER 28

The day after Christmas the Duke and Duchess of Woodborough watched from the main dock as the tall ship carrying Stephen Bennett back to Virginia sailed out to sea.

Alex visibly relaxed, and the heavy tension eased from his brow. His hand held Caroline's small gloved one tightly in his, while the cold ocean wind whipped around them, sending her skirts billowing wildly out behind her. She gripped her bonnet tightly to her head with her free hand and smiled at Alex squinting in the sun.

After their convincing charade for the Parkridges and successful aversion of a public scandal over their marriage, they had celebrated the engagement of Emma and John at the Talbots' ball and Madeline Parkridge had not since uttered a word about Caroline and Stephen. No one in the *ton* was the wiser about her brief visit to Newgate. With Stephen Bennett standing by his explanation that his supposed marriage to Caroline was nothing but a joke, Madeline had no way to prove his story otherwise.

Two days later, as they had arranged, Caroline

and Alex accompanied Stephen to stand before the magistrate to clear Caroline's name. With Geoffrey Claypool's invaluable assistance, they were able to see the magistrate in his private chambers first thing in the morning.

The magistrate was an elderly man with a kind and wrinkled face, wearing the required white wig and long, dark robes. He listened intently to the same story they told the Parkridges and was puzzled by the unusual set of circumstances surrounding the pretty Duchess of Woodborough. However, he became quite irate that she had been arrested based solely on rumors from a countess and then outraged that she spent even one minute in Newgate for such unsubstantiated charges. He had never heard of such a scandalous incident and promised to have Constable Jones questioned about his conduct. The magistrate angrily declared Caroline's arrest baseless, since the marriage to Stephen Bennett had been a completely fabricated ruse. He then acknowledged that her marriage to the Duke of Woodborough was quite legal and lawful in every sense.

His compassionate, pale eyes looked over at Caroline. "This young American has done you a terrible wrong with his slanderous joke, Your Grace. It is within your rights to file charges against him."

Caroline regarded Stephen for a moment. His brown eyes silently pleaded with her, while Alex squeezed her hand in silent affirmation that he would support her in any decision that she made. She could punish him for what he did to her. But what she really wanted was for it to be over and for Stephen to be gone from her life once and for all. She lifted her head and spoke clearly. "No, thank you, my lord. It was simply a ridiculous prank, after all is said and done."

Upon leaving the court, they escorted Stephen to where the ship was docked. Alex was taking no chances that Stephen would somehow change his mind and remain in London. After all he had put them through, Alex wanted the man out of the country and the vastness of an ocean separating them. And he wanted to see him leave with his own eyes.

Caroline wished Stephen luck and said good-bye. Stephen apologized again for hurting her. Alex unmistakably reminded Stephen, with his words and manner, to never return to England. Stephen, markedly silent, nodded his head in agreement. They watched as he boarded the ship that would carry him across the Atlantic Ocean.

As it drifted away, Caroline felt an enormous sense of relief. If she hadn't found out the truth, she might have been on that ship with Stephen, believing she was his wife. Sailing away to a strange life in Virginia. Never seeing Alex again. Her chest constricted at the thought. Instead, Stephen Bennett was going without her, for she had never been legally married to him at all. The invisible weight that had been on her shoulders for over two years finally dissipated. She breathed deeply of the cold sea air and squeezed Alex's hand in gratefulness. She was so grateful for Alex's love. She was grateful for Stephen leaving her life. She was grateful for the way everything was resolved, without a public scandal.

And she was not completely disgraced in the eyes of her family. They still loved her: her grandmother, Emma, the Dowager Duchess, her aunt and uncle. They had all forgiven her for her mistakes and did not think less of her. Oh, they had admonished her for not being honest with them from the start, and she had to agree with them on that fact. But they had managed to avoid another family scandal, for which she was profoundly grateful.

With Stephen Bennett gone, it was as if a significant chapter of her life had finally ended. And she was glad of it.

For now there was a new chapter.

She looked toward Alex. The sun was shining on his incredibly handsome face, and he was smiling at her. That smile still caused a deep fluttering in her stomach and an increased pounding of her heart. She never thought she could love anyone as much as she loved him. And he was legally her husband, forever and ever. Incredibly, he still loved her through all of it. She unconsciously placed her hand over her abdomen. On Christmas Eve, they learned from the doctor that she was expecting their first child. Just when she thought her heart couldn't hold another ounce of happiness, she was blessed with Alex's child.

"Let's go home," Alex shouted with a grin over the rush of the wind.

As Caroline tilted her head up to kiss him, her little bonnet blew off her head and sailed breezily into the blue water. Her golden hair came tumbling around her face, whipping madly in the wind.

He laughed at her. "You lost another hat."

"Just as long as I don't lose you," she replied.

"Never," he assured her, looking into her eyes. He had everything he had ever wanted right there in his arms, and he would never let her go. "Now that there are no more secrets between us."

She shook her head, brushing her wildly blowing hair from her face. She echoed his words in the wind. "No more secrets. Ever."

About the Author

Kaitlin O'Riley fell in love with historical romance novels when she was just fourteen years old, and shortly thereafter, she began writing her own stories in spiral notebooks. Fortunately, none of those early efforts survive today. Kaitlin grew up on the New Jersey shore, but now lives with her family in Southern California where she is busy at work on her next book. **Secrets of a Duchess** is her first novel. You can visit her Web site at kaitlinoriley.com